MW00618910

Copyright © **2019** by **Jordan Taylor**

Typewriter Pub, an imprint of Blvnp Incorporated
A Nevada Corporation
1887 Whitney Mesa DR #2002
Henderson, NV 89014
www.typewriterpub.com/info@typewriterpub.com

ISBN: **978-1-64434-041-7**

DISCLAIMER

THE BROKEN VOW OF SILENCE

JORDAN TAYLOR

Dedicated to my parents and grandparents
who have supported me from my first word on paper
and to my beautiful readers who have followed me from a rough draft to here.

CHAPTER ONE

Another scream escaped from my lips as Morgan's foot made a hard contact with my ribs, sending a sickening crack through the air. The blood that filled my mouth was as familiar as the air in my lungs. I could feel the sharp pull of the tears that were gathering in my eyes and begging to escape.

"And this is for being the worthless piece of trash you are!" he yelled as his fist collided with my cheek, which caused me to fall flat on the floor wheezing for air as my tears and blood became one on the floor.

He scoffed as he wiped the sweat from his forehead.

"Now get up and make yourself presentable," he said as I continued fighting for precious air to reach my starving lungs. "I said get up!" He growled angrily once he realized that I hadn't moved and delivered yet another kick to my ribs.

A whimper escaped from my lips as I forced my weak arms to hoist me up. Morgan laughed at me as I stumbled and fell a couple times. Once he realized that I couldn't get up on my own, he roughly grabbed me by my brown locks and pulled me up. I had to bite my bottom lip to keep the scream that was climbing up my throat at bay as my scalp burned.

"Your dress is in your room. Make yourself presentable," he whispered harshly in my ear before he let go of my hair and stalked off. "And how good you clean up tonight determines when your next beating's going to be."

I nodded silently as I watched him disappear through the door that led to the rest of the pack house. I mutely stood there for a good three minutes before I hurried out of the annex of the pack house, stepping over the whips and other things that Morgan used to beat me with. I hurried through the maze of hallways and stairs before I finally emerged into the pack house where the pack members were laughing and joking, but all of the laughter and smiles stopped once I walked in.

I kept my head down and silently made my way through the kitchen and hurried up the stairs toward my room. People thought that I was Morgan's prized possession and that we were a loving couple who'd give up anything for each other because that was what he wanted them to see. That was why he never hit my face too hard, and when he did hit me, he made sure that it was light enough for it to easily heal over by the time I made it out of the annex.

I cradled my ribs, pain moving through me like a wave as I did, causing me to silently hiss as I made my way up to my room. I flipped on the lights to see an elegant dress draped across my bed. I could already tell it would reveal more of me than I was comfortable with.

My room was the smallest in the whole pack house despite everyone's belief. My bed was barely big enough to hold me, and my sheets were covered in dirt and blood from my beatings. I didn't have a TV or any nice furniture. I only had a bed, a closet full of beautiful clothes which I was only to wear when Morgan instructed me to do so, and a single picture that I had stashed between my mattress and my bed frame.

I effortlessly pushed the dress aside and pulled the special picture from its hiding spot. It was the only thing that distracted me from my awful life or brought me peace. In the picture was a handsome man and woman with bright eyes and warm smiles. Their laughter forever frozen in time. In their arms rested two young children; one boy and one girl with smiles that matched their parents'. A small smile spread across my lips, causing my face to ache from the once familiar action.

I gently caressed the photo as the memories came flooding back.

It was our pack's twelfth anniversary, and the pack threw a grand celebration for my parents; Alpha and Luna Carter. One of the pack members took a picture of my parents; my older brother, Chris; and I. Grief wrapped its fist around my heart. Its fingers slowly constricted around it until it easily replaced the blood in my veins.

It had been about five years since the fire that claimed my parents' and my brother's lives. How it started was never officially confirmed, but I had a feeling Morgan had something to do with it. One minute, we were all asleep in our house that was separated from the rest of the pack, and the next minute, the fire was reaching toward the sky from every door and window.

The orange-red flames filled the night as I sobbed in the front yard with Morgan's arms around me preventing me from jumping into the fire that was feverishly consuming what used to be my house—my home along with my family. Too bad his intentions for saving me weren't pure.

Their screams still haunted my dreams sometimes.

When my parents' bodies were found, they were burned to a crisp. I would never forget the sight of their blackened skin clinging to their bones. They never found my brother's body, or what was left of it. They said that his body completely burned to ashes.

I could still see his vibrant green eyes and hear his joyful laughter, and no matter how hard I tried to push the thoughts away, they always filled my mind.

Why didn't I burn to ashes with them? Why am I the lone survivor? Why wasn't I good enough for the fire's wicked flames? Why did they leave me here with Morgan?

Morgan was their beta at the time of the fire. Ever since my family died and he became alpha, he had been abusing me and blaming me for my parents' "mistakes" like not treating him with the respect he deserved or for not giving him the power he wanted.

I pushed back the tears that were blurring my vision as I tucked the picture back into its hiding spot, unable to continue looking at it. I quickly wiped my eyes and focused on the task at hand. In about an hour, one of the strongest alphas in North America named Shane Chase would be coming in search of his mate, whom he had been searching for the past two years. Morgan wanted me to be his arm candy.

I rolled my eyes as I looked at the expensive looking dress, hating myself for being so weak that I couldn't stand up for myself and allowing him to use me as his silent prize. And what I hate most is how good I am at it: being silent. I haven't uttered a word since my family's death.

I forced my tired legs to carry me to the bathroom where I quickly started a bath in the standard sized tub. I turned and looked at myself in the mirror, noticing how almost every bruise on my face had already healed except for the one on my cheek, which I would have to cover with makeup. I slowly lifted up the hem of the oversized red shirt I was wearing, revealing a giant purple bluish bruise on my ribs, which would take at least a week to heal.

I sighed as I walked over to the bathtub and turned off the water. The steam rose from it and collected on my face. I stripped down carefully to avoid the sensitive spots before I slid into the tub, allowing it to wash away all the dirt and terrible thoughts.

I slowly sank deeper and deeper into the water until the water was just below my nose, and I closed my eyes, trying to imagine what life would be like if my parents were still alive, and if I was lucky enough to have someone to call mine forever. A mate was what we call them—two lucky people who were mated together by the Moon Goddess. To have and to hold . . forever.

I felt a small smile grow on my lips at the thought. What a luxury that would be.

*   *   *

It was five minutes until our designated meeting time with Alpha Chase when Morgan knocked on my door.

"Open up, mutt, or I'm coming in," he said harshly from the opposite side of the door.

I looked at myself one final time in the mirror to make sure that everything would be to Morgan's liking, to avoid a beating. My makeup covered my bruises and blemishes to hide every imperfection, the way Morgan instructed me to. I wore red lipstick and mascara with a bit of eye shadow, but I had to make it look natural to meet Morgan's standards. My brown hair flowed down just below my shoulders, and my dress hugged my figure and cut down so low that it almost reached my belly button.

I did have a figure, but it didn't work in my favor. It was just another thing Morgan could use to objectify me. I bit my bottom lip, took deep breaths, and told myself that it would be over soon.

"I'm giving you three seconds," Morgan growled lowly, pulling me back to reality.

I quickly hurried out of my bathroom, nearly falling in the ridiculous heels Morgan forced me to wear before I finally made it to the door. When I opened the door, I could feel Morgan's rage radiating off of him.

"Next time, come when I call," he growled as he wrapped his arm around my waist and forcefully pulled me into him, his fingers digging into the wound on my hip he'd given me yesterday. I had to grit my teeth to prevent a scream from coming out.

We made our way to the giant foyer where all the girls from our pack waited. Their voices were buzzing and hopeful. As Morgan walked me down the stairs, I instantly put on a mask of happiness and adoration like I'd trained myself to do despite my hatred toward him. I learned that the better I performed, the more mercy he showed once the curtain fell.

The girls we walked past looked at me with envy and whispered about how they wanted their mate to treat them like Morgan did me, but they did not know what they were wishing. I wouldn't wish this on anybody. Not even Morgan himself.

"You look beautiful," Morgan whispered but said it loud enough for the other girls to hear him.

The corners of my lips turned up into a fake smile before he tenderly placed his lips on my forehead, causing the girls to let out a series of "awws," letting me know that I was selling it. Morgan continued walking me through the sea of girls, all of them giving me wishful glances except for one.

Tracey, the plastic Barbie of the pack, glared daggers at me, which caused me to shrink back a bit. She knew that Morgan and I were just for show, and she even joined Morgan in beating me sometimes. Even though she saw what a horrible person he was, she still hated me for being "with him."

I tried to shrug her off, but it was hard when her gaze was burning into my back like a laser. Eventually, we were in the very front of the crowd, waiting patiently in front of the doors for our guest to arrive.

After a few moments, Morgan's beta, whose name I did not know, rushed up to us and whispered that he was here, which caused my heart to speed up for some weird reason. I quickly shook the feeling away, knowing that I was being ridiculous. I couldn't be mated to one of the strongest alphas in history, and even if I were, which was impossible, he would reject me upon sight. I couldn't even stand up for myself, let alone help to lead a pack or bear pups. Plus, I already knew the cruelty of one alpha, and I didn't need to learn another's.

A sigh pushed past my lips as Morgan's grip suddenly became tighter around me, letting me know that it was game time. I straightened up and took a deep breath, causing the most addicting scent in the world to rush into my nose and my inner wolf, which had basically been dormant for the past five years, to immediately go crazy. The smell was a drug consisting of fresh rain and cinnamon, and I couldn't get enough of it. It was like I was addicted.

The large front doors opened, revealing a man who took my breath away with about eight warriors from his own pack following closely behind him. He was tall, standing at about six-foot-three with an incredible build, and the face of a model. He had hazel-green eyes framed by his thick eyelashes and perfectly arched eyebrows. His nose was perfectly straight, and his lips were soft looking. The blade he called a jaw was covered in black stubble that matched his obsidian black hair that my fingers were itching to run themselves through. As my eyes wandered down his body, I could see that his muscles were bulging underneath his black short-sleeved t-shirt and I could even see the outlines of his abs. Dominance radiated off him in waves, and he didn't even have to say a word for you to know that he was a force to be reckoned with.

"Mate!" my wolf screamed, and I froze, fear taking over me as my body slightly began trembling.

I couldn't have him as my mate. I refused to. Yeah, he was gorgeous, and he made me feel ways I thought were impossible to feel just by looking at him, but I couldn't. The man was attractive, but looks could be deceiving.

Morgan taught me that.

I tried to hide behind Morgan, but he firmly held me to his side, determined to show me off. I prayed to the Moon Goddess above that Morgan's scent along with all the other girls would be

7

enough to mask my scent. As soon as he walked through the doors, he froze with his muscles taut.

"She's here," he whispered, his velvety voice sounding like pure music to my ears. I could listen to him talk for hours and never get bored . . .

No, Ariel. Snap out of it! I scolded myself. *You can't do this to yourself. Not again. Just keep your head low and don't make a sound.*

He took a deep breath as he slowly made his way down the rows of hopeful girls, getting closer and closer to where I stood. I closed my eyes and bit my bottom lip so hard that the metallic taste of blood filled my mouth, but I remained still and silent.

His addicting smell was soon in front of me. I could feel his eyes burning into my being, and I had to keep the tears that wanted to escape at bay. Suddenly, I felt his index finger gently hook itself underneath my chin. Sparks almost as addicting as his scent rushed through me, causing me to open my eyes with a small gasp. Instantly, I was met with his eyes, and my knees turned to mush. He looked even more handsome up close.

A small smile grew on his face as he looked at me. "My Goddess, you're so beautiful," he whispered as he repositioned his hand so that he was now cupping my cheek, his thumb lightly caressing it.

Butterflies exploded within my stomach as I became lost in his eyes and drowned in his voice.

"*What?*" Tracey shrieked in her annoyingly high voice, causing us both to snap out of our trance and turn to look at her. "You did not just say that that tramp is—"

Within a second, he was standing in front of her, his tall, muscular body looming over her tiny weak frame.

"You will not disrespect my mate like that," he said in a deathly low voice, sending shivers down my spine. His warriors stood beside him, ready to assist if need be. "Apologize," he demanded, but she was paralyzed with fear. "Apologize!" he said louder as her face began turning red.

"I'm s-sorry," she stammered out, and as soon as she did, he gave her a curt nod though hatred burned in his eyes.

"If you ever disrespect my mate like that again, pup, I won't be so merciful, and I'll have your head," he spat. "Everyone, out!" he yelled, and instantly, all the girls filed out until only me, him, his warriors, and Morgan remained.

He slowly made his way back over to me, his features much softer than they had been mere moments ago, but fear still rose in my chest.

What if I did something he didn't like? Would he do that to me too . . . or worse?

He must have noticed my attitude because he gently cupped my cheek once more and looked me in the eyes, which made a feeling bloom in me that only he could. Despite how much I hated it, he calmed me down instantly.

"What's your name, love?" he whispered as he gently wrapped his arm around my waist and took me from Morgan's grasp.

"Ariel Anne Carter," Morgan said in a tight voice, anger radiating off of him in waves. "She doesn't talk."

"Ariel." Shane mused. As he continued caressing my cheek, more addicting sparks moved through my being. "What a beautiful name for a beautiful girl."

I couldn't fight the smile on my face as I found myself leaning into his calloused hand, loving the feeling of it on my cheek. We just stayed there for a few seconds, enjoying the feeling of each other's skin when suddenly Shane stopped, his body tensing.

"What's this?" he questioned as his eyebrows furrowed and his thumb moved against my cheek. When pain shot through my cheek, I knew that he'd found my bruise.

A low growl escaped from his lips before his hands left my body, and in the blink of an eye, he had Morgan pressed against the wall. His face was mere inches from Morgan's.

9

"What have you done to her?" he growled loudly as he squeezed Morgan's throat to the point his face started turning blue. "What did you do?" he growled lowly once more, causing Morgan to do something that I never thought he'd do.

He wheezed out a laugh.

That simple action made Shane livid. His once hazel-green eyes turned pitch black, which let me know that his wolf was rising to the surface. He drew his fist back and delivered a solid punch to Morgan's face, which knocked him to the ground. Then another. Then another.

Blood was now covering Morgan's teeth and leaking from his nose, but that didn't satisfy Shane, especially because Morgan still had a smile on his face. A string of curse words spilled between Shane's lips like water as he delivered punch after punch. Kick after kick. He showed no mercy even after Morgan's bones cracked.

I was frozen in pure terror as I watched as he beat Morgan the way Morgan had done me. I thought that Shane might do the same to me if I made a move he didn't like or if I didn't act the way he wanted me to.

I brought a shaky hand up to my mouth to silence the cries that threatened to escape from my mouth as my eyes desperately looked for somewhere to run until my eyes landed on it: the door. I glanced back at Shane before I bolted for the door and saw that he was still preoccupied with Morgan, and Shane's warriors knew better than to try to break them up.

I slid out of my heels as I clumsily ran to the door before throwing it open, and thankfully Shane's warriors didn't try to stop me. A blast of cold air hit me in the face like a hard slap and goosebumps arose on my skin, but that didn't stop my bare feet from running out the door and onto the rough, uneven earth.

My wolf screamed for me to turn back and she even started pushing against her boundaries, causing pressure to build up behind my eyes and a scream to escape my lips.

"Mate! Mate!" she chanted in my head as I covered my ears trying desperately to block her out, but that just sent another wave of intense pain through my skull.

Despite the pain, I forced my legs to move faster, not caring that my dress was being ruined or that my lungs were crying in protest. All that I cared about was getting as far away from Morgan and Shane as humanly possible.

Suddenly, Shane's stupidly addicting scent rushed into my nose. Before I knew it, two strong arms that sent sparks dancing across my skin and tingles down my back gently wrapped themselves around my waist and pulled me close to his body.

"Why did you run, love?" he whispered gently in my ear, genuine concern and hurt in his voice.

A million reasons surfaced in my mind, but I didn't turn them into words. I allowed the silence that fluttered between us to talk to him.

"Please . . ." He trailed off, words failing to complete his sentence.

Despite how comfortable I felt or how perfect our bodies fit together, I pulled away. Shane's hands helplessly fell to his sides, but I knew that they'd still be around me if he really wanted them to be. We stood there in silence, the moonlight that trickled through the branches of the trees cascading over us.

"I wish I could've gotten to you sooner," he whispered, regret saturating his voice. "If I had known where you were. What you're going through . . ."

He reached out for me once more, but I stepped back and shook my head, not wanting any contact with him. I knew that if I let myself drown in the ocean that was his touch, no life preserver or lifeguard could ever bring me back.

"Love, just . . . just please, let me get you out of here. No one deserves to go through what you went through," he said gently as his hand found its way back to my cheek, and no matter how

11

much I wanted to pull away, it was like his hand was a magnet. "Please, Ariel."

I broke eye contact with him and stared at the tree that rested just beyond his head.

"I know that we need to take things step by step and I'll do that. I'll do anything for you. Just please, let me take you out of here, and after that, you never have to see me again if you don't want to. I'll respect that."

I looked into his eyes, searching for any possible reason for me to turn around and run away again, but I saw none. I sighed before I slowly nodded, causing a knee-weakening smile to grow on his handsome face, and that was it.

I was in hook, line, and sinker.

CHAPTER TWO

Shane silently walked me back to the pack house where he sent me up to my room to gather my things while he talked to his warriors. I was on high alert, my eyes scanning every nook and cranny in fear of Morgan, but once I made it to my bedroom, I relaxed.

That was my first mistake.

"You might be safe for now," Morgan lowly said from behind me, which caused me to jump and quickly turn around to see his beaten and bloody face. Even beaten, Morgan still scared me to death. "But this is not over, mutt." He growled before he stormed past me and out of my room.

I was left alone with tears trailing down my face and a million thoughts fighting for dominance in my head. I slowly sank down to my knees as silent sobs escaped my lips as it dawned on me. No matter where I run or hide, Morgan would find me. Morgan was smart and strategic, and eventually, he would find a way to get past Shane and back to me . . .

I couldn't silence the scream like noise that pushed past my lips as I hugged my knees and placed my forehead on my knees. Despite my eyes being squeezed shut, tears still escaped and rolled down my cheeks. For the second time today, Shane caught me off guard by wrapping his arms around my body and pulling me into his body.

"What happened, love?" he whispered as he cradled me in his arms like a fragile baby. I wanted to do something to respond, but all I could do was sob and bury my face into his broad chest.

"Shh, it's okay," he whispered as he rocked me and gently rubbed my back. "I can smell his scent in here," he stated lowly as he held me tighter. "That sick mutt won't hurt you. Not anymore."

I silently nodded in response and looked up into his calming eyes that had affection swimming in them. He cautiously brought his hand up to my face, his eyes searching my face for a negative reaction, and when he found none, he gently rested his hand on the side of my face before his thumb gently danced across my cheeks. He wiped the tears off my face. I found myself leaning into his touch as I closed my eyes, allowing myself to get lost in time and drown in his scent.

"Are you ready to get out of here?" he asked, and I nodded, my eyes still closed.

He repositioned my body in his arms before he picked me up bridal style. I almost let him lead me out of the room before I remembered what I'd come in there for. I opened my eyes and looked at the determined look on his face. He was determined to get me out of here.

I hesitantly tapped him, worrying how he'd react to me touching him without permission, but he simply turned to me and stopped walking, concern etched into the features of his face.

"What's wrong, love?" he asked softly, and I motioned toward my bed. "You want to go over there?" he asked, and I nodded.

Once he walked me over there, I carefully shimmied my way out of his grasp until my feet hit the ground. I felt Shane's eyes on me as I lifted up my mattress and gently removed the picture from its hiding spot and held it to my chest, hiding it from Shane's view.

"Is there anything else?" he asked, and I shook my head. "Do you at least want to change out of that dress? I can't stand the thought of other males trying to look at your body like an object."

I felt a small blush light my cheeks as the corners of my lips tugged up into a small smile. He wandered over to the closet, and a look of confusion overtook his face as he fingered through my clothes.

"Where are your regular clothes?" he asked as he looked back at me.

Shame washed over me in waves as I limply lifted my arms and pointed to the torn and bloodied clothes that rested at the foot of my bed.

Shane looked at me in shock as he slowly walked over to the pile and took a once white shirt that was stained scarlet red with holes in it. It was the shirt I had worn today that was hidden underneath the over shirt Morgan forced me to wear to hide it.

"This is from today, isn't it?" He growled lowly, his eyes turning the soulless black that they had been when he went after Morgan.

When I didn't respond, he became rigid as he got up, dropping the shirt in the process.

"I'm going to rip him apart," he said in a deathly calm voice as he walked past me and toward the door.

I gently placed a hand on his chest to stop him. He looked down at me with his black eyes, his jaw constantly clenching and unclenching.

"Let me go," he said lowly, even though we both knew that he could continue on his way with a simple shove, but he chose to wait for my consent.

"Please, don't," I begged silently, mouthing the words and causing him to slowly relax underneath my hand.

15

"Why?" he asked, the stony expression slowly crumbling away. "He hurt you, Ariel. I can't just let him get away with hurting you like that."

"Don't," I silently said again, mouthing the word and causing his eyes to slowly return to their normal color.

He started analyzing me for any hint that I meant the opposite of what I was saying before he sighed and nodded. His features turned soft, that which I'd become accustomed to though anger was still prominent in his eyes.

"Alright." He sighed. "But if he ever dares to even look at you again, I will slowly kill him without a second thought."

I nodded in response and hoped for both Morgan and my sake that he didn't look at me ever again.

"Now for step two," he said as he effortlessly took off his shirt, revealing his model-like body. "I know it's not the best—and I promise, love, we will get you the best—but for now, if you want it, you can change into this until I can get you some clothes." He offered his shirt to me.

I looked from the shirt then back to him, before my eyes finally rested on the shirt.

My wolf screamed for me to instantly take it and allow myself to drown in his scent, but I still hesitated, not knowing what it'd mean for me. This was a symbol. This was him offering himself to me, and if I took it, I didn't know what would be in store for him or me.

My eyes moved across the small room I'd grown to know over the years before it landed right back on the man in front of me who had hope shining in his eyes. And I made my decision.

I carefully took the shirt from his hands and offered him a nod of thanks. He returned it with a smile, flashing me his perfectly straight teeth. Then he turned around and placed his hands over his eyes like a little kid playing hide and seek.

My eyebrows furrowed in confusion, and before the question fully formed in my head, Shane answered it.

16

"I promise I won't look," he said. "Just let me know when you're done, okay?"

I knew he couldn't see me, so I didn't nod. Instead, I simply shimmied my way out of my dress, avoiding the still healing bruises I'd received a few hours ago. Then I slid his massive shirt over my little body. It fell down to my knees and was overflowing with his amazing masculine scent. I felt my wolf start to push to the surface, but I quickly pushed her back before she took complete control and made me do something I would regret.

I gently tapped his shoulder, and he immediately turned around with a look I couldn't decipher. It caused me to instantly feel self-conscious and shrink back to hide.

"No, don't," Shane said quickly, stopping me in my tracks. "It's just . . . God, you look so beautiful in anything." He smiled before he placed one arm behind my shoulders and the other under my legs and picked me up once more.

A small squeal escaped my lips due to the sudden action, and I instinctively held down the shirt so that I'd be covered before a light giggle pushed past my lips.

"Oh. She laughs?" he questioned, causing me to roll my eyes as I unsuccessfully tried to suppress the smile that stretched across my face. "And she smiles." He chuckled as he started carrying me downstairs.

I lightly bit my bottom lip to prevent the smile from growing even bigger.

"You have a beautiful smile, Ariel," he commented as we made it back to the foyer. "I hope I get to see a whole lot more of them."

Shane carried me right out the door and to one of the three giant black SUVs that glistened in the moonlight. His warriors had already packed themselves into the other two. He gently put me into the passenger seat before he leisurely walked around the car, the moonlight cascading over his body and showing off his amazing abs and muscles.

17

My body instantly missed his.

The car slightly rocked as he plopped down into the driver's seat before he dug the key out of his pockets and jammed it into the ignition. The car let out an even hum as it vibrated beneath me. The air turned on as fog quickly filled the windshield.

"Are you ready, Ariel?" he asked as he looked at me, and I nodded. A smile grew on his lips before his massive hand reached over and touched mine, which caused me to tense before I quickly withdrew my hand. A look of hurt flashed on Shane's face as he slowly withdrew his hand. "Sorry," he apologized, and I nodded, a weird feeling of guilt gnawing at my heart.

I slid the seatbelt across my body before I looked out the window to shield myself from the look on his face, though I could still see the reflection.

"Brace yourself, love," he said as he reached into the back seat and grabbed a jacket. "It's going to be a long ride, about five to six hours." He gently draped the jacket that was almost as saturated in his scent as the shirt I was wearing was. His eyes never left mine as he did so.

After a few more moments, we were going down the road that was leading me out of the purgatory I'd been living in for the past five years. I looked back through the window, watching as the pack house became smaller and smaller until it simply disappeared through the thick trees. I hugged the picture of my family close to my chest as the gates that led out of our territory quickly approached.

As soon as we passed through those gates, I would be free with my mate and hopefully, be proven wrong: That all alphas weren't cruel, power hungry monsters.

I watched as the trees began thinning out until it was just me, Shane, and the open road. Even though I knew that there wasn't much to see, I watched in awe as the outside world I'd missed so much passed by me in a blur of color. I caught Shane sneaking a glance my way every now and then, causing a small grin to spread across my lips.

"There's that smile I love so much," he commented, causing me to roll my eyes as I leaned back into my chair and pulled his jacket closer to my body. "Do you want something to eat?" he asked after a few minutes of riding in silence as lights grew in the distance.

I bit my lip and watched as the lights grew closer. I hadn't eaten since yesterday evening but on the other hand—

My decision was cut short when my stomach let out a low growl, causing a wild blush to go ablaze on my cheeks.

"I take that as a yes," Shane said with a slight grin, causing me to sheepishly nod as I looked away to avoid eye contact. "Hey, don't be embarrassed. It happens to the best of us."

I allowed my hair to fall across my face to discreetly hide my blush as Shane turned into a small empty restaurant with flickering neon sign.

"I know this won't be the best thing you'll ever taste, but I hope it'll do for now."

I nodded as he rolled down his window and placed an order before pulling forward to the window. After a few moments, the smell of artificial meat filled the air as he pulled a large bag into the window followed by two drinks. He thanked the server before we drove away and went back on our long journey.

"Let me warn you. This human food tastes a bit weird at first because a lot of them use artificial crap instead of catching it fresh like we do," he warned as he pulled out the food wrapped up in a paper-like cover. "But when we get home, I will make you the best food you'll ever eat." He flashed me a bright white smile that caused my heart to flutter.

It was a nice feeling; having someone looking out for me and talking to me like a person and not just a body for showing off or a punching bag to let all their stress out on.

19

I snuck a glance at Shane before I carefully unwrapped the unfamiliar food. Back when my parents were the alpha and luna of my pack, my old pack, they would help the pack members cook so that we'd have handmade meals each and every day. Preservatives and fillers were non-existent where I was from, and smelling it and seeing it in front of me made me feel like I was from another world, which I kind of was.

I carefully held the food in my hand, careful not to let any of its contents fall out of its fragile shell. I took a quick bite out of it and it instantly set fire to my taste buds, but I swallowed it. As soon as the horrid thing was out of my mouth, I washed my mouth out with the drink Shane had gotten me, which I soon identified as fruit punch.

Once the burning had disappeared, I took a deep breath as I narrowed my eyes at Shane. After a few moments, he eventually felt my heated gaze burning into the side of his face and turned to me. His eyebrows furrowed for a mere moment before something clicked in his head.

He let out a string of curse words before he looked at me with an apologetic grin. "I'm sorry, love. I just got you what I usually get, and it slipped my mind that you weren't ready for the hot ones. Forgive me?" he asked as he shot me a lop-sided grin, causing me to chuckle as I nodded.

I continued eating, getting more and more used to the burning sensation that came over my tongue with every bite until there was nothing left.

"I'm proud of you," he told me, causing me to grin to myself as my hair fell into my face to hide it. "Hey, don't hide your face from me like that," he said as he gently pushed the hair away from me and tucked it behind my ear.

His thumb gently swept over my cheek as he drove. I winced slightly as his thumb tenderly touched my bruise. Another curse escaped his lips before he apologized and pulled over.

"Give me your hand," he instructed gently.

I looked at him in confusion before I slowly obliged, afraid of the repercussions if I didn't. I gently slid my small hand into his large calloused one. He focused on my hand as he put his other hand on top of my hand and closed his eyes. Suddenly, my hand grew unfamiliarly warm before small bursts of electricity moved through me, causing me to gasp as my heart beat faster. But I couldn't let go of his hand.

Soon the small bursts turned into what felt like bolts as the bruise on my face, as well as the ones scattered on my body, began feeling uncomfortably warm until the weird sensations were replaced with the amazing sparks I usually got when Shane touched me. He let out a labored breath before he let go of my hand and leaned back into his chair, breathing heavily.

I gently brought a hand up to my face and cautiously touched my face where the bruise was, expecting to feel the tender skin. Instead, I felt soft, smooth skin. I removed Shane's jacket from my body before I lifted up my shirt, finding that all my bruises were gone.

"Mates can heal each other," Shane said, answering my unspoken question.

My eyebrows furrowed as I looked at my hands, studying them seeing if there was any change in the lines that decorated them or the color that covered them, but nothing had changed. I held my hands to my chest as Shane let out one more breath then pulled back onto the street.

"Rest, love," he said gently as he reached over and readjusted his jacket back onto my body, his eyes never leaving the road as his skilled hands worked around my body. "We have a very long journey ahead of us."

I nodded as I repositioned myself in the seat and closed my eyes, allowing myself to drown in the ocean that was his scent.

CHAPTER THREE

It was still dark when I woke up in Shane's massive arms.

"I'm sorry, love. Did I wake you?"

I shook my head in response as I readjusted myself in his arms, resting my head on his still bare chest.

"We're home," he said as he used his head to motion to the giant house that loomed in front of us. It was too big to be a pack member's house but too small to be the pack house.

It was the alpha and luna's house.

The moon hung high in the sky above us accompanied by stars sprinkled across the dark blue canvas as he carried me up the stairs before he dug in his pocket. He pulled out a small silver colored key then opened the door.

The house was dark, but I didn't need a light to know that it was huge and lined with expensive and nice things. He carried me through the dark foyer and up the stairs, the only light coming from the moonlight that spilled through the windows. He walked down an impossibly long hallway before we came to a stop in front of a large wooden door.

Shane gently set me down before he opened the door. A wave of his scent rushed into my face.

"Welcome to your new home," Shane said as he gently placed his hand on my lower back, sending sparks through my body, and led me into his—our room. He momentarily left me before a lamp was flipped on, illuminating the room with a soft light.

It was a large room with dark walls and furniture. A king sized bed sat against the wall with a large flat screen TV on the wall across from it. There was a dresser underneath the TV, and a small bookshelf on the other side of the room next to a door that led to what I guessed was the bathroom.

Shane sat down on the bed and patted the space next to him while he motioned me over with his head. I slowly walked over to him, and as soon as I was within arm's length of him, his large arms encircled my waist and pulled me into his lap, causing a small yelp to escape my lips. Shane let out a deep laugh as he swept my fallen hair from my face.

"My God. You're so adorable, Ariel," he whispered as he held me closer. Suddenly, his soft lips came into contact with my forehead, causing me to tense up as the sparks moved through my body.

I didn't know how to react to the sudden action, so I didn't. I just held my breath and hoped for it to be over soon.

The last person who kissed me beat me senseless.

Almost as if he realized what he was doing and how scared it made me, he pulled away. "I'm sorry love. I just keep forgetting—"

I stopped him by gently pressing a finger to his lips, not being able to stand the hurt that appeared in his eyes or the feeling of regret that rose in my chest because I freaked him out.

His lips pulled into a smile underneath my finger before he gently removed my finger from his mouth and intertwined his hand with mine.

"Fine. I'll shut up," he stated as he stroked my knuckles with his thumb, his eyes staying on me and studying everything

23

about me. Every breath I took, every curve and fall in my face, every movement my eyes made, he followed.

Suddenly, his body tensed up as his eyes glazed over, which let me know that someone was using the link—a means of communication between the alpha and his pack through their minds. But this link with them was nothing compared to ours . . . if I let him mark me first.

After a few moments, the clouds cleared from his eyes and a low rumbling noise sounded from deep within his chest.

"I have to go take care of someone," he stated bitterly as he stood up to leave, but my grip on his hand tightened. "What's wrong, Ariel?" he asked as he sat back down next to me, concern evident in his voice.

I chewed the inside of my cheek as I tried to figure out a way to communicate.

"Is everything okay?"

I nodded as I pressed my finger to his lips once more. Gears started turning in my head before the idea came to me. I repositioned our hands so that the palm of my hand was pressed against the back of his. With his palm opened and exposed to me, I used my index finger from my other hand and gently drew letters on his hand that strung together into words and sentences.

"Are you sure?" Shane asked, and I nodded before I gave him the puppy dog face, causing him to sigh in defeat. "Goddess, Ariel. You're going to be the death of me," Shane almost whispered to himself as he ran his hands down his face. "But fine." He relented, and I smiled. "First, we need to get you some pants."

A small blush grew on my face once I remembered that I was just wearing Shane's shirt and my underwear.

"I'll be right back," he said as he got up and walked into the bathroom.

Mere moments later, he returned with two sweatshirts, a pair of sweatpants, and a pair of shoes.

"Here," he said, and I gratefully took a sweatshirt and sweatpants.

We both turned away from each other and put on our clothes, me with my new shirt and pants and him with the sweatshirt, unfortunately covering up his amazing body. When I tapped his shoulder letting him know I was done, he looked at me the same way he had when he first met me and the same way he had when I changed the first time, causing my wolf and inner self to go wild.

"Alright. Let's go," Shane said as he slid his hand into mine once more before he led me through the dark house once more and out the door.

We started walking a short distance toward a giant house that peaked over the trees of his territory, and I found myself leaning in closer to him for warmth as the cool air moved over my body.

"Stay close to me, okay? I don't want any unmated males getting close to you."

I nodded in response as my grip on Shane's hand became tighter.

Soon we were on the front steps of the pack house, and I could already hear the laughter and chatter of the pack members who resided within its walls.

"Are you ready, love?" he asked, and I nodded before taking a deep breath.

Here goes nothing . . .

Shane casually opened the door and strolled in. All the new noise overwhelmed me. Shane was greeted by pack members who showed an immense interest in me. I waved and offered a small smile when Shane introduced me to a handful of them. Relief washed over me when he didn't mention the fact that I didn't talk or my past.

Everything was going fairly well. A few smiles and laughs were exchanged until a terrible scent filled my nose. Soon a she-wolf with pin-straight hair, full pink lips, and a cocky smile plastered across her mouth. She had an icy gaze and confidence radiated off her.

A low growl escaped my lips as I held Shane impossibly tighter, feeling overprotective over what was mine. She smirked as she walked over to us, happy to see that she'd caused me to react the way I had.

"Ugh. Why did you bring this mutt here?" she snorted as she looked me up once and scoffed. "I didn't realize you did charity work."

A low warning growl rumbled deep within Shane's chest, causing all laughter and conversation to instantly stop as all attention fell on the three of us.

"Woah. Relax, Fido," she mocked, causing Shane's eyes to grow black due to the disrespect she was dishing.

"This is my mate, Ariel," he said in a low voice, his control hanging by a small and fraying thread. "And you will not disrespect her or me ever again. Do you understand, Stephanie?"

"Are you serious?" She laughed, ignoring Shane's warning, which caused him to go rigid as his grip on me tightened. "I'm surprised you haven't rejected her and gone after someone more . . . your class. Familiar," she said, batting her fake eyelashes.

"I would never reject her. She's stronger than you'll ever be and this is your last warning. Don't disrespect your luna or there will be severe consequences. Do you understand?"

"If she's so tough, then why isn't she defending herself?"

An unsettling darkness took place on Shane's face as another angrier growl escaped from his lips before he made a move to go after her. Before he could, I gently placed a hand on his cheek causing his feet to become stuck in place even though his heated gaze was still set on Stephanie.

"Let me go," he growled lowly, his eyes still never leaving her.

I used my hand and gently moved his head so that his focus was now on me instead of her.

"No," I said, soundlessly mouthing the single word and causing him to clench his jaw.

I felt the foreign need to prove myself not only to her but to Shane and the rest of the pack as well. I wanted to show them that I wasn't a weak little girl anymore, or that I was at least trying to change. Before he could say anything, I grabbed his hand and wrote.

Me and her.

"No," he instantly said, shaking his head. "You still need time to heal, and you don't know what she's capable of."

"Neither do you," I said calmly, mouthing the words before I turned to Stephanie and walked to her.

A smirk decorated her lips as she approached me too. "This is going to be too easy," she said cockily before she launched at me, but I easily sidestepped, causing her to fall on to the floor.

Once she got up, she let out an angry growl, which I returned with a loud one I didn't know I had. She tried to throw a punch, but I grabbed her fist and elbowed her lower back, then threw her on the floor.

I tried to figure out where I'd learned all of these things from before I came to a horrid realization. The things I was doing to Stephanie were the exact same things Morgan had done to me when I'd tried to fight back or escape.

A small shiver ran down my spine, but I couldn't marvel in my thoughts much longer because Stephanie was trying to get up. I quickly straddled over her, pinning her down, and let out a deep growl in her face daring her to try anything.

And she did.

She extended her claws and raked them across my cheek, causing me to hiss in pain, but it healed quickly due to its shallowness. I quickly drew my fist back and punched her square in the nose, causing her eyes to roll back in her head as she became limp. The delicate skin under her eyes turned blackish purple.

Before I knew what I was doing, I let out another loud growl warning anyone else who wanted to try me. After I was certain that they got the message, I sighed as I stood up and placed a strand of hair behind my ear. Only then did I realize that all of the pack members that were there had gathered in a circle around me and were now bowing in respect and submission . . . even Shane.

After a few moments, they all looked up before giving me respectful nods then slowly going back to what they had been doing before. I made my way back to Shane, who had a look of pure shock on his face. He was brought out of his trance when my hand slid into his.

"My Goddess . . ." He trailed off as he looked down at me, amazement shining in his eyes. "I guess they were right when they said that big things come in small packages."

I offered him a small smile before I started dragging him toward the direction of the door, not wanting to be the center of attention for any longer.

"Take her to the cells and immediately let me know when she's awake."

"Yes, Alpha," two men said in unison before one of them threw Stephanie over his shoulder and walked out of the house.

I couldn't help but feel bad because not only did I possibly break her nose, but now she had to deal with Shane.

My mind wandered to what he might do to her. He was furious when she insulted and disrespected me and if I hadn't stopped him . . . I tried to convince myself that Shane couldn't possibly snap on her the way Morgan snapped on me, but the look on his face mixed with the anger that was in his eyes and etched on his face told a different story.

I shook my head in an attempt to shake the thoughts from my mind.

No matter how far away Morgan was, he still struck fear in me. His memories and the trauma affected how I viewed Shane and myself.

We walked back to the house in silence while Shane's thumb gently caressed my knuckles.

"I will show you around the pack grounds tomorrow, okay?" he said as we walked into the house, and I nodded. "Are you hungry? I mean, you did sleep through almost six hours of driving."

My eyes grew wide at his words, and he laughed.

"Don't worry. You're a cute sleeper."

I sighed as I tried to fight the smile that was growing on my face and shook my head to his question.

"Suit yourself."

We walked into the heaven that was our bedroom, and I let myself fall onto the bed as I closed my eyes.

"You ready for bed?"

I nodded, not opening my eyes.

"Okay," he said as he switched the lamp off. The sound of shuffling fabric followed before the bed dipped beside me. I opened my eyes, and a small sigh escaped my lips as I saw him sitting on the edge of the bed taking off his shoes, his back muscles flexing and stretching as he did so.

I slowly sat up and kicked off my own shoes followed by the sweatpants since Shane's sweatshirt came down to my knees. I carefully slid under the covers, making sure that I stayed as far away from Shane's side of the bed as possible. I was still getting acclimated to this whole mate thing, and I wanted to take it slow.

A few moments later, Shane joined me under the sheets. Picking up on the vibes that I was sending his way, a quiet sigh pushed past his lips before he said, "Good night, love."

I slipped into the most peaceful sleep I'd had in years.

CHAPTER FOUR

When I woke up, I was lying on Shane. When I said lying on him, I didn't mean an arm or a leg on him. I meant that my whole body was lying on top of his with his massive arms encircling my waist and holding me so close that I couldn't tell which heartbeat belonged to whom.

My first instinct was to get off of him as fast as possible, but I was stopped when my hands landed themselves on his stubble covered jaw. To my surprise, he didn't wake up or flinch. Instead, he nuzzled into my hand, and my heart jumped. My thumb slowly started wiping over his cheek in steady motions as I studied him like I'd never had the pleasure of looking at his face.

"I could wake up like this every morning," Shane suddenly said, his voice heavy and husky from sleep.

A small gasp exited my lips as I instantly pulled my hand back. My cheeks burned from embarrassment at the fact that I'd been caught.

Shane's eyebrows furrowed as he opened his eyes. His lips poked out in disappointment. "I didn't say you had to stop," he said as he removed one arm from around my hips and held my hand in his own before gently placing my hand back onto his cheek. His eyes never left mine.

My thumb slowly started moving on his jaw like it had earlier until it got its own rhythm.

"I want to know you better," Shane suddenly whispered, breaking the silence that had formed between us.

I used his chest as a canvas instead of his hand like I did last night and brought my finger down to spell a simple word.

What?

Shane looked like he was in deep thought as I continued stroking his face.

"How old are you?" he finally asked.

Twenty.

"Twenty-one," he responded. "What do you like to do?"

It took me a while to come up with a valid answer to that question since I'd been locked up for so long that I'd forgotten what my life had really been before waking up and going to sleep to beatings.

I don't know. Been too long.

A look of anger crossed Shane's face, causing me to tense. I guess it wasn't the answer he was looking for.

"I wish you would've let me kill him for what he's done to you," Shane said in a deathly low voice that caused a shudder to move through my spine and throughout the rest of my body, but he didn't seem to notice. "Alright. The final question that determines how this relationship will go from here on out," he said, his words pushing away the tension that filled the air.

I nodded expectantly and awaited his question.

"Baths or showers?"

It took me a few seconds to come up with an answer that would satisfy the question. *Baths or showers* . . . After I'd finally decided on my answer, I brought my finger down to Shane's chest to write the simple letters.

Bath

After I crossed my "h," Shane gasped in mock horror. His hand flew to his chest just above his heart. "How can you like baths? I mean, you just sit in your own dirt and rub it back on to yourself!"

I chuckled before I wrote.

Relax.

Shane rolled his eyes and looked away from me. "I honestly don't think I can look at you right now."

I sighed as I began pushing myself off of Shane, but instantly, his arms encircled my waist once more and pulled me closer than he had before.

"I didn't say I wanted you to leave," he said softly as he slid his thumb across my cheeks like I did to him, causing my heart to beat a million times faster.

A small grin graced his lips as he continued looking at me.

"You're truly beautiful, Ariel," he whispered, causing me to blush as I looked away while shaking my head. "What do you mean no?" he asked, annoyance thriving in his words.

I shrank back a bit, but Shane turned my head so that I was looking him dead in the eye. He held me captive there.

"Ariel, no matter what your past is or how bad you think you look, it doesn't hold a candle to the shining beauty that you hold."

I felt my heart leap at his words as his thumb slowly started moving across my cheek once more.

32

"You are absolutely gorgeous, Ariel. Never let anyone, not even yourself, tell you any different."

I couldn't fight the small smile that took place on my face, causing Shane to smile as well.

"There it is," he whispered. "There's that beautiful smile. Come on. Let's get some breakfast."

I carefully climbed off of him and out of bed. He followed soon after. As soon as we stepped into the hallway, I was instantly lost. The hallway was impossibly longer than I remembered it to be. It was probably because it was so dark and I was a bit distracted by Shane.

Shane led me down the wooden stairs and into the massive foyer where two long hallways awaited us. He took me through the hall on the right. After passing eight or so rooms, we were in the massive kitchen that had another room, which I assumed was the dining room, branching off of it.

Suddenly, without warning, Shane grabbed me underneath my thighs and effortlessly placed me on the counter. No matter how many times he did it, I couldn't help the frightened gasp that escaped my lips every time.

He chuckled before he leaned against the counter. With his hands on either side of me, his mind-numbing scent rushed into my nose.

"I'm going to make you a special breakfast that you're going to like way better than that human junk," he said before he pushed himself off of the counter and started rummaging through cabinets in search of what he needed.

After a few moments, pans lined the counter along with various ingredients for various foods. Shane's skilled hands moved like lightning as he picked up ingredient after ingredient. My mouth started watering not only because of the yummy smelling aromas that filled the air but also because of the handsome man in front of me working his magic with his muscles on full display.

Just the way they pulled and flexed and the way the light bounced off them just right . . .

I didn't realize that he'd turned around and caught me until his deep chuckle filled the air as he approached me. I wanted to turn away and try to play it off, but I was simply frozen.

"Don't do that, love," he said as he leaned over me like he had before.

Confusion filled my mind before he lifted his hand up and gently released my bottom lip, which had found itself caught in the grasp of my teeth.

"It makes me want to kiss you too badly."

This time I was actually able to turn away as a blush burned itself onto my cheeks.

"If you like your eggs scrambled, nod yes. If not, shake your head," he said as if he didn't say what he had.

I quickly nodded, trying to distract myself from my massive blush.

Once the eggs were done, Shane started filling two plates with every food that he cooked. He then prepared two glasses of orange juice. Shane carried a plate and juice over to me and placed them in my hands before he got his own. He plopped down next to me on the counter, placed his plate on his lap, and looked at me expectantly. My eyebrows furrowed in confusion. A whisper of a laugh escaped his lips before he picked up the fork that rested on my plate and picked up some of the eggs off my plate.

"Open up," he stated as he lifted the fork up to my mouth.

I smiled before I did as I was instructed to do. Shane effortlessly placed the fork in my mouth with the eggs on it, and as soon as they hit my taste buds, I knew that I was in my own heaven.

"You like it?"

I nodded in response before I took the fork from Shane's hand and greedily started digging into my food, not caring about how much of a pig I looked like.

It'd been a while since I'd been allowed the luxury of real food. Morgan had only allowed me to have stray food scraps or rotting meat and the junk Shane gave me yesterday was not food, but this was amazing. After I got down to wolfing down the eggs, I moved on to the butter and syrup covered pancake then finally to the delicious bacon that I'd missed so much over the past years.

Once I'd washed everything down with the orange juice, a dull ache broke through my stomach because I'd eaten more than I had in the past few years. It was a welcome ache. An ache that reminded me that things were changing, and so far, they were changing for the better.

I sighed as I gently placed a hand on my stomach, applying a slight amount of pressure to counter the pain that was growing in my stomach.

"Do you want some more?" Shane asked, and I instantly shook my head. "Me either," he said as he took all of our dishes and piled them on top of each other before he carried them to the sink, preparing to wash them.

I slowly pushed myself off of the counter and stood next to him at the sink. I instantly ran the water and watched as it slowly filled the sink. I filled the sink with dish soap before I placed both Shane's and my dishes in the high white bubbles.

"Relax, love. It's my job to take care of maintenance, and it's your job to relax."

I couldn't help it as my heart skipped a beat and the hoard of butterflies flew in my stomach. I reluctantly nodded before I climbed on the counter that was right next to the sink.

Shane's hands easily glided over each dish as he removed every trace of food that was once there. A few moments later, the sound of the doorbell rang through the house. Shane's eyebrows furrowed together, which formed a small crease between his eyebrows. Then he wiped his hands with a towel.

"I'll be right back," he said as he walked out the door, leaving me alone in the kitchen.

35

A few moments later, I heard the faint sound of the door opening followed by the muffled sound of voices through the air. Soon, the door closed and Shane returned to the kitchen, running his hands through his hair.

"I have to take care of some things, okay?" he said, and I nodded before I hopped off of the counter and walked side by side with him back to our room. Shane quickly threw on a shirt as I sat down on the edge of the bed and watched him. "I'll be right back, okay?"

I nodded despite how much I wanted him to stay with me and never leave. Shane gave me a small smile before he disappeared out the door and my heart instantly dropped. I couldn't help but miss him though he hadn't wandered far.

I started looking for a distraction to take my attention from the loneliness that slowly crept into my system as Morgan's threat repeated itself in my head.

"This is not over, mutt."

A small shiver ran down my spine. I wished Shane never had to leave my side.

I sighed quietly before I got out of the bed and wandered into the bathroom to get ready for the day. As soon as I turned on the light, a huge bathroom greeted me. There was a huge shower with a tiled floor, and two shower heads right next to each other, all enclosed within those glass squares that blur everything from the outside. Next to it was a large jacuzzi that was just begging for me to get into it. I bit my bottom lip, debating whether or not to give in to my desires without gaining permission from Shane first.

He said he wouldn't hurt me and I hoped he kept his promise.

Moon Goddess, please be with me. I silently prayed before I started running the warm water. I added some bubbly soap as the water continued to rise, and when the tub was almost full, I turned off the water.

I stripped slowly, remembering my bruises and scars that decorated my torso. When I didn't see the familiar ugly scars on my ribs, my mind went back to when Shane healed me. A small smile snuck onto my face as the thought crept into my mind.

After I shed the last of my clothing, I slowly crept into the water. A few hisses escaped my lips as the hot water rushed over me. As soon as I made it all the way in, a relaxed sigh pushed past my lips as I sank in a little deeper until the water was just below my nose. I closed my eyes and allowed the hot water to wash my worries away.

After a few moments of relaxing, I grabbed the soap and started bathing. I hummed a random tune before I started shampooing my scalp, giggling as the small bubbles fluttered in front of my face and popped on my nose.

As soon as I was done, I pulled the drain and watched as the water swirled into oblivion before I pulled a large towel off its rack. I dried myself then secured it around my chest. I walked over to the sink and found an unopened toothbrush pack. I opened it and quickly applied toothpaste then brushed my teeth. I hoped Shane wouldn't be upset.

When I completed that task, I wandered through the door that led to what I hoped was the closet. My hopes were confirmed when Shane's scent rushed into my nose and racks upon racks of his clothes came into view after I flipped on the lights. I hugged my towel close to my body as I let my fingers gently skim each article of clothing I passed.

Eventually, I settled on a hockey jersey and a new pair of boxers, which I hoped he wouldn't mind that I opened. I looked at my appearance, being as satisfied as I could wearing oversized clothes that swallowed my little body whole.

I wandered back into the bedroom. I aimlessly walked around the huge room while my fingers touched everything that I came across. After doing that for a while, my legs took me back to the bed where I crashed with a thick book in my hands. I crossed my legs and opened the book. Almost instantly, the words on the page captured me like a spider to its prey and swallowed me whole.

*   *   *

I'd been reading for nearly two hours when Shane's scent filled my nose. My eyes immediately left the book's pages, hoping to see him standing at the doorway with a breathtaking smile on his face, but I had no such luck.

My eyebrows pulled together as I looked around and took another deep breath. Along with Shane's, another horrid scent that I recognized filled my nose, causing me to growl subconsciously.

A few moments later, the door flew open, revealing Shane with a stone cold look on his face, and in front of him stood Stephanie with a pained look on hers. I was confused before my eyes landed on Shane's hand, which was digging into her arm with his claws fully extended and blood was dripping down her arm.

"Say it," Shane growled lowly, causing her to finally make full eye contact with me.

I straightened up and made solid eye contact with her.

"I-I'm sorry about yesterday, Luna," she said, pain obvious in her voice. "It's just that I'm protective over Shane because he and I had a— AH!" She suddenly screamed as Shane's fingers dug deeper into her skin. "Take it easy! You're lucky I even agreed to come and see your pathetic, ugly mutt of a—AHHH!" She screamed once more before she collapsed to her knees with Shane's claws still very deep in her arm.

"I warned you. Didn't I?" Shane said lowly, anger clinging to his every word.

Stephanie growled before she ripped herself out of Shane's grasp. Unfazed by the amount of blood and flesh she'd lost in the process, she came at me without a moment's hesitation. "He's mine!" she growled as she landed on top of me with unprecedented grace. Her eyes were pitch black, letting me know that her wolf was about to take control.

I became paralyzed in fear. Everything that I'd "learned" from Morgan instantly left my brain, leaving me at Stephanie's mercy.

She must have noticed my fear because she smiled and laughed. "I'm going to have fun ripping you to shreds and hearing you scream for mercy, mutt," she spat before a growl so loud and deep rang through the room that it caused the floor beneath my back to shake.

Without warning, a black blur tackled Stephanie from on top of me followed by screams and growls. I quickly sat up to see a giant black wolf on top of Stephanie. A dark and murderous look raged in its eyes, and I instantly knew it was Shane.

His wolf had the same obsidian black hair and hazel-green eyes. It was huge and muscular, and I could feel its power radiating off him like I could when he was in human form. I was so enamored by his wolf that I didn't realize what he was doing to her.

She had blood all over her to the point that I saw more blood than actual skin and her screams had grown silent because she was unconscious, but that didn't slow him down. I quickly scrambled to my feet before I started stomping as loud as I could on the floor, trying to get Shane's attention off of her and onto me. He merely glanced at me, seeing that I was in no harm before he started growling at her bloodied body.

If he didn't stop now, he would kill her. I took a deep breath before I used every ounce of courage in my being and walked up to him before grabbing him by his nape. Before Shane could fully realize what was happening, I used every bit of strength I had to throw Shane's massive beast off of her. He landed a few feet away, and pain exploded within my shoulders from how heavy he was.

As soon as he was down, he got right back up. His low growl ripped through the air as he bared his fangs. Despite the fear that was swallowing my being, I stood my ground, looking into his eyes, which one was never supposed to do to an alpha because they took that as a challenge. But instead of pouncing on me like I expected him to do, the sound of cracking bones filled the air as he began to shift back, causing me to look away not only because the sight of it made my stomach churn, but also because he'd be naked after shifting back.

"Why did you do that?" Shane growled, causing me to shrink back and avoid eye contact with him. "I asked you a question," he stated sternly as he placed a hand on either side of my face and gently forced me to look at him.

I finally made eye contact with him and instantly regretted it. I could see the rage swimming in his still black eyes.

"Answer me, Ariel," he said as he offered me his hand, frustration clinging on to his words.

I cautiously took his hand before writing on it.

You didn't stop.

He scoffed as he turned away from me, running his fingers through his hair before he picked up his boxers from off the floor and slid them on. Even though he was fuming, I couldn't help but watch as his muscles continuously flexed.

"Of course I didn't stop, Ariel," he finally said after calming himself down. "I don't know if you noticed, but she was going to kill you and I can't . . . I won't allow her to live knowing that she wants to kill you. It's my job to protect you whether you like it or not, and I will do whatever it takes to keep you safe."

I turned my head and looked at Stephanie. Her chest was steadily rising and falling, and her wounds were already healing. The smell of her blood still stained the air, and it made me want to throw up, but something she had said still plagued my mind.

I grabbed Shane's hand down and wrote.

You and her?

"What do you mean?" he asked, his eyes now traveling to her.

"You and her," I repeated silently. My heart dropped a bit as I wrote it even though I knew that it shouldn't. Shane had the right to do whatever he wanted. *He didn't know me . . . But why did my chest hurt at the thought of his lips on somebody else's?*

He sighed as he closed his eyes. After a few moments, he looked back at me, regret washing over his features.

"Well, I guess I was going to have to tell you eventually." He sighed as he let go of my hand and sat down on the bed, but I remained standing. "So a bit over two years ago, Stephanie was 'mine' per say. Back then, she was different though. She was sweet and caring, not the pain in the neck who spreads her legs open for everyone that she is now," he said, his eyes going to her once more. "I honestly thought that she'd be mine forever, not only for her personality and beauty that she once had before she replaced everything with plastic but also because she met my needs."

Anguish clawed at me from the inside because I knew that I couldn't provide Shane what he needed and because of the almost wistful look on his face as he talked about his past with her.

Did he still like her? I mean, I knew that he said that he'd do anything for me, but did he really mean it? Did he miss what they had? Did he realize that she offered more than I did or ever would be able to?

"We never had sex, though. I wanted to save myself because I knew that someone—you were out there somewhere and I wanted to share my first everything with you."

My eyebrows furrowed in confusion. If he knew that I was out there, why was he wasting his time hooking up with her instead of trying to find me sooner? I knew it was a stupid thought because he couldn't have had any idea where I was or what I was going through, but still . . .

41

"After a little while, I ended it because I knew I should've been spending my time looking for the one who could truly make me happy and I'm sorry, Ariel. I know I should've saved all my love and kisses for you, and I shouldn't have let my wants or anything get in the way of what was right. I'm sorry. Please, forgive me. It was a terrible mistake that will never happen again."

I studied him, looking for anything that'd make me believe that he was lying, but like all the other times I searched, I came up dry. I walked over to the bed and grabbed his hand.

Never again.

"Never again," he promised just as a groan filled the air, causing us both to turn our heads at the same time to see Stephanie regaining consciousness.

A growl escaped Shane's lips as he tensed and made a move toward her, but I stopped him by grabbing his shoulder.

"Don't hurt her," I said soundlessly, causing his jaw to clench.

"But, Ariel, she tried to—"

I gave him a look, and he sighed in defeat before he turned to Stephanie and calmly slung her over his shoulder despite the rage that still burned in his eyes. "I'm taking her back to the cells," he told me. "And we're going to have a little chat. Don't worry. I won't do anything to her unless she gives me a reason to."

"Don't hurt her," I said mutely.

"I will if she tries to come after you again."

I sighed in defeat, knowing that there was no talking him out of this, before I nodded, and he began walking out the door.

"I'll clean up the mess when I get back!" he called from somewhere deep in the house before the sound of the door opening and closing filled my ears. Then I was alone in our room with Stephanie's blood staining the floor.

42

I knew I wasn't going to be able to do anything knowing that her blood was still on the floor, so I dragged myself into the bathroom and looked through every cabinet looking for cleaning supplies and rags until I found what I was looking for.

I spent half an hour cleaning and recleaning the floor and even when I couldn't see it anymore, the smell stayed prominent in the air. I continued cleaning until the only thing I could smell was the terrible smell of cleaning products. After I was done, I washed my hands until they were numb, not wanting a trace of the chemicals on my hands.

I was exhausted by the time I was finished, but I couldn't let myself go to sleep. Instead, I lay down on my back and stared up at the ceiling, trying to find shapes on the paint.

I was so preoccupied that I didn't notice Shane return until I felt the bed dip beside me, causing me to shoot up into an upright position.

"Woah. Didn't mean to scare you," Shane apologized, the smell of Stephanie's blood masking his usually sweet scent.

Her blood on you.

He nodded. "I know, but I didn't do anything to her." I nodded in response.

Take a shower.

"Oh, come on. I don't smell that bad, do I?" he joked, causing me to nod before I pointed to the bathroom door. "Fine." He groaned like a little child before he got up and dragged himself to the bathroom.

Soon the sound of rushing water filled my ears as I returned to my position on the bed, staring up at the ceiling once more. After doing that for a solid seven and a half minutes, the sound of water stopped, followed by the muffled sounds of shuffling before the door finally opened.

I subconsciously sat up and was met not only by a warm blast of air to the face but also the breathtaking masterpiece that was Alpha Shane Chase. His black hair somehow managed to become even darker, wet strands hanging along his forehead with water droplets dropping off the edges and running down the rest of his body.

"Is this better?" he asked as he ran his fingers through his wet hair, pulling my eyes off his body and to his eyes.

I felt a small blush settle on my cheeks as I swallowed the small lump that formed in my throat before I nodded. I allowed my eyes to linger on him as he wandered into his closet, and as soon as he was out of sight, I facepalmed myself at the fact I'd reacted that way.

After a few moments, Shane returned, sporting a hoodie with the hood over his head, some jeans, and some sneakers. In his hands, he held a pair of sweatpants. I looked at him in confusion as he tossed the pants at me, barely missing my face by an inch.

"Sorry," he apologized as he disappeared into his closet before he returned with another pair of shoes. "But I can't have you leaving the house like that."

I slowly slid on the sweatpants he'd thrown at me. My eyes were still trained on him as I impatiently waited for an answer.

"We're going to get you some clothes," he finally stated as he handed me the shoes that had a pair of socks resting inside one.

I nodded as I pulled out the socks, but on the inside, I was screaming with excitement. I'd have contact with the outside world and other people for the first time in a while.

As soon as I was done, Shane offered me his arm, which I gratefully accepted. He led me through the house and out into the already familiar car that I'd ridden in when he brought me here.

"You might want to get comfortable," he said as he pulled his seatbelt across his body. "It's going to be a long drive to the human world."

At those words, my heart dropped as I stopped in the middle of fastening my seatbelt. I'd barely gotten used to freely being back in my world, let alone the human world. A small shiver ran down my spine as the warnings my parents told me rang in my head.

"If they find out about us, they'll kill us on the spot." My father had told me after a human had found him in his wolf form and shot him when I was six. *"They're ruthless. All they care about are themselves and money."*

The memory of my father caused my chest to tighten. I took a deep breath as I tried calming myself down, knowing that if I got too emotional, I was at risk of shifting right here in the car. I started hyperventilating as pressure built up behind my eyes, letting me know that my wolf was pushing against its boundaries and aching to get out.

"Ariel, look at me," Shane said, as he cupped my cheek and made me look at him in the eyes.

Even when I did, the pressure behind my eyes continued growing, causing me to scream in agony as a supernova of pain burst in my skull.

"Ariel, breathe," Shane instructed, eerily calm and focused on calming me down. "I'm right here." He rested his forehead on mine and closed his eyes as he moved his hand from my cheek down to my hand where he intertwined our fingers. "Just breathe with me, okay?"

I nodded before I followed his example. I closed my eyes and started taking deep breaths. Whimpers escaped my lips every now and then when the pressure began building up once more. After a few minutes, I let out an even breath and opened my eyes, relieved that the pain was gone.

"Are you okay, Ariel?" Shane asked as he opened his eyes, still resting his forehead on mine.

I simply nodded before I closed my eyes once more and took a deep breath, allowing his scent to comfort me like it had many times before.

"I'm sorry. I didn't mean to upset you," Shane stated gently. "I had no idea the human world affected you the way it does, and I'm sorry. If you want, we can go back inside, and I can ask one of the female pack members to shop for you?" he said more like a question than a suggestion, but I shook my head.

This was a new beginning for me, and this was a new fear I was going to have to conquer. Especially if I was going to be the luna of this pack. I slowly removed my hand from Shane's grasp before I opened his hand.

Don't leave, I wrote.

"I won't," Shane said as his fingers found their way back into the spaces between mine. "I promise."

I nodded before I leaned back into my seat and took a couple deep breaths as I looked out the window, my grip on Shane's hand tightening.

"If you ever want to come back, we will."

I nodded in response before Shane used his free hand to put the key in the ignition before we started our journey to the human world.

Moon Goddess, please don't let this be a bust.

CHAPTER FIVE

"Love, wake up. We're here," Shane called, causing me to slowly open my eyes, unaware that I'd closed them.

I blinked the sleep from my eyes and allowed them to adjust to the scene in front of me. We were in front of a huge mall with a million scents rushing to my nose, both new and old. I saw boys and girls laughing as they entered the building while some made out against their respective cars. Their actions were careless and wild.

"Are you ready?" Shane asked, giving my hand that still rested in his a light squeeze.

I nodded slowly, both curious and a bit scared of what lingered inside.

"Remember, I'll be right next to you the whole time, okay?"

I gave him another nod before I gently pulled my hand from his to unbuckle myself from the seat. Shane did the same shortly after.

We both walked around to the front of the car where our hands found their way back together like magnets, calming me down. Having physical contact with Shane solidified his promise that he wouldn't leave my side.

As we walked through the parking lot, groups of girls gawked at Shane while some boys narrowed their eyes at him. I couldn't help the weird feeling that built up in my chest, watching other people gawk at what was mine.

Wait. I thought. *Where'd that come from? Why is this affecting me so much?*

I tried to shake the nagging feeling away, but I couldn't, especially when more and more eyes were drawn to Shane. How could I blame them? He was breathtaking.

"Humans are so obsessed with what they can't have that they don't appreciate who they do have," he said, taking notice of the attention he was getting. As he spoke, his thumb gently caressed my knuckles. "But I am completely captivated by the beauty standing next to me."

A light blush stained my cheeks as we walked through the sliding doors of the mall. Instantly, the smell of various perfumes and fried foods rushed into my nose. I even smelled a few lycans here too, which calmed me down a bit.

I looked around me and tried to take everything in, but there were just too many stores and people all around me.

"If you need to step out for a bit, we can," Shane whispered in my ear, but I shook my head.

I wasn't about to let my fear and emotions get the best of me. Being among humans was a part of a normal lycan life, and even though it might be slow, I was determined to become acclimated to this new world.

"So, where do you want to go first then?" he questioned, and I shrugged before I allowed my feet to carry me to the clothing store that was displayed before me.

I slowly walked through the departments, eyeing everything curiously until something caught my eye. I walked over to the baby blue sundress with white polka dots scattered across it and ran my fingers over its smooth material.

"Do you want it?" Shane asked from behind me, and I gave him a look, asking the silent question. "Why don't you try it on?"

I nodded before I picked out my size and made my way to the fitting rooms, my hand leaving Shane's for the first time since we'd gotten here.

"I'll be right here, okay?"

I nodded in response before I disappeared into a stall. I quickly undressed and slid on the dress before looking at myself in the mirror. It didn't expose me too much, but it also didn't cover me up either. It also complimented my figure nicely.

I let my hair fall over my shoulders before I slowly opened the door, anxiously awaiting Shane's reaction. As soon as I opened the door, Shane pushed himself off the wall he'd been leaning on. He slowly walked toward me, and I watched his every move, trying to figure out his reaction.

"My God," he breathed out, breaking the silence that'd grown. "You look beautiful."

A smile worked its way onto my face as those simple words left his mouth. It seemed like the first time every time he said it.

"Go try something else on. I just . . . I just want to see you smile like that over and over and over."

I felt my heart flutter at his words as I gave him another nod, poorly suppressing the smile that was growing on my lips.

We continued wandering through the store, and I picked out clothes that I wanted, including shirts, pants, and underwear. Every time I would try on an outfit and show Shane, he'd say something that'd bring a smile to my face and a hoard of butterflies to my stomach.

After I'd picked out everything I wanted, we went up to the cashier who was male, thankfully because I didn't think that I could handle another girl trying to flirt with Shane right in front of me.

My eyes widened at the total amount we had to pay: over two hundred and fifty dollars. But Shane effortlessly pulled a card out of his pocket and slid it into the machine before punching in a series of numbers and taking all of the bags in his hands.

"Have a nice day," the cashier said as we left, but I was still in shock from not only buying that much, but also from the fact that Shane didn't seem fazed at all.

"Where do you want to go next?" he asked, causing me to give him a look of disbelief. "Today is about you, so we're going to do and get whatever you want."

"Too much money," I said noiselessly, mouthing the words as I shook my head, causing Shane to scoff.

"Ariel, there is no such thing as too much money when it comes to you, okay? I would buy you the world if you wanted it, and it'd all be worth it just to see a smile on your face."

I had to bite my lip to prevent another smile from rushing onto my face.

I've been smiling a lot lately, I thought to myself before I mouthed a thank you.

We went to two more stores where I got a few more articles of clothing along with a few shoes before we headed to the bookstore where I picked up a couple books to keep me busy when Shane had to leave for alpha duties.

"Are you sure you're ready to leave?" Shane asked from behind the mountain of bags he was carrying.

I laughed as I took a few bags from him and added it to the growing pile in my arms before I nodded to answer his question.

"Okay, but if you ever wanna come back, just let me know, and we will."

I gave him another nod as we left the mall.

Surprisingly, it wasn't as bad as I thought it would be. We blended right in with the humans, and when we passed a lycan every now and then, we'd exchange nods.

Despite my protests, Shane continued buying me things not caring how much it cost. On one hand, it was really sweet, but on the other hand, it was really foolish. I shouldn't have let him spend money that he could've been spending on the pack than on me.

Once we approached the car, Shane effortlessly balanced all of the bags before he dug into his back pocket and dug out the key. He pressed a button, causing the lights on the car to flash before the trunk slowly opened. As soon as it was open wide enough, Shane and I both shoved the bags in the trunk. They almost fell out as Shane closed the trunk and I hurriedly pushed the bags back in place. After Shane successfully closed the trunk, he chuckled as he wiped the invisible sweat from his brow.

"That was a struggle I never thought I'd have to encounter," he said jokingly before we went to our opposite sides of the car and got in. "Did you have fun?"

I nodded in response, causing Shane to grin.

"I'm glad you did. Now how about we head home and I'll make some enchiladas?"

I nodded excitedly. Memories of my family and I eating the amazing dish flashed through my mind as my mouth began to water.

He started the car before he reached his hand over to me. Instead of grabbing my hand like I expected him to, he rested his hand on my knee, his thumb slowly moving back and forth. I looked at him, and he looked back, shooting me another small grin before his focus went back to the parking lot.

We passed a ton of couples walking toward the entrance, and I caught a boy squeezing a girl's butt, causing her to squeal before their lips met for a quick kiss and I knew Shane and I would never be like that.

What they did was senseless, and every time Shane touched me, there was a motive behind it. Whether he was trying to calm me down or reassure me or if it was something completely oblivious to me, Shane always had a purpose. My mind wondered what the purpose of this interaction was, but it was soon whisked away. I didn't care what the motive for his actions was. I just cared that he was touching me.

I leaned my head against the headrest of the chair before I placed my hand on top of Shane's, loving the sparks that ignited every time we touched. I gave his hand a gentle squeeze before I allowed my eyes to close, unable to resist sleep any longer.

CHAPTER SIX

"Do you prefer chicken or beef?" Shane asked as I grabbed a pan and a bowl from a cabinet.

"Chicken," I said quietly, mouthing the words, and he nodded before he grabbed some from the freezer.

I looked at all of the ingredients in front of me, making sure that we had everything. Shane reluctantly allowed me to help him, claiming that even though he wanted to spoil me today, if I wanted to help, he'd let me.

We started making the food side by side, and small bolts of electricity moved through me every time our elbows bumped into each other or our hips gently met. We stayed like that for a while until all that was left to make was the sauce.

I was mixing the ingredients together for the sauce when suddenly Shane's arms wrapped themselves around my waist, causing me to suck in a sharp breath as I tensed up.

"Oh, I'm sorry. God, I keep forgetting that—" he rambled as his hands left me, but I stopped him like I had before: by placing my finger on his lips.

I took a deep breath. If I could handle being in a mall surrounded by the very beings I was told to fear, I could handle Shane touching me whenever he wanted. He knew his boundaries.

I jerked my head to the side, motioning for him to do it again before I turned back to my work.

"Are you sure?" he asked, a bit surprised. "I mean, I understand if you—"

He was interrupted by me gently grabbing one of his arms and placing it around my waist like it had been while my eyes stayed on his the whole time. A small smile stretched across his face before he wrapped his other arm around my waist then he hesitantly rested his chin on my shoulder. Once he realized that I wasn't tense or resisting, he relaxed.

As I was making the sauce, Shane's breath danced across my neck as he breathed.

After a few more minutes, it was done. I drizzled it over the top of the enchiladas before Shane slid them into the oven. After we were done cleaning the dishes we used to make the enchiladas, I found myself back to where I always did; on the counter with my feet dangling off the edge. Shane made his way over to me, placing his hands on either side of my waist and his hips lingering in the space between my legs.

"I'm going to show you around the pack grounds after we eat, okay?"

I nodded as my hands found their way to his soft, inky black hair.

"Then after that, we can start planning your Lunar Ceremony."

At those words, my fingers froze. Sometimes I forgot that I was mated not only to an alpha but to one of the strongest alphas in North America.

"Hey, don't worry," he said gently as he took my hands from his hair and held them in his own. "I'll be right there. Plus, the pack already respects you and sees you as their leader, so it's not like they don't approve of you already. Even if they didn't, they'd better not say anything, or else they'll have my fist down their throat."

I shook my head as a poorly concealed grin spread across my face like an infection before I took my hands from his and placed one on either side of his face, using my thumbs to gently caress him.

"Thank you," I said soundlessly, just mouthing the words before he placed his hands on top of mine.

"Don't thank me. It's my job to make sure that you're happy, safe, satisfied, and comfortable no matter what or who you're around."

There was sincerity in his voice and admiration in his eyes.

"You're going to make a great luna," he stated, leaning a bit closer to me. "You're caring and gentle even when it comes to the people who've wronged you, and you care more about other's well-being more than your own. Not to mention that you're also breathtakingly gorgeous and a gift to the eyes. You're just what this pack needs."

I realized that our faces had somehow lessened the distance between them. I felt Shane's breath brush against my lips in soft, smooth waves and a small shiver ran down my back as a result. Shane's intense eyes bore into mine as he cautiously moved closer and I knew what he wanted to do.

One part of me wanted to pull away and create as much distance between us as I could, but a bigger part of me wanted to feel him against me. Feel what a real, passionate kiss felt like from someone who actually cared about me, no matter if people were around or not. I wanted to feel his hands around my body as the kiss became more and more intimate. I wanted to feel love. I wanted to taste love. And I wanted him to be the one who showed me.

Shane must've had the same desire that I had because his eyes started flickering from my lips to my eyes then back to my lips again. My tongue darted out to moisten my dry lips as anticipation rushed through my veins. Shane watched my every move.

By now, we were so close that there was a hair's breadth between our noses. He looked me in the eye, asking me for permission, which I instantly granted without words. Before he could make his final move, the obnoxiously loud timer for the oven went off, causing me to gasp as I instantly pulled away.

Shane let out a couple "choice words" under his breath before he pushed himself off me and turned toward the stove. A small blush made its way onto my cheeks as I silently chastised myself. I shouldn't have let him get that close to kissing me. I shouldn't have wanted him to kiss me as much as I did. I needed to know that I could fully trust him before I could allow his lips to touch any part of my body no matter how much my body wanted to feel his touch or how much I craved the taste of his lips.

I let out a sigh as I ran my fingers through my hair. This mate bond was getting to me and affecting my judgment.

I need to take this slow.

I started repeating to myself as he approached me with a plate that held three enchiladas, which I graciously took.

We both partook of our meals in silence while Shane's eyes found mine every so often. After we'd both finished eating, we washed our dishes, a deafening silence stretching between us the whole time.

"Are you ready for that tour?" Shane asked after a while.

I gave him a simple nod, which made Shane slide his hand into mine.

As soon as we walked out, a blast of warm air hit me in the face like a wave. The sun was setting, dyeing the sky a beautiful watercolor. Shane and I started our journey through the freshly cut green grass past the pack house and toward a dense collection of trees.

"So I guess I'll start with the history of this pack like a true tour guide," he said as we waded through the grass that made it past our ankles. "I created this pack from nothing. My parents were the alpha and luna of their own pack, and they wanted me to take over once I came of age, but they were so . . . cruel. They killed any human or wolf they decided was too weak to carry the pack's name regardless of age or condition. They even tricked me into killing one of our own pack members."

His jaw clenched as those words left his mouth and his eyes lifted to the canopy of tree branches that lingered over our heads, sunlight trickling through every crack it found.

"They wanted me to kill a girl because they thought she was useless to the pack because she didn't develop her physical wolf as early as the others." He scoffed as he shook his head. "They said she was an embarrassment to their pack and needed to be executed, but I refused, and it made them furious. So that night, they banished both of us saying that my brothers would be better alphas than I could ever dream of being and left us at the mercy of rogues," he said, the words bitter in his mouth.

"I protected her like she was my blood, killing anything that was a danger to her. Eventually, I gathered more and more lycans along the way who'd either been cast out by my parents or their own packs but didn't want to go rogue. Soon, I'd gained enough members to form a proper pack, and through negotiation, I gained territory, and it's been growing ever since."

A small smile grew on my face at his success story. Going against your parents who didn't want you to be an alpha, then managing to become an alpha of one of the strongest packs in North America was a huge accomplishment and took a lot of hard work and dedication.

Where is the girl now?

I wrote, and instantly, a shadow fell onto his face.

"She was killed in our first rogue attack," he stated grimly. "She was one of our best warriors. She was protecting a little girl when one of them just came up behind her and plunged their hand into her back and ripped out her heart with no remorse."

57

I couldn't help the sorrow that burrowed into my chest as he spoke. I felt connected to her even though I'd never seen her a day in my life.

Silence fell over us as we continued stepping over fallen trees and ducking under low hanging branches.

"This is one of the pack training grounds," Shane finally said as we passed a large clearing that held over fifty pack members either running drills or sparring with each other.

I saw two men shift into their wolves before lunging and snapping at each other, each with incredible grace and agility. Soon, one man tackled the other to the ground, his jaw wide open ready to finish the latter off, but before anything happened, both of the men shifted back to their human forms.

"You might've won this time, Paul, but you haven't won the war," the guy on the ground said, as Paul, I assumed, laughed as he stood up and offered his hand to his friend.

"If you keep up with that form, there'll be no war to fight!"

Both of them, along with a couple of their comrades, laughed as one girl gave them a pair of shorts since theirs were ripped to shreds when they shifted.

Shane chuckled as he shook his head. "Those guys are always at each other's throats."

He continued showing me around the grounds including the other training grounds and the meeting hall where he held meetings with other alphas and/or betas from other packs.

After that, he showed me the prison where Stephanie, along with other pack members who were a danger to the safety of the pack, was held. No matter how many times I begged him to let me go inside, he refused, saying that it was too dangerous for me to go in there.

"Come on. It's getting late," he said as I looked up, and sure enough, the sky was being swallowed by darkness with only the sliver of the moon lighting the night.

I nodded as I allowed him to lead me back home and I snuck a quick glance over my shoulder at the prison where the girl who tried to kill me twice lingered. That moment, I made the decision that not only was I going to get in there, but I was also going to see her whether Shane liked it or not.

*   *   *

I was so engrossed in the book I was reading when the bed beside me dipped, and Shane's massive arms wrapped themselves around my waist. I squealed as I landed in his lap and his deep laughter filled the air. I narrowed my eyes at him before I hit him in his chest as water droplets from the shower he'd just taken fell from his hair onto his chest.

"I'm sorry, love. Did I scare you?" he asked playfully as he tucked a piece of hair that had fallen from my messy bun behind my ear.

I rolled my eyes before I swatted his hand away as if it were a pesky mosquito on a hot summer's day.

"I take that as a yes then." He chuckled as my attention returned to my book and not his hands that were securely around my waist, sending a million sparks through my body.

"So what are you reading anyway?" he asked, and I showed him the cover. "Oh, the classic Fault in Our Stars."

I nodded in response. John Green just had such a powerful, poetic way with words that I couldn't stop my fingers from turning the pages.

"It's getting late," Shane commented as he reached over and turned off the single lamp that was lighting our room, causing me to pout. "Don't worry. You'll have plenty of time tomorrow to read your book," Shane said as he took the book from my hands.

No matter how much I wanted to yank it from his hands, I knew that his grip would beat mine, so I let him take it without a fuss.

"Now come here," he said softly as he repositioned me so that my head was now resting on his bare chest and his arms were wrapped around my waist.

Physical contact to this extent still made me a bit uncomfortable, but I didn't want to tell Shane that. Instead, I sucked it up and buried my face deeper into his firm chest, his heartbeat creating a strong, steady pattern underneath my cheek.

"Good night, Ariel," Shane said, sleep slowly creeping into his words.

I merely closed my eyes and gently shifted as my thoughts wandered to what tomorrow might hold for my mate and me.

CHAPTER SEVEN

When I woke, I was alone in our bed. A yawn escaped my lips as I sat up and looked around, hoping to find Shane in the closet or hear water running in the bathroom, but I heard nothing. The house was silent.

I took a deep breath, but Shane wasn't in the house. My eyebrows furrowed as I prepared myself to get up, but something caught my attention out of the corner of my eye. On the nightstand was a piece of paper with my name on it.

Sorry, I had to leave, but I didn't want to wake you up. I have to take care of some pack business, but I should be back around noon. See you soon, beautiful.

Love, Shane.

I glanced at the digital clock that rested on the nightstand next to the note. It read 9:06 AM.

I can sneak out and see her, I thought to myself.

Despite the logical part of me telling me that I should listen to Shane and stay away from the prison, I couldn't fight the feeling that I needed to see her. I at least wanted to make sure that she was okay.

No, she wasn't my favorite person in the world, but I understood that she was hurting because she had feelings for Shane. Now that he had found me, she felt hurt and abandoned. It was my duty as the future luna of this pack to make sure that no one felt hurt, abandoned, or neglected because of stupid decisions.

I pulled myself out of bed, causing Shane's sweatshirt that I'd slept in to fall down to its full length, which was just past my knees. I hurried into the closet and pulled on a pair of leggings we'd bought yesterday underneath the sweatshirt. I grabbed two apples from downstairs, one for me and one for her before I started out the door.

As I walked out, the bright sun warmed my face, and the sounds of nature along with the laughter of the pack members filled my ears. Various smells filled my nose, and I couldn't help the relaxation that overwhelmed my being.

I took a bite out of my apple, its crisp taste numbing my taste buds.

I let my feet guide me down the path I'd memorized from yesterday evening. A couple of pack members gave me silent nods, which I returned. Glad that they didn't try to start a conversation or ask why I wasn't with Shane.

What am I going to do when I get there? Do they have a pencil and paper or will she have to read my lips or—My thoughts were interrupted by someone colliding with me, knocking me to the ground, and the apples in my hands rolled away.

"I'm sorry. I didn't see you there," the person, male, based on his voice, said as he offered me his hand.

The first thing that I noticed was the deep crimson that covered his hand and was etched underneath his fingernails. I looked up at him, and my heart dropped. Shane's face came into view, and a look of shock covered his face once he realized that I was standing in front of him.

"Ariel, I . . ." He trailed off as I looked down at the blood on his hands.

I recognized the scent.

It can't be. He said he wouldn't . . . But her blood was on his hands.

"I can explain," Shane said calmly as he reached for me, but I pulled away, not wanting his sin-stained hands to touch me.

Tears sprung to my eyes as I shook my head, hoping that this was all a huge nightmare, but I knew that it wouldn't work. This was a nightmare I couldn't wake up from. Before Shane could make another move toward me, I turned and ran the other direction not caring where I ended up or who saw me.

"Ariel!" Shane yelled as he ran after me, but I didn't want to be near him. I couldn't.

As I ran, I heard the faint sound of rushing water, and I immediately ran toward it, hoping that it was what I thought it was. Soon, a small stream came into my view and I let out a small sigh of relief before I jumped into it without a moment's hesitation. I stayed in the water until there wasn't a part of me that wasn't drenched in it.

Water distorted our ability to track someone by their scent, and I was grateful for the little stream because, without it, I would've been caught. I hurried to my feet before I quickly climbed up the first tree I saw, going as high as I dared.

I saw Shane's giant wolf slowly walk below me, and I pressed my hand against my mouth, fearing that if I breathed too loud, he'd find me. If only I could suppress the sound of my heartbeat. The sound of bones cracking filled the air as I watched his wolf transform into Shane.

He let out an irritated growl before he let out a slur of curse words as he started punching the tree I was in, though he didn't seem to realize I was in it. It shook violently, causing me to hold on to the trunk of the tree for stability. Just before I thought Shane would break the tree in half, he stopped. I looked down to see him sliding his back down the trunk of the tree before he rested his forehead on his knees, his shoulders harshly rising and falling as air entered and left him.

Pull yourself together, Ariel, I thought harshly to myself when the thought of going down there to comfort him crossed my mind. *Remember that he just killed her. He put what you wanted on the side for his own selfish desires.*

But she could've done something. I tried countering myself, but even I knew that would be impossible.

Why would she try something after he almost killed her the first time?

Underneath me, Shane pushed himself off the tree before he shifted back into his wolf and started running through the forest in search of me once more. I let out a soft sigh of relief as I carefully sat myself down on the branch and leaned against the trunk of the tree. I combed my wet hair out of my face and hugged myself to keep myself warm since my wet clothes were now clinging to me.

I had to take some time to sort everything out. I had to take some time to figure out what I was going to do.

*   *   *

It was about seven when I finally decided to return home. I'd cried all the tears that I could, and I sobbed my throat raw. My head hurt because I'd almost shifted about five times. Something inside me told me that I was overreacting, but I couldn't process the fact that someone had lost their life because they made a mistake.

I ran a hand down my face, my now dry clothes reluctantly moving with me.

I knocked on the massive door that loomed in front of me, wanting nothing more than to have a warm cup of cocoa while wrapped up in a big comfy blanket. As soon as the door opened, Shane wrapped his arms around me and pulled me into his bare chest, his neck buried in the crook of my neck. My arms hung limply at my sides despite how much I wanted to hug him too.

"I was so worried," he whispered into my neck. "I couldn't find you, and I thought something might've happened. I was about to call the warriors to look for you." He broke the hug before his hands found mine.

I could not let my fingers tightly lock with his; they were limp and devoid of any feeling.

"Come inside and let me explain what happened, okay?"

I nodded tiredly before I allowed him to pull me into the house. I went into the kitchen and made myself a steaming cup of hot cocoa, ignoring Shane as he begged me to allow him to help. I carefully carried the scorching cup upstairs where I set it on the nightstand to cool while I took a quick shower and changed into a sweatshirt and shorts. By the time I returned, it had cooled down to the point that I could actually drink it without burning my tongue.

"Are you feeling better?" he asked as I settled into the bed. I shrugged, causing him to sigh before he ran his hand through his hair. "I'm sorry, but can you please let me explain?"

I nodded as I sipped my drink, hoping that what he was about to say would soothe my worries and allow me to put this all behind me.

"I went down there to check on her after one of the guards told me that she was causing trouble. I planned to originally talk her down and assign her as an omega until I knew that I could trust her again."

An omega was the lowest rank in the pack. They had to do the worst jobs in the pack, but they still had freedom and privileges even if they were a bit limited.

"But when I opened the door to walk into her cell, she attacked me," he said as he turned his body to display the deep claw marks on his back that were healing slowly. "She started screaming about how it should've been her and me, and how you stole me away from me and all that nonsense."

He scoffed as he returned to his normal sitting position. "She said that she was going to finish what she started before she jumped off of me and ran through the door of her cell. I knew that no matter how I tried to reason with her, all she wanted to do was to kill you. So, I had to eliminate the threat."

His jaw became tight near the end, and his gaze became intense.

"I didn't want to kill her, Ariel. Even though she's made a lot of really bad decisions, she was still one of my pack members, and I knew her for a long time. But she signed her death wish when she tried to come after you again, and I couldn't let her continue breathing, knowing that she wanted to take you from me." He took my free hand and held it in his two hands. "Now you understand why I had to do it, right?" he said, his voice pleading for me to understand.

I nodded slowly even though I wished there would've been another way.

Shane let out a sigh of relief before his thumb gently brushed over my knuckles. "I know you didn't want me to, but I just couldn't find another option and—"

I lifted my finger up to my lips before gently putting it to his. The more I heard him talk about it, the worse I felt.

"I'm sorry. I'm rambling," he apologized as I retracted my hand and wrapped it around my mug before lifting it up to my lips once more.

Shane tentatively watched me as if he expected me to explode on him or something. Instead, I merely grabbed my book and picked up where I left off.

"I'll start with dinner," he said after a few awkward moments. "Any special requests?" he asked as he pulled himself out of bed.

I shook my head. Any hunger I'd had was drowned in the warm, chocolatey goodness that I was currently partaking in.

He nodded before he silently left the room.

66

It kind of hurt my wolf and me to treat him this way, but I couldn't help it. Maybe after I came to terms with what happened, we could return to normal or as normal as we had been. Until then, I had to deal with this the only way I knew how: by pushing him away.

I looked at the picture of my family that I used as a bookmark so that every time I did what I loved, I'd see the people that I loved. As always, a relaxed feeling came upon me when I looked at it. Sometimes, I felt that it was my parents reaching out to me from heaven and letting me know that everything was going to be okay. The corners of my lips tugged up as I slid the picture back in the book.

Let's just hope that I come to terms with everything soon.

Where It Hurts

UNKNOWN

I had to admit that these two were pulling through quite nicely and enduring what I had put them through so far better than I expected. That simply meant I needed to hit them where it hurt. Mess with their heads. Their hearts.

I had to make sure that these two were the right ones before I gave myself up to them.

A familiar blast of pain exploded in my heart, causing me to fall on my knees and let out a scream of pain. My glow was becoming dimmer. My power was fading.

I needed to hurry, or else, I, along with everyone else, was going to die.

It brought my heart pain, knowing what I was going to have to put them through in the next couple of months, but it was necessary to do this.

I hoped they could pull through because if they couldn't, we were all already dead.

CHAPTER EIGHT

It had been a couple days since the whole ordeal with Stephanie and things had slowly, but surely, started shifting back to normal between Shane and me. I'd started giving him the attention I used to, and I didn't pull away every time he'd try to touch or look at me.

I started mixing the frosting in the bowl that sat in front of me as I started humming a random song I'd heard on TV the other day. Not only had I developed a knack for reading but for baking too. It gave me time to think about everything while I was doing something that calmed my ever active mind.

"What are you making today, my beautiful baker?" Shane asked as he wrapped his arms around my waist and rested his chin on my shoulder, his moves calculated and soft.

I motioned to the box of cake mix that rested next to the bowl I was working on.

"Chocolate cake." He mused before the oven beeped, letting me know that the cake had finished baking.

I promptly slid the oven mitts onto my hands before I hurried to the oven and took the cake out. The sweet smell rushed into my nose as I placed it on the counter. I pulled the oven mitts off my hands and then prepared to finish the frosting, just to find

Shane standing with his back to me. A grin tugged at he edges of my lips seeing how eager he was to help me. His arms were moving in a circular motion as he continued mixing the thick frosting. I decided to transfer the cake to a cooling rack as I wait for him to finish. After a few moments, he was satisfied with his work and turned toward me then offered me the bowl, its contents mixed and smooth. There was a look of pride on his face as if the simple topping were his magnum opus.

Tapping the now cooled cake, I gave him a nod of thanks before I started applying it to the cake.

Shane watched silently as I started frosting the cake while happily licking my fingers when the frosting escaped the spatula I was using. I found myself humming as I continued my work. Shane's eyes followed my every move until there was no part of the cake left unfrosted. The corners of my lips curved up a bit as I looked at what I made.

It wasn't the best, but it was good enough for me.

I sprinkled a few chocolate chips over the frosting before I picked up my knife. I was about to cut a few slices for Shane and me when he stopped me.

"Hold on," he said as he gently used his fingertips to turn my head. "You've got something."

His eyes zeroed in on whatever was on my face before his thumb came into soft contact with my cheek. I saw chocolate frosting on Shane's thumb as he removed it from my face before he licked his thumb clean.

I raised an amused eyebrow at him, causing him to give me a confused look.

"What?" he asked. "A wise man always said, 'If there's chocolate somewhere, don't waste it.' "

I chuckled as I slightly shook my head before I started cutting the cake, two slices for the both of us.

I anxiously watched Shane as he took a bite, hoping to whatever god above that he liked it. As soon as the cake hit his tongue, he let out a sigh as he closed his eyes, his features relaxed.

"Oh my God, Ariel. This is amazing."

I smiled before I decided to test that theory for myself and ate a small piece.

Shane was not wrong.

We were indulging in our chocolate heaven when the doorbell rang. Shane excused himself to get the door. Not long after he departed, I heard him chuckle before a new voice spoke so low that I couldn't make out any words.

"Ariel," I heard Shane say before he appeared with another man in tow.

He was short but extremely muscular. Deep brown hair rested on top of his head, and he had equally deep brown eyes.

"Ariel, this is Aiden, my beta. Aiden, this is Ariel Carter, my mate."

"Hello, Luna," he said with a warm smile, which I returned along with a small wave.

"So how did the negotiations go?" Shane asked as he leaned his back against the counter next to me, his arms crossing across his chest making his muscles bulge.

"Good," Aiden said as he duplicated Aiden's actions on the counter that was across from Shane and I. "Everyone renewed their alliance, except one."

"Who?" Shane asked, his eyebrows furrowing, which caused a small crease to grow in between his eyebrows.

"Alpha Morgan."

Those two words shook me deep to the core, and I hated it. It disgusted me how much fear something as simple as a name could inject into me.

Shane wrapped his arm around my waist and pulled me closer to him, and I rested my cheek on his chest.

Shane scoffed. "What a surprise."

"Am I missing something?" Aiden asked, confusion evident on his features and in his voice.

"Don't worry about it," Shane said as his thumb moved in a soothing pattern against my hip, silently reminding me that he was there and he wouldn't allow anyone or anything to hurt me.

I relaxed against Shane.

A small smile stretched across Aiden's face. "You are perfect for him," he stated as he looked between Shane and me. "He's usually not a gentle, touchy-feely person, and I can see you're changing him."

"Alright, Aiden. You can go," Shane said, sounding almost bashful, causing Aiden to playfully roll his eyes.

"Okay. Okay. I'm leaving. It was nice to meet you, Luna," he said before he exited the kitchen then the house.

I turned to look at Shane, and to my surprise, his cheeks were slightly tinted red. I laughed, causing him to blush a bit more before he awkwardly cleared his throat in an attempt to hide it.

"Cute," I said quietly, mouthing the word, and I smiled up at him.

"Aiden has brain damage," Shane stated jokingly, trying to brush his embarrassment off, but I could see the red in his cheeks. "Now, where were we?" he said as he picked up his plate with his cake on it, but I took it out of his hands.

Shane frowned as I took the fork he'd been using and collected some cake onto it before I raised it to his lips just as he did to me a couple mornings ago. His frown quickly melted into a small grin before he greedily opened his mouth, eating the cake from the fork without breaking eye contact with me.

"You are an amazing baker, you know that?" Shane said after he finished his cake, and I merely shrugged as I had some cake off my own plate. "I'm serious! You're like the Harry Potter of the baking world."

I raised an eyebrow at him, but his focus was now on the cake and only on the cake.

After we'd finished our cake and stored the rest away for later, we headed upstairs for bed, moonlight spilling across the floor through the giant windows like milk.

As we walked through the long hallways, Shane snaked his arm around my waist and the mind-numbing sparks that appeared every time we touched were like fireworks. I didn't want the show to end.

Once we were in our bedroom, we changed out of our clothes and into our pajamas. I was in the middle of sliding on my pajama top when Shane suddenly froze with his leg halfway into his sweatpants. His muscles tensed up and his eyes clouded. When the clouds rolled from his eyes, he let out so many "colorful words" that I couldn't keep myself from blushing.

"Sorry you had to hear that," he apologized before he turned and started toward the door, but I quickly grabbed his arm, and his attention returned to me.

I simply raised an eyebrow. The simple action, communicating better than words ever could, triggered a sigh from him.

"There's a rogue at the western border," he said. The venom in his words showed his hatred for rogues.

Rogues were wolves that left the pack life and lived by their own rules. They did whatever they pleased. Kill whomever they pleased no matter if they were human or lycan, and they only gathered if they wanted to attack or cause chaos.

Many?

I wrote on his palm, and he shook his head.

"So far, there's only been one spotted, but there could be more." He took my hands into his own and looked me in the eyes. "I don't want you to go anywhere where there's even a possibility that you might get hurt. Please just wait here for me, okay? I'll be back in an hour."

Without waiting for my response, he quickly kissed my forehead before he hurried out the door. I stood there in shock for a moment with a pleasant warmth on my forehead where his lips had lingered moments ago.

I was snapped out of my trance when I heard the door slam resulting in the floor beneath my feet to gently shake. My feet quickly carried me to the window where I caught him shifting into his beautiful black wolf before he disappeared into the thick cluster of trees.

The desire to follow him clawed at me from deep within. I chewed on my bottom lip, weighing the pros and cons. I looked up at the moon and took a deep breath.

Please don't let him be upset. I prayed silently before I hurried out the house and followed Shane's scent to the western border.

CHAPTER NINE

I heard him before I saw him. The low, thunderous growls of his wolf filled my ears, causing my legs to move faster as the scent gathered in my nose: blood and wet dogs—a rogue.

When I finally got close enough to see, Shane had already shifted back, and one of the border patrol members threw him a pair of basketball shorts to cover himself up. In front of him was a girl about my age with rich dark skin, naked and covered in mud and grass.

"P-Please," she begged, her face shielded by her hands. "I-I'm sorry. I just need shelter."

"Who sent you?" Shane asked, stone-faced and emotionless.

"N-No one," she said quickly. "Please. A group of rogues is after me. They tried to take me from my pack, but I escaped. Please I ju—"

"Save it!" Shane snapped, causing the girl to whimper as she shrieked back. "Do you think I'm stupid?" He growled.

When she didn't respond, he closed the space between them and grabbed her cheeks and forced her to look up at him.

"Do you?" he yelled, and even I shrank back.

This side of Shane scared me, and I couldn't help but wonder if he was going to kill her.

She furiously shook her head and stuttered an apology. Shane scuffed and released her from his grasp.

"You're not the first rogue who's played that card. I've already made that mistake once, and I'm sure not going down that road again."

I couldn't just stand there any longer. I refused to. Just as Shane was about to shift back into his massive wolf and kill her, I ran over to her and threw myself between her and him, knowing that there was a huge chance that Shane wouldn't be able to stop himself and end up attacking me instead, but I didn't care.

I closed my eyes and braced myself for the impact, but it never came. When I opened my eyes, Shane was standing less than a foot away from me, his eyes black and his body tense as he took deep breaths.

"Ariel. Move," he growled lowly, but I shook my head.

"Help her," I said mutely, mouthing the words and causing him to scoff.

"Help her? Do you know what she is? What she's capable of?"

I nodded before I repeated myself, causing Shane to sigh as his eyes returned to their normal color.

"Ariel—" he started, but I ignored him and turned to the girl behind me.

She had short curly brown hair that had mud and sticks sticking out of it and the moonlight reflected off her hazel eyes. Her knees were against her chest to cover her bare body, and she had various cuts and claw marks all over her body.

She looked like me: scared and beaten. I wasn't going to let her get killed by Shane or the rogues that were after her.

I gripped the brim of my shirt and lifted it over my head before I gently slid it over her body. She graciously took it before she muttered thanks. Suddenly, I felt Shane's arms wrap around me before he pulled me into his chest not only because I was getting too close to her but also because I was now only in my bra.

"There are too many males around here," he growled in my ear, causing me to roll my eyes before I tried to break away from his grip but failed because he was stronger than me.

Hospital.

I wrote on his chest before I pointed to the girl, and Shane shook his head.

"The last time I let a rogue in, Aaliyah got killed, and we almost lost half our pack. I'm not going to let that happen again."

Hurt.

I wrote, motioning to her once more.

"Please," I said calmly, mouthing the word.

His jaw clenched as he looked at her while she tried to pick twigs and mud from her hair.

"Fine," he finally said. "But if she does anything, and I mean anything that makes me feel like she's a danger to the pack, I will kill her with my bare hands."

I nodded before I beckoned her over. After a few moments, I caught her attention. She hesitantly calmly got up and slowly made her way over, her weary eyes never leaving Shane's cold ones.

"What's your name?" he asked once she was in front of us.

"Jessica," she said, slightly lifting her chin up.

"Okay, Jessica. This is what's going to happen. We're going to take you to the pack doctor to get you checked out. If you try to run, you're dead. If you try to attack anyone, you're dead. If you do something as little as look at a pack member wrong—"

"I'm dead," she finished.

"Precisely," Shane said before he turned us and started walking toward the pack house. "Come on. I don't have all night."

We walked through the territory with a small number of Shane's border patrol following us, ready to pounce on Jessica if she made any sudden moves. On our way there, Shane gave me one of his spare shirts that he kept hidden in the trees.

Once we made it to the hospital, the border patrols left and resumed their positions at Shane's command. A pack doctor had Jessica take a shower before she began checking her out. After she treated Jessica's wounds and gave her more clothes to wear, she turned to Shane and asked what he wanted to do.

"What do you want to do, Ariel?" Shane asked lowly so that only he and I could hear.

I turned and looked at Jessica to see her fiddling with the hem of her shirt.

Keep her.

I wrote onto his outstretched hand. He nodded.

"I'm trusting your judgment on this one, but this conversation is not over." He turned his attention to Jessica, and I couldn't help but feel like I did something wrong based on the tone Shane used. "As for you, you will be given a room in the pack house. You are now a member of this pack, and as a member, you will respect your other pack members and our rules here. I am your alpha, and she is your luna. You will only address us as Alpha and Luna unless we say otherwise. Is that understood?"

"Yes, Alpha. Thank you," she said with a nod, which Shane and I returned.

"I will have my beta show you to your room. You will have one day to get used to your surroundings before you start your pack duties."

"Understood," she said with a nod just as Aiden walked in.

"Okay. What was so important that you just had to wake me up from my dream about Jennifer Lawrence?" Aiden grumbled, but he froze as soon as his eyes landed on Jessica.

I turned to look at Jessica, and she had the same facial expression on her face. I felt a small smile stretch across my face as Aiden slowly moved toward her, his facial expression not changing.

"My Goddess . . . ," he whispered once he was right in front of Jessica. "You're beautiful."

A smile stretched across her face as Aiden cupped her cheek.

"I've been waiting all my life for you, and it was totally worth it." Aiden smiled.

"It totally was," Jessica said as she bit her bottom lip to contain her smile.

Aiden silently looked at Shane, causing Shane to nod. Aiden wordlessly took Jessica's hand as he led her out of the room, his eyes never leaving hers and their smiles never disappearing.

A good thirty seconds after they left, Shane let out a long breath before he turned to the doctor who was still there with a look of shock on her face.

"You're dismissed," he said, and she hurried out.

As soon as she left, the mask of composure that Shane was wearing crumbled away and revealed the anger that lay underneath, and I prepared myself for a scolding.

"What were you thinking, Ariel?" Shane yelled, causing me to shrink back from his harsh tone. "I told you to stay at home! She could've been dangerous. She could've hurt you. And jumping in front of her like that . . ." He trailed off, taking deep breaths to calm himself down.

He closed his eyes and ran his hands through his hair before reopening them.

"I know you were just protecting her, but Ariel, I could've seriously hurt you or worse. I couldn't bear it if you were the one in this hospital room with way more than a few scratches and cuts."

His arms encircled my waist and pulled me close to him so that our hips were together. "You understand that, right?"

I nodded as I rested my hands on his shoulders.

"Good," he whispered before his lips came into soft contact with my forehead for the second time tonight.

Instead of tensing and pulling away, I selfishly allowed myself to give into him before he pulled away and rested his forehead against mine.

"Come on. Let's go home. This hospital smell is giving me a headache."

A light chuckle escaped my lips before his hand found mine and we made our way back home.

CHAPTER TEN

When I woke, surprisingly, Shane was still right there, his chest steadily rising and falling underneath my head. His arms were still locked around me, and his beautiful eyes were shielded from the world behind his eyelids.

My mind still couldn't process that this overwhelming being was mine. And I was his.

I slowly started shimmying my way out of his iron grip, but his hold on me was too strong.

"And where is it that you think you're going?" Shane asked, his voice deep and tired, and his eyes were still closed.

Bath.

I gently wrote on his broad chest.

"Fine." Shane sighed as he slowly released his grip on me, eyes still closed. "But don't take too long or I'll miss you too much."

I nodded as I climbed off of him, trying to ignore the giddy feeling that bloomed in my chest and made me feel happy all over as his words repeated themselves in my head.

I went into the closet and grabbed some clothes before I went into the bathroom and closed the door behind me. I filled the tub and quickly brushed my teeth while I waited for the water to fill the giant tub. Once it filled, I turned off the faucet and took off my clothes before I slowly slid into the tub full of white bubbles and warm water.

Me being the giant kid I was, I played in the bubbles for a solid ten minutes, laughing as it landed on my hair or on my nose. Once I was finished being a little child, I washed my body and my hair before I climbed out and drained the tub.

The towel wrapped around me like an old friend giving me a hug as I walked over to the sink. I applied deodorant followed by lotion and finally, I dried my hair. I easily slid on my underwear and bra then eased on a blue off-shoulder dress with my hair cascading across my shoulders. I wiggled my feet into my white flats then looked at myself in the mirror. After looking at myself for a few moments, I decided to apply some cherry lip gloss and mascara to pull my whole look together.

Once done, I gathered my towels and dirty clothes in my arms before I quietly made my way back into our bedroom, careful not to awaken Shane as I slipped out the door and to the kitchen.

I gathered the ingredients for waffles and bacon before I began my work.

I wanted to have Aiden and Jessica over for breakfast if Shane would allow it. I wanted to get to know them better and have it serve as an apology from Shane. I was in the middle of placing the items needed for the waffles in the mixing bowl when I heard a long, low whistle. I turned around just to see Shane looking at me from the doorway. He had a slight smile on his face and was now wearing a sweatshirt and basketball shorts. His hair was wet and dripping.

"You look beautiful." Shane breathed as he walked over to me, his eyes taking in every detail of me as he did.

"Thank you," I said silently, mouthing the words as he placed a hand on my cheek.

"The pleasure is all mine," he said. "What are you doing up this early anyway?" he asked as he offered me the palm of his hand.

Breakfast. Aiden. Jessica.

"Are you sure?" he hesitantly asked, and I nodded before I let go of his hand and returned to my work. "At least, let me help." He sighed as he walked over to the refrigerator and pulled out food after food. "I'm making omelets," he said, answering my unspoken question and I nodded.

We worked for about an hour and a half, with my giggles filling the air every time his delicate fingers touched me or his lips found my forehead or cheeks. Soon, mouthwatering aromas filled the house, and I had to keep myself from pigging out and simply eating all the food without Aiden and Jessica.

"Do you think this is enough?" Shane asked as he poured the pineapple cubes he'd been cutting into the fruit salad that we'd been working on.

I nodded as I grabbed the giant bowl and carried it out of the kitchen and into the dining room where we already had everything set up on the table. All we needed were our guests.

"They should be here any minute," Shane said while he wrapped his arms around my waist and kissed my cheek, causing small lightning bolts to strike where his lips lingered. "So what should we do until then?" he asked, his eyes holding mischief.

I shrugged as I slowly started making my way around the table to make sure that everything was perfect. Shane followed my every movement since his arms were still securely around me.

"Well, I have an idea."

I decided to entertain him, so I turned and lazily placed my hands on his shoulders with my eyebrow raised asking him the silent question that I already knew the answer to.

83

"Well, we could watch TV or bake something else, or . . . This one's my personal favorite. We can go upstairs to our room, cuddle a little bit, let me kiss you a little bit, and just do that for a while," he said, his voice soft at the end. "Just you and me."

I gently shook my head as my thumbs slowly started moving against the back of his neck.

"At least, I tried." He laughed under his breath. "I can still kiss you though."

Just to prove it, he placed yet another kiss on my forehead, causing me to chuckle as I playfully pushed him off before I started running from him.

"Ariel, get back here," Shane called as he started chasing me, causing me to squeal as I continued running. "You run fast," he said as his arms encircled me and pulled me back into his chest, causing me to let out a full laugh. "But you can't outrun me."

He buried his face in my neck and planted feather kisses along my neck and throat, causing me to let out a mixture of giggles and sighs.

"I love the sound of your laugh," Shane commented between kisses to my neck. His grip on my hips got tighter, but it didn't bother me. "And your smile," he continued. "The amazing feeling that comes over me when you touch me. How amazing you look, especially in this dress."

He gently kissed my exposed shoulder before he straightened up to his full height, causing me to crane my head upward to meet his eyes. One of his hands left my waist and slowly lifted to my face, where it removed a stray piece of hair from my face and tucked it behind my ear. He sighed as he let his hand fall down to his side.

"They're here," he said just before the doorbell rang. "I'll get it," he said as he started toward the door, but I grabbed his shoulder. He stopped and looked at me, a question swimming in his eyes.

I answered it by pointing to myself then to the door, before I walked past him to the door that separated us from them. Shane's gaze burned into me with every step that I took. I easily unlocked the door before I opened it.

My eyes instantly landed on Jessica who was dressed in a huge sweatshirt that swallowed her frame. I assumed it was Aiden's. Underneath it, she wore a pair of black leggings and some sandals, which I assumed Aiden got from a pack member. Her beautiful curly hair was pulled into a bun, and she had a mix of fear and uncertainty on her face.

I could tell she was especially nervous, judging from how tight her hand was wrapped around Aiden's. I smiled at her as I pulled her into a quick embrace. She tensed for a second from shock, but the shock melted away as she hugged me back. She no longer smelled like a rogue but of chestnuts and cinnamon.

"Good morning, Luna. Thank you for inviting us." She smiled as we broke the hug.

I nodded in response with a grin still on my face.

"Good morning, Ariel," Aiden greeted warmly as he hugged me.

As soon as I was out of Aiden's grasp, I was pulled into someone who I instantly recognized as Shane due to the sparks that erupted on my hip where his hand rested.

"Good morning, Aiden, Jessica," he said, nodding at them as he said their names. "Please, come in."

We stepped aside and allowed them to walk by. I couldn't help but notice how scared Jessica seemed when Shane said her name or when she walked by, but I couldn't blame her. Shane did almost kill her last night.

As soon as they were out of sight, I turned to Shane and took his hand in mine and wrote.

You scare her.

He let out a small scoff. "Ariel, I scare a lot of people. Just give it time, okay?" he said, and I shook my head.

Now.

I wrote, causing him to sigh.

"What do you want me to do?" he asked, giving in after a few moments of silence.

Play nice.

"I only play nice with you, Ariel," he said, causing my eyes to turn into narrow slits. "But if that's what you want, then I'll play slightly less mean."

I gave him a smile before I pushed myself on my tiptoes and gave him a gentle kiss on the cheek, causing a smile that matched mine to grow on his face because that had been my first time to kiss him in any way. I effortlessly took his hand in my own and led him back into the dining room where Jessica and Aiden were already seated. The smile never left Shane's face even when we took our seats.

"Let's dig in," Shane said, and all at once, hands flew, and food was gathered on plates.

But Jessica had a hesitant look on her face, weary and unsure.

"What's wrong, Jessica?" Shane asked, causing Jessica to jump a bit before she started reaching for food.

"N-Nothing. I'm sorry, Alpha," she apologized as she started piling food on her plate.

"Jessica, you don't have to address us as Alpha and Luna anymore," he said gently. "You're family now, so please relax and enjoy yourself. I'm sorry about my actions yesterday, but I was just doing what I thought was best for the pack and Ariel," he apologized, his hand finding my knee under the table as my name slipped passed his lips.

"I understand, Alph—I mean, Shane," she said, discomfort evident on her face as she called Shane by his name instead of addressing him as Alpha.

"Good," he said as he offered her a polite smile before we all started eating.

"Oh, my Goddess! This is amazing," Aiden proclaimed as he took a bite out of a waffle. "Whichever one of you made this is a genius!"

"That would be Ariel," Shane said proudly as he gave me a look of pride, causing me to slightly blush.

"How did you learn how to do this?" Aiden questioned, his mouth full of dough and syrup, causing me to shrug as I cringed at the unearthly sight of chewed food. "Sorry," he apologized, this time using his hand to cover his mouth as he spoke.

Breakfast was filled with laughter and awkward conversations. I noticed Jessica's anxiety and uncertainty fall away as relaxation and happiness took their place.

"Excuse me, but where's the bathroom?" Jessica asked, and before Shane could answer the question, Aiden stood up, and since he was holding on to Jessica, she stood up as well.

"I've got this one," Aiden said before he led Jessica out while whispering something in her ear that made her giggle as she pushed him away, but the blush on her face was evident as they left.

"Oh, Goddess." Shane chuckled as he playfully said, "Let's just hope they don't make out all over our walls."

I gently punched him on the shoulder before I stood up and started cleaning up the table, causing Shane to frown as he lost his grip on me. I gathered all the plates in my arms before I walked into the kitchen and started running the water and putting the dish soap to make it bubbly. Shane's arms went to their positions around my waist. Instead of going to my shoulder, his chin came into contact with the top of my head.

"What do you want to do today, love?" Shane asked as his thumbs started moving in slow circles against my hips.

I shrugged as I placed a now clean plate on a rack to dry.

"Let me finish this up," he said, and without waiting for a response, he picked me up and gently placed me on the counter before he started doing the rest of the work.

I narrowed my eyes at him, but he was so consumed in what he was doing that he didn't notice my glare.

More heat found its way into my gaze before I used my hands to cup as much water as possible then I splashed it at Shane. My mouth fell open due to the amount of water that hit him, which was a lot more than I was planning.

Shane looked at me, his body frozen and his mouth set in a straight line with a certain fire in his eyes. Fear rose in my chest as I prepared myself to run.

"Oh, Ariel," Shane said, mischief evident in his voice as he grabbed my hand.

I tensed up as I braced myself for the slap or punch or kick.

"You are so on!" He laughed before water splashed over me and soaked deep into my clothes.

I looked at him, surprise and shock fighting for dominance in my head.

Shane's demeanor suddenly changed as he took my hand into his soaked and soaped hands. "What's wrong, Ariel?" he asked, but I shook my head, ashamed that I thought he'd do that.

I saw the gears turning in his head before something clicked behind his eyes.

"You thought I was going to . . . ," he realized.

I had to break eye contact to avoid his hurt gaze.

"Ariel, I promised that I wouldn't hurt you, and I'm a man of my word," he whispered as he cupped my cheek with his calloused hand. "Ariel, I've told you before, and I'll tell you until you believe me. I love you with all my being, and nothing you ever do will make me stop or hurt you. You understand?"

I nodded in response before he placed a kiss right next to my mouth, as close to my lips as he'd ever gotten.

"I love you," he whispered before he placed another kiss on the top of my right cheekbone. "I love you so much." He placed his final kiss on my temple, and I closed my eyes while I let out a small sigh. "I'm sorry that I scared you," he apologized. "I'm also sorry I got that killer dress wet."

I chuckled as he released my face before I looked down at my dress, and sure enough, the light blue fabric had turned almost navy.

Change.

I wrote into one of his hands, and he nodded.

"If you're going to go upstairs, could you grab me another sweatshirt? I can't stand the feeling of wet clothes."

I nodded in response, and he easily slid the sweatshirt over his head, causing me to slightly blush.

"Thanks, love," Shane said as he handed me his sweatshirt. A small smirk decorated his face as he noticed my blush.

I offered him a small smile before I clenched his sweatshirt in my hands and hurried out of the kitchen. No matter how many times Shane caught me looking at him, it felt like I was giving in to a terrible sin.

I was halfway down the hallway when I heard a series of dull thuds followed by soft giggles. My heart told me to walk the other direction, but my feet, on the other hand, were already halfway there.

As I turned the corner that led to the foyer, my feet stopped as my eyes grew wide and a blush made its way to my cheeks once more. In front of me was Aiden who was holding Jessica with his hands underneath her thighs while the wall supported her weight. Their lips were caught in an intense battle for dominance. Jessica's body lightly bumped against the wall every now and then followed by her giggles as her fingers combed their way through Aiden's hair.

I quickly lifted Shane's sweatshirt over my eyes before I quickly yet silently turned and ran as fast as I could back into the kitchen. A monstrous blush tinted my cheeks the whole walk back. I couldn't help but feel like I'd witnessed something private. Something special.

What made it worse was that my mind kept playing it over and over again. Instead of Jess and Aiden, however, it was Shane and me.

My giggles filling the air as I ran my fingers through his soft locks. My feet dangling off the ground as he held me against the wall. My lips fighting for dominance against his.

The images that flashed through my head made me blush much deeper.

"Wow. You're fast—" Shane stated as I reentered the kitchen, but he was cut off by me shoving his sweatshirt back into his hands, wanting nothing more than to unsee what I'd just witnessed.

He straightened out his shirt to look at it, but his eyebrows furrowed when they landed on the water stains. He opened his mouth to say something, but again I pressed my fingers to his lips.

"Don't," I said soundlessly, mouthing the word, and he didn't.

He simply shrugged before he tossed his shirt onto the counter and finished up with the dishes. The movement of his back muscles momentarily made me forgot about what I'd seen.

A few moments later, Jess and Aiden walked back into the kitchen. Jessica's lips were a bit puffy, and Aiden's hair was messy from her fingers.

When Shane saw them, everything clicked in his head, and he let out an "oh" before turning to me, saying, "I'm sorry you had to witness that."

"Me too," I said without a sound, causing him to chuckle.

"Thank you, you two, for the breakfast," Aiden said, oblivious to what Shane and I had just said. "But we'll be heading out."

We all exchanged goodbyes before they left, and Shane and I headed back upstairs.

On our way up, Shane said, "At least, they didn't damage our walls too bad."

CHAPTER ELEVEN

"Do you think we should?" Shane asked as he expectantly turned to me.

We were currently in Shane's office looking over pack negotiations and deals. I was seated comfortably on Shane's lap with one of his hands around my waist. His other hand rested on the desk and occupied with a pen.

I looked over the document that rested in front of me, weighing the pros and cons of this alliance.

Mutual protection. Both sides contributing essentials to each other, I thought to myself while reading the offers on the paper.

After reading the rest of the offers and reweighing the pros and cons, I nodded before I signed my name on the line above the word Luna.

I was still getting used to the title.

Shane signed on the line above his title before he added the paper onto the growing pile of papers we'd signed.

"Do you want to take a break?" Shane asked, and I shrugged, not caring if we continued or not. "Let's finish this pile then stop for the day, okay?"

I nodded and looked at the ten papers we had left.

We were in the middle of looking over the next paper when suddenly Shane tensed behind me, and his hand tightened around my waist. I turned to him, but his eyes were glazed over, and his jaw was set. Worry filled my chest as I cupped his cheek. The simple action pulled him out of his trance.

"No," he whispered as he took my hand, but he didn't direct it to me. "They can't be . . ." He trailed off as he made a move to get up, but my body restricted him from doing so.

I quickly jumped off him, and he immediately started toward the door. Since he was still holding my hand, I was dragged along with him. I stumbled as I tried to keep up and Shane threw apologies over his shoulder every time I stumbled or tripped.

I sent him questioning looks, but he was so distracted that he didn't notice.

He led me to the front door and threw it open, revealing a teenage boy about seventeen and a little boy whose age fell between five and six. They all froze. Their shocked gazes locked on each other.

In the background, a black SUV sped away at an unearthly speed.

I couldn't help but notice how they all shared the same brown hair and the same mesmerizing hazel-green eyes. Instead of holding joy like the young boy, annoyance and almost hatred burned in the older boy's eyes.

"Shubby!" the little boy yelled as he threw his arms around Shane, pulling him back to the present.

"Hey, bud." He smiled as he hugged him back, and a smile grew on my face at the sight. "How have you been?"

"I lost my front teeth!" the young boy excitedly said before he opened his mouth, showing off his teeth or lack thereof.

"You're becoming a man." Shane smiled, causing the boy to smile all the way to his eyes.

"Zac lost some teeth, big deal." The older one scoffed unamused.

Shane's jaw tightened as his eyes slightly narrowed.

"Now can you let us in and tell us who that is?" he asked, pointing to me.

"Greg," Shane warned lowly, his patience hanging by a fraying thread.

"Calm down, Lassie. No need to get your boxers in a bunch," the boy, Greg, said with a slight chuckle before he pushed his way through Shane and me, causing me to stumble back a bit in surprise. He scoffed. "Weak."

Shane's eyes turned black as he made a move toward Greg, but I stopped him by gently placing a hand on either side of his face and made him look down into my eyes. His chilling black eyes bore into mine. I could even see my delicate reflection swimming in the never-ending darkness.

Without warning, Shane wrapped his arms around my waist, and he placed his head in the crook of my neck. His breath moved in waves across my neck as air entered and exited his body.

"I'm sorry," he quietly apologized into my neck. "I don't know what's wrong with him. He's not usually like this."

I placed my hand back on his cheek and looked him in the eye before I gently pulled his head down so that his forehead was level with my lips. I placed a gentle series of kisses on his forehead: one on the center of his forehead, one on each temple, then finally, one between his eyebrows.

He sighed as he straightened back to his full length.

"It is okay," I quietly said, mouthing the words, and he nodded before he took my hand in his own and rested his forehead on mine.

"I don't know what I'd do without you," he whispered. "I'm not good with patience, but you just . . ." He trailed off, struggling to find the words he was looking for. "You're gentle and sweet and understanding. I need to work on that more."

I smiled at him.

He was changing or at least trying to, which not many Alphas did.

I was pulled out of my happy moment when I felt a slight tug at the bottom of my dress. I looked down to see the adorable boy holding the hem of my dress.

"Do you talk?" he asked innocently, genuine curiosity in his voice and actions.

"Zac, that's a rude question," Shane said gently as he placed a hand on Zac's little head as he shot me an apologetic look.

In response, I crouched down so that I was eye to eye with his small figure and shook my head.

"It's okay." He smiled. "We can still be friends, right?"

I nodded, unable to restrain my smile.

"What's your name?" he asked.

"Ariel," Shane answered for me. "Her name's Ariel."

"Hello, Ariel," Zac said as he straightened up and offered me his small hand to shake. "My name is Zachary Chase, but you can call me Zac if you want."

I shook his hand, my smile never leaving my face.

"I'm sorry about Greg. He's been really grumpy lately because I think she hurt him."

Curiosity filled my being as he said that last part barely above a whisper like he was talking to himself. I wanted to ask him or Shane about it, but I decided against it because it'd be harder to communicate with Zac, and Shane didn't hear what Zac said. I'd rather wait for Shane to actually hear the news, preferably from Zac or Greg himself before Shane decided if he even wanted to talk about it with me.

"Not that I'm not happy to see you, but why did Helen and Brian send you here?" Shane asked.

"Mommy and Daddy said that bad people are trying to get into our pack," Zac said and his eyebrows furrowed.

Rogues.

"No one will tell me who! Not even Greg." He pouted.

95

I understood why his parents didn't tell him about the true monsters that lurked in the land between territories. Zac was innocent, and they wanted to preserve that for as long as possible.

My parents did the same thing.

"Speaking of Greg, I need to talk to him," Shane said, pulling me back to the present. All softness in his voice was gone, replaced by coldness.

I gave him a warning look.

"I won't do anything," he said before he headed down the hall where Greg had walked down.

I quickly closed the door before Zac, and I followed him.

We found Greg in the kitchen eating some leftovers from our breakfast.

"Hey!" Shane snapped, causing Greg to roll his eyes before he lazily turned his head.

"What?"

"I don't know what your problem is, but the way you entered my pack, my *home*, was unacceptable. You won't disrespect me, and you *definitely* won't disrespect my mate. Got it?"

By the time he was done with his rant, he was in Greg's face with an angry expression.

"I'm so scared of the Big Bad Alpha and his pathetic excuse for a mate."

A low growl escaped my lips, causing Greg to give me an amused smirk.

"Oh, cute. It thinks it's tough."

Anger coursed through me like water in a stream not only because of his disrespect but also because he called me "it." Before my anger could get the best of me, Shane already had Greg pinned to the wall by his shirt like a stereotypical middle school bully.

"Gregory, my mate is a she, not it. You need to stop before I can't control my anger," Shane growled out, obviously struggling to keep his rage at bay.

"Why do you need to control it?" Greg taunted, not caring that a punch in the face was in his near future. "What? Has she made you soft?" he spat. "Weak?"

Without missing a beat, Shane delivered a solid punch to Greg's face, knocking him down to the floor and causing Zac to cry out. Shane straddled over him and pinned Greg down. Deep crimson was running from Greg's nose and slowly dripping over his teeth, staining them.

"You're lucky you're my brother because if you weren't, I would've—"

"Shubby, stop!" Zac cried, causing Shane to freeze but he remained taut and ready to spring back into action at a moment's notice.

"Zac, stay out of this. He disrespected my mate and me, and now he has to deal with the consequences," Shane stated tightly. "When you're older, you'll understand."

I quickly, yet cautiously, approached Shane before I forced his focus to me. I refused to gaze away from his eyes even though rage burned within them. As I looked deep into his eyes, his rage started fading away until he closed his eyes and took a deep breath. When he reopened them, he was visibly calmer.

"Apologize to her," Shane commanded calmly, but power and authority were still evident in his words.

"But—"

"Now," Shane commanded. His hands balled into fists, ready to punch Greg in a split second.

"Sorry," Greg apologized dryly, emotions and honesty vacant from his face while the simple word was hollow and cold.

Shane looked at me expectantly, awaiting my response. I gave Greg a curt nod, knowing that if I did so, Shane would be satisfied and get off him, and he did just that.

"You know where your room is. Go," he said as he got off of Greg and offered him his hand, though his voice was still hard.

"Whatever," Greg retorted as he got up, rejecting Shane's outstretched hand.

Greg was on his way out of the dining room when Shane stopped him.

"Wait, Greg. Why did they send you here?"

Greg scoffed. "They claim it's a rogue problem, like they actually care. We all know that it's because we're not the picture perfect sons they want us to be. They ultimately kicked us out . . ." He trailed off as a small smirk grew on his lips. "Just like they did to you."

"Leave," Shane said lowly, causing Greg's nauseating smirk to grow since he knew he hit a soft spot before he left.

Shane tightly pulled me into his embrace, not to the point that it hurt, but I also knew I wasn't escaping any time soon.

"Your scent calms me," Shane whispered, washing away the confusion that stained my thoughts like fresh rain washing the dirt off a car.

I closed my eyes and allowed my scent to calm him down, my body slowly getting used to how tight his arms were constricted around my being.

After a couple moments, Shane's grip slackened, but he didn't let go of me completely.

"Shubby," Zac said quietly, reminding me that he was still in the room with us. "Can I have some food? We've been driving since yesterday afternoon, and I'm hungry."

"Of course, you can," Shane said as he momentarily let go of me and got Zac a plate with one of everything on it while Zac climbed into a chair. He set the plate in front of Zac, causing Zac's eyes to go wide based on the amount of food on it.

"I'll get you some orange juice." He walked out of the dining room, and Zac turned to me.

"Shubby's lucky to have someone like you," he suddenly said, catching me off guard. "You help him in ways he can't. You kept him from hurting Greg without saying a word!" he said, throwing his hands in the air with the last sentence. "He should be grateful for you and he better treasure you."

A smile made its way onto my lips as a warm feeling spread through my chest before I gave Zac a big hug. Both he and Aiden voiced how I'd changed Shane, and it made me wonder what he was like before I was here. At the same time, something deep within told me that I already knew.

Killing foreigners upon sight, poorly handling disrespect, threatening people . . . No one else was going to die. Not if I could help it.

I released Zac just as Shane returned with a tall glass of orange juice along with a pitcher filled with the orange liquid. He set the glass and pitcher in front of Zac before the latter dug into his breakfast. He practically inhaled the food like it was air and he'd just come above water after staying under for five minutes.

"So what do you want to do today, Zachary?" Shane casually asked as he plucked a piece of bacon off of Zac's plate and bit into it, disregarding Zac's annoyed look.

"Don't call me that." Zac pouted as he crossed his arms. "You don't have permission."

"Oh, yeah. I forgot." Shane chuckled. "What do you want to do today, *Zac*?" he repeated, and a satisfied smile grew on Zac's face.

"I wanna watch a movie!" he announced as he finished his food.

"Which movie?"

Zac took a few moments before his face lit up and he announced, "Big Hero Six!"

Shane groaned before he childishly pouted. "We watched that last time!" he whined, causing me to use my hand to muffle the laughs that were slipping through my lips. "I wanna watch something else!"

"What do you want to watch then?"

"Froz—"

"No!" Zac yelled, cutting Shane off. "No Frozen ever. We're going to watch Big Hero Six, and that's final!" He declared before he hopped out of his chair and ran out of the dining room toward the unknown.

"Zac!" Shane chuckled before he grabbed my arm and started chasing Zac.

It was no use trying to contain my laughter now as we followed Zac's chuckling figure down a series of hallways that I'd never been down before.

Finally, we followed Zac into a pitch black room, and Shane said, "Zac, I told you I don't like you running around here in the dark," as he flipped on the backlights revealing a gorgeous in-home movie theater.

In the back was a mini snack bar with a few drinks too. There were about six rows of reclining theater seats, and a few yards from the screen were bean bags and pillows. Zac's little body was comfortably sprawled across three bean bags, and a pillow, his giggles filling the air as Shane lightly chastised him.

"Do you like it?" Shane asked, noticing my amazement and I excitedly nodded.

I'd never seen one like this before.

"Find a seat and get comfortable. I'll be over there in a second," he instructed, and I nodded before I chose a seat in the second row behind Zac.

The fluffy seat was soft, and I practically sunk into it like quicksand. I pressed a button on the side, and my legs were lifted and my back slowly dropped. Once I was comfortable, I let go of the button and watched Shane's silhouette quickly move from Zac back to the snack bar back to Zac then finally back to the bar. He spent a few moments back there before he made his way back to me with something huge in his hands.

When he made it over to me, he silently draped the giant blanket over me before he retreated once more. My eyebrows furrowed and I watched as he returned slightly struggling with the items in his hands.

I made a move to help him, but he quickly said, "Don't worry. I've got it."

I looked at him for a second before I slowly resumed my position. He slowly continued making his way toward me. A quiet curse escaped his lips every time he stumbled or tripped, causing me to giggle. I silently thanked the Moon Goddess that the previews were already rolling for the movie so the vulgar language wouldn't reach Zac's ears.

As soon as he made it to me, the sweet and buttery smell of popcorn filled my nose.

"I didn't know if you liked salt, so I just brought it over here just in case."

I offered him a small grin before I gave him a soft kiss on the cheek as thanks.

"You're welcome," he whispered as he handed me a tall glass of bubbly beverage just as the movie started.

As the opening song played, I found myself becoming closer and closer to Shane until I was lying on top of him, my cheeks resting on his chest and his arms tightly around me only leaving when he was grabbing popcorn from the bucket in my lap.

Zac sang along to the opening song as he lifted up a pillow and started singing at the top of his lungs, causing Shane and me to laugh. I couldn't help but wonder if this was what our future looked like; grand morning breakfasts together, watching movies, and laughing. Just Shane, I, and . . . our pups.

A small smile grew on my face as names popped into my head. I closed my eyes and cuddled deeper into Shane as my imagination ran wild about our future and our children.

CHAPTER TWELVE

"Come on, Ari! We have to hurry before we miss it!" Zac's voice called from somewhere in front of me.

I quickened my pace as I ran after Shane and Zac through the woods toward their special spot that Zac wanted to show me. The sun was setting, and its orange-red rays reached across the sky, staining the remaining clouds that lingered and soaked the color up. A slight breeze pushed against me as I ran and blades of grass lightly scratched my ankles.

After a few more moments, I found them in a clearing sitting on a large tree stump, both of their backs facing me. I took a seat next to Shane and rested my head on his shoulder.

"I'm sorry I didn't wait for you. I just had to make sure that he didn't get lost or hurt."

I gave him an understanding nod before I looked through the clearing to see the sun setting.

"Do you see it?" Zac whispered, excitement clinging to his words as he stared at the beautiful display in front of us. "It's amazing!"

"She definitely is," Shane whispered as he turned to me.

A prompt blush appeared on my cheeks at the compliment before he cupped my cheek like he had so many times before.

"Her eyes; like stars. Her smile; the moon. Her skin; a summer breeze and her heart; a delicate and elegant rose."

My mind raced at his smooth, soft words, and my heart was pounding against my chest as poetry flowed from his lips. He slowly leaned in closer, and suddenly, we were in the kitchen all over again. The burning desire to feel each other ate at us from the inside, and our urge danced on a very thin line between controlled and dangerous.

"Her lips teasing and compelling," he whispered, his breath fanning my lips. "And God, there's nothing I want more than to fall under their spell."

I was ready to let myself give in to my selfish desires when Zac let out a squeal. Our attention was now on him and not each other.

"Ew!" he said as he covered his eyes. "At least wait until I'm not here!"

Shane looked at me before a mischievous smile took over his features.

"This isn't over," Shane whispered, strangely sending a shiver down my spine like a shock wave. His smile grew once he saw what effect he had on me before he walked over to Zac and took one hand off of his eyes and held onto it. "Sorry, bud." He chuckled lightly. "How about we make it up to you by taking you back to the house and giving you some chocolate cake?"

At those words, Zac's face lit up. "What are we waiting for? Let's go!" he almost yelled before he got up and started running back toward the house.

Shane shot me an apologetic look, apologizing for leaving me again before he ran after Zac. I took a few more minutes to bask in the twilight before I reluctantly got up and followed after Shane and Zac, taking in nature as I walked.

I noticed the butterflies and bees as they landed on flowers. I noticed the birds flying home for the night to feed and protect their young. I even noticed some pack members in the distance;

two children with their father and very pregnant mother. The man and woman laughed at something they'd said before their lips connected in a sweet, gentle kiss.

I couldn't help the pang of envy that struck my chest. I wanted that with Shane, but I was scared. Scared that I wouldn't be good enough or experienced enough or able to provide what he needed. I was scared of the disappointment I would see in his eyes as his hand dropped from my cheek and he walked away. But what scared me the most was how badly he wanted me. I could see it in his eyes and felt it through his words.

I just didn't want to disappoint him or myself.

I let out a quiet sigh as I continued walking back toward the house, my pace quickening knowing that if I didn't hurry, Shane would get worried.

"You know we won't be able to do that tomorrow, right?" Shane said to Zac just as I walked into the kitchen.

Zac was already occupied with the cake, icing smearing his round cheeks. "Why?" Zac asked, a slight frown showing on his features.

"Because tomorrow," Shane said, snaking his arm around my waist as I got in arms reach, "is Ariel's Lunar Ceremony."

A groan pushed past my lips at the mention of that. Not only did I not want to make a big deal about being Luna, but I was also nervous. The most the pack members knew about me was that I knocked Stephanie out and let out a growl that made even an alpha bow in submission.

What if they don't like me? What if they are only treating me nice because they are afraid of Shane or even me? The thoughts made my head hurt, and I groaned as I rubbed my right temple.

"You can tell she is excited about it." Shane chuckled as he placed a gentle kiss on my left temple, causing amazing sparks to rush through my head and drive away the slight headache. "I know I am," he continued. "I get to show off who I belong to and how amazing she looks in a dress."

My heart leaped as he whispered into my hair.

Who I belong to. Those words repeated themselves, and a welcome warm feeling spread throughout my being while Shane pressed a kiss into my hair.

"You're gonna look so pretty, Ariel," Zac commented, his face lighting up at the thought before he turned serious again. "Not that you're not pretty right now, though. You always look pretty."

"She sure does," Shane agreed, causing a slight blush to grow on my cheeks under their gazes.

I needed to stop doing that so much.

"Come on, Zac," Shane said once Zac had finished his cake. "It's time for bed."

"Do I have to?" he whined.

"Yes, you have to," Shane said with a slight laugh before he took Zac's hand and looked at me. "I'll get him washed up and ready for bed, and I'll be in our room in about fifteen minutes, okay?"

I nodded before I gave Zac a gentle hug, which he graciously returned.

"Good night, Ari," he said as the embrace ended.

I waved goodbye before I left the kitchen and headed up to our room, deciding to let Shane and Zac have their first brother-to-brother moment that they'd had all day.

I washed my face before I rolled on another layer of deodorant then put on my pajamas. I'd just slid my soft, flowing nightgown over my shoulders when the door opened. For some reason, my body jolted in surprise. I tensed up before I quickly turned around, only for my eyes to meet Shane's warm, ever calculating ones.

I relaxed as he swiftly moved through the room, bridging the space between us until there was none left. I felt the heat of his eyes as they slowly moved over me before they finally met mine again. It felt like he was looking into my soul, picking at my thoughts and pulling out my secrets, trying to fit together the many mismatched puzzle pieces that made me up.

"It's like no matter what time of day it is, you look gorgeous," he commented almost to himself as his fingertips lightly brushed down my arms until his fingers found the gaps between my fingers.

His touch alone was enough to relax me.

"I'm going to take a shower," he said as he slowly moved toward the connecting bathroom.

Our hands stayed together until the space between us became too great, and they couldn't hold on any longer.

As soon as the bathroom door closed, boredom hit me like a truck. I let out a groan before I dragged my feet along the floor and got my book before I repeated my actions all the way to the window sill, which was big enough to sit on.

I curled up with my knees crossed and my back against the wall. The gentle sound of rain filled the silence in the air, and I watched it collect on the window, blurring my view of the outside world.

I opened my book and was instantly met by the hauntingly beautiful picture of my family back when we were all happy and together. A suffocating tightness filled my chest as I felt the dam that held back every ounce of my tears begin to waver and shake.

And that was when I broke.

Tears effortlessly leaked from my eyes like a dripping faucet and fell down my cheeks as I let out silent sobs, hugging myself as if it would console me. I cried for my family that I'd lost and seeing Zac, and even Greg reminded me of what I'd lost.

I cried for them, and I didn't hold back.

I held the picture of my family close to my chest, and as if the picture were actually hugging me like my family would be if they saw me like this, I calmed down. My tears ceased, and my breathing steadied. I leaned my head against the cold window and closed my eyes, the picture never leaving its position against my chest.

I stayed there, consumed by my thoughts until I felt a hand on my shoulder. I jumped as I opened my eyes just to meet Shane who was only in a towel with a concerned look on his face accompanied by the water droplets falling from his hair.

"What's wrong?" he asked softly as his fingertips made soft contact with my chin, tilting it toward him. "You've been crying." He noted, the tear trails inevitably still visible on my face. "Why?"

I lifted up the picture, and he pieced everything together, but he didn't offer up a sorry like I thought he would. Instead, he pushed my hand that held the picture until it was in its original position against my heart.

"It's okay to cry for them, Ariel," he stated so softly that even with my enhanced hearing, I struggled to hear him. "It's okay to miss them."

I looked back down at the picture, my thumb slowly moving over the smooth surface. Without a word, Shane simply placed a kiss on my forehead, his lips lingering there for a long while before he slowly pulled away.

"I'll be right back, okay?" he said tenderly as his thumb swept across my chin before he disappeared in the closet.

I let my eyes linger on the picture before I lightly placed it back in its place within the book. I let my legs carry me to the bed, and just as I eased my way down, a low roll of thunder slightly shook the house, causing me to jump a bit.

A few moments later, Shane emerged with a comfy pair of sweatpants on before he turned off the lights and effortlessly slid into bed with me. I settled on top of him as soon as he did.

I found myself slightly jumping every time the thunder bellowed, and lightning ripped through the dark sky. Shane wrapped his arms tighter around my waist as if to say, I'll protect you from it, without using any words. And I believed him. It was hard not to.

I buried my head in his warm, bare chest and simply listened to his breathing and heartbeat, hoping that if I channeled my hearing enough, I'd be able to hear the thoughts that whirled inside that complex, yet beautiful mind of his.

"This is my favorite part of the day," Shane whispered into the darkness that surrounded us, the only light coming from the treacherous lightning beyond the window. "Just lying here with you."

His hands started moving in slow circles, prompting a soft sigh from my lips as I closed my eyes. A whisper of a laugh traveled through the air before I felt him place another kiss on my forehead.

"Good night, love," he said tiredly before he slipped into sleep, his breath even and quiet.

I had almost entered the blissful world of sleep when I was awoken by the low creak of our door as it opened. I peeled my eyes open, but I couldn't see anything in the darkness. Suddenly, I felt the bed dip as soft grunts filled the air as whoever entered our room struggled to get up on the bed, causing me to gasp.

"I'm sorry, Ari," Zac said in a whisper as he finally made it onto the bed, causing me to relax. "The lightning and thunder . . . It scares me," he admitted sheepishly, and even though I couldn't see him, I could practically hear his blush. "Shabby usually lets me stay, but that was before he found you. Will you let me stay?"

I instantly nodded, but then realized that he couldn't see me. Instead, I grabbed a pillow and gave it to him, using where the bed dipped to find his exact location.

"Thank you, Ari," he said before he took the pillow and got comfortable near the foot of the bed.

I placed my head back on Shane's chest and instantly, sleep wiggled its way into my head and took me on a journey.

*　　*　　*

When I awoke, I was without Shane underneath me, or even Zac comfortably curled against my legs. A frown made its way on my face, as it usually did when Shane was gone, while I sat up, combing my fingers through my hair, which was getting way too long.

My eyes instantly fell onto the nightstand in hopes of finding a note like Shane had left last time, and luckily, one was propped against my book. I picked up the thin piece of paper and read the words beautifully written on it.

It's a weird tradition my pack wanted to start to not allow the alpha to see his luna until the Ceremony, so we'll be separated up until then. I will still be close to you, but you will not be able to see me, nor I, you. But trust me when I say this: it honestly kills me to have to wait that long until I get to see your beautiful face.

Love, Shane.

My joy at what I just read brought a smile across my face as my thumb gently passed over the first letter in the last sentence.

Love.

I couldn't help but wonder if that was what I was feeling. No matter how hard I tried to slow myself down, I couldn't help the intense feelings that I'd developed for Shane or the amazing feeling that burst through my being every time he touched, talked, or even looked at me.

Even though I wasn't ready to admit it to him yet, I wasn't going to deny myself the terrifying pleasure of admitting it to myself. I, Ariel Anne Carter, was in love with Alpha Shane Chase. I had to bite my bottom lip to keep myself from smiling too widely. It felt good to say it . . . or at least think it.

I gently set the note back in its original place before I sluggishly got up and went into the bathroom, having no motivation to do anything since my mate wasn't here. Nonetheless, I brushed my teeth and took a bath. Once I was done, I walked out of the bathroom, not bothering to cover myself up since I had no one to hide anything from. I easily slid one of Shane's shirts over my underclothes before I made my way to the kitchen where I made myself some toast along with some hot chocolate.

With my food in hand, I padded my way to Shane's office. His amazing scent overtook my senses as I took a seat in his big alpha chair. As my body came into contact with the chair, I was instantly swallowed into the soft material.

I frowned as I tried to adjust myself, but it was no use. I sighed as I rolled it as close to the desk as possible. My eyes swept over the stacks of papers that rested on the desk: agreements, contracts, security updates, reports.

I sighed as my fingers found their way back to my slightly damp hair. I carefully plucked the first paper on the pile and looked over it. My eyebrows furrowed as I read the words and sipped my hot cocoa.

As I continued looking over the papers, I ended up separating them into two piles: the plans I agreed with and the ones I disagreed with. I started chewing on the inside of my cheek once I realized that my disagree pile was growing larger than my agree pile.

I sighed as I grabbed my empty plate and cup and left the office. The words on the papers threatened to hold me captive in that office if I didn't escape. My eyes looked over the clock on the oven as I set the dishes on the counter, too lazy to wash them at the moment.

Twelve-eighteen.

I let out a frustrated groan. Eight more hours. Eight more hours until I saw my mate. Eight more hours until I get crowned luna.

*   *   *

My heart was beating out of my chest as I looked over myself one last time. A few hours ago, Aiden had dropped off the dress and headpiece I was to wear for the ceremony. Seeing myself in it made everything real.

110

I was wearing an all-white dress that cut low to my mid back. My feet were bare because it was a tradition throughout every pack everywhere. I hadn't decided on what to do with my hair yet, so it rested in a messy bun atop my head. I had minimal makeup not only so it wouldn't take attention away from the ceremony, but also because I knew Shane would get overprotective.

A light chuckle escaped my lips at the thought. *Just an hour and a half until I get to see him . . .*

I let my hair fall messily out of the bun and allowed the thought that I'd been flipping over in my brain since I'd started getting ready. I had more than enough time, and a new, dramatic change in my life deserved a new, slightly less dramatic look.

I nodded at myself in the mirror as I encouraged myself silently, mouthing the words, "You can do this."

I grabbed the tool that would help me complete what I was going to do in one hand and a lock of my hair in the other hand. I let out a slow breath as I lined them up, fully committed. *Snip*, and I watched as a single lock of hair fluttered to the ground.

CHAPTER THIRTEEN

By the time I was done cutting and styling my hair, I had ten minutes until the ceremony started. I took one final look at myself, a grin spreading across my face as I saw my completed look. My hair was now barely brushing the tops of my shoulders and had nice small curls in it. On top of my head rested a crown made of special white flowers that glowed in the full moonlight, woven in intricate patterns and twists.

I was pulled out of my thoughts when a knock filled the air, causing me to jump a bit.

"The ceremony's ready, Ariel," Jessica's gentle voice called from the other side of my bedroom door.

I looked at myself one last time before I hurried out of the bathroom and out into the bedroom. I opened the door, and Jessica gasped when she saw me.

I gently bit my bottom lip, waiting to see her reaction, but when the smile spread across her face, I let out the breath I didn't know I was holding.

"You look beautiful!" she said cheerfully as she wrapped her arms around me, and I instantly embraced her. "I love your new hair! We're kinda like twins now." She chuckled as she motioned to her own short curly hair that she freely wore down.

"But back to the point," she said as she sobered up. "Shane has been going crazy all day without you," she said as she linked arms with me and started leading me down the hallway. "Aiden literally had to hold him down because he tried coming for you," she continued as we walked outside, the dirt and grass feeling almost foreign beneath my bare feet and between my toes. "Call that love. I know Aiden, and I wouldn't be able to do that for sure, especially with the stage we're at."

My eyebrows furrowed as I looked at her, and only then did I realize the scar in the shape of his teeth resting right where her neck and shoulder met. Her mark. They had already marked each other . . .

I had to push down the jealousy that I felt in my chest for some reason. I simply nodded. We continued walking through the trees in silence, our only light coming from the full moon that hung high in the clear sky. After a while, the busy chatter of pack members filled my ears, and I felt my heart beating faster.

"Relax, Ariel," Jessica whispered in my ear as she led me to my assigned spot, which was behind a white curtain so that no one could see me. "You'll do amazing." She smiled before she had to leave.

I took several deep breaths as I waited for one of the biggest things in my life to commence.

Suddenly, a hush fell over the crowd, and everyone was dead silent to the point that I feared the hammering of my heart could be heard.

"Tonight marks a new era for this pack." Shane's smooth, melodic voice rang out, causing my heart to flutter with excitement knowing that I'd be seeing him in a few seconds. "I have a beautiful pack filled with beautiful people, and today, we will welcome the beautiful woman whom I will share not only this responsibility with but also, whom I will spend the rest of my life with. Please welcome, Ariel Anne Carter, your new luna."

At those words, I slowly walked out from behind the curtain and was instantly shocked at the number of people who were in front of me. They were all clapping with smiles on their faces. I slowly walked down the center aisle, my eyes never leaving Shane's who looked amazing in a crisp black tux.

The butterflies in my stomach multiplied at an alarming rate, but as soon as my hand found Shane's outstretched one, they all diminished and were replaced by the warmth and sparks that took over my body every time he touched me.

"You look beautiful, love," he whispered in my ear as he helped me up the stairs that led up to the stage.

His lips came into sweet contact with my forehead once I made it up.

"And I love your new hair." He smiled, taking a curled piece between his fingers. "It suits you beautifully." I couldn't fight the smile that grew on my face before he placed another kiss on my forehead and turned us so that we were now facing the hundreds of pack members whose eyes were watching our every move.

"This is a ceremony, welcoming our new luna into our pack," Shane announced, authority in his voice, "and into all of our lives."

At those words, many people clapped and cheered, causing my smile to widen.

A man draped in black walked forward, and I instantly knew what he was there for. He was the priest of the pack. As he walked up the stairs, everyone became silent knowing that this was the most important part of the ceremony.

"We are here tonight to not only celebrate and embrace Miss Ariel Carter, the new luna that the Moon Goddess has graciously given to us and our alpha," he said, looking at both Shane and I as he stated our names. "But also to celebrate the day that this pack is finally whole."

Shane gave my hand, which was still resting comfortably in his, a quick squeeze and I looked at him. Joy with a hint of mischief danced in his eyes and the small smirk on his lips didn't help either.

"Alpha Shane," the priest said, causing Shane to look serious as he straightened up a bit. "Do you accept your new responsibilities and stress as alpha with your new luna?"

The most genuine smile I'd ever seen spread across Shane's face.

"There's no one else I'd rather share it with," he said, his thumb running over my knuckles. "I do."

"And do you, Luna Ariel, accept your new responsibilities and stress as luna with your new alpha?" he asked, his attention now set on me.

I could feel the pack member's gazes burning into me, awaiting my answer, but I kept my focus on Shane and only Shane. I closed my eyes and took a deep breath.

My last chance to back out was right in front of me.

I knew that I would be breaking the vow of silence I'd made all those years ago. Despite it, I opened my mouth and let two words push past my lips.

"I do." My voice sounded foreign and scratchy in my ears because it'd been too long since I last used it.

Shane didn't notice the shocked expression that fell upon the pack members' faces. Instead, he gave me an adoring smile that made my heart leap and my knees wobble.

"Now, Alpha Shane," the priest said as he recovered from his own shock, his eyes now meeting Shane's, "please, give up your heart to Luna Ariel."

My eyebrows furrowed in confusion at this new concept of giving up your heart. My confusion quickly melted away as Shane raised my hand that rested in his up to his lips, gently pressing a kiss on it.

"Ariel Anne Carter, ever since the first time I had the incredible pleasure of laying my eyes on you, I knew that you would be the best thing that ever happened to me in my life."

I didn't bother trying to hide my smile like I usually did. I didn't have a problem letting everyone—especially Shane—know exactly what kind of effect his touch and words had on me.

"I've become not only a better alpha but also a better person because of you. You've shown me things and made me feel things I'd never thought about in a million years, all without saying a single word. Ariel, I love you with all my being and will never stop even when our hearts stop beating, and I'm proud to say that I am only yours. Now, always, and forever."

By now, my emotions were running wild, and I couldn't keep the wide smile off of my face.

"Luna, please give your heart up to Alpha Shane."

Nervousness almost instantaneously built up inside me, not only because I hadn't talked in a while, but also because I didn't think I could live up to the beautiful words he'd said. But right when I looked into his captivating eyes that were the most beautiful mix of hazel and green that I'd ever seen, it all melted away.

"S-Shane," I started, my voice still a bit shaky and weak, "I can't imagine what my life would be like if you hadn't found me. When you found me, I was broken and scared. I couldn't even go a day without getting new physical and emotional scars, but now that I found you, I'm happy. I'm complete. I'm loved, and that's all I ever wanted. You took me from my own hell and brought me to heaven one step at a time. You helped me find my voice again. You helped me find me again and . . ." I trailed off, debating whether I should admit it. "I love you for it."

A smile that reached his heavenly eyes stretched across Shane's face.

"Say it again," he whispered happily.

"I love you," I whispered back, causing pure joy to dance in his eyes.

"I've waited so long to hear that." Shane breathed.

"Any final remarks?" the priest politely asked, and Shane nodded.

"Yes," he said, his eyes locking with mine, seriousness and adoration radiating from his body, causing me to become nervous. "Miss Ariel Anne Carter," he said gently as he released my hand from his grasp and used it to cup my cheek. "May I kiss you?"

I looked up at him, his intense eyes looking at me through thick eyelashes. I'd been dreaming of this moment, but now it was actually happening. Right here, right now.

A smile grew on my lips, and I nodded.

"Yes, Shane," I said, my voice still dry and scratchy. "Please do."

Without wasting another second, Shane's lips attacked mine, the hunger and longing evident as his lips moved. I slowly moved my lips against him and wrapped my arms around his neck, sloppily kissing him until I got the rhythm of it. I was instantly addicted to the amazing feeling that rushed through every part of my body that was touching Shane's.

Cheers went up in the air as we deepened the kiss. We no longer cared that it wasn't gentle and clean, but rather rough and unpredictable. Uncontrollable.

Shane's hands found their way around my waist and pulled me so close that there was no space between us, not that I minded.

"You have no idea how long I've wanted to do this," Shane whispered into my lips before he continued kissing me.

"Neither do you," I replied, causing him to grin before he attacked my lips once more.

His lips slowly started finding their way along my jawline, and I knew what he wanted to do, but when I saw Zac out of the corner of my eye, I remembered that we were unfortunately not alone.

"Not here," I whispered. The simple words felt like nails in my throat. "Home."

As soon as I said that, Shane was snapped out of his trance and realized that we were in front of the entire pack who'd been applauding the whole time.

"I forgot that we aren't alone." Shane groaned, causing me to chuckle before I gripped the side of his face and kissed his lips once more.

A small groan escaped his lips as I playfully bit his bottom lip.

"Ariel—" he started, but suddenly, a loud, pained howl ripped through the air, and I instantly knew who it belonged to.

Greg.

I'd realized that his seat next to Zac was empty, but what was he—

I didn't finish my thoughts as I started running toward the direction of the howl, not caring about the small sticks and blades of grass cutting into the soles of my bare feet. I suddenly jerked to a stop when Shane's hand wrapped around my arm, stopping me instantly.

"Let me go." That line usually belonged to Shane, but this time, I needed him to let me go. "Please."

"Ariel, you don't know what he's capable, especially if he's in his wolf form," Shane warned, concern evident in his voice.

"And you don't know what I'm fully capable of, especially in my human form," I retorted. "I'm the luna of this pack now, and it's my job to find out what's wrong with Greg."

Shane looked at me, his jaw constantly tightening and untightening as he thought it over before he sighed and gave in.

"I'm not letting anything happen to you, Ariel, and if he tries anything, I will not hesitate to take over," he warned before he effortlessly shifted, the nauseating sound of bones breaking filling the air before his beautiful wolf stood in front of me.

I refused to shift into my wolf not only because I hadn't had much communication with her, but also because it had been such a long time since I had the freedom to do that. I knew it would hurt just as bad as my first shift did, and it hurt. Bad.

He jerked his head, motioning for me to climb on his back, which I did, his soft fur spilling between my fingers as I tightly held on.

He took off. The world blurred past me as we left my amazing ceremony and confused pack members behind, our focus only on Greg.

CHAPTER FOURTEEN

When we found Greg, he was relentlessly beating a tree. The tree cracked and groaned in protest as it began leaning. There was a furious look burning in his black eyes, and a web of sickly purple-grey veins surfaced from beneath his eyes before they retreated beneath his skin once they reached his cheeks. His canines were extended, and it made my skin crawl at how sharp they were, ready to sink into anything that crossed their path.

The simple act of Shane shifting back was what drew Greg's attention to us. A low growl climbed up his throat as he slowly stalked toward us; more specifically me.

"Greg, stand down," Shane growled as he protectively stood between me and the threat, unfazed by the fact that he was naked.

Greg merely growled in response, and the simple action challenged Shane, causing him to tense. He slowly started circling us while Shane's calculating eyes watched his every move.

"Greg, we don't want to have to hurt you," I said, putting as much authority in my voice as I could as I straightened up. "And we won't have to if you stand down."

Another growl escaped Greg's lips as he slowly advanced. I noticed his movement had turned rigid and more calculated, eerily like a rogue's whose only instinct was to give in to their animalistic nature and kill. But they were smarter than sinking their fangs into anything with blood in its veins. They planned their every move and were as light on their feet as possible . . . just like Greg was right now.

"Please, Greg. Stand down," I begged, not only for his sake but for mine too because I knew that I'd have to do some things that I was going to regret.

Instead of coming to his senses like I'd hoped, he let out a growl much like a battle cry before he lunged at me, shifting in midair. I easily sidestepped his clumsy movements, but Greg's massive animal landed on top of Shane who immediately shifted as soon as he hit the ground.

They were engaged in an intense battle. Brother against brother, blood against blood. Greg was mercilessly biting at Shane, not only snapping at his face but at his throat as well. And I could see in Greg's eyes that he wanted blood. Shane's blood.

And that was when I saw red.

I let out the loudest growl I'd ever released before I tackled Greg off of Shane, not caring that it was my human form against Greg's massive, powerful wolf. A mixture of rage and adrenaline rushed through me as I pinned Greg down, my eyes shifting and my canines growing.

"You will not touch what's mine," I growled lowly, causing Greg to growl in return as he tried to throw me off, but it was no use. I was the luna of this pack, and it was my duty to protect everyone, including the alpha. Although I didn't want to hurt Greg, I was fully ready to make my message extremely clear.

I heard a growl come from Shane as he made a move toward Greg, but I looked at him and growled, daring him to step in between us. The fraction of a second that I wasn't looking at him, Greg took advantage of. His hind legs came underneath my stomach, and in one swift movement, I was flying through the air before I collided with a thick tree. An explosion of pain burst within my head as blood filled my mouth.

I felt something dark creep into the back of my head, and panic filled my chest, the feeling dreadfully familiar. I quickly spit the blood out of my mouth as I stood up. The sudden action caused the world around me to spin, but I didn't show Greg that. Instead, I cracked my neck and narrowed my eyes at him.

"You have to try better than that, pup," I spat, knowing that taunting him would be my best shot.

He bared his fangs before he lunged at me again. I waited until he was a hair away from me before I stepped out of the way, allowing him to smash into the tree. I planned to get him to run into as many trees as possible so he'd become disoriented and I wouldn't have to inflict as much physical pain.

I watched as Greg stumbled to his feet. Out of the corner of my eye, I saw Shane give me a worried look, which I returned with a reassuring smile. The moment was interrupted by Greg letting out a loud grunt before he charged at me full speed and I repeated the process I'd just done. A weird feeling bubbled in my chest when I heard him whimper accompanied by the sounds of bones breaking and popping.

"Greg, please stop," I begged gently, knowing that if he didn't stop soon, he could seriously hurt himself . . . or me if I was not careful.

He staggered back up, falling every now and then. His movements had become messier. He'd become more predictable.

I had him exactly where I wanted him.

Greg got in his stance before he threw himself at me and only then did I see the pain in his eyes. But it wasn't just physical. It was mental. Emotional.

I analyzed his every breath and tiny movements as his huge body sailed through the air, and right before he could sink his claws and fangs into me, I wrapped my small fingers around his thick throat.

His pained eyes went wide in shock not only due to the sudden action but also because his air flow had been cut off. I took advantage of his surprise and pressed him against the tree I'd collided with moments ago, his hind legs dangling off the ground by a few inches.

A small whimper pushed past his lips as a few bones in his back popped and cracked, causing a pang of guilt and regret to build up in my chest. But it was instantly driven away by the thought of him lashing out like this on one of my pack members: an adult, an elder, or a child. The thought made my fingers subconsciously squeeze his neck tighter, causing him to choke and gasp for air.

"Shift back. Now," I demanded, my voice low and saturated with authority.

Thankfully, Greg didn't put up a fight, and he shifted back to his human form, causing my grip on him to ease, but I didn't let his feet touch the floor.

"Why are you doing this?" I asked just before Shane's cracking bones could be heard as he shifted back to his human form.

Greg's narrowed black eyes that still had the unidentifiable pain swimming in them moved from me to Shane then finally resting on me. Then he did something I didn't expect him to. He cried. His eyes turned back to the hazel-green eyes that he shared with his brother, and he cried.

No. He sobbed.

Without a second thought, my luna instincts took over. I released him and pulled him into my embrace. Even though Greg had been acting terrible these past couple of days, he was still a pup in my pack, and right now, he was in pain. I wasn't just going to sit back and let him suffer alone.

I held him tighter, giving Shane a wary look. Shane looked confused, his calculating eyes trying to decode the situation.

"What's wrong, Greg?" I asked gentler than before.

123

He tried to compose himself but abandoned the attempt when tears kept falling down his face.

"My mate," he said, trying to keep his breathing steady. "She rejected me."

CHAPTER FIFTEEN

My jaw went slack as I looked at him. The puzzle pieces finally fell into place; how his attitude suddenly changed when he saw Shane and me, the little comment Zac made about "her" hurting him, everything.

"Greg . . ." I trailed off, unable to finish my sentence, so I let my actions do it for me. I wrapped him up in a tight hug, and Shane's massive arms wrapped around the both of us moments later.

The fact that he was bare slipped from our minds.

"Why didn't you tell me?" Shane asked softly, a bit of hurt in his voice.

"Because he was in pain," I answered for the still sobbing Greg.

When wolves got rejected, they lost all sense of everything and the world was replaced by rage. Violence. Pain.

"I loved her so much." He cried, his voice muffled by my shoulder. "And she rejected me because she was in love with someone else," he stated bitterly. "And then I saw you two and I just . . ." He trailed off, and I gently rubbed his back with my hand.

"It's okay, Greg. It's okay," Shane whispered and held on tighter.

"I'm sorry," Greg whispered weakly, his voice worn and tired from crying.

"Don't be," I whispered. "Just . . . next time you're hurting, don't keep it bottled up inside. This may be your battle, but you never have to fight it alone."

Greg nodded. We stood there in silence for another five minutes or so. All I wanted to do was to take the pain away, but I knew that I couldn't so I did the next best thing: I let our embrace say all the words we couldn't.

"Maybe I'll get a second chance," Greg whispered as he pulled out of our arms, his eyes wandering to the full moon that lazily hung among the stars.

"Of course, you will," Shane said as he clapped him on the shoulder.

We all knew that second chance mates were extremely rare and extremely uncommon, but none of us voiced that out.

"You're an amazing brother, and I bet you'll be an even better mate and someday, a father."

Greg nodded before his gaze returned to the stars, taking them in as if it was his last time witnessing their beauty.

"Can I just . . . can I have a moment?" Greg asked gently, and Shane and I nodded instantly. "I'll meet up with you in a bit," he said before he turned his back to us, the moon and stars' gentle light illuminating his handsome face.

A part of me wanted to stay and comfort Greg, making sure that he didn't hurt himself or others. But an even bigger, more logical part of me let Shane intertwine his fingers with mine and slowly lead me away.

"This is so messed up," Shane grumbled, anger evident in his voice once we were out of Greg's earshot. "Many people don't find their mate and the fact that she found him and left is just—"

"Calm down," I whispered as I cupped his cheek.

His skin grew warmer as he got more enraged.

126

"It's just not fair," Shane said in a low whisper, his eyes closing as he nuzzled in my hand. "I found my Ariel. Why can't he find his?"

"Fate has a weird way of working sometimes," I said as I gently swept a piece of hair from Shane's face. "But it always works in our favor at the end."

Shane nodded before he rested his forehead on mine. "Say something that will calm me down," he begged, his voice strained and his skin growing uncomfortably warm against my own, letting me know that his wolf was pushing.

"I love you," I said just above a whisper as if I was trying to keep this conversation between Shane, the wind, and me.

"Again."

"I love you," I repeated easily, relief crashing over me in waves every time I said it. "And I will never stop."

Shane's skin quickly cooled down as a smile grew on his face.

"I'll never get tired of hearing that." He sighed before he took my face in his hands and tenderly kissed me, our lips fitting perfectly together like a key in a lock. His hands eventually left my face and secured themselves around my waist, ensuring that I wouldn't be leaving unless he let me, not that it mattered.

I used my index finger to gently lift his chin so I could have access to him that I wanted.

We fought a long, dangerous battle and I'd somehow ended up between a tree and Shane, my body not minding the wood as it dug into my back. After the kiss simmered down, Shane and I just gazed into each other's eyes as if they outshined any star that was out tonight.

"Do you want to head back to the ceremony?" Shane asked after a few moments in our haze.

"Can we still even go?" I said with a chuckle as I looked down at my now torn and dirty dress. "My dress is ruined, and you're . . ." I stopped midsentence once I realized that Shane was still naked and my cheeks grew uncomfortably warm once I realized how close he was to me.

"Naked?" Shane finished, an amused smile on his face at my flustered state and I nodded. "Don't worry. I have an extra pair of clothes around here somewhere. Plus, they can't leave until the alpha and luna close the ceremony," he explained before he slowly backed off of me, not missing the way I blushed as he did so.

He slowly wandered between trees, looking in branches and in woodpecker holes until he found what he was looking for in a moss-covered log.

"It's not the best, but it'll have to do," he murmured as he shook out the sweatpants in his hands before effortlessly slipping them on.

I turned my head and covered my eyes with my hands to give him some privacy, my cheeks still burning immensely even though I couldn't see a thing.

"You can open your eyes now," Shane said as his hands wrapped around my wrists and gently pulled my hands away from my eyes, and instantly, I became annoyed with how exposed he was.

His broad chest was open for all to view. His muscular body was free for girls' viewing pleasure, and the top of his V flirtatiously peeked from the top of his sweats. His incredible beauty was on display for everyone to bask in and admire. And it irritated me.

"What's wrong?" Shane asked, cocking his head to the side like a confused puppy, but the joy in his eyes and the amusement in his voice let me know that he knew exactly what was wrong.

"You're too exposed," I told him honestly, frowning as I said it.

"Don't worry about it," he said as he wrapped his arms around my waist and pulled me so close that we were chest to chest. "If anyone tries to look at me, I'll do a little of this," he said as he placed a gentle kiss on my forehead.

128

"Maybe a bit of this," he whispered, his lips finding their way to the crook of my neck where he would mark me and numbing sparks ignited on the tip of my nerves. "I might even do this," he said into my neck before his lips captured mine in a breath-taking kiss. "I'll show them all that I belong to the beautiful luna of this pack," he said lowly into my lips. "And if they have a problem with it, then they can tell her about it."

A small smile grew on my face before I placed one more kiss on his lips then pulled away.

Our fingers interlocked and we made our way back to the ceremony where the pack members had been anxiously awaiting our return. All at once, I was swarmed by pack members telling me congratulations and welcoming me into the pack.

"That was amazing!" Zac gushed once he finally made his way up to me.

"Was it now?" Shane asked, pulling me to his side.

"Yeah!" Zac nodded vigorously, his eyes lighting up. "You should've seen you guys! Shubby looked strong and handsome, and Ari, you looked so graceful and pretty, and when you talked, it was like a plot twist I wasn't expecting!"

I laughed at the comparison that Zac used before I said, "Thank you, Zac. One day, this will be you and your luna."

"You really think I can be an alpha like Shubby?" he asked, hope evident in his words, and I instantly nodded.

"You care a lot about the people around you and always want what's best. If that's not the perfect alpha, then I don't know what is!"

He smiled up at me before his attention went to something off in the distance, causing his face to light up before he dove back into the sea of people, bobbing and weaving as he urgently moved toward his destination.

Confusion clouded my head as I watched him, but I instantly relaxed once I saw him run to Greg who affectionately wrapped his arms around him before he said something in Zac's ear that made him nod before they hugged again.

Greg must've felt the heat of my gaze on him because he lifted his eyes from Zac and started scanning the crowd before his eyes finally found me. He gave me a small nod as if saying, *Everything's okay now. I'm okay now.*

I gave him a small smile, which he returned before he and Zac disappeared into the crowd with Zac excitedly talking to Greg as they did so.

More and more pack members continued greeting me, and I talked so much that my throat started burning due to its prolonged use in such a short amount of time.

We dismissed the ceremony by having each pack member, including Zac and Greg, approach the giant bowl that rested on the stage. We used the blade to cut their hand and let them briefly bleed into the bowl before the cut healed.

After each pack member was done, the bowl was over three-fourth full, and I was the last one to contribute. I held out my left hand and held the sharp blade with my right. I pressed the blade into my skin and slowly dragged it. I sucked in my breath as the pain ripped through my hand before I watched my blood fall and mix with the others.

My minor injury instantly healed over, and I set the knife down and took the torch that the priest gave to me.

"Brothers and sisters," Shane spoke for me since my throat was raw. "This represents the new chapter in our lives. A chapter in which we are all bound together not only by loyalty to each other and this pack but also by our trust. Our love. Our blood. This represents the destruction of all hate or bad blood we have for one another and another chance that we're offering to each other. This," he said, sliding his hand back into mine. "Represents a new family. A new pack. A new luna."

Cheers went up, and I knew that was my cue to drop the torch into the bowl. I watched as the blood red flames licked toward the heavens, the wretched smell of burning blood filling my nose. I almost gagged as I dragged Shane not only away from the horrid smell, but also away from the crowd and toward our house. Our home.

"Did you enjoy your ceremony?" Shane asked as we entered our bedroom, and I nodded excitedly, unable to speak unless I wanted to feel knives of pain stab my throat. "You truly looked beautiful up there and how you took control of our situation with Greg . . ." he said, taking slow steps toward me until I was trapped between him and the wall. "It was amazing. You took charge and looked really hot doing it."

I rolled my eyes as he planted his hands on my hips and made a move to kiss me, but I moved my face so that he merely pecked my cheek.

"Playing hard to get?" Shane quirked his eyebrow, causing me to nod before I wrote.

Shower.

Then I pointed at me then him. We still had little leaves and a bit of dirt clinging to us from our fight, and I'd rather not go to sleep with it caking my body.

He childishly groaned before he pulled himself up. "Fine." He huffed as he crossed his arms over his muscular chest. "But when I come back, we're going to finish this."

A blush crept onto my cheeks as I sheepishly nodded and watched a victorious smirk grow on Shane's face as he retreated and headed to the door.

"I'm going to the bathroom down the hall," he announced as he pulled the door shut behind him, leaving me alone.

As soon as I was certain that Shane was gone, I pulled myself from against the wall and hurried into the bathroom, deciding to make another change.

My feet slapped against the cold tiles of the bathroom as I passed by my comforting choice of the bath and reached for the handle of the shower, turning it to hot water. The water pounded against the tiles, sounding like a thunderstorm.

I walked away from the shower and quickly brushed my teeth until the steam fogged the mirror. I rinsed my mouth with water before I stripped down until I was naked then I slid into the shower for the first time in years. Hot water pounded down on me as soon as I got in and a hiss slipped past my lips as a result. It took me a few moments to get used to the hot water constantly raining down on me, and after a while, I found myself closing my eyes and relaxing into it.

I slowly started running the soap over my body and running my hands covered in shampoo through my hair not leaving the shower until I was certain that there was no trace of the fight left on me. I repeated the process that I did every time I was done washing before I made my way into the closet where I slid on a black bra with matching underwear then one of Shane's annoyingly comfortable shirts.

As soon as I walked out, Shane walked into the room, his used towel and old sweatpants in his arms and around his waist was a new pair of sweatpants: black instead of gray. Water dripped down his forehead from his hair, and I realized that he never bothered to dry his hair.

It took him a while to notice that I was standing here. My eyes were hungrily taking in every detail of him. Every scar. Every perfect imperfection. Everything. Then his eyes met mine and that classic smirk spread across his face, the way food color expanded in water. He dropped the articles he was holding to the floor, and in four mighty strides, he was in front me with his hands on either side of my face and his soft lips pressed against mine, the pressure between us growing every second.

My hands wandered down his smooth, defined chest and solid abs before they found the drawstring of his sweatpants. His lips pulled into a smile as I used the drawstring to gently pull him closer to me, not minding that there was now no part of us not touching.

He moved his hands to my waist. As the kiss intensified, he slowly started leading me backward until I felt the familiar pressure of the bed pressing against the back of my knees, causing me to scream as I fell, pulling Shane down with me. We landed on the fluffy mattress, laughter slipping past both of our mouths as Shane propped his body up so that he wasn't lying on me.

"I'm sorry." I wheezed weakly through my laughter, the simple action hurting my throat, once I realized that I'd grabbed Shane so hard that my nails left marks on his shoulders.

Shane followed my eyes. His own laughter pushed to the surface once he realized what I'd done.

"It's fine." He smiled as his thumb gently brushed my bottom lip, his eyes watching me. "Absolutely fine."

We lay there for a moment, every breath blending into one. His body heat seeped through my shirt, and my body craved the feeling of his finger on my lip. Hesitation swam in Shane's eyes as if he were scared he'd ruin the simple, yet beautiful moment if he moved.

A smile grew on my lips at how nervous and careful he was before I lifted my head, so our lips met once more. He moved our bodies so that he was now sitting with his legs hanging off the edge of the bed while I sat on his lap with my legs tightly around his waist and my arms draped over his shoulders with my fingers interlocked behind his neck.

His butterfly kisses traveled down my jaw and throat until he made it to his final destination: the groove between my shoulder and neck. A fire burned in my lower stomach as his lips moved so delicate and calculated across my neck. I gripped the back of his neck tight and drew in a sharp breath once he found the right spot: The spot he was going to mark me.

"Ariel," he whispered against my neck, and I already knew my answer to his unasked question. "Can I make you my luna?"

His lips left my skin before his eyes met mine awaiting my answer. I could see the passion and desire swimming in his eyes, and I was almost sure that I had the same expression. For the Lunar Ceremony to be completed, the Alpha must mark the Luna to seal their connection and unity.

"Yes," I granted silently, mouthing the word as the anticipation growing within me.

He smiled before he placed a tender kiss on my lips then returned to work. He placed open-mouthed kisses where he was to mark me, causing me to sigh.

"This is going to hurt," Shane warned, as he looked up at me as if expecting me to back out.

Instead, I nodded as I gripped his shoulders and moved my neck to the side to allow him full access.

"That's my girl," Shane whispered before his canines fully extended.

I closed my eyes and waited. He placed one more kiss on my neck before a searing pain erupted from my neck. A whimper escaped my lips as my grip on Shane tightened. The familiar stench of my blood hung in the air as Shane dug his teeth deeper into me, making sure that the process was being completed.

Suddenly, the pain turned into a bliss I'd never felt before. I felt a new part of me bloom and reveal itself like a flower showing itself to the world. A quiet gasp slipped past my lips as I opened my eyes, the extraordinary feeling making its way down to my knees and to my toes. After a few moments, I felt Shane release me before his tongue slid over my mark, cleansing off the blood.

"It's done," he whispered before he placed a gentle kiss on it, which sent a shiver down my back and sparks in my cells.

Once we were level again, I placed a quick kiss on his lips before I jumped off him and ran into the bathroom. Shane's chuckles followed me through the air. I flipped on the light, and instantly, the mark stood out. The mouth shaped bite marks had healed over only to the point that you could still see it and know that I was Shane's. The redness of it prominently stood out against my tender skin, making it look more painful than it truly was.

"Do you like it?" Shane gently asked as he wrapped his arms around my waist and rested his chin opposite of the shoulder that bore the still tender mark.

"*Love it*," I said soundlessly, mouthing the words before a small yawn escaped from within me.

"Are you ready for bed?" Shane asked.

I nodded.

"Come on," he said before he suddenly picked me up.

I suppressed the yelp that wanted to come out because I knew it would destroy my throat. Instead, I clung tightly to Shane like my life depended on it. He used one hand to turn off the lights as we passed the switch before he gently placed me in the bed, tucking me in too before he walked over to his own side. He snaked his arms around my waist and pulled me in before he rested his head on my good shoulder before whispering, "I love you, Ariel."

Without thinking, I instantly said it back. "I love you too, Shane." And even though the simple phrase felt like I swallowed a handful of nails, it felt so right slipping from my tongue that it was worth it.

I felt Shane's lips pull into a smile before he pulled me a bit closer and I let the weight of sleep pull my eyes shut.

Observations

UNKNOWN

I watched how Ariel handled Greg with mercy and grace and not brutality or violence. I knew they were the right choice, but unfortunately, I still had one more test I was required to give, and it was by far, the worst.

CHAPTER SIXTEEN

I woke up to a million jackhammers beating my head from the inside out. I groaned as I tried to sit up. The fact that Shane was tightly gripping my waist restricting most of my movements didn't help either. Neither did the bright morning sun that was shining directly in my face.

I forgot about the after effects of getting marked, especially by an alpha. Not only had the mental and emotional link been completed between us, but a new link—a link to the pack—was created so that they could link me anytime they needed me until I put up my walls to block everyone out.

"Is the mark getting to you too?" Shane asked, his arm that wasn't holding on to me lazily slung over his eyes.

"Yeah," I said faintly, my voice still weak from last night.

"Me too." Shane groaned before he let his arm fall from his face. "But if the pain's for you, then it's worth it."

I rolled my eyes at his cheesiness before I placed a quick kiss on his lips. I sucked in a sharp breath as pain shot through my skull like a lightning bolt due to the sudden movement.

"I'm sorry, love," he apologized gently even though he did nothing wrong before he lifted his body up slightly and pressed a kiss against my temple.

Usually, the simple action would make me feel giddy and warm on the inside as his kiss chased the pain away. Instead, all I felt was an ice pick of guilt chipping at my heart, reminding me that I had something that someone I cared about didn't have.

Even though I didn't know it at the time, I was flaunting around what we had right in front of Greg, and now, I have Shane's mark . . .

"Are you thinking about Greg?" Shane asked as if reading my thoughts, and I nodded. "I figured. I could hear some of your thoughts through our link."

My eyebrows pulled together in confusion.

"I'll teach you how to control it, okay?"

I nodded.

Links between mates were more intimate and complicated than that of a pack link. Mates could feel each other's emotions and thoughts at times if what they were feeling was strong enough, while the pack link only worked if you wanted to communicate. Links between mates also felt more natural, while pack links could be jarring and annoying at times. It was all complicated and intricate.

Still not completely used to the new link and my voice still being tired, I grabbed Shane's hand.

Check Greg?

"Of course." Shane nodded before he continued. "Listen, Ariel. The—" Shane started but was interrupted by a loud knock on the door. "Yes?" Annoyance was evident in his voice as he spoke and his arm subconsciously tightened around me.

"Shubby! Greg and I made breakfast for you and Ari! Come on before it gets cold!" Zac explained excitedly from behind the door, and instantly, all traces of annoyance and frustration melted away from Shane's face due to the pure elation and euphoria in his brother's voice.

"Okay, Zac. Just give us a few minutes, and we'll be right out, okay?"

"You better hurry before it gets cold!" Zac warned before the sound of his feet descending down the hallway could be heard.

I looked down at Shane, and he had a giddy look as if he were a child and his parents told him that they had a surprise waiting for him in the car.

"You heard him. We have to hurry!" he said before he quickly started getting up, nearly throwing me off him in the process. "Sorry," he said, though a small smile grew on his face as he said it.

I narrowed my eyes at him, trying to put as much venom into my glare as I could, but I merely ended up laughing at myself. Shane's laughs accompanied mine as I walked into the closet and pulled on a pair of sweatpants. After I was ready, Shane and I made our way to the kitchen, the delicious smell of pancakes and bacon filling our noses as soon as we entered the hallway. The faint smell of something burning hung in the air. Since it wasn't that prominent, we didn't worry too much about it.

"How did you get it stuck up there?" Greg said, trying and failing to suppress a strangled laugh.

"I don't know!" Zac proclaimed. He sounded perplexed. "It just went up and wouldn't come down! I think gravity might be broken," he concluded before he paused, thinking. "Do you think that if I jumped off of the table, I'd fly?" he asked excitedly before I heard him climbing on the furniture.

"Zac, don't!" Shane yelled as we rushed into the kitchen.

We entered the kitchen right as Greg grabbed Zac, preventing him from testing his theory.

"What is going on in here?" Shane voiced the question that occupied my thoughts.

"I was trying to flip the pancake, and it won't come down." Zac frowned as he pointed at the ceiling.

Sure enough, there was a comically big and misshapen pancake stuck to the ceiling, showing no sign of coming down anytime soon without any help. I shot Greg a questioning look, and he merely shrugged as he put Zac back on the ground, causing me to chuckle.

"Well, it's been up there this long, so it won't kill it to stay up there for a few more minutes or at least until we're done with breakfast." Shane shrugged before he turned to the counter where the food was.

His brothers followed him and eventually I did after I spent a few more moments waiting for the pancake to hopefully come down. It didn't.

As we ate, I kept sneaking glances at Greg. More times than one, I caught him wistfully looking at the still tender mark that was now displayed on my neck, and I instantly felt bad.

"How are you feeling?" I asked softly once Shane and Zac had left to scrape the pancake off the ceiling.

"Okay." He shrugged. "My wolf is extremely weak. He's not handling it so well."

I nodded in response. It was normal for the wolf—especially of the male—to become weak following a rejection.

"Can you shift?" I asked, curiosity gnawing at me even though I knew it shouldn't be.

Greg shook his head. "It hurts too much. Last time I tried, I almost passed out from the pain."

"I'm so sorry, Greg. That sounds awful."

"I could feel every bone breaking, every cell changing, and every layer of skin ripping and transforming. Awful is an understatement. More like pure hell."

I wanted to open my mouth to say something to comfort him, but out of all the words that floated around in my head, I couldn't find any that could string together to form a sentence that could soothe that kind of pain. So I didn't. I simply took a sip of the hot cocoa I'd made myself in place of coffee and let Greg talk it out.

"But I guess the pain is good in some aspects. I guess."

I furrowed my eyebrows asking him the silent question.

"The pain from here," he said, motioning all over his body, "takes away from all the pain here," he said, pointing to his heart.

I felt my own break a tiny bit

"Maybe enough physical pain will drown out the emotional pain until I can't feel it anymore," Greg said softly, his gaze wandering out the window.

Without thinking, I got up and wrapped my arms around him, surprising him as much as I surprised myself. "I thought it worked that way too when my parents died," I admitted. "I thought that just one more kick, one more slap, one more blow to the head would distract me from the pain on the inside, but no matter what we do, the pain will always come through. There's no ignoring it. Just controlling it. Just conquering it."

"How do you conquer something that's eating you alive every day?" he whispered into my shoulder, pain evident in his words and body language.

"You refuse to feed it," I said as I gently stroked his hair in a comforting manner. "You let it starve and watch it perish."

Greg nodded as he took a deep breath. "This is why you're the luna of this pack," he stated quietly. "You look out for people like me who've been complete and utter jerks to you. Everyone is the same in your eyes and no one deserves better or worse to you. Everyone deserves love and kindness . . ." He trailed off. "I just hope that I find my Ariel somewhere out there."

"You will," I said, my voice now becoming scratchy and uncomfortable traveling up my throat due to excessive use. "I know it."

"Thank you, Ariel," he said as we both pulled away, and only then did I realize the liquid sadness that was running from his eyes.

141

"For what?" I whispered as I gently wiped his tears away with my thumb.

"For listening to me when no one else would."

I smiled at him and brushed his hair from his forehead the way my mother used to do with my brother and me when we had an emotional moment.

"You're welcome," I said, offering him one more soft smile before I got up and wandered to where Zac and Shane were, leaving Greg to process everything.

Shane had successfully gotten the pancake off the ceiling, and now Zac was playing with it. His eyes were wide and curious as if the pancake was the most magical thing in the universe.

"So you talked with Greg?" Shane asked softly as he pulled me into him so that our legs and bodies were pressed together, and I nodded. "Is he okay?"

"He will be," I said, my voice barely coming out above a whisper.

"Don't stress your voice," Shane advised. "It's too pretty to go to waste."

I rolled my eyes, making it the thousandth time I had done it since I had been with Shane.

"Oh, come on. Don't be like that." He chuckled as he tried to kiss me, but I swatted him away as if he were a pesky fly or mosquito, which he was really acting like. "Fine." He pouted after a few more minutes of persistence. "I won't kiss you but don't come crying to me when you start missing this," he said as he began making kissing faces.

I cringed as I pushed him away.

"No. I'm sorry, Ariel! Love me!" he begged as he began chasing me. My laughter filled the house as my mate chased me, begging me for the love he knew he already had.

*   *   *

142

"So this protocol basically ensures that each pack member, regardless of gender, sexual orientation, etcetera, gets the same training. Understand?" Shane said, pointing to various parts of text on the paper that rested on the all too familiar desk in front of us, and I nodded.

Shane and I took a break from looking over agreements for him to break down all the rules and regulations that this pack was built upon.

I felt the heat that was slowly building up inside me intensify as I felt the familiar pressure of shifting behind my eyes, though my wolf made no effort to communicate with me in a long time. I was incredibly sensitive to everything: my hearing, my sight, my smell. Everything. I was highly irritable too, but I just didn't tell Shane in hopes that this would all blow over soon.

"And this one here . . . ," he continued, pulling out a different paper from the stack but I couldn't focus on a word he was saying.

My sensitive hearing amped up everything, that I could hear the annoying sound of the papers rubbing against each other like two pieces of Styrofoam. No matter how hard I tried to fight the urge, my hands clamped over my ears while my teeth clenched so hard that I found it surprising that they were all still in one piece, instead of pieces. The pressure behind my eyes now felt like jackhammers, and the heat building within me felt like a furnace that I couldn't escape.

"What's wrong, Ariel?" Shane frantically asked as he tightly cradled me in his arms and looked me over for any external injuries, but all I could focus on was the immense pain that was slowly swallowing my body like a snake to its prey.

Suddenly, the door flew open, revealing a breathless and distraught Aiden. "Shane, why haven't you been responding to the links?" he almost yelled.

"Aiden, lower your voice," Shane said in a deathly low voice, reminding Aiden that even though they were friends, Shane was still his alpha.

"Do you not realize what's outside?" Aiden questioned with the same amount of urgency in his voice but at a lower volume.

"Aiden, I don't have time for this. Something's wrong with Ariel, so just spit it out."

"That's the thing." Aiden sighed. "It's the moon. The Blood Moon." At those words, the color drained from Shane's face, and he looked down at me before his eyes found Aiden's again.

"No," he whispered, disbelief clinging to his voice though he knew that it was true. "It wasn't supposed to follow me. The curse was supposed to be broken when my family disowned me." He held me closer as he spoke, the sparks that ignited between us when we touched soothing me a little but not enough.

"We need to hurry," Aiden said. "Everyone in this pack who put their blood in that bowl last night will feel it, including—"

"Zac," Shane breathed. "No, he can't! He's too young. It could kill him or—"

"I know," Aiden said, cutting off Shane's frantic rush of words. "I'll send word out to the pack to meet us in the clearing that the ceremony was held in last night."

"How much time do we have?"

"At most? Fifteen."

Shane sighed before his eyes met mine. "Go," he instructed. "And whatever you do, don't leave Zac's side until I get there. Understood?"

"Yes, Alpha." Aiden nodded before he hurried off.

A shiver ran down my spine, not only from the scared look on Shane's face that I'd never seen before but also from the fact that Aiden addressed Shane as alpha, which let me know that whatever was happening was serious.

"What's going on?" I barely choked out through the pain.

"There was a curse put on my family about ten years ago, four years before Zac was born, and almost every Blood Moon, our pack was forced into a painful, slow shift where we'd remain trapped in our wolf form until daybreak. What makes it worse was that it doesn't happen every year. It's random so we can't prepare ourselves. I hoped that when I left my parents and started my own pack that I'd be rid of the curse, but I guess it didn't just stain our packs but our blood too," Shane whispered. "But now it's here and since Zac's so young and his body's not ready, the shift could—"

"Don't." The simple word felt like fire on my tongue, but I couldn't let Shane finish his sentence. I refused.

"I'm so sorry you have to go through this, love," Shane whispered as he gently pressed a kiss on my forehead. "It's tougher on the females than it is on the males."

A groan escaped my lips as my wolf began pressing harder against my boundaries and worry started replacing the air in my chest. Not only was this supposed to be painful, but I also hadn't shifted in a long time. The last time I did, Roxie almost took over. She was a darkness that lurked in the corners of my mind, telling me to do awful things and had been there ever since my parents passed away. And she almost won.

Tonight, not only would I be trapped in my wolf form, but I would also be vulnerable to her. To the other being in me.

Alexia, I called my normal wolf. *Whatever you do tonight, please don't let her win.*

I didn't get a response as I expected, but I hoped that she heard me.

"You're so strong," he whispered as he cupped my cheek, his words and touch momentarily distracting me from the pain. "I'm sorry," he apologized once more before he gently kissed my lips.

The pain was so intense that even the mere thought of kissing Shane back hurt.

"Just take deep breaths and focus on me, okay?" he instructed, and I barely managed a nod. Shane pulled me closer and whispered comforting things in my ear for a few agonizing minutes before he carefully picked me up bridal style. "We have to meet the pack so that we can lead them during the run, okay?"

I didn't need to nod or speak for Shane to know that I understood him.

He made fast, even steps down the stairs then out the door, going to the clearing we'd just been to yesterday for my Lunar Ceremony. The moon hung high. Its once smooth white color changed into an unsettling crimson color, yet it gave the world a peaceful glow despite the chaos that was about to happen.

Once we made it to the clearing, we were surrounded by the hundred members that resided in the pack. The air filled with pain filled whimpers from the females as they rested in their mate's arms, the males whispering comforting things in their ears to calm them.

Shane scanned the crowd until they landed on Aiden who was with Jess, Greg, and Zac, as he said he would be.

"How much time?" Shane asked lowly.

Aiden looked up in the sky, his eyes carefully calculating as he did so.

"About four minutes."

Shane nodded before he looked down at me.

"Not much longer, love," he whispered as his lips came into contact with my forehead before his attention turned to the pack members before him.

"Members of the Silver Crescent Pack," Shane called, his voice sounding like a deafening scream in my sensitive ears. "Tonight is the night of the Blood Moon. The curse that runs in my veins is now with everyone else in this pack, and for that, I'm sorry, for I had no knowledge that this burden still followed me. I would take all the pain if I could, and I would not knowingly put any of you in this amount of pain." His eyes looked over the dozens of

146

women who were being cradled in their mate's arms before he looked down at me.

I nodded, letting him know that I was okay before he continued.

"But we will make the best of it, rest assured. We will let our wolves run free like our ancestors did hundreds of years before us and truly know what it means to be a lycan."

Shane spoke with confidence and reassurance even when he talked about the unknown future that was at our doorsteps, and I could see why these people made him their alpha. Surprisingly, a chorus of howls and hollers traveled in the air in approval.

"One minute," Aiden reported, and Shane nodded before his attention returned to his pack. His family.

"In approximately one minute, we will be forced into our wolves. As I've learned, it is better not to fight it no matter how painful or hard it may be. Your wolves will take over, hence, why we are in the center of the pack territory. Luckily, we're far enough from the humans, and our woods are filled with animals, but you must control your wolves, or they will control you."

"Yes, Alpha," the pack chorused.

"Thirty seconds," Aiden said, and Shane looked down at me.

"I'll be right here, okay?" he whispered before he gently set me down on the cool grass.

I nodded before a pain I'd never felt before engulfed my body, setting every atom of my being on fire. The screams I'd been fighting so long to keep at bay flew past my lips just as Shane hit the floor. His own screams filled the air followed by the pack. The sound of brittle bones breaking accompanied the screams that filled the once quiet night.

I felt fire replace the blood in my veins and lava fill my skull. That was when my first bone broke. Then the next. Then the next. Another set of agonized screams left my mouth as tears filled my eyes.

Out of the corner of my eye, I saw Shane. His canines were extended, and his eyes were pitch black. His claws were extended through his skin. He screamed as his back broke, taking him from his position on his hands and knees straight down to his stomach where he writhed in pain.

All I wanted to do was wrap my arms around him, but all I could do was scream and cry as black dots danced before my eyes and my body broke and transformed. I felt every bone break and reform, every cell changing its identity and every new hair sprouting from my flesh. And right when I thought that the pain was too much to bear, it stopped and was replaced by a new sensation that I'd never fully felt before. It was like I freed a new side of me.

I felt someone nuzzle into my side and instantly, I knew it was Shane. No one could make the addicting sparks dance across my skin but Shane.

"Are you alright, love?" His masculine voice filled my head through the link as he moved so that he was right in front of me.

I looked at myself through his thoughts. My dark brown wolf had grown a lot since the last time I'd seen it, not only because I was older now, but also because I was the luna of this pack.

"Yeah," I responded though body ached, and slight pressure was building behind my eyes because my wolf was pressing for control.

Out of the corner of my eye, I noticed an extremely small wolf stumbling its way over to Shane and me. It had familiar innocent eyes and deep brown fur. It was Zac.

"Zac?" Shane said, voicing my thoughts.

"Look, Shubby! I'm a wolf like you!" Zac said excitedly, a wolfish grin spreading across his face.

"Indeed you are," Shane agreed before he bent down and took the scruff of Zac's neck into his powerful jaws.

"I'll be right back. I have to take Zac to Greg," Shane explained before he quickly took Zac to a wolf I instantly recognized as Greg.

His wolf looked exactly like Shane's, only smaller and lacking the power that radiated off of Shane.

Greg's eyes met mine, and he gave me a slight nod, reassuring me that he was okay . . . or as okay as he could be right now.

I also caught sight of a wolf whom I recognized as Aiden. His wolf was large but smaller than Shane's and mine. His fur and eyes matched his human form, and he still had that mischievous glint in his warm brown eyes. He was currently nuzzling into Jess's side, causing her to yelp in laughter. She looked almost identical to him, only smaller and more feminine.

"Are you ready?" Shane asked as he made his way back to me, and I nodded.

Without warning, Shane let out a loud and powerful howl, causing everyone to stand at attention before they too joined in, me included.

Shane then scanned the crowd, looking for something I didn't know. After a few moments, he turned to me and nodded before he broke out in a full out run, causing the pack and me to follow him. As we ran, the wind ripped through my fur, twigs crunched under my feet, and the sweet smell of nature rushed into my nose.

Despite the pain that continued growing behind my eyes, I felt my wolf become a bit excited, bathing in the joy of being back where she belonged: the wild.

We continued following Shane through the forest, our paws thundering against the earth like a storm.

"It's time to let down the barriers," Shane announced though he didn't stop running.

He was the first to let his wolf have control, and I could see him slip away as his wolf surfaced. Then one by one, the pack members let themselves slip away, and they started straying from the running formation.

The pain behind my eyes was now unbearable, feeling as if someone was trying to rip my skull apart.

"*Please, don't let her out,*" I begged, referring to Roxie.

"*I won't,*" Alexia said. "*I promise.*"

Even though we hadn't communicated and we were practically strangers at this point, I trusted my wolf more than anyone, and I knew that when she made a promise, she would keep it.

I let my barrier down, and I felt Alexia push me back into the corner of my mind until I temporarily slid off the face of the earth.

CHAPTER SEVENTEEN

I awoke to the beautiful sun pouring its warm light over me. It was quiet, the only sound coming from animals as they hurried by. My body dully ached, and I was idly aware of the metallic taste of blood in my mouth that I instantly identified as an animal's and not a human's or lycan's. But my moment of calm came to an abrupt end when I realized that not only was I naked, but someone was also holding me.

I turned my head, ready to shove the person off when I was met by the sleeping face of my handsome mate who had his arms strategically slung over me so that I wasn't bare for everyone to see.

Shane let out a sigh in his sleep and pulled me closer, his warm breath cascading over my mark. I felt a blush fall over my cheeks, not only from the amazing sparks that bounced everywhere he touched but also because our bare bodies were so close.

To distract myself, I looked around at the dozens of pack members scattered around us; mates huddled close together with dried blood circling some mouths. Some even fidgeted in their sleep.

I was pulled from my observations by a low groan and warm breath dancing across my still sensitive mark.

"Good morning, love," Shane almost croaked, his voice scratchy and dry.

"Good morning," I greeted, my voice equally as gross.

"What a way to wake up, don't you think?" Shane chuckled, causing me to roll my eyes. "I'm merely kidding, love," he assured, though the smile on his face told a completely different story. "How are you feeling?" he asked softly, seriousness replacing the silliness in his voice.

"Sore," I said honestly. "It feels as if I spent all night working out without stretching or taking a warm bath afterward."

"You and your baths." Shane chuckled before he moved his head so that his lips gently touched mine.

I slowly turned my body so that we'd be chest to chest instead of his chest to my back. At the same time, he adjusted himself so that I was still covered and we weren't too close.

"You know that you're breathtaking, right?" Shane murmured into my skin before he placed a gentle kiss on my mark. "You, your wolf, just everything."

A whisper of a laugh pushed past my lips as Shane rested his forehead on my shoulder with his eyes closed.

"We should really get you dressed before everyone wakes up," Shane said, irritation evident in his voice at the possibility of everyone seeing me bare and vulnerable.

"That would be a good idea," I said with a slight chuckle.

"Yeah. It would be a shame if I had to remove someone's eyes because they dared to look at you," Shane mused as he stood up, taking me with him.

"Why do I have a feeling that you're not joking?" I asked, even though I already knew the answer.

"Because I'm not." Shane held me close just in case anyone woke up as we quietly stepped over them to reach a stash of Shane's clothes.

After a few moments of wandering, we found some of his clothes shallowly buried at the base of a tree. I easily slid on a t-shirt

152

that swallowed my body whole along with some basketball shorts, while Shane opted for a pair of sweatpants.

"Are you hungry?" Shane asked, and I shook my head.

"Alexia had a feast last night," I said as I patted my stomach.

"So did Axel," Shane agreed, referring to his own wolf.

I opened my mouth to say more when a frantic—still naked—Aiden rushed up to us, fear and confusion swimming in his eyes.

"Aiden, what's—"

"It's Greg and Zac," Aiden cut in, his eyes jumping from Shane to mine before resting on Shane's.

"What happened to them?" Shane asked, his eyebrows furrowed and confusion hiding behind his calm voice.

"They're not breathing."

CHAPTER EIGHTEEN

"What?" I yelled, not caring that there were over a hundred sleeping pack members that I probably just woke up.

Shane was frozen, still processing the words that'd just come from Aiden's mouth.

"I don't know what happened! When I woke up, Greg was bleeding from his nose and mouth, and Zac wasn't responding. When I checked, I couldn't hear them breathing or—"

"Take me to them," Shane growled, though his voice was still deathly calm. "Now."

Aiden didn't waste any time taking us to where Zac and Greg lay. When I saw them, I had to put my hand over my mouth to prevent me from screaming. Greg was lying face up, eyes glued open and empty while blood trickled not only from his nose and mouth but also from his ears. Even worse, I didn't hear him breathing or his heart beating.

Zac wasn't much better.

His eyes were open, void of any joy or emotion. Instead of bleeding the way his brother was, his skin had grown a sickly white color, almost gray. His lips and fingertips were tinted blue as if he'd frozen to . . .

No. I was not going to think about that word because they were not. I would've known if they were. But every moment, every second of not knowing felt like another dagger through the heart.

"Oh my Goddess. . ." Shane trailed off as he sank to his knees, and for the first time, I saw a tear run down his face as he looked at his brothers.

My mind wandered back to when I was a child at my family's funeral, and I asked Morgan why he was the only one not crying, and he told me that a real man never cries. It showed vulnerability and weakness, but he was wrong. Crying showed just how strong that man was. And Shane was no different.

"Where's the pack doctor?" I demanded, struggling to ignore the suffocating tightness that was in my chest.

"I-I don't know," Aiden stammered. "As soon as I saw them like this, I called her, and when she didn't come, Jess went to find her and—"

"I found her!"

I heard Jess's distraught voice as she came into view, latching tightly onto another woman's arm who I vaguely remember as Samantha, the pack doctor. Her dirty blonde hair was a mess, and she winced slightly as Jessica dragged her to Greg and Zac, undoubtedly because of how tight Jess was gripping her.

A couple of men and women followed behind them, which I guessed was Samantha's help. Aiden's jaw clenched at the sight of at least four naked males surrounding his also naked mate.

"Where have you been?" Shane growled lowly as he stood up. His eyes were inky black though tears were still silently falling from them, making him look much more intimidating.

Samantha's eyes grew wide as she shrunk back. "I-I'm sorry, Alpha. I was—"

"I don't want to hear your excuses!" Shane roared angrily, his wolf slowly getting a grip on him.

155

I gently cupped his cheek and directed his forehead to my own, silently reminding him that yelling at them wasn't in our best interest right now. He took a deep breath and closed his eyes.

"Just tell me what's wrong with them and fix it," he said, his voice tight and strained.

"We'll have to take them back to the office to do that, Alpha," she explained as she squatted down to examine Greg and Zac's condition, not at all bothered by the fact that her body was bare.

"I don't care what you do, just get them to breathe," Shane demanded, his forehead leaving mine and his hard eyes locking with Samantha's.

"Yes, Alpha!" Samantha and her posse of assistants said in unison before the four men shifted and the ladies climbed on their backs, carefully positioning Greg and Zac so that they wouldn't fall off.

"Samantha, I swear to the Moon Goddess herself that if anything happens to them." He paused and looked at each and every nurse and assistant. "I will kill all of you. Understood?"

"Understood, Alpha," Samantha confirmed in a steady voice, though fear resonated in her blue-green eyes. Then they were off to the hospital.

"Jessica, Aiden. I need you guys to stay with Zac and Greg. Don't let them out of your sight."

"Of course." Aiden nodded before both he and Jessica shifted and followed after them.

As soon as they were gone, Shane turned to me and the strong, tough act crumbled away as he collapsed in my arms, sobbing and cursing into my shoulder, not caring who saw or heard him.

"It's going to be alright," I whispered as I gently stroked his hair and back, gently kissing his head every now and again. "They're going to pull through."

We sat there for a while, Shane's heart-shattering sobs echoing in my ears and his shaking shoulders chipping at the foundation that I was trying to be for him. Tears welled up in my eyes, but I quickly blinked them away. Despite the terrible scenarios that were running wild through my head, I had to stay strong and calm. For Shane.

"I don't want them to go," he whispered into my shoulder, his voice broken and scared. "I can't lose them."

"You won't lose them," I whispered as I tenderly kissed the crown of his head. "They're strong. They're fighters, and they wouldn't give up that easily."

Shane nodded before he sat up, his eyes red and puffy.

"Are you ready to see them?" I asked softly as I brushed his hair from his forehead and he nodded before he stood up with me following him.

I looked away as he stripped out of his sweatpants before he gave them to me and effortlessly shifted into his beautiful wolf. I climbed on top of him, and for a brief moment in time, I allowed myself to relax as the wind ripped through my hair and Axel's soft fur spilled between my fingers.

It didn't take us long to get to the tall, gloomy hospital, and as soon as I climbed off of Shane, the weight of fear and uncertainty fell on my chest, getting closer to crushing me with every breath.

I quickly offered him his pants once he shifted back. He barely had them on when we stormed in. The receptionist took one glance at us before instantly directing us to where Zac and Greg were.

"Let me see them," Shane demanded to the nurse who was in the private waiting room we'd been assigned.

"Alpha, I—"

"That's an order."

She silently weighed her options before she sighed and opened the doors that said, "Authorized personnel only".

157

"You must stay behind the yellow line, or you'll be putting them both at risk," she explained as we walked down a long hallway. "The risk is high enough with so many unsterilized people in there already, but—"

"How are they doing?" Shane interrupted, not caring about the nurse's complaints.

"I don't know," she answered honestly. "I was assigned to wait for you as soon as they were brought here."

We stopped in front of a huge door with windows that I could see Greg and Zac through.

"But I do know that they're through these doors."

"Thank you," Shane breathed before we entered the sterile room.

Relief washed over me when I heard heartbeats that not only belonged to Aiden, Jess, and the doctors that were working on the boys but also two strong heartbeats that belonged to none other than Greg and Zac.

"Their hearts are beating," I whispered as I looked at Shane then Jessica and Aiden.

"They brought them back a few minutes ago," Aiden said, his voice weak from the crying he'd been doing. His face was tear-streaked.

I looked at Shane, and I could tell he was struggling to stay behind the yellow line as he'd been instructed to do. His brothers were just a few yards out of his reach, and I could tell it was killing him.

"What happened to them?" Shane asked Samantha as she connected them to an IV containing a multicolored liquid I didn't recognize.

"Greg's wolf was too weak to withstand the shift, and his body began shutting down not long after the shift," she stated as she grabbed two towels from the nurses that were helping her before she placed one on Greg's forehead and the other on Zac's. "As for Zac . . . I still haven't figured it out."

158

"What do you mean?" I asked, my eyes instantly drawn to Zac's pale figure.

"He has no internal or external injuries or trauma. I've never seen anything like this . . ." She trailed off, looking down at Zac. "We've got their hearts started and steady, so that's a start. Greg should wake up any minute, but Zac . . . will take longer."

Almost as if on cue, Greg's eyes slowly peeled open as a scratchy groan escaped his lips.

"Wh—" he started, but Samantha stopped him.

"Everything's alright, Gregory," she said gently as she adjusted the towel on his forehead. "Just relax and hang in there, okay?"

The gentle tone and soft look she was giving Greg almost made Greg submit without question. Almost. But he saw his brother lying motionless beside him, and he bolted upright, a wince escaping his lips as he did so.

"Gregory, please just—"

"What's wrong with Zac?" he demanded as he tried to make a move toward his brother only to have the needles attached to him and Samantha stop him.

"Greg, listen," she said with a bit of force behind her words. "Your brother is in critical condition right now, and you need to take things slow, or else your wolf might shut down again. You wouldn't be doing Zachary any good if you killed yourself, now would you?"

Greg's eyes met mine, and I gave him a small nod, telling him to follow her instructions, causing him to reluctantly do as he was told though his eyes didn't leave Zac.

"What happened to him?" he asked quietly, still refusing to look away from Zac.

"We . . . we don't know," Shane admitted truthfully before I intertwined my fingers with his once he slowly started pushing past the yellow line.

"You can't," I whispered through the link. *"We still don't know their status and walking past the line could put them at risk."*

Shane looked at me, emotional and physical fatigue floating around in his almost empty eyes before he warily returned to my side.

"How are you feeling?" I asked Greg, trying to ease through the heavy tension in the air.

"Weak and sore," he answered flatly, his eyes watching the line spike up and down on Zac's heart rate monitor.

"You'll be fine soon," Samantha comforted. "All you'll need are some—"

"I don't care about myself. Just Zac!" he snapped, causing a look of hurt to flash across Sam's face, but almost as fast as it came, it was replaced with an expressionless professional mask.

"Alright. This is what we're going to do," Sam said to her team, but her words faded into the background as I looked at Zac's sickly pale body.

What if this was the end? What if he didn't wake up? What if his life became nothing more than machines breathing and eating for him accompanied by the tears and sobs of those who love him?

My mind began reeling with thoughts, and my vision blurred with tears. I tried to hold them in, but after the first tear broke free, the rest followed like a relentless downpour that caught me in the worst possible moment. Shane simply wrapped his arms around me like I'd done for him mere moments ago, allowing me to cry until there was nothing left to cry.

"It's okay, love," Shane whispered into my hair and held me close to his bare chest. "It's okay, Ariel. Just breathe," Shane continued comforting me, his iron grip remaining strong even when my sobs ceased.

"I need to get some air," I said, my voice coming out muffled and soft as I spoke into Shane's broad shoulder. "I just can't handle being in here right now."

Shane pulled back a bit, though his grip didn't falter or move as he looked down at me. "Do you need Jessica or me to come with you?" he asked softly as he gently ran his thumb across my cheek, obviously not wanting to leave me alone with my emotions.

"I'll be fine," I confirmed as I wrapped my hand around his. "You guys need to stay here with Zac and Greg, and if anything happens, let me know."

Shane, Aiden, and Jess nodded, which I returned.

I looked at Greg. Silent tears were falling down his still face as he watched over his brother.

"Be careful," Shane gently warned as he pressed a kiss to my forehead then let me go.

I made my way out of the heavy room and out the hospital, ignoring the questioning glances pack members gave me as I wiped my tears away. As soon as I stepped into fresh air, it was like a weight had been lifted off my shoulders and the pressure had left my chest.

All I wanted to do was shift into my wolf and let everything out. I reached for the hem of my shirt to take it off, but I quickly withdrew. I barely knew how to control Roxie when I was level headed, let alone high off my emotions. Just one moment of weakness and someone's blood could be on my hands.

Instead, I simply wrapped my arms around myself and allowed my legs to take me where they wanted me to go. As I ventured further and further away from the hospital, my thoughts became harder and harder to ignore.

What if that was the last time you ever see him alive?

What if you could've stopped this?

Why are you running away like a coward instead of being there for your mate?

What if he loses his temper with Sam while you're gone and no one's there to comfort his aching heart or calm his racing mind?

What if it's too late?

161

What if he's already—

I let out a frustrated yell as I pounded my head.

"Shut up! Shut up! Shut up!" I yelled at myself, hoping the pain would silence the relentless thoughts. "Just stop," I begged, on the verge of letting tears fall once more, but I held them in.

I didn't have a real reason to be crying right now besides the simple fact that I was acting pathetic and weak. Just like Morgan always said I was. And I wasn't going to give him the satisfaction of being right.

With those thoughts in mind, I took a deep breath and furiously wiped away my tears before I straightened up. "I am Ariel Carter, Luna of the Silver Crescent Pack, and I will not fall victim to myself . . . or anyone else," I said, not only as a promise but also as reassurance to myself.

"That's it. Don't worry."

A honey-sweet voice whispered in my head, causing an odd relaxation to wash over me though I didn't know who it was. It couldn't be a pack member because my link with the pack hadn't finished fully forming yet.

"I won't let him go just yet. But I must warn you, he may not be the same Zac you knew before. Hardships are coming your way and I, nor anyone else, can't help you. All you can do is trust Shane and stay strong."

Confusion washed over me in waves, and my mind tried to piece everything together, but I simply came up with nothing.

"Who are—"

"I must go now, but please don't lose faith."

"But who are—"

The connection was lost along with all my hope of getting answers. My mind was now going a thousand miles an hour with Zac and the mysteriously calming voice that had invaded my thoughts mere seconds ago.

I was pulled out of my thoughts when a loud *snap* rang through the air, and only then did I realize how close to the southern border I'd wandered. Shane had warned me to never enter within five meters, but now, I was less than five feet away from the unknown creatures that roamed here. Despite my thundering heart, I focused my hearing and smelling.

That was when I smelled it: blood and wet dogs. A rogue.

Without a second thought, I turned and started running back to the hospital, pushing away the urge to shift even though I knew it would get me there faster.

"Shane, I'm near the southern border, and I think that there's—"

My mind link to Shane was cut short when suddenly someone tackled me from behind. Fear gripped me as my heartbeat pounded in my ears. It was over. With a couple slashes to the ankles and I'd be at this rogue's mercy, unable to escape.

I let out a scream as the rogue flipped me over before he covered my mouth with his dirty hand, his vibrant green eyes boring into my own.

"Please don't. He'll kill me," he whispered, his voice urgent and familiar.

But he couldn't be . . .

It was impossible. I watched them lower his casket into the ground.

"You can't be . . . ," I whispered into his hand.

"I think I can be, Ariel," he said, a mischievous grin growing on his lips as he removed his hand from my mouth. "Hey, baby sister."

CHAPTER NINETEEN

I looked up at him in shock.

"Chris?" I whispered in disbelief.

"The one and only." He beamed before his arms wrapped around me in a tight hug. "I've missed you so much," he whispered into my hair.

I embraced him tightly; excitement, confusion, and a bit of anger fighting for dominance in my mind as I buried my face into his bare shoulder.

"I thought you died in the fire," I whispered, tears springing to my eyes for the fifth time today. "No one could find you. I even watched them bury your coffin," I croaked, causing him to merely hold me tighter.

"I thought the fire killed you," Chris admitted. "I couldn't handle staying there without you, Mom, and Dad. So I ran away for a while. But a couple of years ago, I went back to our old territory, just on the edge so I wouldn't be detected. I wanted to see what had become of everything that Mom and Dad had worked so hard to build and then I saw you and Morgan. It was some kind of pack gathering or something. I don't know. But the look on your face . . . you seemed so happy without us and I didn't want to ruin that for you and bring all the drama and baggage back into your life, so I left."

A mixture of shock, confusion, and a bit of betrayal stirred inside my chest as I looked at Chris. Anger slowly sparked within me, though I knew it shouldn't. He had no idea what Morgan had done to me but the fact that he was there and had done nothing made my heart ache. But it was like I couldn't find words.

"I'm sorry, Ariel. You just seemed so happy with him and—"

"I wasn't happy with Morgan," I said in a low voice, the very name tasting bitter on my tongue. "Every second with him was like my own personal hell. You have no idea what he put me through: the pain, the hurt, the prayers to the Moon Goddess to just end it all. All while you just watched." I pulled away from him, the small spark of anger now a raging fire within my chest.

Chris opened his mouth to defend himself, but I didn't give him the chance.

"You want to know why I'm here instead of our old pack? It's because I was saved from Morgan's awful abuse, day in and day out. Because my mate, unlike you, actually cared enough to look for me and reach out to me, and not just judge my life on what it looked like. Everything I've had to endure and now you just show up and . . ."

My words became lost somewhere between my jumbled thoughts. I was conflicted whether I should hate him or not for something he didn't know while angry tears streamed down my face.

"Why didn't you come back for me?" I whispered as I looked up at him through blurred eyes.

"I had no idea," he whispered before he wrapped his arms around me, and this time, I didn't resist. I just allowed myself to collapse in his arms.

"I'm so sorry that I left you with him, Ariel."

"Just don't leave me again. Ever."

"Trust me, baby sister. I w—"

Suddenly, a black mass tackled Chris to the ground, causing me to yell in surprise. Instantly, I recognized Shane's black, snarling beast on top of my brother. He quickly shifted back, though his stance on Chris didn't change, not caring that both of them were naked.

"I should kill you right now, not only for entering my territory but also for putting your hands on her, you filthy waste of—"

"Shane, he's alright." I interrupted, as I placed a hand on his tense shoulders.

"How do you know?" he asked, his narrowed eyes still focused on a terrified Chris.

"Because he's kind of my brother."

There was a mix of confusion and shock on Shane's face as his eyes traveled between me to Chris, then finally landing back on me.

"I thought he was dead."

"Well, it turns out he's not as dead as I thought," I said with a slight humorless chuckle.

"And I'd like to keep it that way, Mr. Alpha, sir," Chris rambled nervously, pearls of sweat popping up on his forehead.

"How do you know you can trust him?" Shane asked skeptically.

"I don't . . ." I shrugged. "But he's my brother, so that has to count for something, right?"

Shane narrowed his eyes as he slowly climbed off of him. "Fine, but I want him under surveillance until we know we can fully trust him."

I rolled my eyes.

"Are you okay?"

"Yeah." I nodded as I looked over my arms that had little cuts from the grass blades and tiny sticks that littered the ground. "Just a couple of scrapes."

"I was worried about you, and I came as soon as I got the link, but I couldn't find you. It was like your scent was coming from everywhere, but nowhere at the same time and—"

I cut him off by placing a gentle kiss on his lips. "You're fine," I whispered, my lips gently brushing against his as I spoke. "I'm fine. Thank you."

Out of the corner of my eye, I saw Chris's jaw go slack as he looked at us.

"H-He's your mate?" he questioned, causing me to nod with a laugh at his shocked expression. "Wow. Well, that makes sense. No one can calm an alpha down like their mate."

"I second that," I said as I turned to Shane, causing him to roll his eyes. "Can you get Chris some clothes?"

I hadn't seen him naked since we were younger and took baths together, but now, after all these years, it was kind of weird.

He nodded and said, "Yeah. I'll see what I can find." Then he turned to Chris and gave him a pointed look. "Don't touch her or do anything to her while I'm gone. Do you understand?"

"Yes, Alpha. And, um, thank you for not killing me."

"Only because she told me not to," Shane grumbled before he disappeared through some trees.

"Your mate's so charming," Chris stated sarcastically.

"He's not usually like this. He's just emotional and really doesn't like rogues."

"I can tell. He was so warm and welcoming. But that is enough about Mr. Big Bad Wolf. How have you been, baby sister? You found your mate. You've let him mark you. Tell me everything."

I told Chris everything as he requested, from Morgan to Stephanie to Greg to now, with Zac.

"Goddess." Chris sighed. "I'm so sorry that I wasn't here for you. Instead, I ran like a coward and went rogue without thinking about you and your needs. I'm so sorry, Ariel."

"Please. Let's not talk about that, or I just might punch you in the face."

Chris threw his head back and laughed, but I wasn't sure if I was joking or not. A bit of anger still simmered deep within me and my fists were itching to bury themselves in Chris's face just to give him a taste for what I had gone through, but I refrained.

I couldn't. I couldn't blame him for what he didn't know though it was hard at times not to.

A few moments later, Shane returned and offered Chris a pair of sweatpants while he wore black and gray basketball shorts. Chris mumbled a thank you before he slid on the sweats. They were a bit baggy on him especially because he was a lot smaller than Shane.

"So, you're my sister's mate," he mused before looking between the two of us.

"That I am," Shane stated proudly as he wrapped his arms around my waist.

"You've gotten as far as marking her, so I presume you've already had her Lunar Ceremony."

"A couple nights ago, yes." Shane looked down at me. "And she looked breathtakingly gorgeous."

Those simple words compelled a smile to grow on my face before I brought my small hand up to his cheek.

"Looking good wasn't hard when I had a handsome alpha next to me." I smiled up at him, causing a smile that matched my own to grow on his lips.

"Aww!" Chris softly said, causing me to laugh as Shane raised a slightly amused eyebrow. "Sorry, but you guys are so cute that you remind me of Mom and Dad."

At the mention of our parents, a small hole dug itself into my heart, but I kept my emotions at bay and offered him a small smile.

"But don't get me wrong, Mr. Alpha. I might be slightly scared of you, and I'm not afraid to admit that, but if you do

168

anything to hurt my sister or do anything to even make a tear fall down her face, I will rip you apart. Whether you're an alpha or not." A deathly serious tone stood out behind Chris's words, letting me know that he wasn't kidding in the slightest, and Shane picked up on it too because he too became serious and straightened up a bit.

"Of course," he said. "But you should know that I love Ariel deeply and would never do anything to hurt her physically, emotionally, or mentally."

He looked down at me as he spoke, truth and adoration swam in his hazel-green eyes. I was slightly surprised that he didn't try to kill Chris for threatening him, but nonetheless, I smiled up at him.

Suddenly, I felt Shane become taut against me and his eye glazed over.

"What's happening?" Chris asked as he furrowed his eyebrows and eyed Shane with concern.

"He's being linked." I furrowed my eyebrows as well.

"We have to go," Shane said as soon as his eyes cleared, urgency written all over his face.

"What happened?" I asked as he began stripping out of his basketball pants.

"It's Zac," he breathed, and I instantly tensed, preparing myself for the bad news I was almost certain was about to come.

Reuniting with my brother momentarily distracted me from the problem at hand.

"He woke up."

CHAPTER TWENTY

I didn't waste any time taking Shane's shorts before I climbed onto his massive beast after he transformed.

"What's going on?" Chris asked, reminding me that he was still here in the little time I forgot.

"Zac's awake," I rushed. "Hurry up and shift so that we can get to the hospital."

Chris gave me a curt nod before he too stripped and tossed me his pants then shifted into his huge brown wolf with fur that matched his messy hair. Without thinking twice, Shane bolted toward the hospital, not even bothering to make sure that Chris was behind us. As soon as we made it to the hospital, Shane and Chris slid on their clothes before we practically ran through the maze of hallways of the hospital until we made it to the giant doors that read "Authorized Personnel Only".

"Chris, wait here," I instructed. "We'll be out as soon as Zac is okay. Alright?"

"Of course." Chris nodded.

"Don't leave this spot," Shane said sternly. "You may be my mate's brother, but I still don't know if I can trust you. You are a rogue after all," Shane said, spitting the word rogue as if it were sour on his tongue, causing Chris to growl before I pushed Shane through the doors while I reminded him of the problem at hand.

As soon as we got in there, the first thing I noticed was the number of people crowded around Zac. Doctors, nurses, Jessica, Aiden, and even Greg had somehow managed to get out of his bed and stand even though he needed to lean on Zac's bed for support.

Zac's big doe eyes looked around in confusion. They didn't seem as bright and youthful as they had been before, and fear shone from deep within them.

As soon as his eyes landed on Shane and me, he visibly relaxed though urgency was written all over his face. My thoughts instantly went back to what the voice had said.

"He may not be the same as you knew before . . ."

Nonetheless, I rushed over to him and threw my arms around him despite the looks of disapproval the nurses and doctors were giving me.

"Oh my Goddess, Zac!" I sobbed into his shoulder as he wrapped his arms around me in a tight hug and I let a whole new wave of tears loose. "I thought I lost you." I held him as tight as I could without hurting him as I sobbed, causing him to frown.

"Relax, Ari. You couldn't get rid of me even if you tried," he said, causing me to cry even harder at the fact that he didn't know how close he was to death.

"Hey there, buddy," Shane greeted gently, causing a smile to grow on Zac's face.

"Hi, Shane." He smiled, and Shane's eyebrows knitted together in confusion.

"What happened to Shubby?"

Zac shrugged. "I grew out of it, I think. I hope that's okay with you," he said, sounding more mature than he should be at his age.

"Sure, bud," Shane said.

I could tell that he didn't like it one bit, but that didn't stop him from wrapping his arms around Zac in a tight embrace. Zac

171

returned his embrace, but it was clear there was something else on his mind.

"When can we take him home?" I asked Samantha who was scribbling something on the clipboard she was holding in her hands.

"After we run a few tests and make sure that all of his vitals are where they need to be," she said as she looked up at me. "If we determine that he's okay and stable enough to leave, then he could go home as soon as a few hours. But if he doesn't check out, we'll have to keep him a bit longer."

I nodded as I gently stroked Zac's hair, his eyes closed as he and his brother embraced each other.

Then the voice's words kept running through my head like a marathon runner, and I couldn't help the worry that grew in my chest, though its source was unclear. Something told me that a big change was coming. Something that none of us were prepared for.

*   *   *

Zac had changed a lot over the last couple of days.

His eyes didn't hold the same joyous spark that they used to, and he wasn't as energetic and outgoing as he usually was. He still refrained from calling Shane Shubby and even stopped calling me Ari, instead opting for our full names along with Greg's. Every time we'd be playing with him or simply spending time with him, it was evident that something else was on his mind and it worried me, especially when he started murmuring to himself incoherently. To be honest, it scared me. No, that word was too simple. It *terrified* me.

"There you are," a gentle voice said from behind me, causing me to jump. "Sorry. I didn't mean to startle you. It's late, and you need to be in bed with me," Shane said as he sat on the couch next to me and wrapped his arms around me.

172

I nodded. I'd been staking out on the couch in hopes that Zac would come out and join me for cartoon marathons like he used to while we cracked dumb jokes and ate greasy, buttery junk food. But I had no such luck.

"Were you waiting for Zac?" Shane asked as he gently picked me up bridal style, and I nodded before I nuzzled his neck, his intoxicating scent rushing into my nose and slowly started relaxing my nerves.

As we walked up the stairs and down the hall toward our room, the loud snores of my brother bounced through the halls. Shane was slowly warming up to him, but they weren't exactly best friends yet.

"We really need to get him a soundproof room," I muttered.

Shane chuckled lightly as we passed his room before he said, "It is."

I looked at him in shock. "Really?"

"No," he said as he shook his head, a grin growing on his lips. "Ours is the only soundproof room in the house."

"What do you . . ." I trailed off as the gears in my head started turning. Within a few seconds, everything made sense and my cheeks grew warm. "Oh."

"Are you sure you understand because if not, I can elaborate if you need me t—"

I covered my ears and furiously shook my head, telling him that he did *not* need to elaborate, though I could hear his laughter despite my hands still being over my ears.

As we walked into our room, my blush was still prominent on my face, causing me to bury my face in his chest to hide it. He used his foot to gently close the door behind us and gently set me down so I was standing on my own two feet. We both changed and met back in the bed, but as soon as Shane saw me, his eyebrows furrowed.

"What's wrong, love?" he asked gently as he put his hand on my back, his fingers dancing in soothing patterns.

"Is it that obvious?" I groaned, and Shane nodded.

"Now tell me what's going on in that beautifully chaotic mind of yours?" he questioned gently.

"It's Zac," I whispered. "He's just so . . . different. It's like he's not the same little boy I met a little under a month ago, you know?"

"Of course, I do," he said, and instantly, I felt stupid.

Of course, Shane knew. Zac was his brother.

"He's my baby brother and to see him like this, so . . . so distant, it kills me."

I could feel his sadness and confusion seeping from his words, causing my heart to drop. So I did the only thing I could: I hugged him.

"Things have already gotten worse, I think. So now, things have to get better, right?" I whispered into his ear, causing him to shrug in response.

"Maybe . . ." He trailed off, his breath tickling my neck as he spoke. "I just . . . Zac says that something big is coming and things are changing, and I think he's right. Ariel, I feel that things are changing and I fear that I wouldn't be able to protect you from them," he whispered as he looked me in the eyes and gently touched my chin. "I don't want you to slip through my fingers."

"Shane," I whispered as I removed his hand from my face and kissed his knuckles. "You'll always be there to protect me, and I know that for a fact. Even if there's a reason you can't, I'll still love you unconditionally and know that you did your best and that you're still fighting for me." I placed a gentle kiss on his forehead before I rested my forehead on his. "I love you, Shane."

"I love you too, Ariel," he whispered back. "And I promise, no matter what, I will protect you with my life."

"Promise?" I asked, even though I knew the answer.

"I promise, love."

174

The Test

UNKNOWN

It was almost time for the test. I had options, but they were too harsh for my liking. Then again, this was terrible, but I had to do this for all of my children. All of lycan kind. I sighed as I made my choice final, whispering into my poor pawn's head, planting the seeds for a necessary evil to grow.

I knew Shane was strong. There was no doubt about it, but he was at his strongest when he was with Ariel. Ariel was strong, but she was at her strongest, physically and emotionally, when Shane was right by her side. I have to separate them.

I had to break them down, shatter them, and watch them put the shards back together without cutting themselves. I needed to know that they could take care of themselves and possibly others even when they were broken down and defeated. It hurt knowing what I was putting my children through, but I honestly had no other choice.

My once powerful and dominant glow had faded, and my fluorescent white hair had turned into a dull gray. It became harder and harder for me to do my job. I was fading. Disappearing.

"I'm so sorry my children," I whispered, though I knew that they couldn't hear me. "But I have to, or everyone will perish."

I felt a tear roll down my cheek. I saw what lay ahead of them and it was terrible, painful, and heartbreaking, but then again, so were my other options.

I closed my eyes and focused on what little power I had left and released it, setting the series of horrid events into motion at any moment. I felt pain dig its way deep into my chest, as it did every time I used my power. A scream escaped my lips, but it merely echoed through the emptiness that surrounded me.

My body gave out, and I collapsed onto the floor with a dull thud and quiet whimper. I just hoped that they passed before it was too late for everyone.

CHAPTER TWENTY-ONE
The Test: Day One

ARIEL

"Are you really positive that you'll be fine here by yourself?" Shane asked as he loaded the last suitcase into the trunk of the car.

He had a sudden alpha meeting that he had to attend a couple packs over. Though he wanted to bring me along to show me off and get me acquainted with our allies, someone needed to stay to watch over the pack and Zac, who was making very little progress.

"I'll be fine," I assured. "I have Aiden, Jess, Greg, and Chris, not to mention the rest of the pack to look out for me. I think I'll be alright." A chuckle pushed past my lips before Shane's lips met with mine in a tender series of kisses.

It didn't take long for his hands to travel from the low of my back to my inner thigh. With one swift movement, my feet were off the ground, and I was trapped between my mate and his car.

"Shane, stop. You're going to be late." I giggled into his lips, causing him to let out an irritated groan as his grip on my thighs tightened.

"Who cares if I'm a few minutes late?" he grumbled into my mouth. "Or a couple hours . . ." Kiss. "Or a couple days . . ." Kiss. "Or if I don't show up at all and stay here with my incredible mate . . ." Kiss.

"Shane," I drawled as I pulled away, causing him to groan as he reluctantly pulled away. "You'll only be gone for three days."

"Three agonizingly long days without you." He pouted like a child.

"You know I'll always be with you here," I said as I pointed to his chest. *"And here,"* I said through our link, causing him to nod before he cupped my face and gently caressed me with his thumb.

"Please stay alert and be careful, okay? I know that you're going to be within pack grounds, but you still never know what could happen. I don't know what I'd do with myself if something happened to you while I was gone . . . Just promise me that no matter what, you'll stay alert, and if anything happens, no matter how big or small you may think it is, you link me, and I'll be there in a heartbeat."

I gently placed my hand on top of his and nodded. "I promise."

"Good," he whispered before he placed one more sweet kiss on my lips. "I love you, Ariel."

"I love you too, Shane," I said easily as I looked up at him. "Now go! I'll be fine here, but you've got a very important meeting with some very important alphas to get to."

"You forgot to mention super boring," he grumbled.

"Nonetheless, you don't want to be late and create a bad impression."

At those words, Shane threw his head back and laughed. When I say "laughed," I didn't mean a small chuckle. He laughed so hard that his neck, face, and ears became a bit red. I crossed my arms and waited for him to finish.

"Are you done now?" I asked flatly once his laughter was reduced to wheezes.

"I'm sorry, but you're just so funny, Ariel," he said as he wiped the invisible tears from his eyes. "When I walk into a room, everything stops and all eyes are on me. Most of those alphas are scared of me and have even told me that themselves. Thanks for the concern, love, but I think I'll be fine if I'm a couple minutes late."

I rolled my eyes. "Whatever, Shane. If you don't do it for you, then do it for me."

Shane gave me a confused look.

"The sooner you get there, the sooner you come back home to me."

"I like the sound of that." Shane grinned before he gave me one final *final* kiss. "I love you, Ariel."

"I love you too," I responded without missing a beat, making Shane smile before getting in the car.

A low hum rang out once the car sprung to life. It was soon accompanied by the low crunches and cracks from the earth as the truck's tires rolled over it. I watched as the truck drove off until it disappeared through some trees.

I sighed as I turned back to our giant, lonely home. I would be lying if I said that I didn't miss Shane already even though he hadn't even left the territory yet.

"Don't worry, love. We'll be together soon," Shane said through the link as if he read my thoughts, which he probably had since I hadn't blocked the connection.

I kept repeating those words in my head as I walked into the empty house. Greg had taken Zac for a walk around the pack to try to get him to open up again, and since Shane requested surveillance on him at all times, Chris was forced to tag along. I didn't think it bothered him too much though. He and Greg had been bonding, and the forming friendship distracted Greg from his rejection. I didn't know where Jessica and Aiden were because they were gone before Shane and I woke up, but I had no doubt they'd be back soon.

179

I made my way into the kitchen and decided to cook some lunch to distract me and hopefully keep my mind from wandering to Shane every five seconds.

I was in the middle of gathering all the materials I needed when I suddenly heard a low thud, followed by a scent so terribly putrid and strong that tears actually sprung to my eyes. Before I could do anything, an arm wrapped itself around my neck in a choke hold, and a terrible smelling cloth was being pressed against my nose and mouth. I tried to pry their arms off of me and fight back, but I failed because of the angle that the attacker had on me.

"Shane! Someone's——"

My link was interrupted when a vaguely familiar voice said, "Inject her."

Without missing a beat, a piercing pain seared through my neck before a burning pain unlike anything I'd felt before began running through my veins like blood, causing me to scream as I fell to my knees. The person who was holding me moved with me so that I remained trapped.

The edge of my vision began to blacken as my limbs felt as if they were being pulled down by a million weights and my head felt like someone was trying to drill through it. My lungs were burning from whatever I was breathing in from the cloth that was still blocking off my airways.

A figure crouched down in front of me, but my vision was so blurry that I could only make out their outline.

"Oh, this is going to be fun," the figure said, causing my heart rate to increase due to the tone of his voice. "I told you this wasn't over, mutt."

Those were the last words I heard before I was engulfed by darkness.

*   *   *

When I came to, I was in a dirty bed in a dimly lit room that smelled of dirt and mold. I could see that the ceiling used to be white, but it was ruined by dirt and sickly orange water stains.

"Finally, you're awake," a male voice said, causing me to snap my head in the direction it came from.

I saw his silhouette stand from his chair and once he stepped into the dim light, my heart jumped into my throat. I thought I'd never have to see him again, yet here he was standing in front of me with a smirk on his face.

A growl escaped my lips as I made an effort to lunge at him—something I would've never thought of doing a few months ago—but I had restraints around my wrists, torso, and ankles that were attached to the bed I was in. I winced as the Wolfsbane they were laced with rubbed into my body with my every movement. I also noticed a deep cut on my hand that was slowly healing.

"Down, girl." He laughed as he took a step closer, causing my blood to boil and another growl to rumble deep within my chest.

"Don't get any closer," I warned as I narrowed my eyes at him, my wolf itching to take over and rip his head off.

"That's cute." Morgan laughed. "The mutt thinks just because it has a title, it's scary. That's cute."

A wave of hatred moved through me, not only because he called me by my old nickname, but also because he called me "it".

"Don't underestimate me, Morgan." I seethed before I channeled all the strength I had within me and my wolf. I broke out of the restraints, ignoring the burn of the Wolfsbane, before I tackled Morgan to the ground. My canines and claws were extended to their full length as I did so.

He had a look of complete shock and fear on his face as I growled at him, daring him to challenge me. A weird feeling of pride grew in the pit of my stomach at the fact that he was scared. He should be.

I was getting ready to rip his throat out and end him then and there when I felt something spread throughout my body from the back of my neck. I whimpered as the pain moved throughout my body once more, and Morgan took the opportunity to throw me off of him.

"Thank you, Tracey," he said, breathing heavily as he tried to hide the fact that he was rattled.

"This mutt deserves it," she sneered, a syringe in her hand.

"I think she just needs a reminder of where she stands," Morgan muttered before he grabbed both of my legs and Tracey grabbed both of my arms.

They started carrying me out of the bedroom, and through dirty halls that I didn't recognize. I tried reaching out to my wolf, but it was as if she were gone. I tried to link Shane, but that only caused a supernova of pain to explode behind my eyes, causing me to bite my lip to muffle the scream that traveled up my throat.

"It's no use," Morgan said. "If you try to mind link or shift then you'll basically be asking to get hurt. The harder you try, the more pain you'll have to endure until you die." As he spoke, I could practically hear the smirk in his voice.

They continued dragging me, and we started passing cells that held sickly thin people inside. Based on how secure the cells were and the number of guards that were on post, I knew exactly where we were. We were at the off territory prison that held the worst of the worst or in Morgan's case, the people he really didn't like.

I couldn't help but think how long I'd been out. This prison was very far from the pack grounds to protect packs from its dangerous inhabitants. My parents had negotiated with the other alphas and lunas, and they got a small portion of the neutral territory to build the prison so that it wasn't near anyone's pack so that no one could get hurt.

Despite not wanting to, I allowed them to continue dragging me without protest while the inmates' curious eyes watched me.

"Have fun starving to death, mutt!" Tracey laughed as they harshly dropped me onto the dirty ground.

Before I even had time to push myself on my hands, they were already outside the cell. Morgan pressed an extremely long code into the keypad next to my cell, ensuring that I wouldn't be getting out unless he wanted me to.

"Why are you doing this?" I asked, causing him to let out a humorless chuckle.

"That is for me to know and you to suffer from," he said, and without another word, he turned on his heels and casually strolled away with Tracey trailing after him like a lost puppy.

I took a deep breath and tried to reach Shane again, but just like Morgan said, pain erupted throughout my skull. Tears jumped to my eyes as it settled in. I was without my mate, my wolf, or any means of protection. I was vulnerable, and I knew that Morgan was going to take full advantage of my weakened state.

I choked on a sob as it traveled up my throat, and I pulled my knees into my chest. I was alone. I was afraid. No, I was terrified of what the future and Morgan had in store for me.

"Everything's going to be o-okay," I whispered to myself once I'd cried all the tears I could. "I'll get out of here. Shane will be here soon. I know it."

I kept repeating those words to myself, but no matter how hard I tried, I couldn't believe the lies I told myself. I was truly on my own, and not even Shane could save me from what lay ahead of me.

CHAPTER TWENTY-TWO
The Test: Day One

SHANE

My stomach dropped, and my heart was hammering in my chest. My knuckles had turned ashen because of the intense grip I had on the steering wheel, but I didn't care. My mate was in danger, and it was all my fault. I should've trusted my gut feeling that told me not to leave her alone, but I allowed her sweet talk and charm to distract me—a mistake I wouldn't make ever again.

The car had barely stopped when I jumped out and frantically ran into the house, terrified of what might await me inside. My terror only increased when a wretched, metallic smell filled my nose, causing my heart to drop down to my toes.

Blood. Ariel's blood.

I didn't waste a second following the scent into the kitchen where Zac, Greg, Chris, Aiden, and Jessica were already gathered, staring wide-eyed at something on the floor; the source of the horrid smell.

Please, Moon Goddess. Don't let me find my mate on the floor. I silently prayed as I silently pushed through their little circle and what I saw completely and utterly broke me.

The Test Has Begun. Time's Running Out.

It was written in Ariel's blood on the kitchen floor. I felt rage boil in my veins and cloud every thought in my head. I let out a frustrated growl as I felt my wolf start to surface.

"Why weren't any of you here watching her?" I roared as my eyes turned black from my fury, causing everyone even Zac, who'd been almost numb to everything at this point, to shrink back.

I instantly felt bad, but I couldn't help it. Someone took my mate and was doing Goddess knows what to her. The very thought caused a surge of pain to rip through my skull as my wolf made another attempt to take over, and I knew that I couldn't let him do that. He'd kill any and everything in his path out of pain and rage. But I didn't know if I was any better at this point either.

"She's just . . ." Chris trailed off, his eyes glued to the mess on the floor. "I saw her this morning, and now she's just . . ." Tears filled his eyes and rolled down his cheeks as he sank to his knees and sobbed.

All the color had drained from Zac's face as he stared blankly at the message and Jessica was leaning on Aiden for support as she clamped a hand over her mouth to silence her sobs. Greg closed his eyes and furiously shook his head, refusing to believe what was in front of him. But it was real. This horrid nightmare was real.

"A-Aiden," I choked out, my throat tight and tears welling up in my eyes threatening to spill onto my face. "Let the pack know of the situation," I ordered.

"What is the plan, Alpha?" he asked, his eyes locked in with mine.

"I'm going to call for an emergency alpha's meeting," I said lowly. "We're going to find the mutt that took her, and when we do, I'm going to kill him."

185

CHAPTER TWENTY-THREE
The Test: Day Two

ARIEL

I woke up to an ice cold blast to the face. I gasped as I shot up, the cold water seeping through my skin and settling deep into my bones. I looked around, but only darkness surrounded me. Confusion and fear ran through my system. I didn't know where I was. But then my eyes landed on her, and horror flooded back to me like a river.

"Oh, good. You're awake," Tracey said in her annoying voice as she stood outside my cell.

It prompted a growl from deep within me, but since I'd forgotten that Morgan and Tracey had kindly blocked my wolf, it came out as a weird choking sound, causing Tracey to laugh.

"Your mate may be one of the strongest alphas in the world, but here, you're nothing. And even your Big Bad Wolf can't save you now, but I doubt he'd want to anyway. Not after we're done with you at least." She smirked with an unsettling glint in her eyes, causing a cold wire to weave itself down my back.

"What do you want from me?" I said, barely above a whisper, looking up at her through my eyelashes. Dread bubbled in my chest seeing that I had no control over myself or my future.

"Personally, I don't want anything from you," she said with a shrug as she boringly tossed the bucket she'd used to splash water on me from hand to hand. "I just get the pleasure of seeing you suffer and rot."

A satisfied grin stretched across her lips as she said that, obviously pleased at the fact that she was out there, healthy and dry, while I was in here, scared and now freezing.

"W-What did I do to you?" I asked. My teeth now started to chatter due to the cold.

"First, you stole Morgan from me. Then, you stole the man that was meant for me: Shane."

My blood boiled at her calling my mate hers, but I didn't let it show. We both knew who had the upper hand in this situation, and I didn't want to give her the satisfaction of having the chance to prove it.

"Tracey. You don't have to do this," I pleaded. "Your mate is out there somewhere, looking for you. You just have to wait until they find you and you'll be—"

"Bull!" She snapped, cutting me off. "You seriously don't get it, do you?" she asked before she let out a humorless chuckle. "Shane was mine. But you stole him, just like you stole Morgan. Every man that I wanted just fell into your hands and you just—"

"That's enough, ladies," Morgan's voice cut through the darkness before he appeared by Tracey's side, the dim lights illuminating his face. "Get up, mutt."

Despite the fear that pumped through me, I decided to stand my ground and be strong, like Shane would want me to do. Like the luna I was. I refused to let him see my fear. He thrived on fear, and I refused to give him the ammunition he needed. Instead of complying to his demands, I simply crossed my arms over my chest and folded my legs, looking him dead in the eye.

187

"You dare disrespect me?" he growled as he opened the door and stormed into my cell, anger radiating off him in waves. "My, Ariel. I thought you'd learn by now. I have the upper hand in this. I am the superior power. And at the end of the day, I am the one who decides your fate. It'd be in your best interest not to test my limited patience, mutt."

"Why should I listen to you, Morgan? You're not my alpha."

That sentence struck a nerve because Morgan visibly tensed before he let out a breath through his nose.

"What do you want with me anyway?" I continued. "I don't have or know anything useful to you."

"I need you to get leverage over Shane," he said. "But you're walking on extremely thin ice right now, and a change in plans seems to be in order soon," he said as he grabbed something from his pocket, but since the lighting was so dim, I couldn't make out what exactly it was. "I think it'd be a lovely idea to send Shane a little gift. Don't you think? A lock of hair. A limb. Or my personal favorite, we can send you in a body bag. That'll leave him vulnerable, and with one snap of the neck or one swift slash through his neck, he'll be finished."

At those words, my heart dropped, and tears blurred my vision, knowing that Morgan was very capable of doing everything he'd just described. But I kept my poker face on even when Morgan cupped my face and gently started caressing me with his thumb, causing Tracey to shoot me a venomous look.

"But if you help me, he and the rest of your pack will remain virtually unharmed," he continued. "You can help me get to Shane. Without his mate, he'll crumble and fall apart, leaving him and his pack vulnerable. Then I can take him down along with his pathetic pack, and once everyone knows that I took down one of the strongest alphas, they'll respect me. Fear me. I'll become the strongest, most feared alpha in America, and you, my stupid little mutt, will be my trophy."

I instantly pulled away from him and narrowed my eyes.

"No," I said in a low voice, putting as much venom in my voice as possible. "I won't be your stupid little pawn, and I definitely won't be your trophy, Morgan."

"That's Alpha Morgan to you, pup." Tracey snickered.

"Quiet!" Morgan snapped, as his eyes turned black. "*Tsk, tsk, tsk.* You've been very talkative since the last time I saw you," he said, shaking his head as a sadistic smirk grew on his face. "I'm going to have to fix that."

Once again, he pulled out the unidentified object, but when he moved closer, a stray beam of light found it, and my eyes widened as I saw what he held.

"Morgan, get that away from me," I said as I scooted as far away from him as I could until my back hit the wall, causing me to jump.

"No one tells me what to do, especially not you," he growled as his tall figure loomed over me before he wrapped his fingers around my throat and slammed me to the wall.

My breath caught in my throat, and I clawed at his hand, but he didn't waver or budge.

"Any last words?" he spat as he lined up the syringe with my neck.

I tried to keep a straight face as a tear slid down my face. "I'm . . . going to kill you." I gritted out, causing him to laugh.

"I'd love to see you try, mutt."

Without another word, he plunged the syringe into my neck and pushed down the plunger. My body was instantly on fire as the Wolfsbane and silver ran through my veins, causing me to let out the loudest scream of my life. As soon as Morgan let me go, I crumpled to the ground, my body contorting in weird positions as I tried to evade the pain that was consuming me.

"Oh, you think that's bad?" He laughed as he stood up and brushed the dirt from the floor off his pants. "You haven't seen anything yet." He leisurely strolled out of my cell while I screamed

189

and cried before he whispered something to Tracey then to a guard before he and Tracey walked off, leaving the guard at the door of my cell.

My body felt like it was consumed in flames. My nerves were burning, and my head felt like it was going to explode. It felt like I was experiencing the Blood Moon over and over and over and there was no release. The edges of my vision were becoming black as my eyelids became heavy. I felt my body begin to shut down. I felt dizzy, and the oxygen in my lungs was limited.

This is it, I thought to myself. *I can't hold on. I'm sorry, Shane. I love you and I always will.*

Then everything went black.

*   *   *

When my eyes peeled open, I was surprised I was still even alive. The dose that Morgan gave was lethal. I should've died, but I didn't. I was still trying to decide if that was a blessing or a curse.

Suddenly, the nauseating smell of blood rushed into my nose and I instantly recognized it as my own. The sticky crimson liquid pooled around my head and tangled in my hair, caking a good portion of my body.

"What the—" I started to say but was interrupted by an immense pain raging through my throat.

I screamed in pain, but no sound came out, and the pain only grew, causing tears to flow off my eyes as my hands wrapped around my throat. Blood instantly stained the palms of my hands and slid between the cracks of my fingers and that was when I felt it. A straight, almost surgical line jutted out of my skin, burning as my fingers gently skimmed it. And I'd realized what he'd done.

I bit my bottom lip to prevent myself from screaming and sending another wave of nails down my throat. Morgan took the only thing I had left. The one thing I'd worked so hard to get back: my voice.

"I see you've discovered my little gift," Morgan said, causing me to sit up.

I ignored the pain that traveled through my body from the sudden movement and narrowed my eyes at him, an unprecedented amount of hate flowed through my being as I looked at him. He was casually leaning against the wall on the outside of my cell, tossing what I identified as a small pocket knife up in the air and catching it. I burst into tears, my sobs silent and feeling like lava in my throat.

"There's no need to cry," Morgan said with mock gentleness as he abandoned throwing the knife and settled for twirling it in his hands. "I've taken away the only thing that could get you killed, so you're safe . . . for now."

I could practically feel his villainous smirk as his perverted eyes looked at me up and down.

I stayed silent—not like I had a choice—and narrowed my eyes at him though tears were constantly pouring out of them.

"So," he continued as he started pacing back and forth in front of the silver laced metal bars that separated him from me. "What does it feel like to be taken to your highest point just to be brought back down to the very bottom where you belong? Just to watch your beloved mate and pack be broken down and mercilessly ripped to shreds, hearing them beg for mercy. Just to know that it is all your fault."

My chest became tight at the thought of Zac being put through that and Morgan not thinking twice about ripping his little body apart piece by piece until there was nothing left of him. Their blood would forever be on my hands. And for what? Power?

Power wasn't a material thing. It was a feeling that was worthless compared to family and the amazing feeling of love.

"Here," Morgan said, causing my attention to return to him once more. "Eat up." He carelessly kicked a metal tray beneath the bars, causing it to fly around the floor until it slammed into my knee, coming to a halt.

It smelled horrid, but I knew that I had to eat it to get my strength up. I had to get out of here, maybe not today, maybe not tomorrow, but when I did get out, I needed to be at full strength.

I reluctantly grabbed the first thing I could and quickly ate it, the taste and texture of the rotting meat making me want to throw up, but I forced myself to swallow it anyway.

"Good girl," Morgan said as I gulped down the small metal cup of water to wash out the taste from my mouth. The only thing left was a liquid slop that had a mixture of multiple different things, not all of them safe to eat. "Eat it," Morgan ordered, seeing my hesitation.

I shook my head.

"Ariel, don't make me come in there. I said eat it," he growled, annoyance and anger clear in his voice.

With whatever courage I had left, I kicked the tray back over to him. The force caused the bowl to fly off the tray and get all over Morgan, causing him to let out an enraged growl. Other inmates whimpered as Morgan barged into my cell. I tried to get as far away as possible, but my effort was cut short when his foot came into hard contact with my ribs, causing a sickening crack to ring out as an intense pain spread throughout me like food dye spreading through water.

I tried to scream, but that merely caused more pain to erupt within me.

He didn't stop there. He continued kicking me, not caring that since he blocked my wolf, I couldn't heal the multiple bones he was breaking.

"I warned you," he growled lowly as he straddled over my broken frame and delivered a punch to my face, causing blood to fill my mouth. "But you just wouldn't listen."

He delivered another punch to the side of my head, causing the world to spin and white dots to dance in front of me. His long fingers then wrapped around my neck, causing my fresh wound to scream in protest before he carelessly threw me against the wall. My back cracked and my head bounced off the wall from the impact before I slid to the floor. I was surprised I was still conscious and breathing.

He stalked over to my broken, bruised body and knelt down beside me and harshly whispered in my ear, "Next time, I won't be so gracious."

I looked away from him, unable to bear seeing my broken reflection in his soulless black eyes.

"Good to see that things are back to how they should be," he said before he delivered one more kick to my ribs.

Pain consumed my body, its jagged teeth burying themselves deep into my soul. My body felt heavy as if my blood had turned to iron. I squeezed my eyes shut and let my tears fall. I felt empty and powerless. Alone and abused. Afraid and worthless. I felt blood trickle from somewhere on my face and fall onto the floor along with the rest of my blood. As each drop fell, I felt myself fading more and more.

I weakly brought my fingers up to my mark, hoping that the amazing sparks I felt every time I touched Shane would wash over me and chase away the pain like a dog to a cat, but I felt nothing. Nothing at all.

I was all alone, and I doubted that Shane would come. Even if he were looking for me, he wouldn't be able to find me. This prison had a special charm on it that blocked our scents. I curled into a small ball and continued to cry like I used to back when I was Morgan's slave. I slowly felt my body weigh down and my eyes slowly closed, taking me back into another black empty sleep with my mind racing and my heart empty.

CHAPTER TWENTY-FOUR
The Test: Day Two

SHANE

I took a deep breath as I looked at the alphas and lunas that were seated around the table that rested in front of me. As soon as I sent out the message, many of the pack leaders rushed here with many more still on the way.

I readjusted my sweatshirt and instantly, Ariel's scent flooded my senses, causing a mix of sadness and relaxation to fall over me like rain. This was Ariel's favorite sweatshirt of mine.

"As you all may know, my mate, Luna Ariel, was taken yesterday from our home while I was on my way to the original Alphas' Conference."

A few gasps filled the air as my words fell onto unknowing ears. No matter how many times I'd practiced this spiel, a lump always formed in my throat as the sentence formed on my tongue as horrid images and thoughts of what they could be doing to her at this very moment came into mind. But I forced myself to keep going because I knew that I wouldn't be doing her any good if I didn't.

"We need to find her as soon as possible. Her first heat is due any week now and if the mutt who took her touches her . . ." I had to stop myself as rage filled my being from head to toe as if I were drowning in it.

Heat was a seven day period when we would crave each other until we were consummated. If we didn't complete it within those seven days, it would come back every month, each month stronger than the last, until it became too strong and we'd die. The thought of her going through that around someone else . . .

I balled my hands into fists as my claws extended on their own accord, the stench of my blood slowly drifting into the air, but the pain calmed me down a bit.

"Just please, help me find my Ariel," I begged, looking at all of them in the eyes. This was the weakest and most vulnerable I had been in front of these alphas or any alpha in general, but I didn't care. "I . . . I can't get through this without her. She's my everything."

Tears gathered in my eyes, and at that moment, as my chest became impossibly tight, I didn't care if they saw me cry. I didn't care if they saw me have a complete mental breakdown and slip into insanity without her. All I cared about was getting my mate back, no matter what I had to do.

"Of course. We'll help you, Shane," a deep voice said, which I knew belonged to none other than Alpha Clayton, the alpha of the Blue Moon Pack, the fourth strongest pack in America.

I could see how much pain this brought him, especially because his first mate was killed in a rogue attack. Luckily, the Moon Goddess gifted him with a second-chance mate, which was extremely rare. The only reason Luna Shawn, his new mate, wasn't here was because she fell gravely ill and was at home heavily guarded by their beta and their pack warriors, which I should've done with Ariel.

The other alphas and lunas nodded in agreement with his statement. "You're our brother, and you've done more than enough

195

for all of us, especially for me when Sara passed," he said, his voice becoming soft at the end, causing the alpha on his right, Alpha Samuel, to gently clap him on the shoulder.

"Thank you," I said, giving him a gracious nod, which he returned before I started filling them in on every detail that we knew about Ariel's disappearance. "The captor was able to make it pass our border patrol without being seen or even leaving a scent, letting us know that he had access to some kind of—"

Without warning, an immeasurable amount of pain washed over me through the link I previously hadn't been able to connect to Ariel through. The torment was so great that it caused me to collapse to the floor and scream in agony. My head was pounding with my heartbeat and pain pierced through me like a needle through the fabric. In my nerves. In my blood. Everywhere.

"Shane, what's—" Aiden asked frantically as he appeared by my side, concern written all over his face, but he was interrupted by my scream as my back arched off the floor.

It felt like my insides were melting into mush inside my body as my throat closed, restricting oxygen from getting to my lungs. A mix of foreign emotions started clouding my mind, and my heart raced.

That was when I realized it.

I was feeling her. Every emotion I was feeling was hers. Every tear that was rolling down my cheeks was hers. Every ounce of pain I was feeling was hers.

I gritted my teeth together as another wave of pain shot through me like a bullet.

"It's Ariel," I managed, causing some eyebrows to pull together in confusion and some gasps and low whispers. "The pain. It's hers."

I'd barely managed to finish that sentence when a sharp, almost knife-like pain slashed across my throat, causing me to let out a pain-filled yell as my hands wrapped around my throat that felt like it was bleeding, but I felt nothing. Then, almost as fast as it

196

came, the pain disappeared. I coughed and gasped as my throat expanded, allowing the oxygen to get to my lungs once more as I sat up, a thin layer of sweat covering my forehead.

"No . . ." I trailed off as I desperately tried to reach out to Ariel through the link, but I didn't feel anything. I couldn't feel Ariel. "Goddess, no," I begged as tears gathered in my eyes and easily spilled over onto my cheeks. "Don't do this to me."

"Shane, what happ—" Aiden started, but once again, he was interrupted.

This time, it was by someone linking me. My eyes glazed over as my body tensed.

"Hello, Shane." Morgan's nauseating voice filled my head, causing me to growl. *Since Ariel's marked, I assume that your link to each other has been completed and you felt that.*

At the mention of Ariel, my blood boiled. I should've known Morgan took her. He threatened her before we left and he wasn't too pleased when I took her from him.

"You're right. I did feel that," I growled lowly through the link. *"And I promise that you'll feel more than that when I find you."*

"Not too fast, my fiery alpha," Morgan said, and I could practically hear the smirk in his voice. *"If you want your sweet mate to stay alive, you, your pack members, and those other alphas better stay away from me and my pack, not that you'd be able to find us anyway,"* Morgan bragged, causing my wolf to quickly surface, wanting nothing more than to mercilessly rip Morgan joint from joint.

"What if I don't play by your rules?" I growled, hoping to call his bluff.

"Shane, we both know that I'm always sixteen steps ahead of you. I have eyes everywhere. The moment you even think of a plan to get Ariel back, she'll already be bathing in a pool of her own blood if I don't decide to have some fun with her first."

I let out a loud growl at the last sentence, even though I knew he just added it to get under my skin.

"Fine." I sighed in defeat, giving into him knowing that even though I didn't want to admit it, Morgan was far more clever than I was. Far more ruthless too. I also knew that he wouldn't hesitate to fulfill his promises.

"What do you want? I'll give you whatever you want for Ariel. Just . . . Please, don't hurt her anymore."

"I know you will," he stated cockily, causing my fingertips to itch in desperate need to strangle him. *"But as far as what I want, I think I'll let you suffer a little longer and get back to you on that one."*

"No. Morgan, please—" I begged, but he cut me off.

"I've warned you, Shane. One wrong move and Ariel's dead."

"Wait. Please—"

It was too late. He cut the connection, leaving me teary-eyed and enraged, but there was nothing I could do. If I tried to fight back, Ariel would die. If I sent someone else to get her, she would die. If I said one thing Morgan didn't like, Ariel would die. All I could do was wait, and it killed me knowing that my mate was out there somewhere going through hell at his hands. I was caught between a rock and a solid mass, and all I could do was wait until either the rock moved, or the mass caved in.

"What happened?" Aiden asked as the clouds cleared from my eyes just for them to become blurry with tears.

"Morgan's got Ariel," I whispered, causing a shocked expression to settle on everyone in the room.

"Then what are we sitting here for? Let's get her!" Aiden declared as he stood up from his crouched position beside me, but I instantly grabbed his wrist and brought him back down so that he was back on the floor.

"We can't," I said weakly, utterly defeated, the words crushing me like a boulder as they left my lips. "If any of us make any attempt to get to her, he's going to use her then kill her." The words felt like poison on my tongue, and my heart broke with every syllable.

"We will figure this out, Shane," Aiden said. "We will win."

"That's the thing, Aiden," I said. "I fear that when it comes to Morgan and his wit, the battle has already been won before we even had a chance."

CHAPTER TWENTY-FIVE
The Test: Day Two

ARIEL

Fear.

An unpleasant emotion caused by the belief that someone or something is dangerous and likely to cause pain or a threat.

Fear. That was all that was coursing through my veins. Morgan had been coming in here every day with a routine. He would ask me to help him take down Shane, and when I refused or was too weak to respond in any way, he'd proceed to beat me relentlessly before he injected me with a Wolfsbane and silver concoction. It was a miracle that I was still alive.

Morgan also gave me smaller and smaller meals until I was surviving off of meager portions of rotting meat and barely enough water to moisten my tongue. Since I didn't have my wolf, it was taking an enormous toll on me. My skin was slowly starting to cling to my bones since I'd barely begun gaining back weight from when Morgan had me before Shane. My stomach was constantly hurting, reminding me just how empty it was, and I didn't have the energy to fight back anymore.

A series of whimpers erupted from the inmates, and I instantly knew that he was coming. I quickly dragged myself into the shadows, silent winces escaping my cracked lips due to the pain that shot through me every time I put weight on the wrist that I was almost positive Morgan had broken yesterday.

I pressed myself against the wall as far as I could, hoping that it would simply swallow me up and make me disappear, but I had no such luck. Morgan stopped in front of my cell and punched in the impossibly long code that unlocked my cell before strolling in with something in his hands. My eyes widened as my body started trembling.

Was it another dose? Had he finally gotten tired of my defiance? Was it a gun?

A million different thoughts rushed through my head as he slowly walked toward me, slowly extending what he had in his hand toward me. I squeezed my eyes shut and pressed my body as hard into the wall as possible, ignoring the excruciating pain that shot up and down my bruised spine.

I heard a dull thud before he said, "Eat."

I opened my mouth and saw the faint outline of a tray in the darkness.

"You need some meat on your bones. You won't be doing me any good if you die on me."

Something within me told me not to trust him, but a bigger part of me told me to do it, or else a punch or kick might be in my near future. I grabbed whatever was on the plate—something that felt like a sandwich—and shoved it into my mouth. It was bland and almost tasteless with a powdery substance in it that had an awful taste to it. As soon as I swallowed the first bite, my body went numb, and I fell over, not able to even move my fingers, only my eyes. I'd fallen right into his trap.

The low light highlighted the malevolent smirk that flourished on his face.

"I knew you were stupid, Ariel, but I expected a little more than that." He laughed before he delivered a hard kick to my ribs, causing a nauseating crack to ring out, but I couldn't even flinch to represent the agony I was feeling. "Good. You can't move. I need you to be completely powerless for this."

Panic rose in my throat as I hysterically tried to thrash out of his grasp, but my body didn't move. Not even an inch. Horror clouded my mind as he sat down next to me and put my head onto his lap. He gently moved my messy hair from my mark, which had completely lost its comforting spark.

"Interesting," he mused as his disgusting fingers gently swept across my mark. "This is going to be fun." His canines extended and his eyes turned black. "I was hoping you'd eventually cave in, but you're just too stubborn, and I'm tired of waiting."

He shifted my body so he could have access to my neck and with dread, I realized what he was going to do. And there was nothing I could do to stop him.

"Welcome to the pack, Luna Ariel," he spat before he savagely dug his canines into my neck.

A scream rang through my head unable to escape as I felt every layer of skin and muscle being penetrated and broken. Tears instantly started leaking from my eyes as I internally screamed and sobbed, but all Morgan saw me as was territory waiting to be claimed.

As Morgan's canines left my skin, the smell of my blood made me dizzy as it rushed into my mouth. It was hard to breathe, each breath a battle on its own. Morgan growled some words under his breath once he realized that it wasn't healing like he initially hoped. Since he wasn't my mate, he couldn't heal me. Morgan roared in outrage as my very being started slipping from my grasp with the blood. My eyes closed and I was surrounded by a black, soundless void.

If this didn't kill me, I didn't know what would.

CHAPTER TWENTY-SIX
The Test: Day Two

SHANE

Panic and anguish were eating me from the inside out. I hadn't been able to get a blink of sleep ever since Morgan sent that message, not that I really wanted to. Sleep was useless unless I had my mate sleeping right next to me. The other alphas and I had been trying to figure something, anything, but every plan resulted in a chance that my mate might die and I refused to go through with any plan that even had a tenth of a chance of getting her killed.

Chris had refrained from talking or even looking at me ever since the day we found out she'd been taken. He blamed me for everything, and I accepted every bit of it. I should've had guards with her at all times. I should've made sure that Aiden was by her side at all times. Goddess, I'd do anything to have a do-over.

I held one of her shirts up to my nose and took in her scent. My heart felt empty. I missed her soft butterfly kisses and her breathtaking smile and her angelic voice and her *everything*. I missed Ariel. I missed my luna. Tears welled up in my eyes, as they did every time I thought about Ariel, and I ran my fingers through my disheveled hair.

"Moon Goddess, I don't know if you can hear this or if you even care, but please, I'm begging you. Bring her back. She's my everything. The air in my lungs, the blood in my veins, everything."

It'd become a ritual to ask the Moon Goddess for help every day, yet every day I get nothing. No sign. No help. Nothing. But I did it anyway, praying that the outcome would be different than the last.

"Please bring her back to me. I just love her so much, and it hurts not having her with me. I just need . . ." I choked on my tears, and I didn't try to keep them from falling. "I need her."

I sobbed and held her shirt as close to my chest as possible. All at once, pain erupted throughout my body, and I knew it was Ariel's. I'd been feeling almost unbearable bursts of pain every day since her disappearance. It killed me knowing that she was going through this all by herself with no one to protect her from Morgan's wrath, but it also gave me a spark of hope. Every day that I felt this pain let me know that she was still alive. That she hadn't given up.

Pain sprouted from my ribs and my back like the kicks I knew she was receiving. After a few moments, searing pain exploded from my shoulder, causing me to scream as the pain bore into my shoulder. My head started spinning, and my breaths became labored as a bonfire of pain went ablaze throughout my body, embers burning through my soul.

The fire slowly died as Ariel slipped into unconsciousness, no longer able to feel the pain. I sighed as I blankly stared at the ceiling of the bedroom I shared with Ariel, sweat drenching me.

"I'm going to kill him," I growled, solidifying the promise I'd made to myself the second I found out that Ariel was missing.

Three loud knocks sounded from my door, and I instantly knew who it was.

"Come in," I called, not bothering to get up since my body was slowly regaining its strength.

"I heard the screaming. All too familiar, my friend," Alpha Clayton said as he walked into our room before he extended his hand to help me up. "I felt it when Sara died."

I took his hand, and in one movement, I was on my feet. The room spun, and my legs wobbled, about to give out, so I quickly leaned against the bedpost to keep myself from ending up back on the floor once more.

"It brings me comfort though, knowing that she's alive," I breathed out.

"We're trying to figure something out, and we won't stop trying until we figure it out," he said, gently clapping my back and I nodded.

"I know. Thank you."

He nodded in response before asking if I needed anything. When I said no, he left me alone with my grief and my wild thoughts.

CHAPTER TWENTY-SEVEN
The Test: Day Thirteen

ARIEL

I awoke to a persistent beeping sound. I felt a soft material wrapped around my body and underneath my fingertips. I slowly curled my fingers around the material and held onto its warmth and comfort. I wanted to stay here forever, ignorant and shielded from what would happen to me once I opened my eyes. But I knew I couldn't do that, no matter how badly I yearned to.

I slowly peeled my eyes open and was instantly greeted by blinding lights, causing me to immediately close my eyes to shield myself. After a few moments, my eyes adjusted and I slowly opened them once more. As soon as I opened my eyes, I realized that I was in a hospital room with multiple IVs and needles prodding at me.

"You're awake," the voice that made my skin crawl said.

I turned my head and saw Morgan rising from the chair he'd silently been sitting in. As he approached my bed, I pressed myself as far away from him as I could, sharp pain cutting through my still broken body as the IVs moved inside me.

My hands flew up to my neck where he'd bitten me. It was covered in some kind of bandage, but I could still feel the warm blood seeping through it. I bite my bottom lip to prevent me from crying. Another male had marked me that wasn't Shane. Dread moved through me. I felt so dirty and sinful.

"Don't worry," Morgan said as he walked around to the right side of the bed. "You'll be fine. They've been feeding and hydrating you. You're lucky that I got you here when I did, or you would've bled out," he said as he ran his knuckles against my cheeks, and I instantly pulled away, hating the feeling of his skin on mine.

He spoke as if he'd saved me when he was the force that was pushing me closer and closer to the edge of oblivion.

"Ariel, listen to me and listen very closely because this will only get worse for you if you don't," he said as his eyes bore into mine, causing my heart to race with fear. "You will be my luna, and you will help me take down Shane. You will tell me everything I need to know, and when we do take Shane down, you will be my luna, and you will bear my pups. Do you understand?"

His words terrified me, but not nearly as much as the calloused look in his eyes. The very thought of bearing his pups made me want to throw up, but I knew that I couldn't say that. I didn't need his warning to know that if I didn't agree it'd only get worse for me.

But I could also use this to my advantage. I might not know everything about the pack, but I knew enough. I could throw Morgan off. Maneuver him so he'd fall right into my lap. I just had to execute it properly.

I looked at him and slowly nodded despite my body yelling at me to shake my head, causing a smile to grow across his face.

"I knew you'd come to your senses."

He had no idea.

He called in a doctor to look over me before she released me. Morgan placed one of his hands under my legs and the other on my back. He instructed me to hold on tight, and despite the urge to pull away, I complied without putting up a fight, causing a faint smile to grow on his face. He carried me out of the hospital, my knees instantly coming together to cover myself since I was only wearing a hospital gown with nothing on underneath.

I prayed to the Moon Goddess that Morgan didn't see me bare, but then again, I had been praying to her for a while, and she hadn't delivered. So why would this time be any different?

Morgan carried me back to his house, the alpha and luna's house, which had been rebuilt after the fire. My chest became tight as the once familiar house loomed over us. They'd rebuilt it to look exactly the same. This was the house I shared with my parents and brother once upon a time. Or, it looked like it. I wondered what the insides looked like, but I knew I'd be finding out soon.

"Welcome home, my luna," Morgan said as he opened the front door, causing an invisible shudder of disgust to run down my back.

It killed me to hear someone other than Shane call me that. It was like he was rubbing it in my face that I was trapped here with my mate so far away.

Did he even know where I am? Has he realized that I'm not home? Does he even care? I had to stop those thoughts from working themselves into my brain or else I'd start crying and botch everything.

Of course, he cares, I thought to myself. *Every word had compassion behind each syllable, every kiss had meaning, and every touch had a purpose. He'll find me. I know he will.* Those thoughts held me together as we walked into the house.

The interior structure was the same, but everything was just *wrong.* The once beautiful, happy walls were redone in black and gray. The shelves that once held our family portraits, our happy moments trapped on a single piece of paper, were wiped clean with nothing but dust collecting on them. The lavender scent that once circulated through the house had disappeared, overtaken by Morgan's.

"Are you hungry?" Morgan asked softly as he gently set me down, this level of humaneness was foreign and unsettling.

I hesitantly shook my head, not wanting to fall for another one of his traps while also not wanting to set him off.

"Ariel, please eat. I promise no more gimmicks or beatings unless you do something to deserve it. But you need to eat."

I had to resist the urge to roll my eyes as he took my hands in his own. Instead, I slowly nodded. I had to show him that I was still vulnerable and completely loyal to him. I had to make it seem like he'd completely beaten me down and broken me. Like he'd won.

He sighed as he looked at me, his thumbs gliding over my knuckles. "I'm sorry," he said, causing a wave of shock to move through me.

Morgan never apologized. Ever.

"But I had to do what had to be done." I offered him a small smile despite wanting so badly to roll my eyes. "Can you forgive me?"

No.

I nodded.

"Good," he said as he placed a kiss on the back of my hand, causing my skin to crawl. "Let's make you some dinner."

He led me to the kitchen. As we walked in, all the memories from my childhood came flooding back. The time when Dad was making pancakes and almost burned the house down, or the time he was making dinner and almost burned the house down, or the time he was putting waffles in the toaster and, you guessed it, almost burned the house down. I laughed at the memories, instant pain ripping through my throat as I did so, but I kept the tears at bay.

"Put up one finger if you'd like peanut butter and jelly sandwich, and put up two if you want ham and cheese," Morgan instructed, and despite my lack of appetite, I lifted two fingers, and he nodded. "Please. Make yourself comfortable. This will only take a moment," he spoke as if we were old acquaintances. "Would you like some water?"

I nodded before I watched him prepare my sandwich, analyzing his every movement to make sure that he wasn't trying to slip anything in it. He didn't.

Once he was finished, he effortlessly cut off the crusts and cut the bread diagonally across the center, from the top left corner to the lower right corner.

"I remember you liked your sandwiches like this when you were younger," Morgan commented as he slid the plate over to me, and I nodded as more memories from my childhood flooded over me.

Morgan used to be around my family a lot since he was my father's beta. Before Morgan, Morgan's father was my father's beta, but I never knew what happened to him and never planned on asking.

Morgan had an almost eager look in his eyes as he waited for me to eat the sandwich he'd prepared. I took slow bites out of the sandwich, tasting for anything out of the norm, but I tasted nothing. I continued eating, offering Morgan small nods and smiles through the whole endeavor. When I was done, I quickly drank the water, a substance that I'd had very little of over the past few days.

"Are you full?" Morgan questioned, and I nodded. "Then let's get you some clothes."

I nodded in genuine agreement. I felt so bare even though I had the hospital gown draped over me. Morgan didn't waste any time calling a female pack member to bring me not only a pair of underclothes but also a silky, overly revealing nightgown that I recognized from the wardrobe I used to wear when I was here.

"Go change into this," he instructed after he led me into his bedroom that consisted of dark walls and bed sheets. "The bathroom is just over there."

I nodded and made my way into the bathroom that my parents had shared. I walked to the mirror, the tile floor feeling cold

210

against my bare feet. Once I looked in the mirror, I realized how haggard and tired I looked.

My short brown hair was like a bird's nest, sticking out in all directions with dirt from my cell mixed with my blood clinging to my hair. I had healing bruises and cuts on my face, including a black eye that turned a bit green. The horizontal cut across my neck had turned a deep red, painfully standing out against my skin. Once I looked at the bandage that covered the side of my neck onto my shoulder, the anger I was suppressing began rising along with tears. I wanted to scream and thrash around, but I knew it wouldn't make anything better. Instead, I looked myself in the eye and took a deep breath.

"You can do this, Ariel," I said mutely, mouthing the words to myself as I rigorously wiped the tears from my face and forced myself to straighten up. "You are a luna. It's time to start acting like one."

With that in mind, I quickly ran a shower, vigorously washing my skin raw, desperately trying to get every speck of dirt and every trace of Morgan from my skin before I did the same with my hair.

Once I finished cleansing myself, I slid on the lacey undergarments Morgan had ordered for me before I slid on the nightgown. It was a black silk material that stopped just below my butt, the slightest movement and I would be revealed. I trembled as I tucked my damp hair behind my ear. I felt disgusting.

Let's get this over with.

I slowly opened the bathroom door, and I crossed my arms across my stomach to prevent the gown from moving in ways that would leave me bare and vulnerable. A disgusted feeling wormed around in my stomach as Morgan's eyes hungrily swept over me. He took slow, calculated steps toward me, his breathing becoming loud as he began losing his composure.

I couldn't meet his eyes.

"Move your arms," he instructed.

211

He was so close to me that his breathing brushed my forehead. When my arms stayed where they were, a frustrated growl escaped Morgan's lips before he roughly grabbed my wrists and pushed me against the wall with my arms pinned next to my head.

"Yes," Morgan mused, causing tears to jump to my eyes, but I quickly shut them to keep the tears from falling. "Look how much you've grown in a few short months," he murmured, and I could feel his gaze burning into my chest.

He placed a soft kiss on my neck opposite of my bandage, causing me to gasp as my eyes shot open not only from shock, but also because my neck was one of the most sensitive parts of my body. Morgan smirked against my neck as he kissed me again, his tongue feverishly dancing across my skin, causing anger and disgust to move through me as my knees became weak.

"I know all your soft spots, Ariel," Morgan whispered into me, generating tears from my eyes, and I let them fall freely. "I know what drives you wild."

I pushed against him, causing him to stumble back in surprise. Instead of yelling at me or slapping me like he would usually do, he merely chuckled. I narrowed my eyes into slits and glared daggers at his smirking figure.

"All in good time," he mused as he took off his shirt before he slid into bed. "It all comes at the right time, Ariel. Now get over here."

Despite the rage that was shaking my whole body, I forced my feet to walk to the other side of the bed. I forced my body to settle into the sheets, staying as far away from Morgan as possible. Swiftly, two muscular arms wrapped around my waist and pulled me into a chest before his head rested in the crook of my shoulder.

"Good night, my luna," Morgan's sleep filled voice whispered before he drifted off to sleep.

And that was when I let everything out.

I sobbed and silently screamed as what just happened replayed over and over again in my mind, the pain that erupted in

212

my throat triggering more tears to jump to my eyes. It felt like my skin was burning everywhere Morgan touched, and I wanted nothing more than to wash my skin raw and cleanse every inch he tainted. But all I could do was helplessly lie there, wrapped in the arms of the man that I hated the most, and cry myself into an empty sleep.

CHAPTER TWENTY-EIGHT
The Test: Day Thirty-six

SHANE

Broken.

That was the only word I could use to describe myself right now.

I hadn't felt anything from Ariel in three weeks, and many of the alphas and lunas had packed up and left, including Clayton. And I couldn't blame them. They had their own packs and mates to attend to. Though some still had hopes and pitch ideas, mainly Clayton, most of them, however, thought she was dead, but I refused to believe it.

Ariel couldn't just die. She wouldn't. She was too strong. Plus, I would've felt it if she'd died . . . Right?

I also hadn't heard anything from Morgan either, and I couldn't reach out to him either. I would give Morgan anything for Ariel, and he knew it. He was simply baiting me, watching and waiting to see if I'd make a move. Waiting to see if I'd put Ariel in danger, and there was nothing I could do for her but sit and wait.

"Shane, come on. You've been in there for over two weeks," Greg said from outside my office door, and he was right.

I had been in my office relentlessly, trying to come up with ways to get my luna back, but every plan had a hole in it. Every plan had a chance of Ariel getting hurt more than she inevitably was. I'd only left to eat and take showers every now and then. Other than that, I had been in my office with a stash of Ariel's clothes to keep me sane.

"No, Greg," I stated hoarsely. "I'm not coming out until I have a plan to get Ariel back."

Greg sighed from the other side of the door. "You need to at least get some rest, Shane. You won't do Ariel any good if you die from lack of sleep, now would you?"

Now it was my turn to sigh. I knew he was right. I hadn't slept in Goddess knows how long, only taking naps not longer than an hour every few days.

"Fine." I relented.

"Good," Greg said before his footsteps began descending down the hallway, but they fell short. "We're all worried about her, Shane. We're worried about you too."

"I know," I said barely above a whisper.

"You'll find her, brother. You always do." With that, Greg started walking once more until his footsteps could no longer be heard.

I ran my hands down my face and let my head fall into my hands, Greg's words ringing in my head like sirens.

"You'll find her, brother. You always do."

It got harder and harder to believe with every second that ticked away, and she was not in my arms.

After a few moments of sulking, I pushed myself out of my desk chair and forced my tired legs to carry me back to our bedroom. Ariel's scent had almost completely been taken over by mine. The only things that still held her scent were her clothes. But even those were starting to lose their comfort since I'd been handling them so much and my scent was starting to taint them.

I took a quick shower before I slid into the bed that felt empty without Ariel there.

"Please, let me find my luna," I whispered into the night as the sleep I'd desperately been trying to escape fell over me like a cold dark blanket.

*   *   *

I woke to a furnace burning within me, the flames licking at my nerves with an insatiable hunger. Every time I took a breath, daggers buried themselves within the spaces between my ribs and my blood burned like a wound after alcohol had been pressed against it.

My wolf, who'd been silent ever since our mate had been stolen from us, was screaming. Her name was ricocheting throughout my skull as he relentlessly pushed against my wall in desperate need of taking control. As he did so, an unidentifiable feeling slowly seeped into the depths of my body, settling deep in the pit of my stomach.

I clenched my teeth as a wave of pain ripped through me like a knife to butter. Sweat quickly beaded my forehead. Another tidal wave of pain crashed over me, its poisonous waters rushing down the bones of my spine, causing my back to painfully arch off the bed in torment.

"Must get to mate," my wolf chanted in my head as he pushed harder, pulling a scream from my lips that I couldn't suppress. Then it all dawned on me.

Heat.

I was going through heat, which only meant one thing; my mate, my Ariel, was alive. With Morgan.

Anger burned within me at the thought of that monster going anywhere near my mate, let alone at a time like this. But I had to hold my anger at bay. Too much emotion and my wolf would take control, and I couldn't let that happen. Not yet.

216

"Aiden," I called over the link as I forced myself to get up despite the pain that was clawing at me. I instantly got a response.

"Yes, Alpha?"

"Tell all of the warriors as well as anyone else who can fight to meet me in the clearing," I ordered.

"What's the plan, Alpha?" he questioned as I made it outside, the cool air that wrapped around me contrasting with the blazing fire that resided within my bones.

"Ariel's going into heat," I growled. *"And we're going to get her before that mutt can lay a finger on her."*

"Yes, Alpha!" Aiden said before I cut the link.

I wasted no time shifting into my beast, my clothes ripping in the process before I made a dead sprint for the clearing. Not long after I got there, wolves were pouring in by the dozens. Almost three-quarter of the pack was there including Greg and Chris, which relieved me.

"This is all of them," Aiden reported as his deep brown wolf appeared next to me, and I nodded before my attention returned to the wolves in front of me.

"I'm going to keep this short because we don't have a lot of time," I announced, making them stand at attention. *"As you all know, your luna has been captured, and up until now, I haven't been able to do anything about it."* I sighed before continuing. *"But she's about to go into heat, and I'll die before I let another male touch her. So we're going to take her back and bring her back to her family where she belongs."*

Howls of approval filled the air before another wave of pain ripped through me. A whimper pushed passed my lips. We were running out of time.

"Move out!" I commanded before I started running as fast as I could in the direction of Morgan's pack with the thunderous sound of hundreds of feet behind me.

Every time a foot hit the ground, a new detail of the plan emerged, and with every new detail came a new spark of hope.

217

It killed me putting Ariel's life in danger, but not as much as it killed me knowing that Morgan was right there waiting to pounce on her when the time was right. Luckily, a six hour drive would be a four hour run, considering we had to abide by the human world's rules. This was our best bet. But four hours might be too late for Ariel.

My feet moved faster. The pain became more intense, but I pushed through it. I had to.

Don't worry, love. I'm coming for you.

CHAPTER TWENTY-NINE
The Test: Day Thirty-seven

ARIEL

I awoke to an uncomfortable pressure in my lower abdomen as if someone were sitting on me. Heat was running up and down my spine and feeding it into the rest of my body, and it didn't help that Morgan was holding me flush against him. Sweat was already forming on the back of my neck, and the pressure was slowly becoming painful as if the person sitting on me decided to stick millions of needles in me as well.

A silent whimper escaped my lips as pain shot through me like a lightning bolt, my silent cries acting as the thunder.

Morgan groaned into my back where his face was buried as his arms constricted around my waist. I'd trained myself to not shudder every time he touched me.

"What's wrong, babe?" he asked lazily into my skin, and his voice never failed to nauseate me.

My mind whirled, trying to come up with a feasible answer, but everything came back to one thing.

No, I thought to myself. *I can't. I'm in my human form. It's not possible.*

"Is everything alright?" Morgan asked, making me realize that I hadn't answered.

I waved it off before I mutely said, mouthing the word, "Bathroom."

It had taken him a while to get used to reading lips since I refused to write on his hand, not wanting to touch him more than I had to do. *I could make him believe me.*

"Are you sure you're alright?" he asked, and I nodded.

His eyes narrowed and searched my own eyes, looking for any sign not to believe me. He released me.

"Don't be too long," he muttered as he closed his eyes and settled back into the bed.

I let out a silent relieved sigh as I pushed myself out of bed. I sucked in a sharp breath as anguish moved through me with enough power to take me off my feet. But I willed my legs to stay strong and carry me the few strides to the bathroom.

As soon as I safely made it into the bathroom with the door locked behind me, I collapsed and allowed my body to succumb to the throbbing pain that had spread throughout my body like a virus. Silent screams parted my lips as I curled up into a ball in a desperate attempt to find a position that would keep the pain at bay, but I failed.

Heat.

That was what I was going through.

A seven day period in which pain overtook both mates and didn't go away until they mated. If they didn't complete the mating process within seven days, it would come back stronger each month until eventually, both mates would perish.

I pushed the thoughts out of my head as I crawled toward the shower on all fours and started a cold shower; something my mom had told me that helped with the heat. I wasted no time stripping and jumping into the ice cold shower, relief washing over me with the water, but it was short lived when what Morgan had told me last night bombarded my thoughts.

He'd told me that today would be the day he was going to attack our pack and take Shane down. Over the past couple of days, Morgan had briefed me, presenting me with multiple maps of our pack, each with its own details. He asked me questions about every aspect of our pack like where the weakest defenses were and where all the warriors usually were during night time.

It was easy to give him false leads on things like security like how I told him the weakest border was the west, even though I knew it was the strongest. In addition to the multiple warriors and border patrol that were looking over it at any given moment, it was the closest to our house, meaning that if anyone or anything came within a hundred-yard radius of the border, then Shane could easily find them.

But on other, more complicated questions, I had to make up something on the spot and hoped that it wasn't true. As far as I knew, Morgan bought everything and even brought me to meetings he was holding with his own warriors and soldiers on the forthcoming attacks. Hopefully, I misguided them enough or else my pack, my family would crumble into oblivion.

Despite the comfort it brought, I reluctantly dragged myself out of the nice cold shower. I knew that if I stayed in the shower any longer, Morgan would become suspicious. As soon as I left the cold canopy of water, the pain overcame me. My lips parted as I silently screamed while I leaned against the wall, my knees too weak to bear the overwhelming weight of my body. I used the wall to support me as I took small shaky steps to grab my towel before I headed toward the minuscule closet that was within the bathroom. With trembling hands, I managed to slide on my clothes despite the affliction on my body.

After I took a few minutes to compose myself, I slowly made my way out of the bathroom, praying that Morgan couldn't smell the heat that was radiating off of me in excruciating waves.

221

When I walked out, Morgan was no longer in bed, but rather brooding by the window with his exposed back facing me, his muscles flexing every now and then.

I couldn't deny the fact that Morgan was an attractive man with his extremely muscular body and tall frame. He had a rugged kind of look and a fire always blazing in his eyes. His red-brown hair was up and sticking out all over the place, but it didn't look bad. If he walked into the pack like this, he'd have dozens of the girls falling head over heels for him.

Too bad such a handsome face belonged to such a hideous personality.

His back muscles suddenly tensed, but almost as fast as it happened, it was gone. "How was your sleep, my luna?" Morgan asked as he turned away from the window and faced me, his eyes slowly looking me up and down as he did so.

I looked down at my feet and tried to hide. That did not go unnoticed by Morgan.

"You will not hide from me!" Morgan roared, and in one swift movement, I was pinned against the wall with my hands all the way above my head and Morgan's body flat against my own. "You are mine now, Ariel, and you can't hide what's mine from me!"

I cowered against the wall in an attempt to make as much room between Morgan and me as possible.

"Do you understand?" he said, seething in rage and his morning breath invading my nose and his spit flew onto my face.

I quickly nodded, and he harshly let me go. I instantly started rubbing my wrists where bruises were starting to form due to how often he pinned me against the wall whether it was to scold me or to force me into long kissing sessions with him.

A small shiver ran down my back as I remembered a few nights ago when Morgan forced his rough lips onto mine. Despite the nausea that filled my being, I made myself play along with it, and I instantly hated myself after. I felt so guilty allowing another man to kiss me.

I shook the thoughts from my head.

I'm doing what I have to, I kept repeating to myself, but there was only so much reassurance one could give.

After Morgan took a quick shower and we ate breakfast in the silence we'd become accustomed to, Morgan took my small hands in his and slid his long fingers in between mine.

"Come on, my luna. We must finish preparing the final details for our plan."

I didn't respond as Morgan led me out of the house and into the meeting hall. I was too wrapped up in the pain that overtook me with every step. Every breath.

Throughout the meeting, the pain didn't let up one bit. Every moment I spent sitting there, the pain grew stronger and more unbearable. Fire was rushing through my veins and an invisible weight was pulling on my bones. Pain pulsed through my head with every heartbeat, and it felt like someone was punching my lower stomach with knives between their fingers.

Morgan obviously noticed my discomfort and the sweat beading my forehead, but he didn't utter a word. Instead, he continued to lead the meeting, which I was grateful for. However, the other males in the room didn't seem interested in the meeting or final details of the plan at all. Their attention was on me rather; there were small smirks and grins on their faces, which sent shivers down my spine although there was a fire gnawing at me from deep within.

As soon as the meeting was over, I practically ran out of the meeting hall, unable to take all the hungry gazes I was receiving. They knew what was happening. And so did Morgan. That alone caused me to practically run from him into the house and into the bedroom while his sickening laughter followed me all the way.

As soon as I made it into the bedroom, I desperately tried to close the door. But before I could even get the door halfway closed, Morgan pushed it open with such force that it actually caused me to stumble back and almost fall. Thankfully, I managed to stay on my feet knowing that if I fell, then it would be over.

"Oh, Ariel." Morgan chuckled as he shook his head and closed the door, locking it in the process.

Fear slowly crept up my throat and gripped me tight as I took slow steps away from Morgan, fear and pain fighting for dominance within me.

"You know you can't outrun me. I thought you would've learned that by now," he mused, shaking his head as he lifted his shirt over his head. "Consider this your final lesson."

He continued advancing towards me. The next article of clothing that came off was the belt that supported his jeans.

"The moment you woke up, I could smell it on you," he continued just as my back hit a wall, causing me to gasp. He took the opportunity to pin me against the wall, his signature smirk plastered on his face. "It took every ounce of control I had within me not to take you the moment you walked out the bathroom, but I'm glad I did."

He brought a rough hand to my cheek and gently stroked it. I sucked in a sharp breath and pressed myself as far against the wall as I could, my back crying in protest as I did so.

"It'll get me riled up before the fight. Keep me motivated."

In one swift movement, he ripped the shirt I was wearing off my body, causing me to silently yelp as goosebumps arose on my skin.

Morgan's eyes hungrily took in my breasts, and I felt tears in my eyes.

Goddess. Please, no! I begged silently as tears streamed down my cheeks, but I knew that no matter how much I begged and cried, I knew that I was on my own.

"We're going to have a lot of fun tonight," Morgan whispered as he lowered his head so that his lips could meet my jaw, traveling all the way down to the top of my breasts where he placed multiple kisses and light bites.

More tears fell from my eyes and onto my cheeks, rolling down off my face and landing in his hair in small droplets. I felt so disgusted and objectified. I felt so dirty and used and defenseless.

I thrashed and kicked underneath him, but it had no effect on him, merely causing him to smile.

"I just wish I could hear you scream my name . . ." He trailed off as he used one hand to restrain my arms and used the other to pull off the sweatpants I was wearing, leaving me in only the bra and underwear he'd forced me to wear. "Are you ready, my luna?" Morgan asked after eyeing me up and down, and I frantically shook my head no.

I knew that Morgan hated me, but I never thought he'd go this far.

He scuffed. "Don't worry, Ariel. I'll show you things that pup Shane could only dream of."

His eyes wandered down to my underwear, and his fingers gathered the material in his hand, ready to remove those as well. I wanted to stop him. I wanted to fight back. I wanted to run. But it was as if my body was numb, my thoughts and instinct gone and replaced by static and white noise.

I was powerless. Helpless.

"This is going to be fun," Morgan mused, about to take full advantage of me when suddenly, I felt a supernova of pain burst through my skull and pressure building behind my eyes.

I felt fire ignite within my bones and sparks dance on the ends of my nerves. Power surged through me like an electric current, and a tingling sensation moved through my body, especially where my bruises and scars were, including my neck and throat.

I could feel every bruised and scarred cell fall away and slowly try to heal themselves. I felt every wound tingle and become numb. I felt every fiber of my severed vocal cords reach out for one another like hands, becoming whole once more so that they could

225

produce the sounds and pitches that was my voice. Although joy and strength circulated throughout my body as all of my enhanced senses returned, panic filled my chest. This feeling was all too familiar.

Before Morgan could make another move, a great wave of power washed over me, and my arm shot out and grabbed him around the neck, my now extended claws digging into the sensitive flesh of his throat. Before I could register exactly what was happening, something or someone pulled me back into the depths of my mind as it pushed forward and took control.

Roxie.

Morgan's eyes were wide, holding a mix of shock and horror.

"Ariel?" he choked out in disbelief, his blood now trickling from his mouth and down my arm.

"No," Roxie said, her deep voice mixing with mine in perfect harmony. "Roxie."

Without missing a beat, Roxie hurled Morgan into the wall with such force that his body actually made a dent in the wall and the sound of several breaking bones filled the air.

"It feels good to finally have full control," Roxie mused as she cracked our neck. "I finally get to accomplish what Ariel was too weak to do."

She walked over to Morgan in two mighty strides. He was still dazed, and blood was now leaking out of his nose in addition to his mouth, a few broken bones visible.

"St-Stay away from me, or you'll regret it, mutt," he spat in an attempt to sound unfazed, but Roxie and I both could see the fear swimming in his eyes.

"No one tells Roxie what to do," she growled before she effortlessly grabbed Morgan by the throat and hoisted him in the air so that his feet were no longer touching the floor. "You've caused Ariel too much pain," Roxie growled as Morgan desperately clawed at our hand, his face turning a deep red color as his air supply was

226

cut off. "You've abused her. You've kidnapped her. You almost took advantage of her, but now," she growled lowly, holding Morgan so close that they were face to face, "I'm going to do what I should've done long ago."

Swiftly, she changed Morgan's position so that she had him in a headlock with a hand positioned on either side of his head.

"Any last words, Morgan?" she spat, causing Morgan to merely chuckle.

"Oh, Ariel. You're just as stupid as your parents were." He laughed before he dug his canines deep within our arm, and though I felt nothing, Roxie howled in pain and instinctively let Morgan go.

Surprisingly, he didn't run. Instead, he got into a fighting stance as if he didn't have multiple broken bones or had blood dripping out of his nose and mouth.

Roxie growled. "Don't you dare talk about our parents, coward," she spat as the bite quickly healed. "They were stronger than you'll ever be. You had to murder them to be where you are," she said, the truth burning on our lips as it slid past them.

"And I should've let you die with them," he growled before he shifted into his giant red-brown wolf and lunged at us.

It was like time itself slowed down. Roxie didn't move a muscle, her keen eyes watching every movement Morgan made. While Morgan was in midair, his eyes wild and his canines bared, Roxie effortlessly grabbed him by the neck and slammed him into the ground with such force that the floor shook beneath our feet, cracks webbing out and carving themselves into the ground.

Nauseating cracks filled the air, and his wolf looked up at us in horror before bowing its head in submission, but he missed that opportunity long ago.

"Shift back, now," Roxie ordered, and Morgan did so without hesitation, not looking her in the eye once he'd done so.

"Please spare me," he begged. "I-I'll do whatever you want. I'll l-leave you alone fore—"

"Silence!" Roxie roared, rage boiling within us.

Morgan whimpered as he thrashed around in an attempt to free himself from Roxie, but her grip was firm, and she refused to waver.

"To think you made our life purgatory and now you're begging us to let you off easy." Roxie scuffed. "I think it's time for us to return the favor."

Without another word, Roxie mercilessly started breaking Morgan's bones, ignoring his blood-curdling screams or his bones breaking through his delicate skin or the stench of his blood that filled the air. She continued despite my pleas for her to stop, I even pushed back further in my head sometimes because the scene was too horrid. Too barbaric.

When I could finally bring myself as far forward as Roxie would allow me to, almost all of Morgan's bones were broken and bent in different ways. Blood smeared all over his body and face like paint over a canvas. It was a miracle that he was still alive.

"Roxie, please stop! He's had enough!" I begged as Roxie took his forearm in our hands and effortlessly snapped it like a twig, sickness waving over me as Morgan's agonized cry filled my ears and echoed throughout my head.

"He deserves it, Ariel," Roxie hissed as a sickening smile grew on our face.

She was proud of her work.

"He's beaten you for years and took away your happiness. Your freedom. Now he must pay. Dearly."

She curtly put Morgan's broken body into a choke hold once more and positioned his head between her hands, power radiating through my body. I knew exactly what she was going to do. My heartbeat sped up, and I screamed at her to stop, but she blocked me out. She was high of the blood and the screams and wanted more, not willing to stop until she got exactly what she wanted.

My fingertips tingled.

"Any last words, mutt?" Roxie spat venomously, throwing the old nickname he used for us back at him.

"P-Please, l-let me go," Morgan barely choked out through the blood and pain.

"Hmm, let me think about it." Roxie cruelly teased as our fingers started applying pressure to Morgan's skull.

No!

Before I could utter a word of protest, I was thrust into the very back on my being, unable to see or do anything except to hear his horrified screams accompanied by the sickening sound of bones breaking.

I felt the stomach-turning feeling of warm blood and the oddly soft feeling of his flesh spilling between our fingers. After a few seconds, I felt Roxie release him before once again, I was pulled back to the furthest point Roxie would allow me to go.

I refused to look at what she'd just done. I couldn't handle it.

"He got what he deserved, Ariel," Roxie said, her words once again flowing from our mouth. "He'd taken too much away from you already, and I was not about to let him take advantage of you."

Part of me was glad that she'd done what she'd done, but another, much larger part of me was horrified and angry even. I knew what Morgan was going to do was terrible, and I knew that I wanted Morgan dead, but I wanted it to be on my terms, my way. Not Roxie's.

Roxie was about to say something else but was interrupted by the door of the bedroom breaking open, causing our attention to snap to it. Standing there with a terrified look on her face was Tracey, frozen in fear.

"O-Oh my . . ." She trailed off, her lips quivering along with the rest of her body. Her eyes quickly filled with tears as they left what used to be Morgan and looked up at us, pure grief swimming in the swimming pools of tears in her eyes. "Y-You just—"

"Leave. Now," Roxie commanded.

Roxie didn't want anything to do with Tracey since she hadn't been half as bad as Morgan, just blinded by her unrequited love for him. But she would kill Tracey if she made a move toward us.

Unfortunately, she did.

"You killed him!" she screamed.

A small shiver ran down my back at the haunting image of her black eyes overflowing with tears, pure anger etched into her face while anguish burned in her eyes. "I'm going to kill you!"

She lunged at us, but Roxie merely grabbed her neck the same way she'd grabbed Morgan's. In one swift motion, she broke Tracey's neck and dropped her now lifeless, breathless body to the ground, her face still wet with tears.

"I told you to leave," Roxie growled down at the corpses that lay at our feet before I was thrust back into control of my body so fast that my head spun for a few moments.

As soon as my equilibrium stabilized itself, tears instantly formed in my eyes while they wandered down to my sinful, blood-drenched hands. An earth-shattering scream escaped my lips as I saw what Roxie had done, and my newly healed vocal cords cried in protest.

My hands started shaking as I fell down on my knees and desperately wiped them on the floor, but it only made things worse as my hands met more of Morgan's blood that had pooled around their bodies, slowly making its way toward me.

Sobs escaped my lips as I got up and pressed myself against the wall furthest away from the corpses. A small part of me was happy that I'd killed them; that I protected myself when it counted; that I survived. But a greater part of me was horrified and scared; that part of me wanted to burn off every cell of my body that touched Morgan and Tracey and file my brain down to bloody nubs to forget what I'd done. But I couldn't. I'd killed them both, and I would live with that forever.

I shook my head to get the images that kept replaying themselves in my head. I couldn't stay here anymore. I willed my shaking legs to carry me out of the bedroom and out of the house. It was dark when I emerged outside and the cold instantly wrapped around my body since I was still only in my underwear and bra.

Without a second thought, I ran into the forest, not caring where I would end up as long as it wasn't here. Tears blurred my already terrible vision as the scenes relentlessly replayed over and over. The putrid smell of his blood forever burned into my nose and the feeling of his flesh between my fingers eternally carved into my fingertips.

The deeper I ventured into the woods, low growls followed by the sounds of combat filled my ears. The sounds became louder as I neared the border. That was when I saw it.

In the darkness, I saw the silhouettes of hundreds of wolves in close combat, each aiming to kill the other. I recognized some from Morgan's pack and some from my own.

I quickly hid behind a large tree far enough that no one would see me. Tears sprung to my eyes as I watched my pack members bite and scratch and fight the men and women I recognized from Morgan's meetings. Even the thought of him caused a new wave of tears to emerge. I was so distracted by the scene in front of me that I didn't notice the mind-numbing smell of cinnamon and fresh rain approaching me at an alarmingly fast rate.

Alexia, my wolf who'd returned after Roxie's departure, screamed at me to run toward my mate and melt in his comforting arms, but I couldn't. I didn't know if Roxie could still gain control of me and I didn't want any of my pack members to get hurt because of her unpredictable nature, especially not Shane.

Instantaneously, I turned on my heels and began running the opposite direction from Shane, not only breaking my heart but also causing Alexia to push against my boundary. Pressure quickly escalated behind my eyes as Alexia tried to gain control, but I wouldn't let her. I refused to let anyone or anything have control over my body ever again.

"*Ariel!*" Shane's heartwarming voice called in my head, confusion evident in his voice. "*What's wrong? Why are you—*"

I cut off the connection, unable to handle hearing his broken voice. As soon as the connection was cut, a loud howl ripped through the air like a bullet, and I instantly knew it was Shane.

I forced my legs to move faster although the pressure was becoming unbearable.

"*Our mate is in pain! Need to soothe mate!*" she growled, and I shook my head.

"*I don't know if she still has control! I don't want to risk her hurting Shane.*"

Suddenly, a thunderous growl came from somewhere in front of me, and I instantly stopped in my tracks. My heartbeat sped up not only because it was the growl of an alpha, but because it was the growl of my alpha.

I heard the leaves crunch beneath him, and branches snap as his huge beast stepped on them. I turned my head toward the direction of the sounds, and I saw his wolf emerge in all its glory. My eyes grew wide as he slowly advanced on me, baring his fangs as he growled. Panic crawled up my throat once my eyes met his pitch black ones.

All I wanted to do was run to him and let him hold me and whisper sweet things in my ear, but I knew I couldn't. She could still be inside me, waiting for the perfect opportunity to strike. I made a move to run, but my foot didn't even meet the ground when I felt two familiar arms wrap themselves around my waist and pull me into a firm chest. The sparks I'd missed so much shot through everywhere our bodies touched.

"Why were you running from me, Ariel?" Shane asked, his voice low but hurt pulsed through every word.

232

I opened my mouth, but instead of words coming into fruition, I choked on my silent sobs. Shane growled in frustration with my lack of an answer before he craned his neck down so that his lips were next to my ear.

"You're practically bare, and I can smell him all over you, Ariel!" he spat angrily, causing me to jump a bit. "Tell me where he is, and I'll kill him. I'll rip him joint from pathetic joint."

"That's the thing, Shane," I said as I finally turned to him, tears once again falling over my cheeks and my voice shaking uncontrollably.

Shane's hard eyes and demeanor instantly softened as I looked him in the eye.

"Sh-Shane, I . . ." I trailed off, and Shane wordlessly wrapped his arms around me and pulled me into his broad chest. I sobbed as I cradled my sin covered hands to my chest.

"What happened, love?" Shane asked frantically as he looked me over, his eyes growing wide as they landed on my blood soaked hands.

At that moment, my legs could no longer support my weight, and I let my body collapse into Shane's comforting arms.

"Ariel, are you alright? Tell me what's wrong," Shane begged as he effortlessly held me up.

"Am I alright?" I repeated before I slipped into an insurgent series of hysterical laughter that were easily contradicted by the endless tears falling freely down my face.

"It's alright, Ariel," Shane comforted as he held me impossibly closer, and my laughs turned into ugly sobs. "Now can you please tell me what happened so I can make it better?" Shane asked as he looked at me with concern, blood from the slowly healing gaping wound on his forehead leaking from the nasty cut and running down his face and gathering in his eyebrow.

"You can't make it better," I whispered, shaking my head side to side as I looked up at Shane with tear filled eyes. "I killed them. Morgan and Tracey. He was going to take advantage of me, and I didn't know what to do so I had to and then she just came at me and—"

"Shh," Shane cooed as he used his massive hands to cover mine. "It's alright, love. It's over now. Okay, Ariel?"

I nodded.

"You did it in self-defense. You said it yourself. He was going to take advantage of you, and she was going to attack you. You didn't do anything wrong."

His arms became increasingly tight around me as he nuzzled into the groove of my neck where the mark he gave me was and where the scar Morgan left once resided before Roxie healed it.

"I missed you so much," he whispered as he looked down at me. "Every day without you was a struggle and every night alone was torture." He sighed and held me tighter. "Just please never leave me again."

"I-I missed you too," I stammered with a hoarse voice from screaming and crying. "And I won't. I can't."

Shane's finger softly met my chin and tilted my head up so that his lips could find mine. Even though chaos and death were raging around us, I found peace in his lips. The kiss was tender, though it screamed passion and love, telling more than words ever could. I even forgot the fact that Shane was bare from his shift.

I didn't care. I was with my Shane. My mate. My everything.

"I've missed doing this." Shane sighed as he rested his forehead on mine, and almost as soon as he said that, the world caught up with me and an excruciating pain shot through me like lightning.

My knees buckled, and my body went down, but Shane caught me right before I made an impact with the ground. A few curses slid past his lips as he held me close to his chest, the pain lessening the more we touched.

"I almost forgot," he said in a strained voice, pain evident in his words and movements. "Hold on tight," he instructed before he took off in a deadbolt through the dark woods.

I buried my head in the groove between his neck and collarbone. I could see the outlines of wolves locked in deadly combat. Some even made a move toward Shane and me, but before they could even get into position, one of our pack members already killed them. A smile made its way onto my lips in spite of the pain I was in. This was my pack, my family, and it warmed my heart to see them fighting so hard for me, a luna they barely knew.

"We're taking over this pack," Shane stated as he continued running, gracefully weaving in and out of trees as if he weren't in any pain at all. "Chris is the rightful alpha, but he said that he'd much rather let us take this pack in since he claims he has a lot to learn about being a leader."

I pulled myself closer to him as the pain intensified.

"Aiden, Greg, and Chris are at the pack house right now, gathering all willing pack members while whoever else doesn't agree with the new rules are going rogue."

"Where's Jessica?" I asked right before a bolt of pain filled my chest and ran up the side of my throat resulting in me biting down on my bottom lip to prevent a scream from pressing past my lips.

I drew blood.

"She's back home with Zac," Shane explained as the pack house came into view with a big truck with bright lights in the front of it. I recognized it as one of the cars that belonged to this pack.

Shane hurried to it, and the closer we got, I saw that Chris was sitting in the driver's seat, nervously drumming his fingers against the steering wheel. He visibly relaxed once he saw Shane and me.

"How is my baby sister?" Chris asked frantically as Shane gently placed me in the backseat in the car so that I was lying on a few of his sweatshirts that he must've had someone bring from the pack.

It lessened the pain a bit but wasn't as good as Shane actually holding me.

"She's in heat," Shane growled as he tugged on a pair of basketball shorts. "Now Chris. Listen to me carefully and don't argue with me because I'm not in the best state of mind right now and won't be held responsible for my actions if you don't oblige."

The words were tight as they pressed from Shane's lips, his eyes flickering between black and their natural hazel-green color.

"I need you to get out of the car and stay away from Ariel until her heat passes, along with the other males, or else I just might do something I will regret."

"But she's my—"

"Chris," Shane said in a warning tone, causing Chris to bow his head in submission. "I'm doing this to keep from hurting you or any other male who dares to look at what's mine. It's not personal. It's just—"

"I understand," Chris said, before his eyes wandered to mine, causing a deep growl to rumble in Shane's chest.

"Don't look at her!" Shane roared, causing a small whimper to press from Chris' lips. I knew Shane wouldn't normally be like this, but he and his wolf were feeling very protective of me.

"I'll be f-fine, C-Chris," I stammered as the pain increased, and Chris nodded in defeat. "I love you."

Shane growled again.

"I love you too." And Chris was gone.

Shane slid into the driver's seat and started driving. The world and all the chaos in it flew by in a blur.

"I'm going to get you home. Alright, love? I just need you to rest. If you rest, the heat will be stalled until you wake up once more."

I nodded and closed my eyes.

"Oh and Ariel?" Shane said gently, causing my eyelids to lift themselves. "I love you."

A weak smile formed on my lips as I closed my eyes once more, not needing to use words to let him know the boundless amount of love I had for him.

CHAPTER THIRTY

"Ariel?" Shane called softly as he gently nudged me.

My eyes slowly peeled open, but I quickly closed them once more due to the bright light that poured into them.

"Sam, turn down the lights," Shane instructed, and through my eyelids, I could see the light dimmed.

I peeled my eyes open once more and was able to keep them open. Shane was gently cradling me in his arms, his fingers gently playing with my hair. The pain of my heat had greatly decreased, but I could already feel it beginning to intensify.

"Are you okay?" he asked, and I nodded as I took in the room around me, and I instantly knew where I was. The pack hospital.

"Shane, what am I—"

"I wanted to make sure that you're okay," he stated gently as he gently readjusted me on his lap.

While I was sitting on Shane's lap, I noticed that I had been changed into one of his comfy gray sweatshirts that fell past my knees as well as the lack of blood on my hands, which I was immensely grateful for. I also noticed that we were sitting on a hospital bed.

I shook my head. "I-I'm fine, really. I don't need to be in here," I said, panic rushing through my veins as the time I woke up in a hospital with Morgan at the foot of my bed replayed in my head.

"Ariel, I know that you're not fine," Shane whispered in my ear as his grip around me tightened. "As your mate, it is my job to make sure that you're alright. As soon as I know you're okay, we can leave and do whatever you want."

I bit my bottom lip before I slowly nodded.

"Just promise me that you won't leave," I said, looking up into his eyes.

"I just got you back, Ariel. I'm not leaving your side for a while."

I smiled before he placed a soft kiss on my lips.

"How are you feeling, Luna?" Samantha asked once our lips parted after several long moments.

"Okay," I admitted honestly. "And please, call me Ariel."

"So why don't you tell us exactly what happened, Ariel," Samantha said, seeming uncomfortable calling me by my birth name.

My eyes met Shane's, and he nodded. "Don't worry, love. You can stop whenever you want to."

I gave him a small nod before I took a deep breath and spilled every detail of what happened; from the day Morgan took me to the horrendous events that happened mere hours ago, broken bones and all. By the time I was done, my hands were shaking, and tears were rushing down my cheeks.

"I-I can't. I need to stop," I whispered.

"It's alright. Just breathe," Shane cooed as he used his thumbs to wipe my falling tears away. "Just follow my lead."

Our eyes locked and he took a deep breath in and slowly let it out like he'd done when I had that panic attack going into the human world. I wordlessly followed him while his fingers

239

continuously wiped away my tears that fell until I became calm and my tears ceased.

"Lun— I mean, Ariel. I need to look you over for any injuries."

A low growl of protest rumbled deep within Shane's chest, and his arms became impossibly tight around me.

"Relax," I said as I cupped his cheek, causing him to relax a bit under my touch. "She's just helping me. Like you said, we need to make sure I'm alright."

Shane looked at Samantha before his eyes landed on me. "Alright, but Samantha, don't hurt her more than she's already hurt . . . Please."

A look of shock washed over her face at the fact that an alpha, let alone her own alpha, said please. But almost as fast as it came, it disappeared, and Samantha nodded.

"Of course, Alpha."

"Shane. Call me Shane."

I chuckled at the shocked expression on her face, causing her to slightly blush before she started checking me over. I climbed off of Shane though I kept my hand in his to make my heat more bearable. I allowed Samantha to remove my sweatshirt and looked at the deep bruises that were taking longer to heal.

"You poor thing," Samantha whispered as she looked over me. "I'm going to apply slight pressure on your bruises and wounds. Let me know if it hurts even the slightest bit, alright?"

I nodded, and she proceeded. As she examined me, Shane growled in frustration and anger as his eyes swept over me.

"If that useless mutt weren't dead, I'd kill him with way less mercy than you gave him."

My eyebrows furrowed. What I did was not merciful in the slightest.

"You allowed him a quick death. I would've slowly tortured him, only giving him enough time to heal himself before I did it all

240

over again every day until I got tired of his pleas for mercy. Then I'd kill him."

"Too soon," Samantha whispered, causing Shane to snap out of whatever angry trance he'd been in and apologized. "Luna, I need you to lie on your stomach so that I can check out your back."

I silently obliged, slight winces escaping my lips as she applied pressure on the bruises I'd sustained from Morgan constantly slamming me into walls and bedposts. Shane growled as his grip on my hand tightened to calm himself down. She then continued inspecting my throat where it was cut then finally where Morgan tried to mark me, causing many growls and choice words about Morgan to slide past Shane's lips as he held me impossibly tighter.

When she was finished, I slid Shane's sweatshirt back over my body before I beckoned for him to sit next to me on the bed. Once he was comfortable, I climbed back onto his lap with my back against his chest and both of his hands laced with mine.

"You seem to be healing alright though the process is slower than most, but I'll just pin that on the circumstances." Samantha mused as she peeled the blue gloves that'd been covering her hands off. "You just need to take things easy and keep Shane with you since you're in heat. I'd also like to recommend counseling or at least talking to Shane about what you went through because you've been through a lot in the days you were gone, and you can't keep it bottled up inside you. It's not healthy."

I nodded reluctantly even though I didn't really want to relieve what happened over and over again with a shrink.

"Shane, I trust that you'll take good care of her."

"Is that even a question?" Shane said into my neck where his head was buried.

"Of course not," Samantha said. "But keep her fragile state in mind during your heat process. I know it can be compelling but always put her physical state first."

"Understood," Shane said with a nod as a blush ran to my cheeks at how easily the topic of my heat slid from her lips. "Thank you, Samantha."

"No problem." She smiled before she made a move to exit the room, but I stopped her.

"Wait, Samantha . . . how do I control Roxie or whatever this thing is that's inside of me? I just . . . I don't want this to happen again, especially not around the pack. I don't want to hurt anyone else."

"Roxie is only an extension of you, Ariel," she explained gently. "She's not some uncontrollable being. It's just your survival side that seems to only come out in dire situations. But it's still you. Still your motives and wants and actions. Right now, it's not a matter of controlling her. It's a matter of being in control of your emotions and actions."

I let out a shaky breath and nodded, though it was hard to believe that it was me who did all those terrible things to Morgan and Tracey. The revelation caused my heart to race as everything began playing in my head again.

"But hey," she said as she gently placed a hand on my knee, interrupting my racing thoughts, which I was grateful for. "What you did wasn't a bad thing. You protected yourself. It's just not in a way you're used to. That's all. And that's okay. Like I said, you just need to talk with someone and figure this part of yourself out, okay?"

I nodded once again. "Thanks, Sam."

"My pleasure. And I will make sure to let the pack know not to bother you while you're in recovery." She smiled before she left the room.

"That was a lot to take in, Ariel," Shane said softly after a few moments and I nodded. "Are you sure you're alright?"

I nodded. "As alright as I can be, given that I was kidnapped, tortured, and I murdered two people with my bare hands," I said with a humorless chuckle.

242

"Ariel, I'm serious," Shane pressed. "We're already at a vulnerable place right now with our heat and with everything you've been through . . . I need to make sure that you at least feel safe and okay."

"Of course I feel safe," I said quickly. "But really, Shane, I'm okay. Just a little sore and the healing process is taking longer than usual due to the circumstances, so—"

"Let me heal you." Shane interrupted. "I've done it before, and I'll do it again."

"No, Shane. I'm fine. Plus it takes so much out of you and—"

"I wasn't asking."

Mere seconds later, I felt bolts of electricity ran up my body, the intense heat gathering where my bruises were. Within seconds, the heat turned into pleasurable sparks, and Shane let go, breathing heavily like he had when he healed me the first time.

"You didn't have to do that," I whispered as I turned in his lap so that I was now facing him. "I would've healed eventually." My fingers started tracing the features of his face. All of his battle wounds had healed, leaving nothing behind but smooth, flawless skin.

"I know," he stated, still breathing heavily. "But I couldn't let you endure the pain that I knew I could take away."

I grinned before I placed a gentle kiss on his lips. We moved in perfect synchronization, communicating how much we'd missed each other through our kisses without the need of words to act as a middleman.

Shane took handfuls of the shirt I was wearing, holding onto it tight. "I need to stop." He sighed into my lips. "The heat is making it too hard, and I don't want to hurt you."

I pulled away reluctantly, and he buried his head into my neck next to the mark he'd given me. I held him close to my body and allowed him to calm himself down.

"Are you ready to go to bed?" he asked after a few moments, and I nodded.

"I thought you'd never ask."

Shane led me out of the hospital then drove me back to our house. Our home. I never knew how much I'd miss it until I couldn't go back.

"This house seems so empty without everyone here," I mused as Shane carried me into our big, empty home.

"As you know, Greg, your brother, and Aiden are with the rest of the pack, fighting. Zac is staying with Jessica at Aiden's place," he explained as he carried me into the kitchen before he set me on my resident spot on the counter. He then grabbed a glass and filled it with water from the refrigerator then offered it to me, which I graciously took.

"Do you want something to eat?" Shane asked as I took a sip of water.

The kitchen was dark and filled with shadows, silent as the rest of the house besides our voices. I shook my head as I finished my water before I took Shane's hand in mine and led him upstairs. We wasted no time changing into our pajamas, our bodies going through agony every millisecond our bodies weren't touching. As soon as I slid into the bed, my body was flush against Shane's, and our lips were interlocked. The kiss was soft and intimate, yet rough and unpredictable.

Shane's fingers found their way into my hair, which had grown a lot since the last time I'd seen him. His lips created a soft trail of kisses from my lips, across my cheek, along my jawline, and down my neck where my mark laid. He placed kisses on it, softly using his hand to maneuver my head so he could have all the access to my neck that he wanted.

"Goddess, you're so beautiful," he whispered into my mark before he placed another prompt kiss on it, tingles running up and down my spine and gathering in my fingertips and toes.

"You are too." I breathed out as I buried my fingers in his soft locks. I felt Shane smile before he strengthened up so that we were lying face to face. We lay there for a few moments, Shane sporting a giddy grin as he looked at me. "What?"

"I've just missed having you here next to me," he admitted. "I never really realized how empty this bed is until you weren't in it with me." He tucked a short lock of hair behind my ear, his eyes following his movements. "It was miserable."

I gently cupped his face and softly traced his eyebrow with my thumb.

"I missed hearing your voice," Shane continued, leaning into my touch. "I missed your laugh, and I missed the feeling of your hands. Ariel, I just missed you so much." By now, he looked like he was on the verge of tears, and it utterly broke my heart into a million pieces.

"I missed you too," I whispered. "I missed your embrace and your killer meals." I chuckled. "And as weird as it may sound, I missed your scent. I missed your kisses and your hugs. I missed lying in bed with your arms wrapped around me. Your head on my shoulder. Your body against mine." I softly brushed his silent tears away. "I love you."

"I love you too," he confirmed before our lips met for a quick kiss. Shane's massive arms wrapped around me and pulled me on top of him and I comfortably rested my head on his chest. He wrapped his arms around my waist and kissed my forehead. "Good night, love."

"Good night."

CHAPTER THIRTY-ONE

SHANE

I awoke to the sound of heavy breathing. My eyes fluttered open right away, and the first thing I saw was Ariel lying on top of me. Her eyes were tightly screwed shut with harsh tears slipping between her eyelids.

"Stop." She whimpered as her nails buried themselves in my bare chest.

"Ariel," I said softly as I gave her a gentle shake in an attempt to wake her up while not startling her in the process.

"Don't!" she begged, more tears escaping. "Please, stop!" Her once soft voice was now yelling with pain evident in it.

"Ariel," I called more forcefully as I shook her once more yet again receiving the same response; nothing.

"Don't!" she yelled as she violently jolted awake, her red puffy eyes falling onto her trembling hands. "No, no, no . . ." she repeated as she shook her head, her voice fragile and shaking like a bridge ready to shatter into a million pieces at a moment's notice.

Without hesitation, I wrapped my arms around her waist and rocked her as she cried. My heart broke at how scared and broken she looked. The image of her face when I got her back flashed through my mind like lightning, hot and bright. How horrified and confused she looked, but that didn't hold a candle to how she looked right now.

"It's alright, my love. It was just a nightmare. I've got you now," I murmured gently, still rocking her back and forth.

"It was just so awful," she whispered into my chest as she began shaking her head once more and her breathing became heavier. "I just can't—"

"Shh, it's okay," I whispered, holding her as close to me as possible, not wanting a cell of her skin not touching my own. "Just breathe, Ariel. Just breathe."

She nodded before she took deep breaths with me, calming herself down.

"Good," I whispered as I kissed her forehead.

"I just can't stop thinking about what happened," she said in a voice raspy from crying. "Not just Morgan and Tracey, but everything before that: the Wolfsbane and silver injections, the endless abuse and starvation, being objectified and almost being taken advantage of . . . I just feel so weak, and I hate it."

"Ariel, don't say that," I begged, pain stabbing me in the heart at how lowly she thought of herself. "You are hands down the strongest, most beautiful person I know. You survived all of this while having your wolf stolen from you. Most lycans die within seconds of getting Wolfsbane or silver and the fact that you not only got both, but you also survived multiple doses is amazing. You misled Morgan and took away any power he had over you or anyone else for that matter. So you definitely are not weak. You're the exact opposite of it, and I'm elated to have the honor of calling you my own." I placed another kiss on her forehead. "You're smart and you used that to your advantage, and even though what happened to Morgan and Tracey wasn't ideal for you, you did everything you had to, as a true luna. Like a true alpha female." I pulled her into a tight hug, and she buried her head in my neck. We just stayed like that for a while.

"Thank you," she whispered into my neck.

"For what?" I questioned.

"Calming me down . . . being there for me . . . believing in me. Everything."

"You've done more for me than I could ever do for you, Ariel," I said in a low voice as I gently stroked her hair. "I should be the one thanking you."

I turned my head and placed a kiss on her cheek, and she held me tighter, her head buried into my neck as she took deep breaths. The same thing I did when I needed to calm down. I simply held her until the sounds of soft snores could be heard and her grip on me loosened.

I couldn't help the soft chuckles that pushed past my lips as I slowly moved her so that we were in the same position we'd been in before she'd been awoken by her nightmare. Her face was buried in my chest like she regularly did, her chest steadily rising and falling against my own. I stretched my neck to kiss her cheek before my thumb gently started stroking her cheek. Despite the drowsiness that was pulling my eyelids closed, I didn't allow myself to succumb to the temptation. I wanted to watch over her, ready to fight away the demons that were her nightmares. The discomfort of my heat started weaving through me, causing the relief of sleep to look even better, but yet again, I refused. Ariel was more important than anything. She'd been bruised and traumatized, which easily outdid my want for sleep.

"I've got you, love," I whispered into the silent night. "I've got you."

CHAPTER THIRTY-TWO

ARIEL

I didn't get much sleep last night. Between the relentless nightmares and unforgiving tears that continuously spilled from my eyes, sleep was the least of my worries, but I had Shane there with me every step of the way. Through every scream, and sob, Shane was right there, holding me close and whispering things in my ear as he gently kissed every tear away.

I looked up at his sleeping face. He was tranquil: his bold eyes tucked away behind closed eyelids and thick lashes, his jaw relaxed, and his face neutral. He looked so peaceful, so calm, and so beautiful. I ran my hand along his jaw, his sharp stubble tickling my fingertips. He shuffled a bit and held me closer before becoming still once more. I smiled to myself before I carefully started working my way out of Shane's embrace, careful not to wake him up in the process.

"What exactly do you think you're doing?" Shane asked, his voice gruff from sleep as he pulled me back on top of him.

"I can't get anything past you, can I?" I chuckled.

"Of course not," he said before he gave me a quick kiss. "But what exactly were you trying to get past me?"

"A bath," I admitted. "I really need one."

"Ariel, I can smell your heat from a mile away, and that means that any other male can too. Wherever you go, I'll be right by your side even if it's in our own home."

"Shane, I just want to take a bath," I whined.

"And you will," he said. "But I'll be right there with you. I know you might not be feeling it right now, but this heat cycle will be intense, and I'm not leaving you alone for a second knowing that something as simple as touching you can make it go away."

"Shane—"

"It wasn't a question, Ariel," Shane interrupted, using the same line he had right before he healed me yesterday.

I guess there was no changing his mind. I sighed. "Fine, but if you insist, then you're going to be following my rules, not yours. Got it?"

"It depends on what these 'rules' are," he said, raising an eyebrow, causing me to roll my eyes as I got up and dragged him into the bathroom.

"You are going to stay right here unless I tell you otherwise," I said, pointing to the edge of the bathtub.

"Sounds fair enough," Shane shrugged.

I started running the bath water, having one hand securely in his. I grabbed my toothbrush and allowed Shane to apply the toothpaste before I quickly brushed my teeth so I could be done by the time the tub filled. I stopped the bath and let go of Shane's hand so that I could strip out of my clothes, my back to him so that he couldn't see all of my "assets."

"I don't understand why you're so shy around me, love," Shane commented as I slid into the bath before taking his hand once more, thankful that it was a bubble bath, so I didn't have to worry about being exposed. "I've seen you bare before, and you're beautiful. What are you trying to hide?" He looked me in the eye, his eyes burrowing into my mind trying to pick me apart.

I turned my head and looked at my toes peeking through the water and bubbles as if they were the most interesting things in the world.

Shane gave my hand a light squeeze. "At least, let me help you," Shane said as he briefly let go of my hand and moved behind me. Before I could utter a word of protest, he already had shampoo in his hands and started working his fingers through my filthy hair.

I couldn't contain my relaxed sighs as Shane's skillful fingers massaged my scalp.

"How's that?" Shane asked softly, and I nodded in response.

I slowly started bathing myself as Shane leisurely washed my hair while using every opportunity he could to tell me how beautiful I was. The pressure was slowly starting to increase in my lower stomach, but I held in the grunts and whines to keep him from worrying about me.

Shane effortlessly cupped water in his massive hands and let it cascade over my head to wash the suds out of my hair, causing me to laugh as the water fell over me. The moment was short lived for mere seconds after Shane's hands left my body, pain ran through my body like a current. I screamed in pain as my spine sharply arched, resulting in water escaping the tub and splashing onto the floor. Within seconds, I was out of the bath and in Shane's arms, but instead of being soothed, the pain intensified. Another scream filled the air as pain ripped me apart from the inside out and tears filled my eyes.

A slur of curse words fell from Shane's lips as he held my bare body as close to him as possible. "We need as much physical contact as possible for this to pass," Shane instructed.

I wasted no time pulling him down to me and kissing him with everything I had within me.

251

Shane drew a sharp breath before he kissed me back, his grip on me tightening. I tightly pressed his face between my slippery palms and pruney fingertips and allowed myself to become lost in the kiss. Shane quickly gained control, his skillful tongue sneaking into my mouth and challenging my own to a tedious battle. My fingers found themselves enthralled in Shane's soft hair and Shane shifted me on his lap so that one of his hands was on the low of my back and the other cupping my cheek. His lips snuck away from mine and tenderly kissed down my jaw until he met my mark. I closed my eyes and basked in the pleasurable tingles that spread throughout my body and subdued the pain. A couple light giggles escaped my lips as his feather-like kisses tickled my skin and his teeth nipped at my neck. By now, Shane was breathing heavily, and his grip on me was as tight as it had ever been, borderline painful.

"I need to stop now, or I won't be able to later," Shane growled out, his struggle with his wolf apparent in his voice and his tense muscles under my skin. Almost on cue, he buried his nose into my neck and calmed himself down. Deep breaths in and out. His chest steadily fell up and down against my own, his thundering heartbeat pounding adjacent to mine. "As much as it pains me to say it, please cover up because I don't know what I'll do if you don't, especially in the position you're in."

I looked at our position, and sure enough, I'd somehow ended up straddling him during all the excitement. The water that once clung to my skin now decorated his bare chest and arms from where our bodies touched. I blushed as I quickly climbed off of him and quickly wrapped a towel around myself before I hurried into the closet and threw on some clothes.

After he and his wolf calmed down, we repeated the process for him, but instead of a bath, he insisted on taking a shower despite my many, many protests.

"Shane, hurry up. My arm's getting tired!" I whined as I used my free hand to rub my aching shoulder. Since Shane was showering, I had to contort my body in weird positions not only so I could hold him while staying as dry as possible, but while also giving him privacy.

"Love, I've only been in here for a minute." He chuckled, causing me to roll my eyes.

"Yeah, a minute too long."

Shane merely laughed before he placed a soft kiss on the back of my hand, causing tingles to erupt all the way down to my toes.

After Shane's irritably long shower, we had a relaxing breakfast that included waffles, juice, and a lot of kisses and giggles. As the day went on, it was becoming apparent that Shane's grasp of his control slowly started slipping between the cracks of his fingers. He kept holding me uncomfortably tight as he desperately took in my scent to calm him and his wolf down.

In the end, we decided to look over pack negotiations as it was the only thing that could distract Shane from the heat that was plaguing our bodies and holding us hostage. I didn't know if my body could handle the unbearable pain anymore, especially not in the state I was in due to Morgan and Tracey, but the only key to completely free us from this was something I wasn't sure I was ready for.

"When will everyone get back from the expedition?" I asked Shane, referencing their trip to not only get me but also to add more people to the pack.

"Soon," Shane answered vaguely. It was obvious his focus was no longer on the task at hand, but now on our heat. He was trying not to let it take control of him and I was trying to distract him.

"When will I be able to see Zac or Greg or—"

"You will see no other male!" Shane growled, causing his grip on me to become very firm and I couldn't help the laughter that spilled from my lips.

"You know I don't want to see anyone else." I chuckled as I turned my body so that I was facing him, a smile on my lips. His eyebrows were pulled together, and his lips were pulled down into a slight frown. "You're cute when you're overprotective." I laughed as I squished his cheeks in between my palms, causing him to roll his eyes and his frown to deepen.

"I'm not cute." He pouted as he wrapped his fingers around my wrists and moved my hands from his face. "I'm tough. I'm a tough man, and tough men aren't cute."

Now it was my turn to roll my eyes, causing him to grin before he placed a quick and controlled kiss on my lips.

"Are you hungry?"

I nodded in response. Shane wasted no time scooping me up in his sculpted arms and taking me down to the kitchen where he prepared dinner, making sure to emphasize how much of a "tough man" he was with every chance he got. I ate sitting on Shane's lap, his face constantly nuzzling my neck with his hands around my waist. His sweet whispers were accompanied by my light giggles as the edge of his nose, and the soft skin of his lips moved along my neck.

"I love you," he repeated for the fourth time into my neck. "I won't ever stop. I want to raise pups with you. I want to grow old and wither away with you. I want to comfort you on your low nights and chase away each and every tear that plagues you. And in the moments that you doubt me and my love for you, I will show you. Again"—he placed a light kiss on my mark—"and again"—*Kiss!*—"and again."

By then, I couldn't focus on the amazing food that rested in my lap. Instead, I tried to control my inner wolf who was going out of her mind and the pressure that was lingering in my lower stomach, heavy and sinister. Without a moment's notice, a blade-like pain, unlike anything I'd felt before, buried itself deep within my abdomen, twisting as it buried itself deeper and deeper into me until it reached the center of my very being. A scream unlike any

254

other pressed past my lips. The pain was so intense that it triggered my eyes to shift into their deep black color. Shane barely had time to react before another scream filled the air, the pain violently jerking my body. The plate in my lap dropped to the floor and shattered into pieces, and the food spilled all over the hardwood.

I doubled over in pain, nearly falling off of Shane's lap and landing on the floor with my broken plate and wasted food, but Shane's grip was too strong, and he caught me before I hit the ground. The coppery, salty taste of my blood filled my mouth due to how hard I was biting into my lip to prevent another scream from slipping out.

"Ariel," Shane said as his finger slid under my chin and forced me to look up at him.

I sucked in a sharp breath as my reflection stared back at me, trapped in Shane's glossy black eyes that matched my own. I could see his desire. I could feel it. What scared me the most was that in my reflection, I had the same yearning and hunger in my eyes that he did.

"Love, please let me help you," he whispered as his thumb softly stroked my chin.

At that simple request, my head spun, and my heart pounded against my rib cage, wanting nothing more than to escape my chest and body. Sweat started forming in the back of my neck as I asked myself the silent question.

Do I really want this? Am I really ready?

The answer escaped me before I could fully process the full weight of it.

"Yes," I whispered.

A look of surprise showed on Shane's face before it quickly melted into one of satisfaction before he hungrily pressed his lips against mine. The pain didn't subside, but his skillful lips thankfully gave me something else to focus on. Pain clawed at me once more, causing me to accidentally bite down on Shane's bottom lip. A deep groan escaped his lips before he pulled my body closer and kissed me harder. Like I weighed nothing, he picked me up and within mere moments, we were in our bedroom on our bed with Shane's massive body on top of mine. As if they had minds of their own, my fingers slid beneath Shane's shirt, hesitating as they wrapped around its fabric.

"Do it," he murmured into my lips. "Do whatever you want. This night is yours."

I smiled before the low ripping noise filled the air and Shane's shirt effortlessly fluttered to the floor. This excited Shane and his kisses became rougher and messier. Untamed and uncontrollable, just the way I wanted it; rash and in the moment.

Before long, my lips strayed away from his soft lips and wandered down his structured jawline. Groans escaped his lips as my lips traveled down to the base of his throat. He pulled my hips to him, and a deep aroused growl escaped his lips as my tongue found the grove between his neck and shoulder. I smiled against his skin. I liked having this effect on him.

"Shane," I whispered, placing wet, open-mouthed kisses on his neck. "Let me mark you. I want everyone to know you're mine and only mine." My voice came out huskier than I intended, but when Shane tensed beneath me, I didn't mind. I knew I was driving him crazy.

"Do it," he begged, longing evident behind his voice. "I want everyone to know that I belong to my beautiful, strong luna."

I couldn't help the pride I felt in my chest as I continued to lick and prime his neck before my canines elongated. It was highly unusual for the female to mark the male and it made me giddy that Shane wanted it so badly. I placed one more soft kiss on his neck before I buried my canines into him.

He drew in a sharp breath as his grip on me became tighter. I held him for a few moments until he sighed and relaxed under my touch, pleasure rushing through me as it ran through him. It was complete.

I removed my teeth and gently licked away his excess blood while my saliva acted as a solvent to help him heal quicker. Once I was done, I placed another kiss on his new mark, causing him to shiver under my fingertips.

"My Goddess, Ariel. You amaze me. Every time I think you can't do something to surprise me, you push my expectations through the roof, and it's extremely arousing," he admitted, causing me to smile before our lips found each other again. "You're just so perfect, my love. Too perfect . . ." he stated as he rested his forehead on mine. "I don't deserve you."

I brought a hand up to his cheek and gently stroked it. "You're perfect, Shane. Don't ever doubt it. I love you."

"Not as much as I love you," he countered before he kissed me once more, a fiery intensity behind it I'd never felt before.

"May I?" Shane asked lowly, my shirt held tightly between his fingertips.

I bit my lip and nodded.

"I can slow down if you need me to," he said, noticing the second's worth of hesitation, but I shook my head.

"I'm ready," I said, barely above a whisper.

A smile grew on his face before he delicately slid my shirt off, his eyes hungrily taking in every detail of my body; every curve, dip, imperfection, and scar.

"You're beautiful," he whispered as he carefully took my waist in his hands as if he were afraid that I would push him away. "I'm so proud to call you mine."

I couldn't fight my smile as he cupped my cheek.

"Goddess, Ariel. I can't think straight when you smile at me like that." He chuckled softly, a small smile of his own spreading across his lips.

"Luckily, you don't need to think to kiss me," I quipped before I pulled his lips back to mine.

That night, we gave ourselves to each other, a priceless gift to claim. Nothing but the moon itself witnessed us or heard our names spill from each other's lips. Shane's kisses found every part of me, and while I wasn't the type to kiss and tell, I could say that Shane showed me a part of myself that even I knew nothing about, and I to him. Even though it wasn't under the ideal circumstances—which would've been our honeymoon after our grand, beautiful wedding—it didn't matter. I knew I truly loved this man and he loved me, and I knew that one day, hopefully soon, we'd be one through marriage.

Thoughts of our wedding flooded my head as we lay next to each other with the moon spilling itself over us, causing droplets of our sweat to be illuminated by its light, and smiles lay across our drunken faces as we held each other close.

"I love you, Ariel," Shane whispered into my neck where he was placing multiple light kisses.

"I love you too, Shane," I whispered back.

We fell asleep in each other's arms with goofy smiles on our faces and endless love in our hearts.

Passed

Unknown

They passed.

They passed.

I had finally found the right mates to take my place and to bear the burdens and stress that came with this job. This sweet dream that could easily turn into a hellish nightmare with one slip up. And now it was time for them to step up to the plate.

It was time for a new Moon Goddess and God.

CHAPTER THIRTY-THREE

I awoke to gentle movements on my back. It moved back and forth in a soothing pattern that earned a gentle sigh from my lips as my eyes fluttered open and I was met by Shane's smiling face.

"Good morning, love," he greeted as his fingers started a new yet equally soothing pattern along my back. "How was your sleep?"

"Amazing," I answered honestly, causing him to grin before he craned his neck down to kiss me. Somehow in my sleeping state, I'd made my way on top of Shane and used him as my own personal bed, not that either of us seemed to mind.

My attention turned to the healing mark on Shane's neck, and I couldn't help the pride that bubbled in my chest.

"I love it," Shane said. "The mark. I like being claimed by you. I also really like your dominant side. It's really hot." Shane's fingers found a lock of my hair, which he twirled between his fingers as I rested my cheek against his sculpted chest and closed my eyes, letting myself indulge in the feeling.

Unlike the pain that came when he marked me, all I felt was a very dull throb. I guess compared to the pain I'd recently endured, a little headache was nothing.

"What is the plan for today, love?" he asked softly, his hand now rubbing the bare skin of my back once again.

"I want to see Zac and Jess," I admitted. "And Greg and Aiden and Chris. I want to make sure that the pack is okay."

Shane let out a soft chuckle before he kissed my forehead, causing my eyebrows to furrow.

"What?"

"You're just like a true luna, always wanting to make sure that everyone else is okay."

"It is my job. They risked their lives for me, so the least I can do is make sure that they're alright."

"You're their luna, Ariel. Of course, they're going to risk their lives to protect yours."

"I know, and I love them for it."

"Well then, you'll be pleased to know that there haven't been any major casualties on our side and we've taken in almost three-quarter of Morgan's pack."

"Good," I said, pride bubbling within me at the fact that our pack was so strong both mentally and physically. I was proud that they were smart and vigilant. I was proud that they were my family. "I'm not surprised though. They did have a handsome and fearless alpha leading them," I added to fluff Shane's ego a bit.

"That they do." He chuckled. "But it was their beautiful luna who truly motivated them."

I rolled my eyes just as his lips met mine. The kiss was soft, though passion pulsed through it like a heartbeat. Shane effortlessly repositioned my body so that he could have access to my lips. My nails dug into his shoulders as the kiss slowly intensified, all while a weird pressure built up in my stomach, all too familiar and the timing all too wrong.

"Shane," I whispered, the sentence I was trying to form dying on my lips as he started placing gentle kisses down my neck. The emptiness in my stomach grew and traveled upward. Before I could pull away or even blink, one of the loudest growls filled the otherwise silent room. Shane instantly pulled away and assumed a protective stance over me as his eyes scanned the room for a threat, but when they landed on my pink cheeks, his lips pulled into a full-on smile. "Sorry. I'm really hungry."

Shane threw his head back and laughed before he released me and allowed me to put on some clothes. I merely rolled my eyes before I threw my legs over the side of the bed and left the safety of the sheets. As I walked out into the open with my body bare and very visible, I felt Shane's eyes burning into my back. Instead of immensely blushing like I normally would, a sense of satisfaction bubbled up in my chest. It felt almost natural to be naked in front of him, especially after how well we had gotten to know each other's bodies last night. Shane's eyes continued to trail after me while he let out a few whistles every now and then until I made it into the closet where I slid on an oversized sweatshirt over my bra and underwear. When I came out from the closet, Shane was out of bed as well, sporting a pair of boxers he'd most likely grabbed from the dresser.

"What would you like for breakfast?" Shane asked.

"Pancakes," I answered instantly, my mouth watering at the thought of the buttery paradise.

"Your wish is my command," Shane said before he led me down to the kitchen where he created a mountain of delicious looking and smelling pancakes. I barely waited until he placed the last one on the top of the mound before I began digging in, inhaling the food as if it were air.

Shane's chuckle pulled me out of the food trance I was in, and I realized that I'd eaten most of the food he'd prepared.

"Did you want any?" I asked, embarrassed that I'd completely pigged out like that.

"I'm fine. Please, continue," Shane said with an amused smile on his lips, causing me to shrug.

"Remember that later when you come crawling back to me trying to jump into my pancake ocean," I said, ignoring Shane's confused expression before I dove back into my syrup and butter covered heaven.

After devouring all the pancakes, Shane and I went up to his office and started looking over more negotiations and pack statistics. Afterward, we got on the phone with Aiden who gave us an extensive and thorough progress report of the battle, including the number of injured or killed on both sides and how many new pack members we had. Like Shane had told me earlier, there had been no major casualties on our side, just scratches and a couple of broken bones, while over three-quarter of the warriors from my former pack were either killed, taken prisoner, or had surrendered.

"We should be back by eight."

"Okay. Good job taking over while I'm here with Ariel. I'm impressed."

"Thank you. Chris also helped immensely," Aiden said, causing Shane to nod.

"I'll keep that in mind. We'll see you at eight, and even though we may be winning, you always need to keep your eyes peeled, understood?"

"Of course, Alpha. Anything else?"

"Don't treat the prisoners too badly unless they come after you first," I instructed. The command caused Shane's eyebrow to raise as he opened his mouth, but I cut him off. "They were just following their alpha's orders just like you are. It's not their fault that they had a murderous and corrupt one."

"But if this would've weighed in their favor, they wouldn't show us any mercy," Aiden argued. "So why should we—"

"Aiden, I might be your friend, but I am also your luna, and as your luna, I made an order. An order that you will follow without question. Clear?"

"Yes, Luna. I'm sorry for questioning you," he apologized.

"Good. You are dismissed."

Then the line went dead, and Shane looked at me, conflict evident in his eyes.

"What?" I questioned, the curiosity about what was going on behind his eyes gnawing at me.

"Not that I doubt you, but I kinda agree with Aiden on that one," Shane admitted. "I mean, come on. If this had gone in their favor, they'd show no mercy. They'd simply kill us and send our heads to our family as a gruesome warning."

"That's why we're showing them mercy," I explained. "It's not their fault that their blood-thirsty alpha taught them to be that way. Will there be punishment for their indiscretions? Of course, but we will also be merciful."

"But Ariel, I—"

"Trust me, Shane. I know what it's like to be a prisoner: locked up, neglected, and abused. I'm not going to let that happen to anyone else who doesn't deserve it to that extent. Not on my watch," I said, my voice now nearly above a whisper as the agonizing memories spread through my mind like dye in water. "Not even our prisoners."

Shane's jaw became tight at the mention of what I'd endured. Nevertheless, he nodded before pulling me closer into his chest. We just stayed like that, trapped in a silent embrace with neither one of us moving or daring to breathe too loudly. I allowed my eyes to slowly shut as Shane's middle finger moved over the skin that rested on top of my spine, gently moving up and down along with my spine's peaks and valleys. The familiar pounding of his heart traveled through my ears, the beat quickly synchronizing with my own.

"You need some rest. Your body still needs time to recover."

It seemed like before I could open my mouth to utter a protest, we were already in our bedroom with Shane gently sliding me underneath the sheets I'd just been under mere hours ago.

"Get some rest," Shane gently instructed as my heavy lids, which had been shut throughout the whole ordeal, slowly lifted a few millimeters.

"Where are you going?" I asked, sleep already weighing down on my words.

"I have to finish up some things. I'll just be in the office if you need me." He placed a soft lingering kiss on my forehead before he walked out of the door, and as soon as he was no longer in sight, I succumbed to my drowsiness and fell into the arms of sleep.

* * *

"How's she doing?" Chris's muffled voice questioned, causing me to slowly peel my eyes open.

As soon as my eyes cleared up, I saw that I was still in bed. The sheet on the other side was turned up as if someone had just gotten out of it, and from the abundance of Shane's scent next to and on me, I knew he'd been there.

"Her body and mind still need time to rest," Shane's voice responded from the other side of our closed bedroom door. "I'm just . . . I'm just so proud of her. She went through hell and back, yet her concerns are of the pack instead of herself."

A small smile grew on my face hearing my mate speak so fondly of me even while he thought I was still sleeping.

"But I can tell it's taking a toll on her though. I can see it in her eyes like a small darkness. I'm just worried that it'll grow and swallow the shine in her eyes. I just hate that I can't even help her except talking with her about it, which I know she hates, but what else can I do?" Sorrow and a twinge of guilt weighed in his words.

"I just wish I could've been there to protect her, so none of this had to happen."

"Me too," Chris agreed. "But she became stronger from it, and though how it happened isn't ideal, she's growing from it. As a luna and a person."

"I guess you're right." Shane sighed, and I could imagine him running his hands through his already messy hair as he usually did.

"So based on how willingly you left her side, I'm guessing she's not in heat anymore?"

"No, she's not. But my Goddess, she's just so . . . amazing inside and out. I don't understand how I got the honor of calling her mine," Shane fondly stated, causing my heart to flutter.

"Dude, that's my sister. I don't need your details!" Chris whined, obviously uncomfortable with the conversation.

"I'm sorry, but your sister is just so perfect."

"She is pretty amazing," Chris agreed. "Just let me know when she's awake, okay? I wanna see my baby sister."

"Of course," Shane said, ending the conversation and letting me know I needed to close my eyes and pretend to sleep. Not less than a second later, I heard him wander into the room and close the door behind him.

I couldn't keep the corners of my mouth from turning up a little when he slid into bed with me and pulled me deep into his deep embrace.

"You heard every word of that, didn't you?" Shane whispered into my ears, causing a full-blown smile to grow across my face as I opened my eyes.

"How did you know?" I chuckled as his lips met mine for a quick peck.

"Your smile gave you away," he replied simply.

"What if I was just having a dream about food or something and I was just smiling because in my dream the food was so good?"

266

"Highly unlikely unless you were dreaming about my food." He gloated, causing me to roll my eyes as he pulled me onto his lap.

"Everyone's home."

A smile instantly rushed to my face at that simple sentence.

"There have officially been no deaths on our side, and all of the injuries are being treated and now healing."

I pulled him in, and our lips met.

"What was that for?" he asked as we parted.

"For leading them." I shrugged, causing Shane to shake his head.

"I had little to do with it. All I did was lead them into battle, everything else was out of their love for their luna."

"Can we go see everyone?" I asked, eager to meet each and every person who put their lives on the line to put me back into Shane's arms.

"Of course," Shane granted, and after taking our shower, we went out.

I stopped by Chris's room, but he was passed out, undoubtedly tired from the tedious battle he fought for me. Instead of waking him up and depriving him of the sleep I knew he needed, I kissed his forehead and made the silent promise of seeing him as soon as he woke up.

Jessica and Aiden were spending well needed time with one another at Aiden's house that I didn't want to disturb either, and Greg and Zac were both sound asleep on Greg's bed, both snoring loudly with their limbs extended as if they were eagles or starfish. Judging from the dark circles that were visible on Zac's face, it seemed like he hadn't gotten a good rest in a long time. Knowing him, it was because he was too worried about me and the rest of the pack. Now he could finally rest knowing we were all safe.

That only left the pack members. When we went to see them, Shane held me tightly by his side, not in an overprotective way, but in a way to show me off. I also didn't miss the way he'd move his head to show off his new mark, which sent tingles throughout my body.

We shared smiles and small talk with every pack member until it was late at night and there was no one left. Despite my protests, Shane carried me all the way home and into our bed where we shared feverish kisses and airy sighs. By the time we'd settled down, we were in our underwear. He was in his briefs and I in my bra and underwear with my head gingerly resting against his bare chest. Despite my efforts to ignore it, an odd discomfort that I'd never felt before settled in my stomach, heavy yet weightless.

"Are you alright?" Shane asked with a soft kiss to the forehead.

"Yeah," I lied. "Just need some more sleep."

"Today was a busy day," Shane agreed. "Good night, Ariel."

I didn't respond, worry and confusion growing in me at the same rate as the weight became heavier and heavier.

CHAPTER THIRTY-FOUR

I woke up to the uncontrollable need to vomit. Before my eyes had even fully opened, I was in the bathroom throwing up whatever was left in my stomach from the night before. Within seconds, my shoulder-length hair was being pulled back from my face as soothing circles accompanied by sparks danced across my back. After about three minutes, I flushed the toilet, disgusted with what had just come out from my body.

"You okay? You want anything to drink?" Shane questioned.

"I'm fine," I lied, the nauseating taste still staining my taste buds. "I just need some fluids."

Shane looked at me with uncertainty. It was extremely rare for a lycan to get sick, let alone throw up with the intensity I had. There was one condition though, and I refused to think about it. It was nearly impossible, so I didn't want to waste my breath on it. Yet, I still couldn't keep my heart from beating a bit faster every time the thought crossed my mind.

Shane carefully carried me to the kitchen as if I'd shatter if he handled me too rough. Despite my unknown condition, Shane held me close to his body as he made me a smoothie. I was thankful that we were alone at the moment. I wasn't sure where Chris, Zac, and Greg were since we'd usually be eating breakfast and cracking jokes with each other by this time of day, but I didn't have the strength to ask Shane.

"It should make you feel better," he said softly as he used one hand to pour the thick liquid into a glass while he held me tight with the other. "My mom used to make this for me all the time when I was younger, and she could still stand the sight of me."

I rolled my eyes at the last part before I closed my eyes and chugged the liquid down my throat, a small shiver moving through my body as the thick substance traveled down. Shane looked at me, holding his breath waiting to see what would happen.

I barely made it to the bathroom.

My body violently shook in Shane's arms as the three gulps I'd taken, grimly left my body, causing me to once again collapse into Shane's arms once I was done since my body felt too weak to stay upright on its own. Shane held me while he gently pressed the back of his hand to my forehead.

"You're not warm . . ." He trailed off as his thick eyebrows pulled together and I knew that gears began to turn deep within his brain. "I need to call Samantha to make sure you're okay. Your body might've been too weak for the heat, and we just got so carried away that we didn't even think about what she said about your body and health and—"

"My body's fine," I interrupted, though that statement wasn't exactly true this very moment in time. "I just . . ." I trailed off, struggling to come up with another reasonable explanation, but it eluded me and only left me with the one explanation that I refused to accept, so I let the sentence fade and die on my lips.

"Ariel . . . ," Shane said. The tone of his voice and the look in his eyes told me he'd come to the same horrid conclusion I had.

"Please don't." I groaned as I ran my hands down my face.

"I mean, it was pretty intense, and we didn't use protection and—"

"Shane," I said, putting a bit more authority behind my voice. "You and I know that there's a very thin chance of it being that."

It tended to be hard for lycans to conceive children during heat because of the weird chemistry in our bodies, but when we did, we knew within a couple days. It was way faster than humans did, meaning that it only took four months until the baby was ready due to its rapid growth and development.

"I know, but just . . . Can you please just take the test so I can have peace of mind?" he asked, his eyes and voice teaming up against me in a way both he and I knew I couldn't say no to.

I nodded.

"Thank you," he whispered before placing a kiss on my cheek. "And if you really are pregnant," he started, and my mind raced with all the possible ways he could end the sentence. "It won't change a thing. There'll just be more of you in this world for me to love."

The corners of my lips pulled up, and air exited my nose. I sighed with relief, a sign that I was thankful. Shane's eyes glazed over as he linked someone before they quickly returned to normal.

"Come on," he said as he stood up and offered me his hand.

"Where are we going?" I asked as I let him help me to my feet.

"Where do you want to go?" he questioned, and before I could even open my mouth to form words, the doorbell rang throughout the house. "That should be Sam."

"That was fast," I said a bit skeptically.

"Yeah," Shane said, awkwardly rubbing the back of his neck. "She was planning to come by anyway to make sure that you're okay. Also, she wanted to make sure when we were 'wrestling'—as she chose to call it—that I didn't 'put you in too tight of a choke hold'—still her words, by the way."

I couldn't help but laugh at her analogies and imagined the raging blush on her cheeks. "Okay, John Cena. Let's go before the ref calls a foul or whatever they do in wrestling."

We walked to the front door, my nerves bouncing out of control, all jokes aside. I reached the door before Shane, and I silently prayed he couldn't see how badly I was shaking. I'd always wanted pups, but now that the time could possibly be on me, I was questioning it.

"Hey, Sam." "Good morning, Samantha," we spoke at the same time as I opened the door.

Shane's arm instinctively wrapped around my waist and pulled me an inch closer.

"Good morning," she greeted warmly before thrusting her hand out that held the dreaded test at me. "How are you feeling?"

"Fine. Thanks," I said as I reluctantly took the test from her. The plastic felt cold and heavy against my fingertips.

"She woke up throwing up this morning," Shane said, causing me to narrow my eyes at him.

"And I'm fine," I said tightly, causing Shane to roll his eyes.

"We'll never know until you take the test, Ariel," Samantha pointed out, and my heart instantly started beating faster.

"Right." I sighed as I turned and headed toward the bathroom with Shane and Samantha right on my heels.

I slowly entered the bathroom, and as I closed the door, Shane and my eyes locked. It was as if his hazel-green orbs were magic and could calm me down with a single look, no matter how long or short it lasted. I took a deep breath as soon as the door was fully closed and looked at the test between my fingers. Lines on a tiny screen would determine how my life would go from here on out. Forever and always. For better or worse.

CHAPTER THIRTY-FIVE

Nervousness was clawing at me from the inside. My leg was bouncing uncontrollably, and my mind was racing. What if I turned out like my father, ruthless and cold toward my pup or even pups? What if I let Ariel down? What if I let them all down?

"Shane," Samantha said gently as she hesitantly pressed her fingertips to my knee. Once she saw that I wasn't going to yell or snap at her, she firmly pressed the rest of her hand on my hyperactive knee to put it to rest. "Calm down. Everything's gonna be alright. You just need to calm down."

"But what if it isn't?" I questioned, uncertainty bubbling up in my chest as words began spilling from my lips. "What if I'm like my father? What if I can't provide them with what they need?" My focus shifted from Samantha to the bathroom door that was hiding my mate. "I don't want to let her down, Samantha," I said barely above a whisper before I looked at her once more. "It's not an option."

"Shane, you'll be an amazing father, rest assured. No matter what happens, I doubt you could let Ariel or the pup, or even pups down unless you honestly didn't care or try."

I took in a deep breath before I nodded. "Thanks, Samantha. Sometimes it's just hard to think straight when—"

My words were interrupted by the faint sound of the door unlocking, but it sounded like a roll of thunder in my anxious ears. Within a second, I was on my feet as Ariel slowly opened the door. Her hand shook ever so slightly as it had when she opened the front door for Samantha. Tears were welling up in her eyes, and I could hear her rapid heartbeat.

"What's wrong, love?" I asked as I quickly approached her and captured her in my arms.

She let out a small chuckle as she looked up at me through tear-filled eyes, a small smile tugging at her lips. "Nothing's wrong," she said before she handed the test over so that I could see the two prominent pink lines streaked across its screen. "Nothing at all."

"I'm a father," I whispered, disbelief rising within me, but it was quickly chased away with excitement and happiness. "I'm a father!" I exclaimed as my arms wound tighter around her and I lifted her off the ground.

Her giggles filled the air as I spun her around. My inner wolf was howling with excitement and joy, but overall, we felt pride for what we'd done together. I swiftly placed my lips on hers, and I could taste the salt from her joy-filled tears.

"Ariel, I love you so much," I whispered into her mouth. "I love you so much."

"I love you too," she whispered back as she pulled away. "I mean . . . I'm a mom. A mom, Shane. I just can't . . . Wow." She chuckled. Then she shook her head as she placed her hands on each side of her head almost woefully.

"What's wrong?" I asked softly, hating to see her like this at a time so happy.

274

"I just . . . I don't know if I'm ready, Shane," she whispered as if she were embarrassed. "I don't know if I'm ready for this yet . . . emotionally or physically."

I opened my mouth to offer words of comfort to her, but what could I say to her to show her how strong she was in my eyes that I hadn't told her before? Instead of using words, I did the next best thing: I hugged her. I gently rocked her side to side as I looked at Samantha who was still sitting on the couch and hadn't uttered a single word throughout the whole endeavor. She simply shrugged, unable to give me any help or guidance, so I simply buried my face in Ariel's hair and allowed her to cry, offering a "there, there" or "it's okay" every now and then.

"I just want to be the best parent I can be for them," she said, her voice broken and hoarse from her sobs. "I don't want to disappoint them."

"You won't," I instantly reassured her as I shook my head and looked down at her. "You could never let them down. You are an amazing mate, luna, and soon-to-be mother. You are strong, independent, and beautiful and, my Goddess, I wish you could just see yourself the way I do because you're simply amazing."

"Don't do that," she groaned as she shook her head.

"What?" Confusion easily clouded my brain as my eyebrows pulled together.

"Say those things. Every time I feel like falling apart you just catch my pieces and put me back together again. And the way you look at me makes me feel so—"

"Appreciated?"

She shook her head. "Loved . . . and I don't deserve the love you're giving me."

"Stop talking like that, Ariel. Just let me do this for you."

"Do what?"

"Love you," I stated simply. "Just let me love you." I gently placed my lips on hers and savored every second our lips were

275

touching and praised the endless sparks that flowed through my body as I simply held her in my arms.

After a few more moments, I forced myself to pull away before I got ahead of myself. "Let's get you checked up so that if I feel like doing a bit of wrestling later, I'll know if it's okay or not," I said in a low voice with a small smile just to ease Ariel's raging emotions, and it worked.

Ariel rolled her eyes though I could see a smile growing on her face as a small blush grew on Samantha's cheeks.

"Fine," she conceded.

"Then after this," I said, gently placing a hand on her belly, "we can tell everyone about the miracle of life growing inside of you."

We sat down on the couch with Ariel resting on my lap and went through Ariel's check-up without a single hitch.

"As for your comment earlier," Samantha said, looking at me, "you probably shouldn't do any 'wrestling' for the time being." She laughed as she used her fingers as air quotes around wrestling.

"Man." I pouted as I wrapped my arms around Ariel and rested my chin on her shoulder. "I really wanted to try some new moves with you."

"Shane!" Ariel gasped, awkwardly laughing to play off her deep red blush, causing me to laugh as I kissed her cheek.

"Thanks, Samantha," I said after I could contain my laughter.

"Of course." She smiled politely. "We'll have another appointment next month to check on the progress of the baby. But Ariel, be aware that the chemistry in your body is going to be thrown off drastically in the first few weeks and the last."

"I understand." Ariel nodded as she gently started running her hands through my hair since my head was still resting on her shoulder.

"Good. Make sure that you avoid any raw meat and alcoholic beverages. If you have any questions or if your stomach

276

starts hurting or you experience unusual bleeding, let me know immediately."

"I will," Ariel said as she pulled herself off of my lap, causing me to groan not only because my chin rest was gone, but also because she removed her fingers from my hair. "Thank you, Samantha. For everything." She wrapped her up in her arms and gave her a hug.

"Of course, Ariel," she said. "You guys are like a second family to me."

Ariel smiled in response before she turned to me, gesturing with her eyes for me to get up, which I obeyed without argument.

"Thank you for looking after my mate and both of my brothers in our time of need," I said as I gently hugged her with genuine gratitude. "Without you, my brothers might not be here."

"It's no problem." She smiled though it was obvious that she still felt a bit uncomfortable with her alpha speaking to her so casually. "Call me if you have any concerns," she said before offering both of us a wave before she let herself out.

"Are you ready, love?" I asked as I pulled her back into me.

She rested her head on my chest and let her eyes flutter closed. "Not in the slightest," she admitted, causing me to chuckle before I kissed the crown of her head.

"You're going to be an amazing mother, Ariel," I reassured as I held her a bit closer. "You're gonna raise strong pups that will hopefully take over for us one day. We'll love and support them no matter what, and when they look back at us, long after we're dust in the ground, they're gonna say, 'Wow. We had great parents. But most importantly, an amazing mom.'"

Ariel chuckled though her eyes were still closed before she buried her face deeper into my chest. "We might as well change and tell everyone the news." She sighed after a few moments of silence.

"That or wait for them to come knocking down our door because they heard it from Samantha and not you." I followed her upstairs and got ready with her, unable to tear my eyes from the

277

incredible work of art that was her body, and knowing that she was carrying what was ours made her that much more incredible.

Excitement bubbled within me. I didn't realize I wasn't moving anymore and was just staring until she turned and looked at me. Her body was only covered with her sweatpants and bra she was wearing.

"What?" She chuckled.

"Nothing." I shook my head. "It's just . . ." I trailed off, searching for words I could use to describe how I was feeling. "I'm so happy that we're starting this new chapter in our lives together."

The corners of her lips pulled up in a smile before she walked over to me and got on her tiptoes before giving me a quick kiss on the lips. Her kiss told me more than words ever could.

*   *   *

Ariel was practically shaking as we prepared to tell everyone the news. It was past noon, and Ariel sent out a message through the link letting everyone know that we had something important to tell them, but now she looked like she regretted it.

"Babe, relax," I said gently as I wrapped my fingers around her wrist to prevent her from the restless pacing she'd been doing and put her hyperactive hand movements to rest. "Everything is going to be fine. We've already established that, have we not?" I asked as I pulled her onto my lap since I was sitting on our bed.

She nodded mutely as she looked down at her hands as she played with her newly grown hair. Goddess, I still couldn't get over the fact that I'd let her slip through my fingers and go through hell for all those wretched days. I shook my head to rid myself of those thoughts as I took her hands in mine.

"Then what's on your mind?"

"I'm just . . . worried, I guess," she confessed as she used one of her hands to tuck her hair behind her ear before placing it back in mine again, but her eyes still refused to meet mine. "I mean

. . . What if their reactions aren't the best? What if Chris's reaction isn't the best? I know that he hasn't been the best brother, but he's still my brother, Shane. As weird as it may sound, I don't want to let him down or disappoint him, or anyone else for that matter." She looked up at me, and I could see how truly tired she was, not just physically but also mentally and emotionally. "Am I crazy? Am I overthinking? It's just . . . Goddess, these past few weeks messed me up so bad, and things that shouldn't be important to me are suddenly all my life revolves around, and now I'm not making any sense, and it's just—"

I placed a soft kiss on her lips to keep her words from flowing from her mouth because I knew if she kept going she'd give herself a panic attack and I didn't want to see her go through that again. It would eat me alive knowing there was nothing I could do about it.

"It's alright. You're alright, Ariel," I muttered into her lips before I kissed her again and again and again until she relaxed under my lips and wrapped her arms around me and kissed me back. "Just breathe, okay? Can you do that for me?" I questioned softly, and she nodded.

I needed to get her a counselor or at least get her to open up and talk to me because she was holding her thoughts and emotions back and eventually they'd all spill out like a broken dam.

"Thank you," she whispered, and I gave her another soft kiss.

"You're welcome."

After taking a few more deep breaths, she nodded then said, "I'm ready."

Instead of asking her if she was sure, I let her lace her fingers with my own and lead me out of our room and down to the family room where everyone was gathered. As we neared the room, we heard light chatter floating among them. Once we entered the room, I saw Chris chatting with them though he looked highly uncomfortable.

"Ari!" Zac cried as he ran to Ariel and wrapped his arms around her legs because that was as high as he could reach. "I missed you so much!"

"I missed you too, Zac." She smiled as she happily embraced him.

All at once, Greg, Aiden, and Jess ran to Ariel and greedily embraced her, all of them talking at once. Chris hung back, seeming a bit uncomfortable and wanting to talk to Ariel alone. Though I had felt a trace of anger toward him for leaving Ariel, he'd shown that he truly cared for her and deeply regretted leaving her alone to face that coward Morgan. Though he'd helped with the pack while Ariel was away and played a major role in helping us get her back, it still seemed like he felt the need to prove himself and was constantly walking on eggshells around Ariel. I couldn't help but feel a bit sorry for him.

"Ariel, I-I missed you so much," Greg confessed, his eyes becoming glassy as he hugged her.

"Aww, Greg. I missed you too," Ariel said as she wrapped him into a warm motherly hug. "I missed all of you. I tried to visit you guys, but you were either asleep or out." She chuckled before her eyes found Chris who still hadn't said or done anything to show how much he'd missed his sister.

"Hi, Chris," she greeted, causing everyone's attention to fall on Chris once they noticed he wasn't among them and not hugging Ariel like they were. "Are you going to join in on this group hug or just stand there like a statue?" She chuckled though she was eagerly awaiting his response.

"S-Sorry," he stammered. "It's just . . . Goddess, I let you down again . . ."

"Chris, it's not your fault. None of you is at fault," she said, her eyes meeting everyone's and lingering on mine a bit longer before she looked at Chris again. "*None* of this is your fault," she repeated as if she were saying, "*I don't blame you for anything. Not even Morgan's abuse.*"

280

A look of relief spread across Chris' face as the edges of his lips slightly rugged up. "Now come over here and give your sister a hug."

A full smile grew on Chris' face before he shamelessly embraced Ariel. I could even see a smile on Ariel's face too.

"Now, what was the big news you wanted to tell us, baby sister?"

Ariel visibly tensed as she looked at me. I could tell she really didn't want to talk about it.

"We don't have to, Ariel. We can wait and tell them—"

"I'm pregnant," she said so softly that even with my enhanced hearing, I struggled to hear her.

"Wh-What?" Chris stammered and almost instantly, I felt waves of Ariel's regret through the link quickly followed by panic.

I hurried over to her and held her in an embrace, placing her head next to the mark she'd given me on my neck. She greedily took my scent in, and she slowly relaxed.

"Ariel's pregnant," I repeated. "We're having pups."

"Oh my gosh . . ." Chris trailed off, and instantly, Ariel looked up at him.

"Chris, I—"

"My baby sister is going to be a mother!" He smiled, causing all sense of worry and panic to melt off Ariel's face and be replaced by happiness and euphoria as he tenderly wrapped his arms around her.

CHAPTER THIRTY-SIX

"Chris, I swear to the Moon Goddess herself if you don't give me those pickles, I will drop kick you!" Were the first words I heard as I entered the house, but I wasn't surprised. I heard things along those lines every day now.

It had been a little over a month since my little mate, and I found out she was pregnant and these past weeks had been a roller coaster, especially with the chemistry in Ariel's body changing so rapidly and her cravings starting to kick in. The baby was growing faster than expected, and she had developed a small baby bump.

The stress was slowly getting to her, but I managed to calm her down each time. We took her to a counselor for professional help, but the counselor said that Ariel merely talking to and having contact with me would do her much more good than sitting down in a room for an hour twice a week. So that was what I did. I stuck by my mate through thick and thin.

I was here for every tear, every cold sweat, and every scream, and I wouldn't trade it for the world. As long as I could be there for my mate in her time of need, that was all that mattered to me.

As I walked into the kitchen, I saw Chris in fits of laughter as he held a large jar of pickles over his head as my pregnant mate fruitlessly jumped in an attempt to retrieve them from his grasp.

"Christopher Alec Carter, if you don't give me those pickles in the next five seconds, my foot will be so far up your rear that you'll be able to taste my toes for breakfast and think about my toenails!"

"What?" Chris asked, his eyebrows furrowing in confusion at Ariel's weird analogy.

"Just give me the pickles, Chris!" She whined as she made another attempt, but Chris was just too tall.

"I don't think I—Ow!" he cried as Ariel delivered a hard punch to his stomach.

As he hunched over to cradle his stomach, Ariel simply snatched the pickles from his now lowered hand. A satisfied smile grew on her lips as she effortlessly popped open the lid.

"What the—"

"Never deny a girl of her pickles." She growled, causing a small chuckle to escape my lips and Ariel's attention to snap toward me with her eyes narrowed. "Are you laughing at me?" She growled lowly as she approached me, and even in her pregnant state with pickles in her hands, she still scared me beyond my wits. And she looked extremely hot.

"Wouldn't dream of it, my luna," I said as I took her free hand and kissed the back of it.

She narrowed her eyes at me before she pulled her hand out of mine and roughly grabbed my collar. "You are so lucky that I love you because if I didn't, you would definitely be feeling my pregnant wrath right now," she grumbled as she dragged me all the way upstairs into our bedroom where she threw me down on the bed.

I gently set the bags full of tubs of ice cream I'd gotten from the store down while she placed the large jar of pickles on the nightstand. She then straddled my waist and savagely claimed my lips while her arms were tightly wrapped around my shoulders as the kiss deepened. I quickly gained control of the dangerous kiss and flipped us so that I was on top, being extra careful that none of my body weight pressed down on her.

"Ariel, you know you shouldn't come at me like that, knowing that it will lead to the very thing Samantha told us to avoid during your pregnant state," I said lowly into her lips, but she silenced me by kissing me deeper. Harder.

Her hands slid under my shirt and set every part of skin she touched ablaze before they roughly gripped my shirt and ripped it off in one swift move.

"Ariel, we need to stop before I can't." I grunted as her lips wandered away from mine as she flipped us back around so that she was straddling me once more.

She started placing sinful kisses on my mark, and I let out a throaty groan as I held her closer. My desires slowly pushed to the surface as my fingers slowly traced her spine and moved toward the brim of her shirt. She sighed, and her warm breath cascaded over my mark and sent a shiver down my spine.

Suddenly, a scent rushed into my nose as it quickly approached us. Before I could pull myself out of my lust filled trance or take my hands out from under Ariel's shirt where she'd failed to put on a bra, the door burst open. Within a second, I wasn't under Ariel anymore but rather in front of her in a protective stance until my brain realized who was in our doorway.

Zac.

"Hey, Zac." I chuckled nervously before I turned to Ariel to make sure she was alright.

Once she nodded, I turned back to Zac who was looking at us in confusion.

"You gotta start knocking. Okay?" I said as I got off the bed and scooped him up in my arms before I turned back to Ariel. "Your ice cream and spoon are in the bag. Enjoy your weird mix of pickles and ice cream, love," I said before I walked Zac out of the room.

"I'm sorry. My hormones got the best of me."

I heard Ariel's soft voice through our link, and I could almost see her blush. The corners of my lips pulled up into a small grin. *"Don't worry, love. I had about as much control as you did and I loved every second of it,"* I admitted. *"I just wish we could've continued without the interruption or without the chance of it affecting the baby."*

"Me too," she agreed before she shut off the connection.

"What did you need, bud?" I asked as I carried Zac downstairs toward the kitchen where Chris was leaning against the counter still recovering from Ariel's blow.

"Remind me not to get on her bad side." Chris groaned, causing me to chuckle as I clapped him on the back.

"I wanted to spend some time with you." Zac shrugged as I put him down. "But you guys were busy." His eyebrows furrowed as he spoke and I instantly felt bad.

He shouldn't have seen that.

"Look, Zac. I'm sorry you saw—"

"Don't worry. I've seen Mommy and Daddy do worse."

*   *   *

ARIEL

"He said what?" I laughed after Shane told me what Zac had told him after our intense moment when I'd foolishly let my raging hormones get the best of me.

"He looked me in the eye and explicitly said, 'Don't worry. I've seen Mommy and Daddy do worse.' " Shane laughed, causing me to press my hand against my lips to prevent my own laughter from escaping.

"Poor child."

"That doesn't even begin to cover it with my parents," Shane said as he reached into my pickle jar and stole one, despite my narrowed eyes following his every move as he did so. "Those heartless monsters are like little bunnies every month or so."

"Ew." I laughed as I crinkled my nose before I rested my head on Shane's chest and continued partaking in my ice cream and pickle concoction. The odd mix of contradicting flavors satisfied my weird craving.

"Oh, don't judge too quickly," he said softly as he took my hand and kissed the back of it. "After you bear our child or children, we'll be like that all night every night."

"In your dreams, Chase." I shrugged off though I knew there was a dash of truth behind it.

He smiled as he used his hand to stroke my cheek. "Ariel Anne Carter, I don't think you understand how strong of a hold you have on—" he started but was interrupted when the TV that we were watching suddenly turned off as our bedroom door swung open.

Within a second, Shane was protectively in front of me like he had been when Zac had barged in, but I knew it wasn't Zac this time. It couldn't be. A heavy mixture of peacefulness and fear hung in the air. The two emotions fought for dominance and I knew I wasn't the only one affected due to Shane's constant tensing and relaxing.

"What the . . . ?" He trailed off as a girl not much older than twenty gracefully walked into our bedroom as if she were an old friend.

Her white dress flowed with her movements. Her long gray-white hair cascaded down her back like a waterfall and was accompanied by her flawless complexion. As I looked at her, her eyes seemed to flicker between every color known to man: gray, purple, crimson red, icy blue. All of them, yet none of them.

A deep growl rumbled deep within Shane's chest, causing her to stop but not out of fear but what seemed like politeness.

"Who are you and who let you into our home?" he growled lowly as he tensed, his wolf ready to come through and attack the trespasser.

"Don't say that you don't recognize me, Shane. You've been talking to me a lot lately," she said in a honey-sweet voice as she flashed a smile. Her perfect straight white teeth were on display, and her accent was clear. I recognized her voice, but I couldn't pinpoint how.

He merely growled in response, but the stranger hardly blinked.

"Ariel?" she questioned, her multicolored eyes focusing on me. My silence was my answer.

How did she know our names?

"Well, I see that they don't educate you, pups about me like they used to in the good old days, but I don't mind introductions," she pleasantly stated with another smile. "My name is Ella, but you guys might know me as the Moon Goddess."

CHAPTER THIRTY-SEVEN

To say I was shocked would be an understatement.

"Y-You're the Moon Goddess?" I questioned breathlessly, shock and confusion sinking deeper and deeper into my system as I looked at the very being I'd prayed to my whole life.

And every time she'd let me down.

"Yes, but call me Ella it sounds less . . . formal," she requested. Then she wandered beyond the doorway of our room, causing Shane to let out a louder more threatening growl, which made her laugh. "Come on, Shane. Don't get your tail in a twist."

"I don't believe you." He growled. "You'd better give me a reason to in the next five seconds, or your blood will stain these walls."

"Oh, Shane. You stubborn wolf." She sighed as she sat on the edge of our bed, not caring that there was a temperamental alpha sitting less than two yards away from her. "But if you insist, then I'll comply.

"You are Alpha Shane Ansel Chase born November 12, 1994, to Helen and Brian Chase who rarely communicate with you or your brothers Gregory and little Zachary. Near the beginning of your time with Ariel, you were forced to kill an old friend of yours due to her indiscretions against your mate, and you told your pack that she was conspiring against the pack and that's why you had to kill her.

"You've mated with your mate over here, Ariel Anne Carter a little bit over a month ago and are now expecting pups. Unfortunately, however, your mate has been struggling from the stress and trauma of her kidnapping and murder of former Alpha Morgan Hills and his sidekick, Tracey Nixon who wanted her back after you took him from him. Even though all he offered the poor girl was years of senseless abuse following the terrible deaths of her parents, Nolan and Annalise Carter.

"She didn't utter a word until her Lunar Ceremony. She's also recently learned that her brother Chris who she'd mourned is not actually dead but went rogue after the horrible fire. And, if this last bit doesn't convince you, then I don't know what will. You've been praying to me for the past month to be with you and help you be the father your pups deserve.

"You're also considering the names Lukas, Luca, and Mathias if the pup's a boy and Lauren, Celeste, and Annalise if it's a girl. Does that sound about right?"

I swallowed. I couldn't deny that she'd laid out perfectly everything that had happened to us since the day we'd met. But the shock quickly turned to anger as my eyes narrowed at her.

"If you knew all of this was happening to us, why didn't you stop it?" I growled out as my wolf easily began rising, begging for a chance to show how much pain her negligence caused us. "I was tortured and almost taken advantage of. I prayed to you, yet you never answered, and now you come into our territory, our *home* like nothing's happened?" I questioned, tears quickly filling my eyes but I blinked them away as quickly as they came.

"You just let my mate suffer all those years and even during those long days while she was fighting for her very life, you just left both of us on our own even when you swore to always be there for all lycans," Shane spat as he gathered me in his arms and held me tightly.

"I'm sorry, my children, but I can explain," she pleaded as she reached out to touch me, but I moved away.

What could she possibly say that would explain why she left us when we needed her the most?

She sighed before she looked out the window at the setting sun. "My children, I fear I have awful news for you, and you'll hate me for the situation that I've put you in, but you must understand that I didn't have a choice." She frowned before her attention returned to my mate and me.

"Out with it," Shane growled. "My patience for you is waning, and since you've done nothing for us, that's what we owe you: nothing."

"I understand, but please hear me out," she begged.

Shane looked at me, telling me that whatever happened next would be my decision. I clenched my jaw and gave her an empty look.

"You have five minutes starting now. Go."

"I have put you through a series of tests since you two have been together. The moment that you two met, I felt a power spawn from you that I'd never felt between anyone in my life. As you grew closer, the bond and potential became apparent, so I put you through a series of tests to see if my theory was correct. I got in Stephanie's head and made her crazy for you, Shane, and to hate Ariel to the point that you would have no choice but to end her to see if you could handle making tough decisions," she admitted, causing Shane to growl.

"You what?" he yelled, anger radiating off him like heat from the sun.

"Shane, relax," I whispered. "Please don't do anything too—"

"Stephanie was my friend. She was like blood to me before you screwed her up!" he yelled, his skin becoming hot and he was a thread away from shifting.

"I did what I had to, Shane. Now calm yourself. Remember that I am the one who holds the power of every lycan in the world, including yours. If you don't listen to your mate and cool down, I'll remind you who's in charge."

Shane narrowed his eyes, and a growl escaped his lips before he suddenly buried his face in my neck and took in my mark to calm himself down.

I held him tight and looked at Ella. "You have three more minutes. I kindly suggest you hurry up or please get out of our home."

Ella sighed and ran her fingers through her hair. "Very well then. After that test, I performed more. I made Greg's mate fall for another and reject him and led his parents to send him and his little brother here so that I could see how Ariel handles challenges and plays the motherly role."

Anger boiled in my veins at how casually she spoke of robbing Greg of his chance at true love and happiness with his mate and all for what? A stupid test?

I felt my eyes shift to black as I clenched my jaw though I said and did nothing besides continue to calm my mate who was also getting angrier and angrier, his grip tightening by the second. All the while, I stared right at Ella. I wanted her to actually see the pain she was causing us and feel our anger.

"The next test was the Blood Moon and as surprising as it may sound, I didn't need to manipulate the moon at all. It just naturally happened as did what happened with your brothers, Shane. I gave little Zac the warning to prepare you, but it didn't do much good now, did it?" She paused and took a deep breath before she turned to me. "And your final test was Morgan and Tracey."

At those words, my body went numb as all the horrible memories came flooding back to me as if they were brand new.

291

"No," I whispered, shaking my head as tears quickly sprang to my eyes. "You didn't damn me to that," I said, trying to convince myself though I knew the truth. "No."

Shane quickly enveloped me in his arms, a deep growl rumbling deep within his chest as he looked at Ella with pure hatred as I sobbed into his chest. The memories of my hellish time there replayed in my head.

"I should kill you for putting my mate in pain and letting that bastard do what he did to her," Shane growled as he held me closer.

"And I should kill you for threatening me, yet you're still breathing."

Shane let out a humorless laugh. "Oh. I'm sorry, powerful Moon Goddess. But Ariel, the woman you mated me with, is in pain and not the kind I can take away from her with a single touch but the kind of pain that will follow her throughout her life. Do you know how that feels? To know your very lifeline slips through your fingers and there's no way for you to correct your wrongs and give her the peace and happiness she deserves?" Shane asked, his voice breaking at the end. "And as her mate, it's my job to want to kill anything and anybody who causes a single tear to fall down her face."

"And as the Moon Goddess, it is my job to do what is right for my people," she snapped. "I'm backed into a corner. Don't you get it? I'm weak and dying, and it's causing far more rejections and complications with lycans than there should be, so I had no choice. I had to administer those tests on you to see if you were ready."

"Ready for what?" Shane asked though I already knew the answer.

"Ready to take on the responsibilities of the Moon Goddess and the first ever Moon God."

"What?" I shrieked, panic numbing my body.

"Yes," she stated calmly as she stood up and casually walked over to the window and looked out. "I tried testing other

mateless wolves in various other ways, but they didn't . . . pass."
She frowned as she spoke.

"No," Shane said firmly, and I shook my head in
agreement. "I can't. We can't. Like you said, we have a pup,
possibly pups to raise and we can't be proper parents if we're
carrying the weight of every lycan in the world on our shoulders. I
hate to break it to you, Ella, but you'll have to find another she-
wolf because this one is mine," he stated confidently before he
placed a soft kiss on my lips just to prove his point.

"I'm yours," I confirmed against his lips, causing Ella to
smile once we parted.

"I did a good job with you two." She nodded with a sad
smile. "I hate that I have to do this to you, but like I said, I have no
choice. I don't have time to wait for another pair of mates because
I'll be long gone by then, and if I die while I'm still Goddess, then
every lycan in the world will endure a slow, agonizing death along
with me, including you two and your unborn."

I sucked in a deep breath as her words hung heavy in the
air. *We had to take over Ella's position, or else everyone I love would perish, no
pressure there.*

"A-Are you sure there's no one else that can take your
spot?" I questioned. My heart rate quickly increased as pressure
slowly started building behind my eyes, signaling a panic attack.
Shane must've sensed it too because he held me tighter. "I mean,
there are millions of us in the world so there must be someone else.
I-I mean maybe you haven't looked hard en—"

"Trust me, Ariel. I've looked high and low, and no one can
fill in the gap quite like you two can."

I placed a hand on my round swollen stomach. "What
about my children?" I asked softly, causing her to bite her lips and
look away from me. My heart sank.

"Ella, what aren't you telling us?" Shane asked slowly,
feeling the heaviness that had filled the air due to her small, yet
huge action.

293

"That's the problem." She sighed as her eyes finally met mine. "That's why all of the Goddesses have been mateless . . ."

"What do you mean?" I questioned, worry fogging my mind as I slowly slipped into a panic attack.

"If you become Moon Goddess and God, you will have so much power and responsibility that anything else will cease to have a meaning to you," she explained carefully. "The only reason I'm dying is that I've simply outgrown my time as the Goddess and I need to move on to be with the elders."

"Ella," Shane warned, telling her to get to the point while worry was evident in his voice.

She sighed once more. "Since you'll have so much raw power and energy moving through you, your child will not make it. It won't survive the power transfer. Even a fraction of the power would cause instant death to whatever is growing in your womb."

I went numb. My child wouldn't be able to enter this world alive. They would never grow up to learn how to overcome the hardships of life and what it had to offer. They would never find their mates and experience the true bliss and security that they had to offer. Our ears would never be blessed with the cries that would spill from their lips as they entered this world.

The very thought caused tears to well up in my eyes, but I quickly blinked them away and shook my head. "T-There has to be another way," I stammered. "Maybe w-we could wait until it's born."

"I doubt I can stay alive that long, Ariel, and I don't want to risk dying while I'm still in my position."

"Ella, please don't take this away from us," Shane begged. "We love the being growing within Ariel and you can't just take this from us after all you've put us through to get here—"

"I don't have a choice!" she snapped, having lost her temper before she took a deep breath and put her head in her hands for a few moments then looked at us again, visibly calmer though her hands were shaking. "Don't you see that? If I don't do this, every lycan, including everyone you love will perish. Do you want that?"

We remained silent, offering only that as our answer.

She let out a breath. "I was hoping it wouldn't have to come to this, but you leave me with no choice. I have approximately three months to live before I die and transfer to the other side. At the end of those three months, my powers will be forced onto you, and there's nothing you can do to stop it."

"What?" I screeched.

"What's wrong with you?" Shane and I said at the same time as he held me closer.

"I'm sorry, but I'm doing what I have to. You have three months," she whispered, and within an instant, she disappeared in a whisper of smoke as if she were never there.

"No, no, no . . . ," I whimpered as I tightly held my head. I felt my wolf trying to break down every layer of defense that I had placed to hold her back, begging to be let free. "I-I can't, Shane. Oh my God. I can't!" I cried as my body became hot and my head started spinning. "I can't do this, Shane!" I screamed as he held my cheeks and rested his forehead on mine, his eyes boring into mine.

"Calm down, Ariel," he said in a deathly calm voice though I could see the pain swimming in the tears that were building up in his eyes. "You have control over your wolf, not the other way around. We'll figure out a way for you to have your pups. Okay? We always do."

"Sh-Shane, it hurts!" I sobbed as she began surfacing. My bones started to break, and my cells started to change.

"Alexia, stand down," Shane growled in his alpha tone, addressing my wolf by her name. "Now."

Hearing our mate's voice, she stopped as slowly returned to her place in the back of my mind though I could still feel her sadness.

"It still hurts." I sobbed as I was enveloped in Shane's strong arms.

295

"It's okay, Ariel. You will gain better control of—"

"I don't mean that, Shane," I stated weakly as I looked at him through tear-blurred eyes. "It hurts here," I explained, placing a hand on my heart. "I-I'm not ready to lose my child after all this. I can't."

"Trust me. I'm not either, but we're going to love what is growing inside of you until we figure out how to get out of this mess," he said softly as he placed a hand on my stomach, which instantly calmed me down. "I love you, Ariel. I love both of you, and I will die before I let anything happen to either of you. Do you understand?"

I nodded. "I just wish it didn't have to be this way," I whispered as I placed my hand on top of Shane's on my stomach.

"Me too, but unfortunately this is one more test we must pass or die trying."

CHAPTER THIRTY-EIGHT

I watched over Ariel's tired figure as she slept. She'd cried herself halfway insane and nearly screamed herself the rest of the way. After some time, she'd finally found rest, but even in sleep, she relentlessly whimpered and held onto her stomach, onto the living, breathing creature we didn't want to let go.

It killed me seeing her like this.

"Don't worry, my love," I whispered as I kissed her forehead. "I'll fight for you," I muttered as I gently lifted her shirt and kissed her belly. "Both of you."

I silently made my way out of the room and searched for everyone who'd been in our home before Ella showed up.

Chris was the first one I saw. He was passed out on the floor of the family room. His chest was barely moving as blood slowly leaked out of his nose and spilled into the growing crimson stain that plagued the carpet. I quickly knelt beside him and looked over him for any injury, but there appeared to be none. This had Ella written all over it.

"Chris?" I called as I nudged him. He didn't move. "Chris," I said with a bit more conviction and headed the same response; nothing. "Chris!" I said in my alpha tone, causing his eyes to snap open as he lurched to an upright position and his chest rose and fell quickly.

"Wh-What-?" he sputtered, raising trembling fingers up to his mouth, causing his eyes to widen once he saw the blood that stained his fingertips. "What happened, Sh-Shane?" Confusion shone in his eyes as he spoke while he continued wiping his mouth until you could no longer see blood. "What happened to me?"

"It's a long story that isn't solely mine to tell," I explained carefully as I stood up and offered my hand, which he graciously took. "I think it'd be best for both of us to tell all of you at the same time, so Ariel doesn't get upset."

"What happened to her? Is she alright? Is the baby okay?" Chris asked frantically, which caused a loose chuckle to push past my lips at his concern, which earned me a strange look.

"I'm sorry it's just that a lot has been going on lately," I explained, clapping him on the shoulder before I ventured throughout our house in search of our other friends.

I saw them all piled in a spare bedroom that hadn't been used in months and what I saw caused me to stop dead in my tracks.

The room was newly decorated. Instead of an old, unused mattress, there lay a crib with delicate stuffed animals inside that would work whether we had a boy or girl. The crib was also big enough for if we had a single child or children. There were toys and childproof shelves that held everything Ariel and I would need for our child. It was beautiful and extremely thoughtful.

Tears quickly filled my eyes, but I quickly blinked them away. Why did they have to be so caring? Why did they have to do this for us the same day we found out that there's a huge possibility that we won't be able to keep our child?

Greg was the first one to wake up, and he too suffered from a bloody nose as did everyone else in the room.

"Shane, what happened?" He groaned as he touched his forehead with his hand and winced. "My head is killing me and what happened to everyone else? All I remember is seeing a lady with white hair and now all of a sudden, I'm waking up with a killer headache and a nose bleed."

"It's a long story," I muttered as I helped him up. "For now, I need your help hiding this. Ariel cannot see this. It could make her upset, and that is the last thing that we need right now. Do you understand me?"

"Shane, what's going—"

"I'll explain later, okay? For now, I need you to trust me on this one," I said as I held him by the shoulders. "Can you do that for me?"

He nodded. "Can you at least tell me if Ariel's okay?"

I couldn't help but smile. Ever since Ariel helped Greg with his rejection, he had been looking out for her and seeing her not only as his luna but also as a mother figure too.

"Physically, yes," I answered, causing him to nod though I saw confusion and concern evident in his eyes. "I'll explain later, but right now, I need your help waking everyone up and keeping this room a secret from Ariel."

Despite the evident confusion on his face, he nodded before helping me wake everyone. They asked the same question about what happened, and they all gave me the same confused face when I told them not to tell Ariel about the new nursery they'd thoughtfully built for us.

"Why can't we tell her?" Jessica asked, and I shook my head.

"That's not important right now. What is important is that—"

"What's going on down here?" Ariel's groggy voice asked from behind me.

299

I quickly turned around to see her rubbing her tired eyes with one hand and touching her bulging stomach with the other. You could still see the pink trails on her cheeks where her tears had streamed.

"Nothing, love," I insisted as I stood in front of her in an attempt to block her view of the nursery, but she merely pushed me aside and took in the scene for herself. Her eyes grew wide, and tears quickly filled her eyes as her lips began quivering in an attempt to keep her sobs at bay.

"Do you like it, Ari?" Zac asked, his voice filled with hope and excitement as he easily mistook her tears of pain for those of joy.

"I love it," she whispered, the words sounding painful as they slid past her cracked lips. "It's absolutely p-perfect." She barely managed before she broke down in my arms. Her loud and painful sobs filled the air to the point everyone in our pack could probably feel her pain.

I hugged her and gently rocked her as I felt tears of my own begin building up, but I quickly blinked them away because I knew I had to stay strong for Ariel.

"What's wrong?" Chris asked, panic evident in his voice as he spoke and his eyes turned to me when Ariel didn't respond.

I swallowed and looked down at my sobbing mate in my arms before I looked at everyone in the room. I tried thinking of a delicate way to say it that could explain the harshness of our possible future without upsetting Ariel more than she already was. But she beat me to it.

"There's a big possibility that we can't have our pup or pups, and there's nothing we can do about it," she stated bitterly, tears still silently slipping down her flushed face.

Aiden was the first to recover from her blunt statement. "What do you mean?"

"As crazy as this may seem," I said, interjecting so Ariel wouldn't upset herself anymore by talking about it. "The Moon

Goddess, Ella, just came to us and is forcing us to take over her role as Moon Goddess and God because she's slowly dying. If she remains in power when she dies, all of us go down with her, including our unborn," I whispered the last part as I placed a hand on Ariel's round stomach. "Even if we do take the position, the baby would be in a limbo-like state so that it'll never grow or be delivered. It'll just be frozen in time."

"Oh my . . ." Jessica trailed out as she pressed a hand to her mouth in shock. Everyone else was at a loss for words.

"I'm so sorry," Greg whispered before he engulfed both of us in a hug that everyone soon joined.

"Me too," Ariel whispered, her voice slightly breaking at the end.

I held her closer and kissed her forehead.

"Why are we sad about the bad part?" Zac questioned, causing all eyes to fall on him. "There's still a chance you can have your baby, right? Let's focus on that instead and be happy!" He smiled. His adorable smile caused one of my own to grow on my lips.

"Yeah. Let's focus on that instead," I agreed as I looked down at Ariel and whispered, "I told you we were going to figure this out, didn't I? Don't go giving up on me yet, okay?"

She nodded mutely, and I placed a soft kiss on her forehead, which relaxed her a little bit.

"I won't give up on either of you," she whispered as she hid her head in the crook of my neck, next to my mark. "I promise."

CHAPTER THIRTY-NINE

ARIEL

It'd been two weeks since Ella delivered the news, but with every passing minute, hour, or even second, it became harder and harder for me to handle it. I'd broken down and cried more in these two weeks than I had in my entire life. I hated feeling absolutely useless when my child needed me most. Shane tried to console me and calm me down, but his efforts only made me feel worse inside, not that I'd tell him that though.

I took a sip of my tea and used my free hand to touch my still growing stomach as I glanced out Shane's office window, my thumb moving in slow circles over my belly. We'd talked to Samantha about delivering the baby early, and she said that it was possible, but it could mean some unseen health risks to our child, and Shane and I didn't want to risk possibly hurting the baby.

"What are you thinking about?" Shane asked gently from his position behind his smooth oak wood desk. His eyes momentarily lifted from the paperwork he was looking at to look at me. The black framed glasses that he rarely wore balanced on the bridge of his nose, making him look even more handsome.

"Nothing," I answered vaguely, not exactly meeting his eyes.

"Why don't you come over here and think about nothing with me?" he said as he pushed himself away from his desk and opened his arms, beckoning me over.

I couldn't keep the smile off my face at how adorable he looked as I slowly stood up, careful not to get up too fast or spill my beverage before I wobbled over to him. Once I was comfortably situated on his lap, he gently placed a hand on my stomach before he slowly scooted the chair back up to the table, careful that he didn't hit the baby.

"Have you narrowed down the names?" he asked as I leaned my back against his chest and nodded.

"If we have a girl, I want her name to be Annalise Serenity, after my mother. She was a strong and beautiful woman, and that's what I'd want her to grow up to be."

"So are you," Shane complimented. "You don't give yourself enough credit." He gently kissed my shoulder. "Have you narrowed it down for if we have a boy?"

"You should come up with a boy name," I said. "You're trying to give me all the work!" I laughed though it was forced. If Shane noticed it, he didn't let onto it. He merely moved his hand along my stomach in soothing patterns.

"How about Luca Ethan Chase?" he suggested, and I instantly nodded, liking the sound of it.

"Perfect," I stated just as the oven went off downstairs, indicating the cake I'd put in was ready to be taken out.

I wordlessly pushed myself off of Shane's lap and slowly made my way down the stairs and into the kitchen with Shane following close behind. I slid on an oven mitt before I carefully slid the hot cake out of the oven and placed it on top of the stove. When I turned around to prepare the icing, I was met with Shane's muscular back as he steadily mixed the icing until it was smooth and thick. After about twenty minutes, the cake was cooled, frosted, and ready. Shane didn't waste any time digging in.

"Babe, calm down." I laughed as he greedily devoured the cake. "You need to control yourself."

"Who needs control when you can have cake?" he questioned. The cake was stashed in his mouth as he spoke, making him look like a handsome squirrel before he grinned.

I rolled my eyes before I partook in my own slice of chocolate heaven.

Shane was right.

Who needed control when you could have cake?

"I wanna do something tonight," Shane said as he wrapped his arms around me from behind before he rested his chin on my shoulder. "I wanna do something with just you tonight," he whispered before he kissed me behind my ear, sending sparks throughout my body.

"Like what?" I asked as I turned toward him.

"Let me worry about that," he said softly before he kissed my cheek, releasing me and swiftly walking out of the room.

"Shane, where are you—"

"I'll be ready by eight. Keep your eyes peeled."

I opened my mouth to respond, but I closed it as soon as I heard the front door open and close. I sighed and looked at the clock on the oven.

1:16 PM.

Great. I got to spend the next seven hours by myself. I sighed before I finished up the rest of my slice of cake before I took care of all of the dirty dishes and covered the cake to preserve it. I was on my way upstairs but stopped at the foot of the stairs.

I placed a hand on my stomach. "Well, Luca or Annalise, this is the bane of my existence," I mumbled as I slowly made the short trip up the stairs and into our bedroom where I threw myself onto the bed, panting.

Being pregnant was a workout. I glanced at the clock. I'd wasted ten minutes, but I still had over six hours to survive. This was going to be hard.

*   *   *

I looked at the clock. 7:42 PM, it read.

I hurried back to the bathroom to look myself over. I was slightly taken aback at my reflection. I'd grown so accustomed to my long brown hair that'd grown back due to my inability to cut it so in efforts to not only kill time but to also regain the style I'd missed, I cut my hair back down to its shoulder-brushing length. I'd also opted for an off-shoulder top that fit perfectly—not too loose, not too tight—along with some jeans and a pair of flats to ensure that I remained comfortable no matter what we did. I also applied mascara and some lip gloss with a hint of cherry flavoring.

I turned to head back into our bedroom and jumped when I saw a trail of flower petals that I was 95% sure wasn't there before. I slowly approached the beginning of the trail and picked up a small white card that was on the floor.

Follow me.

It read in Shane's beautifully, messy handwriting. I quietly chuckled to myself before I followed the instructions and carefully followed the trail that had been laid out for me. A few giggles escaped my lips when I stumbled upon a full rose in the middle of the trail every few meters.

After a slow descent down the stairs, I found the trail leading out the back door.

"What are you planning, Mr. Chase?" I said under my breath as the semi-cold air nipped at my skin.

I continued following the trail through the yard and through the back gate where I was met by a beautiful setup.

How was Shane able to pull this off?

There were lovely fairy lights that hung between the trees running from the edge of the house all the way to the giant tent that loomed further back. In front of it all stood my mate in a black tuxedo with his hair slicked back holding roses with an adorable smile on his face that momentarily rendered my lungs useless.

"Oh my gosh, Shane . . . ," I breathed out as I took it all in, causing his smile to widen as he walked toward me.

"I've missed you," he said as he gently cupped my face in his hands and placed a soft kiss on my lips, causing breathtaking sparks to run through my body as I moved my lips against his. "I've also missed the short hair," he said, taking a strand between his fingertips, causing me to smile. "So, I take that you like the setup?"

"I love it," I said as I looked up into his mesmerizing eyes. I hoped our children would have eyes like his. "But you know I don't like fancy things."

"I know," he answered vaguely before he laced his fingers with mine and led me to the tent. "So I made it to your liking," he said as he pushed open the flap and led me inside.

Inside was a huge mattress covered in big fluffy blankets and pillows and a table full of food Shane had made himself, including various desserts in addition to an amazing smelling pizza. To make it even better, there was a projector projecting the Netflix home menu on the side of the tent.

"You know me too well." I chuckled, causing him to place another kiss on my cheek.

"I know."

"How did you pull this off in such a short time?" I questioned.

"Nothing is too good for you, Ariel," he said as he wrapped his arms around me. "I knew this would be something you liked, so I brought it to life for you with a bit of help from the boys and a lot of determination."

I couldn't help my smile. Shane was too good to me sometimes.

"Today is your day. Whatever you want, I'll give. Whatever you hate, I'll end it."

The way he looked at me made my insides melt, and my heart skipped multiple beats.

"Let's get some food," I suggested since I hadn't eaten the majority of the day.

He led me to the table that displayed all the glorious food he'd made. He then prepared my desired meal then made his own before he headed for the comfy looking bed that was screaming my name.

"You look beautiful," he complimented as we settled into the bed with my back to his chest as he used my lap as his table.

"A bit underdressed compared to you, though," I countered with a chuckle.

"You could wear a trash bag and still outshine anyone in the room," he reassured me before placing a gentle kiss behind my ear, causing a small shiver of pleasure to race down my spine.

We continued eating, and Shane planted his lips on some part of my skin every so often until we were both done eating. Afterward, we embraced each other.

"How's our official first date going so far?" Shane asked earnestly.

I hadn't realized that we'd never gone on our first official date. I was just so used to Shane always being there that I seemed to have forgotten a time Shane wasn't there.

"Perfect," I admitted, meaning it. Whether we were in a fancy restaurant or a makeshift tent in our backyard, every date was the best as long as Shane was right there next to me.

"This is only the beginning. You'll see," Shane said cryptically as he went through our watch list and picked out one of the many movies I'd told him I wanted to see.

I snuggled deep within his arms as we watched the movie with brief kisses, tender touches, and sweet nothings every here and there until the credits rolled. I didn't want it to end. I wanted to lay here in Shane's arms forever. It all just felt so right.

"I have one more surprise in store for you to make this date that much better," Shane said as he paused the movie before he got up and offered me his hand. I took it and allowed him to help me up.

He had a certain excitement in his eyes that matched that of a kid in a candy store, and I couldn't help but share his excitement too. He led me back outside where the lights somehow managed to look even more elegant than they had and underneath them stood Zac, Greg, Chris, Jessica, and Aiden. They all had huge smiles on their faces.

"Ariel, ever since the day I met you, I knew you'd change my life," Shane said as his thumbs rubbed soothing patterns on the back of my hands. "You are hands down the strongest person I know, and you continue to surprise me every day even in the little things you do. You're smart, compassionate, and overall a beautiful person inside and out who I've grown to love more and more with each passing hour of every day. And ever since I laid my eyes on you, I knew I wanted to spend all of my days with you right there by my side, and now I want to make it official. So," he said as he got down on one knee and presented a small black box from his back pocket, causing me to instantly tear up and my heart to skip a beat.

"Oh my gosh, Shane . . ." I trailed off, my brain failing to find the correct words that would capture exactly how I was feeling.

His smile grew.

"Ariel Anne Carter, will you make me the happiest and luckiest man alive and marry me?"

I didn't waste a second and instantly nodded. My words got caught in my throat along with my tears of joy.

He stood up, and I tightly embraced him, letting out all of my happiness in the form of tears.

"I love you so much," he repeated over and over again in my ear as I continued to sob and our friends clapped.

After a few moments, I finally composed myself and let Shane go and allowed him to slip a small silver ring on my finger with beautiful diamonds on it. If you looked carefully enough, you could see tiny moons carved into the band. It was perfect.

He quickly captured my lips in another breathtaking kiss, not caring who saw our passionate, love-filled kiss. By the time we were done, we were both breathing heavily as we pressed our foreheads against each other.

"Thank you," he whispered.

"For what?"

"Saying yes," he said, a drunken smile on his face. "I'm so excited to start this new chapter in our lives with you. All of you," he said, placing his hand on my swollen stomach. "No matter what I have to do, we will have this baby."

"Of course, we will." I smiled as I used my thumb to gently caress his cheek just as I felt a soft tug at the bottom of my shirt.

"Are you and Shubby getting married?" Zac asked, his adorable doe eyes twinkling as he spoke.

A smile grew on Shane's face as Zac called him "Shubby" for the first time since Ella's tests started.

Afraid I was going to get emotional again, I merely nodded as Shane said, "Yeah, little man. You can be the ring bearer if you'd like."

This caused Zac's eyes to grow wide as he excitedly nodded.

"I'm so excited! Thank you, Shubby." He laughed as he hugged Shane's legs.

"Is Shubby here to stay?"

"Yep," Zac said as his smile grew. "I can't wait to grow up and find my mate so I can be as happy as you are."

309

Shane laced his hand with mine and gave it a slight squeeze to make sure I hadn't missed what had just happened, and I hadn't. Anyone could see that Zac was smiling and laughing the way he had when I first met him before our lives became hectic. He was acting like his old self again, and I was glad. We all were.

I couldn't help but smile at his restored state and pure hopes for the future as I ruffled his hair.

"You'll find a smart and beautiful mate who loves you almost as much as we do," I said before I turned to Greg. "You too."

"Thanks, Ariel," Greg said as he hugged me. "Congratulations, you two. I'm really happy for you."

I could tell he meant it. Even after his mate brutally rejected and broke him, he survived and became stronger in spite of it.

"I never thought I'd see the day my baby sister gets married," Chris said as he tightly embraced me, careful not to touch my stomach.

"Me neither," I joked as the hug broke. "The world is full of surprises."

"That it is," Shane agreed as he pulled me back into him so that my arms were wrapped around his neck and we were face to face. "I have a feeling it's going to work in our favor." He leaned in for another kiss when suddenly, I felt a lurch in my stomach.

"Oh my gosh, Shane!" I whispered as I put a hand on my stomach.

"What? Are you hurt?" he asked as his eyebrows knitted together and he looked over me.

I shook my head and quickly placed his hand on my stomach just as another kick came.

"Oh my . . . ," he whispered as he put his other hand on my stomach, and I bit my bottom lip in an attempt to keep my raging smile at bay. "They kicked. Something that we made kicked!"

he said, disbelief still evident in his voice before he kissed me again, earning yet another kick.

I laughed as I too put both hands on my stomach on top of his.

"Ariel, you are so close," he whispered, as he knelt down and looked me in my eyes.

"To what?" I asked though I already knew the answer. I just loved hearing him say it.

He smiled, seeing right through my facade, but played along nonetheless. "To having our pups."

CHAPTER FORTY

SHANE

I carefully tucked my mate in and kissed her forehead. After I'd made the best decision of my life and proposed to Ariel, we all celebrated until Ariel was tired to the point that she could barely sit up. I even had to change her into her pajamas. I couldn't help but chuckle at the thought as I turned and headed toward the door.

"Wait," Ariel called softly, her voice heavy with sleep. "Where are you going?"

"I just have to check on something, and then I'll be right back," I assured her.

She gave me a tired nod before she settled back into the sheets and her chest started rising and falling in a steady pattern. I stood there for a few moments, admiring how tranquil and relaxed she was before I forced myself to tear my eyes away from her and complete the task I'd set out to do. I walked out the door, and I was instantly enveloped by a cool breeze. Goosebumps appeared over my exposed arms and chest, but I didn't mind. I walked to a clearing in the middle of the woods and looked up, momentarily basking in the full moonlight. I felt my wolf stir within me, but other than that he remained serene.

I felt her near. It was like a slight pressure behind my eyes. I'd felt it a lot lately ever since she'd flipped our world upside down and now I needed to confront her, or at least negotiate with her.

"Ella!" I yelled into the otherwise silent night. A roaring silence was my only response, but the pressure had increased. It was working. "Come on, Ella! I know you can hear me. Ella—"

"Do you mind keeping your voice down?" She hissed from behind me. "You don't want to wake up your whole pack, do you?"

"I'd wake up the whole world if that's what it took." I deadpanned. "But that doesn't matter. I need to talk to you." I felt my wolf flare up from within me at the sight of the one who had been causing our mate and I pain, but I kept him at bay.

"Well, you definitely have my attention now," she said, crossing her arms. Irritation was evident in her voice, and it flashed across her multicolored eyes.

"You said you're dying because your time has passed, am I correct?"

She nodded in response.

"And in the past the Moon Goddess role has been taken on by a single mate-less wolf, right?"

She nodded once more.

"Then why not give me all the power, at least for a bit. That way, Ariel can stay normal until she delivers and then I can share the power with her as well. This way we'd be killing two birds with one stone," I suggested.

"I don't know if that will work," she whispered. "This power has grown to be far too much for a single person to handle it. The only reason why I've been able to endure it is because I've gradually grown with the power and I didn't have it all dumped on me at once like you would if we were to do this. And if your body couldn't handle it—"

"Then we'd all die," I said, finishing her sentence for her.

313

She nodded.

"We have to at least try," I insisted, borderline begged. "Please, Ella. You have no idea what we're going through. What Ariel is going through. You've already put us through hell and back. There has to be something that you can do so I can be there for my family. So I can be a better father than my dad. So I can see Ariel's smile as she holds our baby for the first time. I want to hold our baby for the first time. Please, Ella. Don't take that away from us when we're so close."

She sighed and looked at the moon as if asking it for guidance. After a few moments, she sighed and looked me in the eye once again. "I will try," she agreed, causing me to let out the breath I didn't realize I was holding. "But know this: even if it does work, there is no guarantee that your child will survive. Especially with all the stress Ariel's body has been through, so remember that."

"I know," I said.

Samantha had said something along those lines to me in private. She'd told me to keep Ariel relaxed and away from stressful situations to increase the chance of a safe and healthy birth.

She gave me a small nod. "We will meet again at the end of the three months," she said before she disappeared as if she'd never existed.

I sighed as I ran my hands through my hair and down my face in an effort to slow my racing heartbeat. After taking multiple deep breaths, I felt calm enough to head back to the house where my sleeping mate was waiting for me. As soon as I got into our room, I wasted no time slipping into the bed with Ariel and pulled her close to me.

"I hope Ella pulls through," I whispered as I softly pressed my lips to the back of Ariel's head. "Because I really want to meet you," I continued as I placed my hands on her bulging stomach. "Both of us do."

CHAPTER FORTY-ONE

ARIEL

My heart was beating out of my chest. Today was the big day: our wedding.

I let out a shaky breath as I looked over myself in the mirror. I'd allowed Jessica to go all out on my hair and makeup, and I had to admit that she did a great job. My eyes popped, and my lips looked full and delicate. My hair was perfectly curled underneath my pulled back veil. I was wearing an elegant, flowing white dress that not only suited my body perfectly but also showed off my humongous stomach.

I smiled as I placed my hand on it. I'd gone to Samantha yesterday for my checkup, and she'd reported that they were healthy. She offered to tell me the gender and other details like she had the other times I'd come, but I told her the same thing I always did: I wanted it to be a surprise. I was due any day now. Shane had informed me about his talk with Ella, and it filled me with hope. We had six days left until our forced coronation, and Samantha assured me that I was due within the next three days, but it made me feel uneasy that we were cutting it so close. It also made me nervous that we hadn't heard back from Ella since the night she and Shane talked.

I forced myself to swallow down my worry. Today was supposed to be a happy day and stress wasn't good for the baby or my body.

"Don't worry, baby. Mommy and Daddy are trying," I whispered as I looked at my stomach in the mirror. "You will be okay no matter what."

Was I trying to convince myself or my child? There was a thin line between the two.

"Ariel?" a voice I recognized as Chris's gently called as he softly knocked on the door. "It's almost time. May I come in?"

I took one last glance at myself in the mirror before I turned and opened our bedroom door and was instantly greeted by my brother in a sharp black tuxedo.

"Wow. Baby sister, you look gorgeous," Chris said softly as he looked me up and down, tears starting to fill his eyes. "I wish Mom and Dad could see you like this: all grown up, about to get married, and pregnant with pups."

"Yeah, I bet they'd be proud," I agreed as I felt the familiar prick of tears behind my eyes, "But don't cry. If you cry then I'll cry and ruin my makeup, and this whole thing will be a huge mess all because you're emotional," I half-joked.

"Alright, fine," he said as he wiped his eyes. "Just let me hug you one last time while you're still a free woman."

I rolled my eyes but hugged him nonetheless. After a few moments, he let me go and offered me his arm, which I linked with mine. I allowed him to lead me out of our house and toward the clearing where I had my Lunar Ceremony and where my wedding was being held.

The earth felt cold against my bare feet; my parents, and their parents before them had been married barefoot as a sign of good luck.

"Are you ready?" Chris asked as we approached the curtains that made up my waiting area.

I could hear the chatter of my pack from where I stood, and my heart pounded against my ribs. Despite how nervous I was, I nodded. "I think so."

He smiled before he hugged me once more. "I love you, Ariel."

"I love you too, Chris," I said as the hug ended.

He offered me one more smile before he handed me my bouquet of flowers then made his way to his designated spot next to Aiden and Greg. The sight warmed my heart, but also made my palms sweaty because it was another reminder that this was in fact happening.

Soon, the soft music of the quartet Shane and I had picked out began filling the air, efficiently causing a hush to fall over the crowd. I silently peeked from behind my curtain and saw Shane walk down the aisle. I pulled my veil over my face and counted to fifteen before I too revealed myself. Since neither of us had parents, let alone grandparents who could show up, I had to walk alone.

The heat of dozens of eyes burned into me, but all I could focus on was Shane and the genuine smile that stretched across his lips when his eyes landed on me. His smile was contagious. As I got closer to Shane, he extended his hand out for me, which I graciously took. Once we were face to face, Shane slowly peeled back my veil, and his smile grew impossibly wider as he flipped it over my head.

"There's that beautiful face I've missed so much," he whispered, causing a hoard of butterflies to erupt within my stomach as I bit my lip and looked down to hide how flustered I was. "It's already hard enough as it is not to kiss you, yet you insist on teasing me still," Shane whispered with a faint chuckle as he gently guided my head up and released my lips from between my teeth.

I could feel my cheeks heat up.

"We are gathered here today to witness the official bonding of our alpha and luna," our priest from my Lunar Ceremony started. "Before we get to the vows, on behalf of the bride and groom, thank you all for coming to celebrate this special event shared between these two. These two have been through a lot in their relatively short amount of time together, and it means a lot to them how devoted and loyal you are. Now we will commence with the reading for the promises that they are not only making to themselves, but to each other as well." He then looked at Shane and nodded, which was a cue for him to start.

Shane took my hands in his and gently ran his thumbs over my knuckles in a soothing pattern. "Ever since the day I met you, I knew you'd be the one who'd turn my life around," he started before he paused and placed a soft kiss on the back of my hand. "Ever since I was little, I imagined what my mate would be like, but I'd never ever imagined the strong, beautiful, and intelligent woman standing in front of me today. You are my light in the darkness. My sun after the storm. The one that makes every breath I take every second worth it. You've made me a better alpha, brother, and person just by being you, and I love you unconditionally for that. With these vows, these promises, I promise that I will always give you all of me. All my love, respect, and happiness. I can't wait to start a family with you, and I promise that no matter what happens, I will always love and protect you with all my being," he said before he placed his hands on my stomach and smiled. "All of you."

I couldn't stop the tears that filled my eyes, and I didn't try to hide or stop them. I wasn't ashamed to let Shane or the rest of the pack see exactly the effect his words had on me.

He cupped my cheek and used his thumbs to gently wipe away my tears. "Don't cry, love," he whispered. "Tears don't belong on your face."

I couldn't help but smile. He always knew exactly what to say. I grabbed his wrists and gently removed his hands from my face before I kissed his palms then held his hands in mine.

"Shane," I started, my voice a bit faint and wobbly from the crying, "you are without a doubt the best thing that's ever happened to me. From the moment our eyes met for the first time all the way up until now, you've done nothing but love and support me even when I couldn't love myself. You will forever be the angel who saved me from the suffocating darkness, and I will forever be yours. I promise to never stop loving you and to always support and protect you the same way you've always loved and protected me. I promise to always stand by your side and be the shoulder you lean on in hard times. I promise to not only be an anchor for you but for the rest of our family too," I said, placing both hands on my round stomach.

The priest smiled before he said, "If anyone objects to these two becoming one through Holy Matrimony, speak now or forever hold your peace."

Thankfully, no one spoke up.

"Perfect," the priest said. "Bring forth the rings."

As soon as he said that, Zac appeared down the middle aisle dressed in a sharp tux, a cute bow tie, and dress shoes that were too big for him. In his hand rested Shane's grandparent's rings that his grandmother had given to him before she died. He looked absolutely adorable, and I couldn't keep my smile off my face as I watched him approach us. Once he was in front of us, we offered him a quiet thanks before we slid our respective rings on each other's fingers. They were absolutely breathtaking.

"Do you, Shane Ansel Chase, take Ariel Anne Carter as your lawfully wedded wife to love, honor, and cherish her through sickness and health as long as you both shall live?"

"I do," he said confidently, true love and happiness swimming in his eyes as he said those two words that would change our lives forever.

"And do you, Ariel Anne Carter, take Shane Ansel Chase as your lawfully wedded husband to love, honor, and cherish him through sickness and health as long as you both shall live?'

I nodded as tears began filling my eyes once again. "I do."

The priest smiled. "Then I now pronounce you husband and wife," he claimed proudly before turning to Shane. "You may now kiss the bride."

"With pleasure." He smiled before he cupped my cheek and pressed his lips against mine in a tender, yet passionate kiss, causing our pack to erupt in thunderous applause and shouting. We held it for a few moments before we pulled away with the biggest smiles on our faces.

"We did it," I whispered. "We're married."

"Yeah. I guess we are," Shane said before he placed another kiss on my cheek.

"Oh my gosh. You guys are so cute!" Jessica squealed as she ran up to us and engulfed us in a hug with Greg, Chris, Aiden, and Zac not too far behind her.

"Thanks, Jess." I laughed as she released us.

"Congrats," Greg said as he slung his arm over his brother's shoulders. "Never thought I'd see the day when someone decided to torture herself and marry this guy."

Shane playfully narrowed his eyes at Greg before he shrugged his arm off, causing Greg to erupt in laughter.

"It's all out of love," Greg said.

"You and Shubby are married now!" Zac cheerfully stated as he wrapped his arms around my waist. "Does this mean you're my sister now?" he questioned, his eyes lighting up, causing me to laugh as I nodded.

"Yay!" he cheered as he held me tighter, which caused me to laugh a bit more before we were swarmed by pack members congratulating us and asking to touch my belly, which I permitted.

We all talked and laughed with Shane showering me with kisses every now and then. It all felt so right: being surrounded by friends turned family, sharing laughter, and getting advice from pack mothers. This was everything that I'd dreamed of ever since I was a little kid and now it was all coming true. I couldn't fight back my smile at the thought.

Unfortunately, my happy realization was cut short by Shane suddenly pulling me close to him as a low growl came from deep within his chest.

"Shane, what's—" I started, but the words died on my tongue once I saw what, or rather who he saw.

My heart raced. At the very back where I'd walked out of mere moments ago stood Ella with her white hair pulled back in a neat ponytail, wearing her usual dress and shoes.

No. Not today of all days.

We were so close, and the pack didn't even know of the struggle we had gone through, and it wasn't like she could walk into a room unnoticed.

"No," I whispered as Shane held me tighter while she casually walked up to us as if she hadn't been causing us pain and anxiety for the past few months. She had a warm smile on her face as if she were an old friend.

"Ella," Shane growled.

"Hello, my newly-wed lovebirds." She smiled, seemingly oblivious to the hate-filled glare Shane was throwing her and the tears that began forming in my eyes. "I'm afraid we need to talk."

CHAPTER FORTY-TWO

My heart dropped as those words left her lips.

"N-No," I countered as I shook my head. "We still have a few days. I'm due any day now. Please, we just need two, maybe three more days at most—"

"We don't have the time, Ariel." She cut me off. "I'm sorry, but I'm weaker than I thought and the elders want me now. It has to be done today, or we all die."

"We've come too far . . . ," I whispered, my voice weak and shaky as I placed a hand on my stomach. I didn't try to hold my tears back any longer and let out loud, ugly sobs into Shane's chest as he held me.

He pressed gentle kisses on my forehead and cheeks to calm me down.

"Ella, please don't do this," a voice I recognized as Chris's begged. "She's gone through so much already and still has so much ahead of her, which includes starting a family of her own. Isn't there anything you can do? You are still in power and even though you claim to be weak—"

"Watch yourself, Christopher," she warned as she narrowed her eyes on him. "I don't appreciate what you're insinuating."

"And I don't appreciate what you're trying to do to my sister and brother-in-law," he countered, seemingly unaffected by the tightness in her voice or her obvious irritation.

"Look, I know this isn't easy on her or any of you, but you have to understand—"

"Understand what?" I snapped as anger pumped through my veins at her feeble excuses. "Understand that we're about to lose any and all chances of starting a family of our own? That we'll never be able to provide a better future than what was given to us? That the all-powerful Moon Goddess who's held onto her power for centuries through all kinds of hardships can't hold on for a few more days?"

A few gasps rang out at the fact that many of the pack members had no idea what was going on.

"Ariel, please calm down," Shane whispered. "If you get too emotional, it could harm you and the pups."

"I'm fine," I snapped, my eyes never leaving Ella's.

"You should really listen to your mate," she chastised, "because if you continue to defy me, I will ensure that the transfer of powers will be long and tedious—"

"Enough!" Shane snapped, cutting her off mid-threat and looked her dead in the eye. "If you're so eager to alleviate your powers then give them all to me and leave Ariel out of this at least until she has delivered."

"No," I said instantly, remembering what Shane had told me about the night he'd met with Ella. "It's too dangerous. Your body might not be able to handle all that power. You could . . ." I trailed off, unable to bring myself to finish the sentence.

"I know the risks, love," he whispered as he cupped my face in his hands. I hadn't realized that I'd started crying until he gently slid his thumb across my cheeks to wipe my tears. "What did

323

I tell you about crying?" he whispered, causing me to give him a half-hearted chuckle even though I was terrified.

I didn't want Shane to go through it alone even if it were for a couple of days. If all that power crippled him, I'd never be able to forgive myself.

"Are you sure?" I asked, my voice too weak to rise above a whisper.

"Of course." He nodded. "No matter how long or how bad it is, it'll all be worth it to see you and the pups. I love you, Ariel."

"I love you too, Shane." I smiled before I pulled him into a kiss, knowing it could be the last one we shared for a while. After a few moments, he reluctantly pulled away before he knelt down, so he was eye level with my stomach.

"Hey," he said as he placed his hands on my stomach, "I have to go for a little bit, but I wanted to let you know that I love you and I'll miss you very much. Treat your mother right. She's a very, very special woman who also loves you very much." After he said that, there was a movement in my stomach, causing him to smile and I could see the tears he was relentlessly trying to blink back. "Those are my pups," he whispered before he kissed my stomach then stood up and looked out at the pack before he looked at Jessica, Aiden, Greg, Zac, and Chris. "Take care of Ariel for me until I get back, okay?"

"Yes, Alpha," the pack chorused as Jess, Aiden, Greg, Zac, and Chris merely nodded.

"Take care of yourself, alright?" Greg said, his voice shaking and tears evident in his eyes.

"I will." Shane nodded before he kissed my forehead then turned to the pack. "Silver Crescent Pack," he addressed in a loud, powerful voice. "Today, I am taking on a new set of duties as the first ever Moon God. Ariel will follow soon after me once she's given birth to our pups. I know that this is a lot to throw at you with such little context, but all you need to know for now is that I

324

will be back, as soon as I can. While I'm gone, you will listen to Aiden and Christopher."

Surprise was evident on Chris's features, but Shane merely gave him a small nod as if to say "you've got this" before he continued. "Treat them with the same respect you treat me with. And please," he said, looking at me. "Look after my Ariel and our pups until I'm back."

I blinked away the tears that I felt were coming. I had to stay strong.

"I love all of you and will see you again soon."

Shane pressed a gentle kiss to my lips. "I love you so much, Ariel," he whispered so that only he and I could hear before he turned to Ella. "I'm ready."

She nodded. "Kneel," she instructed, and he did. "Do you, Shane Ansel Chase, accept the duty, burdens, and hardships of becoming the first ever Moon God?" she questioned.

"Yes." He nodded, his voice sounding confident and strong while I was prepared to break down any second.

"Then I now pronounce you the first ever Moon God," she stated proudly before she gently placed a kiss on his forehead.

Immediately, the white in her hair was chased off by a jet-black color while Shane's hair turned white. Her eyes became a stunning gray and Shane inherited her multicolored eyes and her pale hue while she got a rejuvenated glow to her skin.

"Come on, my child." She smiled as she linked arms with him. "You have much to learn and a lot of pain to endure." In a whisper of smoke, they were both gone.

I let out the cry I'd been holding in, resulting in both Greg and Chris to rush to my side and hold me up since my legs had given out. I sobbed, my mind racing with the terrible things Shane would have to endure and I could not do anything about it. It broke my heart.

"Where did Shubby go?" Zac asked innocently with his eyebrows furrowed, not fully grasping the weight of the decision that Shane had made.

"I-I don't know," I choked out between tears. "I don't— Ah!" I screamed in pain as my hand flew to my stomach where the pain was coming from.

"What's wrong?" Chris asked as his grip became tighter on me.

"My stom—" I started, but was interrupted by yet another scream as pain tore through my body like a knife to butter.

"She's having contractions," a female voice called before Samantha came into my view. "She's going into labor. We need to get her to my office now."

Despite the intense pain I was in, I couldn't help but let out a laugh in relief and irony. If only she could've waited just a few more moments . . .

"Hold on tight," Greg said. With a small grunt, he picked me up and followed Samantha to her car, Chris on his heels.

"Jess and I will stay here with the pack. Keep us updated," Aiden called as Greg gently settled me in and Samantha and Chris jumped in the front.

"What about me?" Zac asked.

I swallowed down the pain and offered him a weak smile. "You need to stay here with Aiden. This is a large pack, and it requires both a beta and a future alpha."

His eyes lit up when I referred to him as an alpha and he smiled.

"I won't let you down," he promised before he turned and ran back to where Aiden and Jessica stood frantically trying to console the confused and panicked pack.

"Alright, let's go," Greg commanded as he slid into the backseat with me, allowing me to tightly hold his hand as another wave of contractions hit me, but there was nothing I wanted more than this feeling. I was able to have my pups. Our pups. I just wished Shane was here.

Without wasting another second, Samantha floored the gas and made her way through the trees toward the hospital. "Breathe, Ariel. Breathe," she instructed as whimpers escaped my lips.

"I-I need to get out of this dress," I stammered as I fruitlessly started clawing at the top half of my dress. I'd chosen a two-piece dress that looked like a one-piece just in case this happened.

"Do you want my help?" Greg asked timidly, and I nodded. He carefully, yet efficiently got it off.

"We're almost there," Samantha announced. "Chris, Greg, prepare to take her inside. I'll have the staff have a gurney ready for her and I'll meet you in the labor and delivery room."

"Okay." Chris nodded as Samantha stopped the car and rushed into the hospital, no doubt to put on her scrubs and prepare for the birth. Greg and Chris helped me out as instructed while I bit the inside of my cheek to keep my grunts and whimpers at bay.

"Over here, Luna!" a nurse called as she and three other people rolled the gurney toward us and helped the boys gently set me down.

"Keep breathing, Luna. We're almost there. You're doing great," one of the nurses said as they rushed me to my destination. Chris and Greg struggled to keep up.

Suddenly, I felt a low pressure leave my abdomen and moisture slowly leak between my legs.

"Her water broke! Move! Move!" she barked, and they moved impossibly faster.

For humans, the span between labor and birth were long hours, but for wolves, the birth took place mere minutes after my water broke.

I screamed as a pain, unlike anything I'd felt so far ripped through me and tears jumped to my eyes. "Shane!" I cried though I knew he wasn't near me, but his name on my tongue relaxed me ever so slightly and made me feel close to him.

"Through here," a voice I recognized as Samantha's called and the gurney turned. "Tell Chris and Greg to stay outside for a second. I need to make sure that she's stable before I'll allow anyone else in."

The nurses nodded before they gently helped me into the bed then left the room, closing the door behind them and leaving only a few to aid Samantha. "How are you feeling?" she asked as she hooked me up to the heart rate monitor.

"Alright," I answered honestly as the contractions lessened for a moment.

"Are you feeling dizzy? Light-headed?"

"No."

"Let me know if you want to be put on medication to lessen the pain, alright?" She offered as she put on some blue gloves and hurriedly put her hair up in a cap.

I nodded once more.

"Alright, Ariel. Now what I'm going to have you do is—"

"Where is she?" a deep male voice called from somewhere outside the door, causing my heart to jump.

Shane.

I opened my mouth to call for him, but a scream of agony came out instead as a new wave washed over me. Without a second thought, Samantha carefully removed my soiled underclothes before carefully opening my legs.

"Luna, breathe," she instructed as I held my stomach and took harsh deep breaths just as Shane opened the door.

There were dark bags under his eyes, and his forehead was matted with sweat. He looked like he'd gained a year for every minute we'd been apart, and exhaustion swam in his ever-changing eyes. But he was here, and that was all that mattered.

He swiftly made his way to my side and took my hand in his own, but no matter how hard he tried to hide it, it looked like every step was a struggle for him and every breath a battle.

What had Ella done to him in the short amount of time they'd been together?

As if reading my mind, he said, "I'm fine." Then he pressed a soft kiss to the back of my hand.

I wondered how exactly he was here.

"I heard you call," he answered, seemingly reading my mind once more. "There was no way I was missing this. Not for anything."

A smile made its way onto my face before another wave of pain crashed over me, causing me to tightly grip his hand.

"You've got to push, Ariel. Push!" Samantha ordered.

Without wasting another second, I did as I was told. Grunts and pants escaped my lips along with a war cry that topped all war cries as I squeezed Shane's hand with all my being.

"I can hear their heartbeats," he announced, a smile on his face. "Two. You're having twins."

That information alone made me push harder, my breath coming out controlled like the breathing exercises Samantha and I had practiced for weeks leading up to this very moment.

"I can see the head! Don't stop, Ariel. You're doing great," Samantha said, prompting me to go even harder until Sam lifted up my baby so I could see. My heart skipped a beat and I knew that I loved this baby with all my being. She quickly wrapped it up before smiling down at it. "It's a beautiful baby boy," she announced before she handed it to the nurse to hold.

Joy washed over me as I looked up at Shane.

"You're doing amazing, Ariel," Shane said with a smile that matched my own. "I just need you to push a little more. They have separate placentas."

I nodded and did as I was told, squeezing Shane's hand until it was done. Samantha quickly handed it to another nurse

329

before they walked to the other side of the room with my baby to cut the cord and clear his airways. My arms ached for him as his beautiful cries of life filled the air and called for me, but I knew I wasn't done yet.

"You did it, Ariel." Shane smiled and kissed my sweaty forehead. "Just one more to go."

Joy moved through me in waves as our son's cries filled the air, the precious sounds of life. But the moment was short lived due to another wave of contractions.

Samantha gingerly placed her hand on my stomach and felt it for a few moments before she nodded. "They're positioned head first," she confirmed. "You just have a little further to go, Ariel."

I nodded before I started the process all over again, but this time, dots danced before my vision, and I felt the pressure building up behind my eyes.

"Stop. There's something wrong." Samantha demanded as her eyebrows knitted together in confusion. "I can't see it. Prepare for an emergency C-section."

"W-What's happening?" I breathed as I looked up at Shane who was leaning against the bed breathing heavily as something slowly started leaking from his nose, but my vision was blurred like a camera that couldn't focus.

"Don't worry. Things like this happen sometimes, but we will deliver this baby to you safely," Samantha reassured, which caused me to slowly nod before she stuck an IV into my hand and rubbed something all over my stomach.

My heartbeat was pounding in my ears, and it felt like an elephant was pressing down on my chest. What was happening?

"Luna, I need you to keep your eyes open for me, okay?" Samantha said as my eyelids became heavy.

I opened my mouth to speak, but words wouldn't fathom into existence. It felt like my mind was full of static.

"Ariel, stay awake."

I heard Shane beg, and even though he was right in front of me, holding my hand, he sounded like he was miles away. I couldn't feel his touch.

"Ariel? Ariel!" he called as my eyelids shut and I was plunged into an empty, silent sleep.

CHAPTER FORTY-THREE

SHANE

"What happened? Why did she pass out?" I frantically asked Samantha.

"She passed out from exhaustion and stress," she answered, "but she'll be alright. It happens sometimes."

I nodded as I held her hand tighter and thought about the way she'd looked at me when I first walked in and how she instantly knew that something was off.

Ella had taken me to a weird limbo where I was "between planes" as she'd put it, and as soon as we'd gotten there, an immense pain I'd never felt before tore through my body and lit the ends of my nerves on fire. The pleas and screams of thousands of people ricocheted throughout my skull as an immeasurable pain circulated throughout my head.

Ella had been right when she said time had no meaning there. For every minute that ticked by, it was like months and years had gone by, and more pain and pressure was added. She'd assured me that my body would get used to the pain, and it'd take some time. Despite her promises, it had only gotten worse.

I felt a liquid slowly reveal itself from my nose and quickly wiped it away not wanting anyone to see or worry. I didn't have to look because I knew exactly what it was. Silver. My body wasn't handling the power so far and was slowly starting to succumb to it. But it would only be a little while longer until I could crown Ariel and the power would be evenly split among us so that neither one of us would have to suffer.

"Shane, can you help me?" Samantha asked, pulling me out of my thoughts as she placed an oxygen tube below Ariel's nose.

I nodded.

"Put on some gloves and grab four of those white clamps," she instructed using her head to motion to the tray where the materials were located as she used a black marker to draw a long black line on Ariel's stomach.

I did as I was told as she called for the nurse to hand her a scalpel. By the time I was finished, Samantha had just finished cutting a long line into my mate's delicate skin. I had to look away, not able to handle seeing my mate cut open and probed.

"I got it!" she announced as another cry filled the air. "It's a girl," she announced, causing me to smile. "Shane, I need you to place the clamps where I tell you to, alright?"

I nodded and followed her instructions on where to put the clamps on the umbilical cord.

I'd been looking forward to this moment ever since Ariel showed me her test was positive and even though I'd never been very good with babies, seeing the ones my mate and I'd created filled me with pride and joy. But one fear plagued my mind.

What if I wasn't good enough? What if I let them down like my own father had done to me?

"Don't worry, Shane," Samantha said as if she could read my thoughts. "The worst thing that could happen is Ariel getting mad at you for holding the baby first."

I chuckled as Samantha effortlessly cut my daughter's cord then proceeded to remove the liquids from her airways. Her loud cries filled the air, bringing a smile to my face.

"Good. Now, you can hold her," she said.

I allowed her to place the delicate pup in my arms. I couldn't keep a smile off my face as I gently rocked her. She was so soft and pure like her mother. As I held her, I made her and her brother a silent promise that I'd never let them down or abandon them. I promised that I'd be the best father for them and I'd protect them from the harsh and cruel world no matter what it took.

I just wanted to hold her forever. But I couldn't. After a few moments, I reluctantly handed her over to the nurse to run a few tests and make sure that she was healthy. I quickly took off the gloves as Samantha removed the placenta then stitched Ariel back up to aid with her healing. I am the father of two beautiful pups, the husband of a strong and beautiful woman, and the alpha of a strong and unified pack.

"Where's my son?" I asked.

"He should be done with his tests any moment now," Samantha answered as she finished the last few stitches.

I nodded as I took Ariel's hand in mine.

"You did it," I whispered as I kissed her forehead. "We're the parents of two beautiful pups." I couldn't wait to hold both of them with her.

I made a move toward the sink to wash my hands when an overwhelming pain washed over me, causing my knees to buckle and my body to collapse. As soon as I hit the ground, a supernova of pain erupted from behind my eyes, causing me to scream as my hands flew to my head to relieve me from my pain.

Samantha made a move toward me when suddenly she too collapsed and erupted in tortured screams. I felt my airways constrict and it felt like water was filling my lungs. Fire traveled throughout my veins as I choked on the air I wasn't getting. I began coughing and choking, causing a mix of silver and blood to escape from my mouth and my nose. My body was shutting down. About a yard away from me, Samantha started spewing up silver, further confirming my thoughts. I heard screams coming from outside the door accompanied by my pups' cries.

I couldn't let this power overtake me or else it'd kill everyone including those I cared most about. I refused to do that to my pack. My children. I had to power through it. I closed my eyes and focused, drawing on my wolf and reminding myself who I was fighting for and what was at risk. I felt my wolf's strength flow through me, and the pain washed away, and my airways quickly opened. I shot up and gasped for air, coughs escaping my lips as my body tried to take in as much air as possible.

"Wh-What just happened?" Samantha asked as she quickly wiped the silver from her face, her watering eyes looking at me awaiting an answer.

"I'll explain everything later," I said as I jumped up and hurried toward the sound of my crying pups, hoping that they hadn't been affected by what had happened. I followed their cries to the room right next to where I'd just been, relieved to see that they were safe in their bed, unfazed and unharmed.

The other workers that had been in there were slowly getting up, groaning and holding their heads as they frantically wiped away the liquid silver that was on their faces.

"Can you check over them again to make sure they're okay?" I asked as I walked over to my pups and looked at their small, fragile bodies and thanked all that was good that I hadn't caused them harm.

"Yes, Alpha. Sorry for the delay," the nurse who'd been with us in the delivery room apologized, causing me to shake my head.

"It's not your fault. It's more mine than it is—" I was cut off by a scream that shook me to the core, and it came from the delivery room. "Stay with them," I instructed as I hurried out the door and back to the delivery room where I saw Samantha hunched over the foot of the bed frantically sobbing to the point her whole body was shaking.

"Samantha, what—" I started but the words died on my tongue once I saw what she had seen.

Lying there with her eyes wide open, but vacant of color and silver dripping from the bottom of her chin and into the pool that was absorbed in the bed sheets was Ariel. Motionless. Her skin was a sickly pale, and all of the colors had been chased out of her beautiful face, and her once soft lips were dried and cracked. But it got worse still. The worst part was the fact that I could no longer hear the sweet melody of her heart beating or the soft whisper of air as it entered and exited her body.

She was completely still.

"Ariel," I whispered as tears jumped to my eyes and I made my way over to her bedside and took her soft hand in mine. It was ice cold, and the spark I loved so much didn't ignite when our skin touched. "No," I cried as I sank to my knees and buried my head in her chest while I wrapped my arms around her, silently begging for her to wake up. To tell me she was okay. To kiss me again. But that didn't happen.

She remained completely still, and it broke my heart into a million pieces as memories replayed themselves in my head. The day we first met, the day of her Lunar Ceremony where she not only said her first words to me but also confessed that she loved me as much as I loved her then showed me in the first kiss we'd shared, the excitement in her eyes after she said I do. Her smile. Her lips. Her touch. Her.

"Please don't leave me, Ariel," I begged. "I need you. We've come too far. I love you with all my heart, and I can't make it through this without you, so please come back. I need you." Tears were now rushing down my face, and I continued begging her, but she remained still.

I buried my head in her chest and sobbed, not caring who saw or heard. Ariel, the love of my life, the mother of my pups, the luna of my pack, and was to be the luna of all werewolf kind was dead.

And it was all my fault.

CHAPTER FORTY-FOUR

All of us stood in Ariel's room, a heavy silence weighing down on all of us. We'd cried all the tears we could cry and screamed all of the curses that could push past our lips, but nothing made the stabbing pain in my chest go away. Nothing ever would.

Dried tears stained my face along with redness that plagued my eyes and cheeks. My voice was hoarse and scratchy from screaming and cursing. My head ached not only due to my unceasing sobs but also due to the screams and pleas that echoed throughout my skull and buried every memory of Ariel I'd tried to grasp.

It was all because of me. Samantha chalked her death up to her body being weak from the childbirth and our momentary "hiccup" being too much for her body to handle, so it simply shut down. But I knew better. Ariel was dead because of my moment of weakness, and I'd never be able to forgive myself for that.

"Baby sister." Chris sobbed as he held her cold hand. "Please . . ." He trailed off before he broke down in tears once more, causing grief to wrap its fingers of guilt tighter around my heart as I watched tears plague his face that'd been lively and happy mere hours ago.

Zac wasn't much better. He'd been spending his time crying at the foot of Ariel's bed, begging for her to wake up, but like all the other times, she didn't move a muscle. Not when I cried. Not when Chris cried. Not when anyone did. She couldn't.

Eventually, Zac cried himself to sleep, but the tear trails were still prominent against his cheeks.

I could still hear Jessica's sobs through the door even though Aiden took her out when she broke down after taking a mere glance at Ariel. Her screams and sobs echoed throughout the hospital despite Aiden's numerous efforts to try to calm her down. I could practically hear the tears falling down her face.

Greg had stormed out the moment he saw Ariel with anger rushing off him in waves and rage etched into every cell of his body. Even though he hadn't said a single word, pain and anguish were evident in his eyes. It took all of the control in my body for me not to do the same thing: simply storm off without a trace, but I knew if I let my emotions get the best of me, my wolf would easily take over and kill anyone in my path out of torment. I knew that wouldn't change anything or make me feel better. So I'd remained planted where I was, holding her hand in mine and praying for a heartbeat. A breath. Something.

As I held her hand, a million thoughts plagued my mind, but one stood out the most. I thought about my pups asking about their mother.

"Daddy, what was Mommy like?" one would ask.

"She was the most beautiful and caring person you'd ever meet. You couldn't help but fall in love with her," I would respond with an empty heart.

"Daddy, what did she look like?" the other would question.

"She had the softest, most beautiful eyes," I'd explain. "Her smile would light up a room, and her voice could make even the most barbaric and ruthless men stop and listen. I loved your mother very, very much."

After I'd say that, their eyebrows would pull together and ask the question they'd just become old enough to ask and understand. "Daddy, if you loved her so much, why would you let her die?"

339

My throat would become dry, and my heart would drop as I looked them in the eye and replied, "I was careless and let her slip between my fingers."

My chest became tight as I looked down at her. A wedding, two births, and a death all in one day. A whole lifetime played out within a single day.

Suddenly, the door opened slowly, revealing Samantha's red tear-stained face. Silent tears continued falling down her otherwise emotionless face.

"I need to take her now, Shane," she said, her voice still weak from crying.

I looked at Ariel's soft and still face before I looked back at Samantha. "Can I just have a few more minutes with her?" I said, the words feeling like knives as they traveled up my throat.

"Of course." She nodded before walking back out the door with a hiccupping Chris right behind her carrying Zac in his arms.

As soon as the door closed behind them, I turned back to Ariel. It looked like she was merely sleeping, ready to wake up and kiss me at any moment.

"I'm so sorry that I let this happen to you. I broke my vow to you. Instead of protecting you, I'm the one who led you to this," I whispered as yet another tear fell down my face. "I love you, and I will keep on loving you, Ariel, and I will tell our pups of their strong, smart, beautiful mother who left too soon," I promised as I leaned forward. "I love you, Ariel Anne Chase," I whispered before I placed a gentle kiss on her forehead. Some of my tears falling from my face cascaded over her forehead.

I allowed my lips to linger there for a second before I slowly let go of her hand before I wiped my tears and reluctantly left her to meet with the others. They were gathered in the waiting room, hugging and attempting to comfort each other.

"I don't know what I'm going to do without her," Chris said softly, sorrow etched in his features. "I've already lost my parents, and she was the last family I had left . . ."

Without wasting a second, Greg pulled him into a hug, which Chris graciously accepted.

"We're your family too," he comforted. "This pack is your family. Got it?"

Chris nodded before they both broke the hug and Chris wiped his newly shed tears.

"Come on, guys," I said, trying to sound strong though I was an emotional mess on the inside. "We all need to think some things out and get some rest. I'll stay here with the pups, but you guys need to get out of here and clear your heads."

They nodded reluctantly as they started heading out when suddenly Chris stopped and turned back to me. "We're here for you if you need us. None of us blame you for this, okay?"

I nodded though I felt differently. "Thanks."

He nodded in response before everyone disappeared through the exit to grieve in their own respective ways. As soon as I was sure everyone was gone, I ran my hands through my hair, causing another wave of tears to fall down my face but I quickly wiped them away. Crying hadn't helped anyone today, and it certainly wouldn't help now.

I made my way back to where my pups were. They were in their crib, sleeping with their chests rising and falling at a steady pace, completely unaware of what had taken place in the room right next to them. I smiled down at them. These two beautiful creatures were the only parts of Ariel I had left. They looked so beautiful. So serene. So much like Ariel. I bit my lip to keep myself from breaking down. Not here, not now.

I pulled a chair next to their crib, watching them before I took a deep breath and buried my head in my hands, blocking out the voices that continually bombarded my brain. I tried to focus on dealing with not having her by my side. The smell of disinfectants burned my nose and hung heavy in the air, almost as heavy as my grief. The sounds of machines sound like the screams of agony in my head.

I felt my wolf push against its boundaries, his anger and sadness seeping through my veins and needing a way to escape.

"Let me out," he begged, and I knew if I didn't grant him control, he would take it by force, putting my pups and the staff here in danger. I needed to get out of here.

I quickly stood up and made my way out of the door and down the labyrinth of twisted halls before I finally made it out of the stuffy hospital and into the woods right behind it. I wasted no time stripping out of my tuxedo and shifting into my wolf. He'd become two times larger, and his fur had changed from a dark black to a crisp white color. He radiated a different level of power than he had before. He let out a pained howl, effectively letting the whole pack know of the loss of their luna before he bolted deep within the woods in search of anything he could sink his teeth into.

He was currently stalking a large buck, getting into position to attack, when out of the corner of his eye, he caught sight of a bigger target. A wolf. I instantly recognized its brown fur. It was Greg.

"Don't," I commanded as I tried to gain control, but he'd refused to listen as he crouched down behind a bush as Greg let out a pained whimper.

Greg was weak. Vulnerable.

And my wolf attacked.

He pounced on Greg, knocking him down with us on top of him, caging him between our four legs so Greg couldn't escape. My wolf let out a deep menacing growl, which Greg returned and my wolf took it as a challenge. He snarled in Greg's face and bared our sharp, dangerous canines that could easily end Greg in one swift motion. Greg whimpered before he bowed in submission, but my wolf refused to let him go. He wanted Greg dead.

My wolf had become much stronger since Ella crowned me. But luckily, so did I. If I allowed something to happen to Greg at my hands, I'd never forgive myself. I began pushing for control with all my strength, and I felt my wolf slowly start to back down

342

just as the most incredible scent filled our senses, and I felt a weight lift off me. It was the sweet smell of fresh strawberries and vanilla. It was addicting.

That was all it took for my wolf to give me full control again, causing me to shift back into human form, and one word slipped past my lips as I stood up.

"Ariel?"

CHAPTER FORTY-FIVE

ARIEL

Darkness was all I could see while a loud silence was all I could hear. I felt an overwhelming sense of coldness, but fire licked at my fingers and toes at the same time. I didn't know how long I'd been stuck like this, but it felt like hours though it could have been mere minutes. Regardless of the position I was in, all I could think about were Shane and the pups.

Were they okay? Were they experiencing the same fate? Had I successfully delivered the second pup? Was it a boy or a girl? What would it feel like to hold them? Kiss their cheeks? To just be with them?

I sucked in a sharp breath as the fire became hotter and dizziness filled my being. Without warning, I felt the warmth move over various parts of my body as if someone were touching me, yet all I could see was darkness. Within another second, the addicting sparks Shane and I shared spread through me, starting with my forehead. As the sparks flowed through my body, so did an oddly addicting wave of power and a foreign strength. But too soon, the sparks disappeared as did all the comfort they brought with them. I wanted to cry out and beg for my mate to come back though I could not see him, but like every other time I've tried to talk, words failed me, and my mouth remained sealed shut.

In the blink of an eye, I was abruptly thrown into a world of color or a world of a single color. I was surrounded by a nauseating pure white with nothing stretching in each direction. I finally had control of my body, but my joints were aching, and my muscles were weighed down. I realized that I was now dressed in a flowing white gown that pooled at my feet and perfectly blended into the white floor I was standing on, making it hard to tell if I was wearing white or if it had reached up from the ground and wrapped itself around me. I also felt a lightweight on the top of my head, and when I carefully plucked it off, I realized it was a crown made of the same flowers used for my Lunar Ceremony, but it had a completely different aura about it. Confused, I cautiously placed it back on my head.

"Hello?" I called out as I continued to take in my surroundings.

"Ah, finally," a voice said, sounding directly behind me.

I turned and was surprised to see Ella standing there looking healthier than she did when we'd last met and a little younger too. She was wearing a dress identical to mine, but it was red instead of white, and a crown of red roses sat on top of her long black hair.

"I was starting to think you'd never show up," she teased with a playful grin.

"Where am I? What happened to me? Are Shane and the pups alright?" I asked, firing off all the questions that'd been occupying my mind while I slowly walked toward her.

"Don't worry, Ariel," she said with a warm smile as she placed a hand on my shoulder in a comforting manner. "We're in a limbo that I made for you. Your body was too weak for your delivery, and your heart stopped, so to prevent you from completely dying, I made this space for you so your body can find its strength until Shane crowns you."

"What?" I said in utter disbelief.

"Relax," she cooed. "Your body is almost healed, and Shane has already crowned you whether he knows it or not. His coronation is what sent you here." She smiled and took my hands as I tried to wrap my head around the whole situation. "I knew I'd chosen the right pair to take my place. You two have a strong and beautiful bond that can keep our kind afloat. I know I didn't give you much of a choice, but I'm so proud that you guys stuck together and toughed it out until the very end."

"Are you sure we'll be able to do this?" I inquired. "I mean, we don't even know the first thing about running a whole species or how to mate people or—"

"Ariel, relax." She chuckled. "You're far stronger than you give yourself credit for. Besides, I've already given Shane the 'Moon Goddess and God 101,' but if you still need my help, you can always reach out to me through a link," she explained as the world around us started to fade.

I nodded. "Thank you for saving me. I hope you find peace in your new world among the elders."

"Thank you, Ariel." She smiled. "I hope you find peace in yours."

Those were the last words I heard before all the white disappeared and I was hurled back into a black void. The smell of sterile air burned my nostrils as it entered my lungs and I could feel the full weight of my body again. I slowly opened my eyes but quickly shut them once more due to the intense light that invaded them. After a few moments, I sat up as I tried again. I felt power surge through my body like lightning as my mind was plagued by thousands of different voices saying various things at once.

I held my head as I took a deep breath, taking in my surroundings. I was still in the same hospital room with silver coating the sheets and clinging to my skin, but it didn't burn like it should have. Out of the corner of my eye, I caught a glimpse of a white strand of hair. I gathered it in my hands and realized that it was mine. I caught a glimpse of my reflection in a metal tray that held bloodied medical tools. My hair was an icy white, and my eyes were continuously changing.

"Hello?" I called, realizing that my room was void of any other soul other than mine. "Sam? Shane?" I called as I stood up, almost falling over due to the intense needle-like pain that plagued my legs.

How long had I been out?

"Is anyone he—" I started just as the most intoxicating scent rushed in my nose and was approaching quickly.

Shane.

The door quickly swung open, revealing a bare Shane. He looked at me with shock and disbelief evident in his eyes then finally happiness.

"Ariel," he breathed out before he approached me, and in two mighty strides, he scooped me up in his strong arms that reminded me of home. Then he did something I didn't expect him to.

He cried. No. He sobbed into my chest as his grip became impossibly tighter as did mine. I wanted nothing more than to wipe every tear off his face.

"Please don't leave me again," he whispered between sobs, causing my heart to clench as I tangled my fingers in his white hair that matched my own.

"I won't. I promise."

After a few moments, he composed himself, and his breathing returned to normal as he looked at me just like he did the first day we met: loving eyes, an adorable grin, and an expression that read I love you so much.

I used my thumbs to gently wipe the tears from his now red face, and all the while, his expression remained the same. He continued looking at me as if I were a rare jewel that'd disappear in a whisper of smoke if he looked away.

"I missed you so much," he confessed in a whisper as he leaned in and gently placed his lips on mine.

I felt new sparks dance between us, making my insides heat up and render my knees utterly useless. He pulled me closer with an urgency I'd never felt from him, and his hands wandered all over my body like he was trying to embed the feeling of my body within each of his cells.

"I love you," he murmured into my lips before he rested his forehead on mine.

"I love you too." I smiled as I slid my hands into his.

"How are you feeling?" he asked softly as he kissed the back of my hands.

"Better now," I stated honestly, causing him to kiss my forehead just before the door opened.

Both of us turned toward the sudden motion and saw my brother in front of Aiden, Jessica, Zac, Samantha, and Greg, who was only wearing basketball shorts. Greg shared an unreadable look with Shane before they both nodded in mutual understanding.

"Oh my gosh, Ariel," Chris said barely above a whisper before he shamelessly wrapped his arms around me and sobbed into my chest. "I-I thought I lost you."

"You'll never lose me," I promised. "I'm right here."

"Please never leave again," Zac begged as he wrapped his arms around my waist.

"I won't. I promise," I said, causing them to smile.

"I'm guessing you want to see your little ones," Samantha suggested, and I nodded feverishly.

"Please," I said as I began following her. "I want to meet my pups."

CHAPTER FORTY-SIX

My heart raced as I was led to the room where our pups rested. The others decided to give Shane and me some space so that they wouldn't be overwhelmed by the number of people surrounding them, which I was grateful for.

"Are you ready?" Shane asked softly as his hand rested on the metal doorknob.

"Yes," I confirmed with a small smile, and he pushed the door open.

I hurried into the room, and my heart swelled at the sight. My two pups rested in their little cribs; eyes closed and bodies stretched out. My smile grew as tears rushed to my eyes while I walked to the one closest to me, my baby girl. I gently picked her up, careful not to wake her from her sleep, and cradled her in my arms. She unconsciously moved closer to my heart in her sleep.

"She's beautiful," I whispered as I lightly touched her cheek with my index finger.

"She gets it from you," Shane commented with a smile, causing me to roll my eyes. "Do you still know what you want to name her?"

I nodded. "Annalise," I responded. "The name of a strong and important woman in my life," I said before looking down at the sleeping angel in my arms. "Now it's yours, Annalise Serenity Chase."

"Annalise Serenity Chase," Shane echoed as he wrapped his arms around my waist and rested his chin on my shoulder. "Perfect." He gently placed a kiss on her cheek before he walked over and picked up our baby boy. "I guess that makes you Luca Ethan Chase, little guy." He smiled as he gently rocked the newborn who was drowning in Shane's massive arms, but neither of them seemed to mind. "You're going to be a strong alpha," he whispered softly to him. "You're going to love and respect your mother, and you're going to protect your sister from knuckle-headed pups for me, okay?"

I couldn't help but chuckle at the demands Shane had before he continued.

"You're going to protect people even when it seems like they don't deserve protecting. And when you find your mate." He paused, looking up at me. "You're going to hold on to her and never let her go."

I smiled as Shane walked over to me and placed a gentle kiss on my lips, each of us holding the most important beings in our lives.

Without warning, the door suddenly opened, causing us to quickly pull apart and for me to hold Annalise closer to my chest, but I relaxed once I realized who the culprit was.

"What?" Chris asked, raising an eyebrow with a mischievous look in his eye. "Bad timing?"

I narrowed my eyes on him. "If we weren't in front of children, I would slap you right now," I said, though we both knew it was an empty threat. "Come in, but be quiet. They're sleeping," I said, using my head to motion that he, along with everyone else, was welcome.

They all quietly washed their hands before they approached our babies and us.

"They're beautiful," Jessica whispered.

"What are their names?" Aiden asked softly.

"This little girl right here," I said, slightly rising her in my arms, "is Annalise Serenity Chase, and Shane is holding Luca Ethan Chase."

"Can I hold Annalise?" Chris asked faintly, his eyes never leaving the little angel in my arms.

"Of course." I nodded though I never wanted to let her go. "Hold her like this," I instructed as I showed Chris how to handle my fragile child.

"You named her after Mom," he observed, and I nodded.

"She's going to be like her too. I can tell. Kind, strong, courageous, and loving. Stubborn too, I bet," I joked.

"I know she will be," Chris said with a slight chuckle. "Because her mother's like that too."

I gently punched him in the arm before I took in the sight before me. Jess was talking to Aiden and Greg about throwing a baby shower that I never got to have while Zac sat in Shane's lap talking to him in an excited voice while Shane held Luca.

"I'm an uncle?" he asked, disbelief evident in his voice and a light shining in his eyes.

"Yes, you are, little buddy," Shane confirmed before using one hand to ruffle Zac's hair.

I smiled to myself as I took it all in. This marked the start of a new chapter of something wonderful. Of course, it was going to have its ups and downs, but as long as I had my pack, my family right by my side, I knew I was going to be just fine.

EPILOGUE

SHANE

"Luca Ethan Chase, get your naked butt back in this bath!" Ariel's voice yelled from upstairs of our new house. "No, Annalise! Get back here!"

I heard the laughter of our two rascals as their bare feet pounded against the floor above me. They were headed toward the stairs. I smiled to myself as I quickly hid around a corner at the base of the stairs and prepared myself to strike. Within moments, I heard four tiny feet padding down the stairs, contagious laughter filling the air as they did so.

As soon as I heard their feet hit the hardwood floor, I jumped out from my hiding spot and quickly scooped up their wet, sudsy bodies. "Now what have we got here?" I questioned as I looked at them both giggling uncontrollably.

"Daddy, let us go before Mommy gets us!" Luca squealed as they both feverishly tried to escape my grasp.

"Luca! Annalise!" she growled from the top of the stairs, causing their happy, giddy looks to quickly melt into those of fear.

"Daddy, please," Annalise begged as she gave me a look that she knew I couldn't resist. This was going to come back and bite me in the butt. Nevertheless, I sighed and put them down, causing them to scream and run in the opposite direction just as Ariel made her way down the stairs.

I was in trouble now.

"Where are they, Shane?" she demanded in a tight voice, bath suds in her hair and water soaking her clothes. She looked so adorable minus that murderous rage that burned in her eyes. "I know you know."

"Woah, Ariel, calm down," I said, raising my hands in surrender.

"Don't tell me to calm down!" she snapped. "Look at me!"

"You look adorable." I smiled down at her as I wrapped my arms around her waist and pulled her in, not caring that she was getting me wet or that she was obviously cross with me for helping our kids escape.

"Shane, I'm serious. Let me go," she whined like a child, weakly trying to get free.

"Only if you give me a kiss," I bargained with a smirk, causing her to roll her eyes before she tried to break free once more. I didn't budge.

"Come on, Ariel. I can stand here all day." I taunted, causing her to let out an aggravated sigh before she roughly grabbed the back of my neck and kissed me.

Sparks erupted throughout my body as Ariel's aggression melted into pure compassion. My hands firmly planted themselves on her hips, and she tightly gripped my shoulders. Our lips moved perfectly in sync with her soft lips fueling the fire that was ablaze between us. As the fire grew, so did my hatred for the space that burned between us. I wanted it gone, bad.

Luckily, before I could let my ecstasy get the best of me, a small voice said, "Ew! Mommy and Daddy are kissing, Luca!"

We pulled apart to see Annalise and Luca staring at us with looks of disgust plastered on their adorable faces.

"Ew!" Luca laughed, wrinkling his nose to enhance his disgust.

"I'm gonna get you guys!" Ariel laughed as she started chasing them with me right behind her.

They screamed and laughed as we chased them throughout the house, water and bubbles leaving a trail everywhere they went. It was especially hard to catch them due to their werewolf genetics starting to kick in giving them enhanced speed and strength, but after about ten minutes of chasing them, I scooped up Annalise, and Ariel got Luca.

"Gosh, you guys have a lot of energy." Ariel chuckled as she made her way upstairs with Annalise and me following her.

"Don't make us go back," Luca whined as we re-entered the bathroom.

"It's no use. The water's cold anyway." Ariel sighed as she put Luca down and pulled the plug on the cold bath while I grabbed their towels and wrapped them around their naked bodies.

"Go put on your PJs," I instructed. "Mommy and I will be right behind you to tuck you in."

"Okay, Daddy."

"Okay," Anna and Luca said at the same time before they raced out of the bathroom.

"Come on," I said as I took one of Ariel's hands in my own.

"Next time, you're on bath duty." She chuckled, causing me to sigh.

"Fine," I agreed reluctantly as I led her out onto the patio that overlooked the pack.

The full moon peeked out from behind the clouds, giving everything a somewhat eerie glow. I looked at Ariel, and her eyes were glued to the moon, its light illuminating her silvery hair and bouncing through her colorful eyes.

"We're starting to get the hang of this," she murmured, her eyes still glued to the moon.

I nodded, understanding what she meant. We'd learned how to silence the agonizing screams in our heads and dived out our strength to those in need, though there were still some nights where she'd wake up screaming in a cold sweat from nightmares, completely emotionally and physically drained. We also learned how mating essentially took place in the back of our heads without much effort, but we'd also learned the extreme pain that came with intentionally mating two people together like we had for Greg, Zac, and our children.

Blood leaked from our eyes and filled our chests until it almost suffocated us. But it was worth it for our family even though we didn't know exactly who they were or when they were going to meet. Ariel had offered to mate Chris, but he refused to put either of us in pain and said that he'd be happy with whomever he was naturally placed with.

And we did this all while managing our growing pack rather than giving it up completely and retiring to the realm between realms like Ella did when she was in power.

"We're trekking through it," I agreed as I snaked my arm around her waist and pulled her close enough for her to rest her head on my shoulder. "We always do."

She nodded before turning to me. "I love you," she said as she kissed my bare shoulder and without a moment's hesitation, I said it back.

"I love you too." I slid my hand into hers as we looked over the pack grounds where our pack rested. We heard wolves running about in the forest and pack members sharing memories and laughter with one another.

It was pure bliss.

"Come on," I said, leading her back into the house. "They should be done by now."

She nodded in agreement and allowed me to lead her into Anna and Luca's room where they were throwing pillows at each other, one laughing as it hit the other's face.

"Alright, settle down you two," I said as I caught one of Luca's airborne pillows before I set it back on his bed.

We both tucked them in and took turns kissing their foreheads. "Good night, Luca. Good night, Annalise."

"Wait, Daddy!" Annalise called as we began walking out the door. "You and Mommy need to tell us a bedtime story!"

"Yeah!" Luca agreed, light filling his eyes and excitement lacing his voice.

I raised an eyebrow at Ariel, asking her the silent question and she just shrugged before she took a seat at the end of Anna's bed with me on the end of Luca's.

"Okay," she agreed. "Once upon a time, there was a girl who had a mean alpha. He would bully her and say really mean things to her that would make her cry. He even bullied her into not speaking!" she started, causing Anna's eyes to grow wide.

"I don't like him," she decided, as she crossed her arms.

"Me neither," Ariel agreed.

"Then one day," I continued. "Another nice, strong, handsome alpha came and found out that the girl was his mate. She was the most beautiful girl he'd ever seen, and he knew he loved her immediately," I said, smiling at Ariel causing her to playfully roll her eyes.

"After the nice alpha beat up the mean alpha for hurting the girl, the nice alpha and the girl went back to his pack where he vowed he'd protect her and build her up again. Unfortunately, there was a bully in his pack too. She was mean though it wasn't her choice, but the girl defended herself and showed the bully that she wasn't going to be treated badly anymore," Ariel said as she punched the air, causing Luca to giggle.

I couldn't help the tightness that grew in my chest any time Stephanie was mentioned as memories of what Ella had made her do plague my thoughts, but I forced myself to swallow it down and continue. "The alpha and the beautiful girl began falling deeply in love, and even though they had trouble sometimes, they made it through and made a lot of good friends on the way. She even started talking again."

"But one day, the mean alpha came back and kidnapped the girl again, treating her even worse than he had before," Ariel said softly as her hand gently touched her neck where Morgan had slit her throat. The very mention of him made me enraged.

"But she showed him how strong she'd become and he never bothered her again. She got back to her mate and pack, and he promised to never let her go," I quickly finished, knowing that was the part of the story Ariel hated the most.

"And he didn't." She smiled at me. "Soon they got married, and the girl gave birth to a couple of pups named Luca and Annalise before they both shared the responsibilities of all lycan on their shoulders."

"Hey, that was a story about you!" Luca called, causing him and his sister to giggle.

"I knew that story sounded familiar," I joked as I rubbed my chin in mock thought, causing them to laugh harder and I couldn't help but laugh along with them before we gave them one more round of kisses.

"Love you," Ariel said.

"Love you."

"Love you too," they both said in unison as we exited their room, closing the door behind us before we headed into our room right next door.

I stripped down to my boxers while Ariel changed into a silk gown I'd gotten her for our fourth anniversary earlier this year.

"What?" She chuckled once I realized I was staring at her.

"You just look so beautiful," I said honestly, causing her to roll her eyes though a smile took place on her lips.

"Whatever, Shane."

Within a moment, I was behind her, my arms around her waist and my mouth close to hers. "Stop putting yourself down. You're beautiful," I whispered before I skillfully placed a delicate kiss on her mark and her body shivered under my touch.

"You know what happened the last time you did that," she chastised, causing me to chuckle as I gently turned her around.

"Your point being . . ." I trailed off as I placed a mixture of soft and rough kisses all over her face and shoulders.

"Stop!" She giggled, but no matter how many times she told me to stop, she knew I never would. I loved the sound of her laughter too much. "Shane, it's late, and I'm going to wake up the kids!" She giggled.

"Fine, you party pooper." I frowned, finally giving in.

"Come on," she said as she grabbed me by the hand and led me to the bed, the light from the moon silently spilling through the window and perfectly illuminating her body.

We settled into bed, and I wrapped my arms around her and held her as close to me as possible. Amazing sparks moved through me everywhere we touched, and her mesmerizing scent sent my wolf and me into a frenzy. I gently placed a kiss on her cheek before I said, "I love you, Ariel."

"I love you too, Shane," she said sleepily before she closed her eyes and welcomed the world of sleep.

Even though we had said those simple words over a million times, each time it escaped our lips I knew that it was true and always would be. I loved my wife. I loved my children. I loved my family and my pack. I loved my life, and even though it was harder than most, as long as I was surrounded by the people I loved and my beautiful mate and children were there with me every step of the way, the world could fall apart around me, and I wouldn't care.

I wouldn't want it any other way.

FREE DOWNLOAD

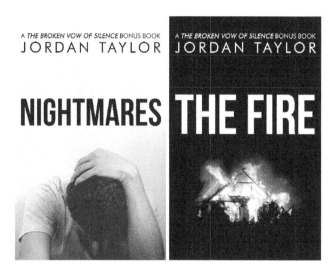

Can't get enough of the story?
Get these two bonus chapters when you sign up at
typewriterpub.com/author/jordan-taylor

Do you like werewolf stories?
Here are samples of other stories
you might enjoy!

Yolanda Jolante

Luna Catherine

CHAPTER ONE

He had taken everything from me yet I'm still here. My own brother, Ronan.

Ronan lost himself a long time ago, and selfishly enough, he dragged me down along with him. I was of pure innocence, and he corrupted me. He made me bear witness to the most heinous of crimes, filling my mind with nightmares. I watched him in silence as he went down a black hole, returning to be what he secretly feared the most—a man with a dark soul.

He's claimed to not fear anything; a rebel who lives off instilling fear into others. He feeds off the control he has, the adrenaline rush he gets when a life ends by his hands. He can be irrational at times, a loudmouth, cocky, stubborn, dark, and twisted, yet still, he can't control one thing.

His love for me.

In his own twisted way, he loves me. He's done so much hurt and pain. He's been cruel and left me bare at such a young age, but still, he keeps me close. He feeds off my strength and breathes calmly in my silence. Now that he's grown, he can't find it in him to destroy me any further than he already has.

A murderer, a selfish and cruel man, and many more titles to everyone else but a frightened, confused, and an out-of-control little boy in a man's body, right in my view.

A storm is brewing, I can feel it. He knows it too because I told him before. He's tried so many times to ignore me, but today, he can't because, like always, I'm right.

A crash sound comes from the living room. He's breaking stuff again. He's earned everyone's attention, all movements still, in his outburst.

I watch him silently by the doorway while he loses his cool once again. He throws a glass to the nearest wall and makes one servant gasp in shock.

"Everyone, out!" he demands.

Not needing to be told twice, every present person scurries out of there, leaving us alone. Right after everyone has gone, he walks over to the drinks cabinet, pulling out a bottle of brandy.

I finally enter, walking over to stand by the large windows, not even sparing him another glance.

I hear him shuffling close, then the sound of liquid being poured before glass is slammed hard against the wooden table.

He loudly gulps down his drink. He's frustrated, I can feel it.

"Be careful, brother, before you kill yourself," I say.

He growls in answer, wanting to ignore me but he can't. I know he wants to have another, and if he does, he might lose his senses. That's never a good sign, especially today. A drunk Ronan is the worst Ronan.

"You've done wrong, brother. Now, you just might meet the outcome of your actions," I tell him calmly, like always.

"Shut up!" he growls in warning.

I do.

He paces up and down now.

"Damn troublemakers."

More like you, I want to say.

A cold, icy chill runs down my spine, and my body tenses in the process.

"The storm is coming. The storm is near."

I hear a growl before I'm spun around to face him, and his brown eyes darken. I don't even wince when he tightens his grip on my arm.

"Stop talking gibberish and say what you mean!" he seethes, his alcoholic breath fanning my face.

Like a lightbulb clicking in my mind, a certain wind washes over me. It's them. They are close. I don't know who they are, but they come with a mission.

"Be prepared . . . for just about anything," I tell him.

He growls in anger before he backhands me across the face, sending me flying and landing hard on the floor.

"If you have nothing better to say, then shut the hell up!" he shouts, leaving the room.

He has listened.

I close my eyes for a minute, blinking back tears and softly rubbing at my burning cheek.

"Oh no, miss!" Cara—one of the omegas—says, rushing over to help me up. "Please sit and let me treat you."

"There's no time. Please take care of the glass and then go into hiding."

Her eyes search my own until she gulps in realization of the situation. "Trouble is coming once again," she mumbles.

All I do is stare at her.

"You've always been the calm one out of everyone here, and the most truthful. Ha!" She sighs. "I will do as you say, Luna."

I close my eyes, holding back my tongue from telling her to stop referring to me as Luna.

Leaving her alone to attend to the scattered, broken glass, I decide to leave and go to my room, wanting to treat my cheek and to try to look presentable because I know Ronan wouldn't be pleased with me if I wasn't.

Coming back down the stairs in a long black jumpsuit with ballet pumps, I feel them really close, though I may not see them. It's a matter of time before they appear. I remain in the living room with half of my body visible through the window.

His footsteps echo as he appears, looking cleaner in dark jeans and a white shirt that hugs his muscles. I can feel his gaze on me.

"What the fuck are you wearing?" he shouts, and I almost jump out of my skin.

I turn to face him, opening my mouth to say something, when the cold chill comes at me like a bullet going through my chest.

"You have visitors, brother," I tell him, turning to face the window.

I hear his footsteps come closer.

"Shit," he curses before storming out of the door.

Ronan with his styled, cut, light-brown hair appears into view, standing on the front yard with about ten to fifteen men. A few minutes pass and no one shows up, making Ronan glance over his shoulder at me. His eyes narrow and I notice him try to fight off a smirk.

This is a promise that there'll be consequences if I'm lying, but I'm not. He's doubting me yet again.

All too soon, a group of tall men appear from the forest. Ronan's demeanour changes and his body tenses when he turns back front. Amongst the approaching men, I notice the one in the middle—the leader.

He is the most muscular out of the men; he's breathtakingly handsome with his midnight black hair, striking emerald-green eyes that meet mine, a strong jaw, and sculpted blank face. He shows no emotion to the onlookers, yet I can sense him. I'm stronger than him in this.

He is feeling everything, and he thinks I can't. His scent is of fresh pine and woods—earthy and pleasant to my nose.

I know without a doubt that he is my mate, the one I'm destined to be with, my soulmate. Yet what he represents, what he stands for, his views on mates, and all he's been till now forms a defensive shield against the bond.

He is just like my brother.

I sigh and slump in disappointment and defeat.

I watch the interaction between my brother and my mate. It's intense and doesn't seem like something good will be concluded. It's been a few minutes now, and I hold no hope for what may be.

Turning away from the window and meaning to walk away, I stop in my tracks when I sense it—a strong and intense gaze. I glance over my shoulder at the precise moment he nods my way. My heart flips at his intense eyes.

He has just caused the first real reaction from my already still heart.

When Ronan glances over his shoulder, I'm suddenly grabbed by arm and dragged out of the house, earning frightened eyes from pack members and hard ones from my mate's company. I'm shoved hard towards the ground, only for someone to grip my arm strongly to prevent me from going down any further.

Sparks erupt throughout my body, and I gasp at the contact. It's him, my mate.

I almost whisper it out but bite down on my tongue, not wanting to expose anything. Being pulled up, I sneak a glance to my mate. My breath hitches at the sight of his beautiful green eyes. I notice a small but deep and permanent scar on the side of his face; it still doesn't take away from his captivating looks. His scar is a sign of things he's gone through and conquered.

He catches me looking at his scar, and that makes his eyes harden with anger laced in them. I'm spun around to face my brother whose eyes are trained on me.

"So are we talking now?" My breath hitches when something sharp is pressed hard against my neck.

My eyes are only on my brother.

"What do you want, O'Connell?" my brother grunts, clearly annoyed by the situation we are currently in.

"You know what I want, Black. It's been long overdue now. Give me back my beta."

"Dead or alive?" Ronan arches his brow.

"Don't play games with me and give me what I want." My mate's deep voice sounds calm but deadly.

"Or what?" Ronan asks, clenching his hands into fists.

"Do you really want me to answer that? Alright, let me demonstrate." Without any warning, the sharp object is shoved into the side of my neck and pulled out. I'm immediately thrown across the yard, my body slamming hard against a nearby tree.

Growls erupt, bones crack, and bodies collide. I glance up from the ground to the horrific scene in front of me. Werewolves are everywhere; there's so much blood and fighting between my brother's wolf and my mate's right in the centre.

Pack members scream and run around, trying to get to safety.

Pain erupts from my neck and reaching up to where I was stabbed, a wetness coats the wound. Soon, I'll be bleeding out.

My attention diverts when I sense it, my brother's life is hanging in the balance. I sit upright, pressing against my wound and facing what now looks to be my mate's dark-gray gigantic wolf standing over Ronan's midnight-black one. My mate's eyes connect with mine just as he digs his teeth in my brother's wolf's neck.

My heart hammers hard against my chest. He won't hesitate to kill Ronan, but his eyes tell me that I've only got one chance to do something.

He's daring me to do something.

"Stop! Stop please!" I plead, struggling to rise on my feet.

I stagger close to them. A few of my mate's men remain, looking rather threatening.

"Alpha, I have a proposal. Let him go please." My brother's eyes narrow in threat, but I avoid his eyes, looking at my mate's.

I'll deal with my brother's wrath after. Right now, I need to manage the situation. Though it may be my first time being given the platform.

My mate doesn't let up. He puts pressure on my brother's neck, earning us both a growl and whine from my brother. Time is of the essence; I can almost hear him say.

"Your beta will be released, so long as you release our own." I take a ragged breath. "I will take upon any punishment and everything your beta endured in time of his captivity. I will accept with no argument or fight. The length of time he stayed here is the length of time I'll remain there."

I gasp when I feel myself really bleeding out now. I watch my mate's eyes take notice of this before he growls and takes a step back, loosening his grip.

"Please, release my brother. Brother for a brother." I gulp though I choke a bit.

My mate shifts into his human form, and I look away from his nudeness. From the corner of my eye, I see one of his men take a pair of grey sweats to him.

I'm getting dizzy now.

"What. Do. You. Think. You're. Doing?" my brother growls, his body shaking in anger. He is injured but I know he'll heal soon.

"I'm doing what's best, brother. You might not agree but it is. I-I will take my punishment once I return." I wish I didn't have to say this out loud, but it's for Ronan to clearly hear me and understand.

Ronan grunts before instructing one of his men to fetch the beta.

I sigh in relief for that—knowing a person will get to go home to his family. I stagger back due to the dizziness and almost fall, but my arm is gripped hard to the point of pain by my mate's men.

I mistakenly whimper due to the pain, but then, there's a growl. The grip on my arm is loosened and is being replaced by pleasurable tingles that I almost sigh out in relief.

The beta is soon brought out, beaten and bruised yet still standing. His fellow troops help him to one of the cars. I take a much-needed breath in preparation of me looking like him when I return. Well, if I don't die out due to all the bleeding.

Maybe I might just die here. That'll be fine with me.

"My beta," Ronan grunts.

All too soon, his beta is thrown at his feet, being helped up and taken in the house probably to the pack doctor.

I can't even watch anymore. My vision gets blurry, and my body weight takes over. I feel myself falling, only to land in someone's arms. The sparks give it away.

Before I can slip into darkness, I hear the parting words between my brother and mate.

"You know that I'll come back for her. She belongs here."

"No. She's mine now."

If you enjoyed this sample, look for
Luna Catherine
on Amazon.

WOLFBORN

CRISTAL SIEBERHAGEN

CHAPTER 1
The Lost

They bound Devon Creed in place with silver-plated chains and cuffs crafted from solid steel. The touch of that precious metal seared exposed skin, insidiously poisoning her bloodstream and draining her will to fight until she stopped defying the bonds holding her on her knees. The stone's sun-warmed and blood-soaked abrasive texture bruised her lower legs, not allowing her to find a comfortable position to ease the aching needles and pins of restricted blood flow.

Earlier, her father's guards positioned her in the center of the "Circle of Justice", an honor reserved for heinous offenders like mass murderers, kinslayers, political rivals that stir rebellion, and traitors—all of which Marcus accused her of, turning her into a villain the likes of which the werewolf kingdom had not seen in a thousand years.

Devon never met a werewolf so devious or thought one existed.

Marcus framed her with minimal effort, orchestrating each detail to perfection.

His timing was almost surreal, always putting her in the wrong place at the wrong time, with no excuse for her presence and no idea of what she would find.

Then she received that bloodied letter from Maria, pleading for her help.

Dear Devon,

My husband has gone insane again. This time, he threatened the children. Please come alone. I don't want to set him off, and Malvern always listens to you. Don't let your father see this letter. Burn it as you always do. You know what he thinks of Malvern and his temper.

Yours always,
Maria

It was not the first time Lord Malvern drank too much and threatened his wife, but he never did it to the children.

Only Devon could restore him to reason.

She didn't think twice about the letter. It was Maria's familiar writing on the parchment, her seal and her words.

She left her tasks undone, hurrying to the aid of her family. When she arrived, she found the castle doors ajar with no signs of forced entry. A bloodied sword lay abandoned in the foyer, and the scent of blood permeated the air. The blade belonged to Malvern, and she picked it up without thinking.

The most pungent smells came from the Great Hall. Devon ran in that direction and pushed open the enormous oak doors that led to this room; but unlike the front doors, they were torn half off their hinges with some unknown force as if to resist the intruders. Blood from the broken wood smeared her hands without her even noticing.

She took three steps into the room and froze.

They were all dead: Maria, Malvern, the children, his men-at-arms, the servants, and even the dogs before the hearth.

Despite her horrified shock, something drew her attention: Marcus' symbol drawn in blood. It was near Malvern's body and half obscured by the scuff mark of someone's boot.

She had no time to process the loss of Maria, who was her best and only friend since childhood, before Marcus and his men stormed into the room.

Startled, Devon tried to get away from them. As she did, she tripped over one of the corpses and fell to the floor, smearing her dress with her family's blood.

"Drop the sword, Princess. We caught you in the act of slaying your kin, and these bodies are still warm." The smug tone of his voice brought her to her senses.

"That is Malvern's silver-edged weapon you hold, is it not? Is it the same weapon you drove through his heart?"

Until he mentioned it, she had forgotten the heavy sword in her hands.

His predatory gaze made the pieces come together in her head. She had reacted like a soldier entering a dangerous situation, not a princess surrounded by enemies.

"As the King's Chief Advisor, I lay the charge of high treason against you, Princess Devon Elizabeth Creed, kinslayer. Do not bother denying the allegations. We witnessed the aftermath of your brutality, and we were too late to save your victims."

Despite her shock, she could see the picture he painted with such forethought.

"We've been on to you for months, and the evidence is damning. Do not speak and condemn yourself any further. We are not fooled by your pretty face or partial to your lies," Marcus warned with a smirk touching his lips.

She watched him smear the bloody emblem with his boot, shifting Malvern's body over it and using his finger to draw hers instead.

"So, you found out your father would not allow you to rule alone. To avoid marrying me, you did this instead? The common folk might have forgotten that you are not all werewolf, but they will remember now. They won't forget that Elizabeth, your mother, betrayed her husband, your father, King Wolfgang by leaving." The glee in his tone and the victory in his eyes said more than his words.

The smirks on his men's faces warned her that contradicting Marcus' lies would do her no good.

*   *   *

The towering monoliths stood sentinel to the ages for a thousand years, mute witnesses to man's unashamed cruelty, brazen folly, and unmatched arrogance.

The werewolves used this haunting monument, isolated within the no-man's-land between two rival territories, to punish those who broke the kingdom's most sacred rules.

This strip of land belonged to *The Circle*, dividing the vampire and werewolf kingdoms. Both sides freed outcasts, criminals, and rogues into this hinterland, allowing their royalty to hunt the damned without consequences.

Its type of justice knew no mercy, not even for the disavowed daughter of the high king of the lycan empire, ultimate ruler of all twelve werewolf domains. It dispensed the same punishment to Devon as it would to a common murderer, making no exception.

No one would relieve her of her suffering. No sane person would dare to enter this place with those red and black flags lining the road. Their presence proclaimed Wolfgang's will: strictly forbidding any interference at the penalty of death.

If the king wanted to make an example of someone, whose standing in their society justified the arduous journey to this desolate ruin, they found their way here to face Wolfgang's justice and inevitable verdict. *The Circle* offered its occupants the guarantee of a slow, painful, and humiliating death.

Devon struggled to keep track of time. Minutes dragged into hours, and hours passed in the blink of an eye.

She lacked the energy to raise her head, not that she needed or wanted to do any such thing. She already knew what she would see—the innocents condemned with her.

These were people whose execution Wolfgang forced her to witness. He punctuated each murder with a lash of his silver-studded whip, not even bothering to wield the weapon himself.

With her suspended from the whipping post through a pair of thick, rusty chains clamped on her wrists, Marcus took the "honor" of flaying her, brandishing the ornate tool with such wicked relish.

The black leather thong split her skin with every crack of the whip, and he coerced her into counting aloud the loss of each life to avoid doubling her punishment.

It was not her first whipping, just the most brutal.

Thirty-two rotting corpses littered the ground. These were the desecrated remains of blameless souls who had the misfortune of belonging to Devon's court.

The vicious lies of greedy backstabbers and brutal half-truths of false testimony delivered this sheer terror and denied them the honor of burial. It robbed them of the justice that every citizen deserved while Wolfgang's hatred kept their kin from getting closure.

Hostile spectators abandoned Devon to her fate. Trapped amid the chaotic destruction of death, she was a helpless observer to scavengers feasting on the decaying dead, gnawing on sun-bloated cadavers infested with maggots. Guilty horror overwhelmed her. She saw similar things in the past; but those bodies did not belong to her friends, comrades, servants, or their families.

Soon, she would face an agonizing end, their fates a mere foreshadow of her future.

Her continued survival was not rational, even as a testament to the power of her line.

She no longer saw her tenacity as courage but a curse denying her entrance to the tranquil fields of eternal rest.

She wanted fate to release her from the painful reality of mental and physical anguish that was slowly driving her to delirium.

Devon closed her scratchy, swollen lids; and the faces of the recently gone flashed before her mind's eye in a never-ending collage.

The memories of happier times, their lives, and their families provided no respite to her aching heart.

Devon's tormented spirit and ravaged body instinctively resisted the fatigue dragging her into oblivion even as she prayed for the kindness of that final twilight. The nothingness of not existing beckoned just beyond her reach.

A studded whip never left a clean wound, releasing trace amounts of silver into each deep laceration.

These metal shavings prevented her cuts from closing or healing, causing the injuries to leak blood, infected pus, and gore.

The relentless pressure of the cuffs hurt. The chain's roughened edges chafed Devon's skin until it oozed ichor, piercing deeper with each shift of her weight.

Someone, probably a blacksmith, had designed these devices to cut into the muscle and intensify the victim's suffering by merely attaching a few simple counterweights. Pain, time, and gravity did the rest.

After the unbearable destruction caused by his whipping and before assigning guards to shackle her into this torturous contraption, Marcus had her right ankle tethered to the stone with a six-foot-long chain.

He stalked Devon, chasing his prey and tripping her. If his actions triggered her instinct to fight, he pelted her with his fists. It was something easily achieved in her weakened condition. Then he'd give her some space, followed by a few kicks to hasten her reaction, all the while telling the crowd what he thought of her and what he intended to do after breaking her spirit.

Devon's inner werewolf gave her the determination to drag herself to her feet, mindlessly driven to survive and defend itself.

Tired of the game, Marcus unexpectedly caught the chains, tumbling Devon face-first into the dirt. She hit her temple against an outcropping of rock, seeing stars as she drunkenly crawled to her knees.

He gave her no chance to gather herself. His foot connected solidly with her jaw, spinning her onto her back.

Her body grew slack, but she was not unconscious, only dazed.

Marcus tore the remains of her flimsy shift from her, grabbing her neck in a one-handed chokehold Wolfgang taught him.

He straddled her and grinned, his eyes dancing with smug pride while she uselessly tried to pry his grip from her throat. She could not even shift her hands into claws.

She hated no one more than him.

He warned her the day she denied his marriage proposal that she would regret it; but safe in her innocent, self-important little world, Devon had no idea of what Marcus was capable of doing.

He shamed her while suffocating her; and his animalistic violation ground dirt, filth, and stones into her open wounds.

Would she have felt any less abused in the privacy of their bedroom day after day? Some rational part of her mind wondered.

He enjoyed hitting her, and she suspected that she was not the first woman he beat up or raped.

This was nothing more than an inferior wolf proving himself superior over a so-called pureblood princess despite his pretense of doing it for the spectator's entertainment.

Her disgrace was his victory lap. Marcus triumphed over Wolfgang, and her father did not even realize it.

Worse than what Marcus did to her broken, bleeding, and abused body was the fact that Wolfgang, her father who was supposed to protect her and be on her side no matter what, turned his face away from her as if she were not his daughter and allowed Marcus to do whatever he wanted.

Something inside Devon shattered, destroying the fight in her. He was never the best father, but his heartlessness crushed her.

Her empty stomach grumbled, distracting her from the horrors in her head.

Starvation had become a familiar companion. It teased her wolf into rising and kept it dominant.

Wolfgang tasked Devon with acting as the royal executioner in the months before her trial as a form of punishment, and he used this duty to paint her as a heartless killer to their people.

He also appointed Marcus as her handler. Marcus used starvation, along with the increasing dominance of her wolf, to manipulate her ferocity when enacting her duties as royal executioner.

They tasked her with killing those Wolfgang condemned and who did not deserve the spectacle of *The Circle*, a job usually left to members of the royal guard who wore masks to protect their identities. Devon received no such consideration.

The blistering sun burnt down from the azure sky, reflecting off the light-colored dirt. It cracked her lips and increased the bloodshot sensitivity of her painful eyes.

In her current condition, a human could kill her with his bare hands.

She recalled the chants of enraged hostility coming from the surging crowd and could still hear the ferocity of their insistence that Wolfgang should end "Devon Creed, the kinslayer."

The unjustified betrayal of the memory broke Devon's heart.

She could scarcely believe that her subjects denounced her with such relish, condemning her and the others without compassion.

The change in her circumstance seemed surreal. They captured her like the dregs of an awful nightmare. The girl in her thought they made a mistake while the woman realized she would never wake up in the safety of her bed again.

When humans and vampires called werewolves brutes, Devon corrected them, fighting for her kind's rights and reputation as a specie.

Bitter ashes of disillusion replaced those beliefs.

The depths of terrifying darkness that slumbered inside the most civilized lycanthrope was knowledge she could have lived without.

Devon did not belong to the werewolf nation any longer. Even if they had spared her, she wanted no part of them.

They destroyed her trust, and her experiences created an unbridgeable emotional distance.

A monster lurked beneath the surface of their skins, an unforgettable lesson that changed her world. She saw pure evil in the eyes of ordinary wolves that chilled her soul and severed her kinship to her kind even before they turned on her like feral beasts. The darkness in their spirits clarified her vision, revealing their thirst for violence and quicksilver temperament. It shocked her to admit that only her rank kept her safe all these years.

Devon thought that maybe her impending doom was a good thing. How does one live with what she had learned?

If you enjoyed this sample, look for
Wolfborn
on Amazon.

CHAPTER 1

I have thought about my death for the better majority of my life. I had thought about how I would die, who or what would kill me, and how much time I had before it happened.

For a long time, it was an obsession, something I could not stop thinking about day in and day out. It was always hanging over my head, always lurking around some corner.

The only thing I thought about more than my death was that I would never get to see my family again. I couldn't watch my sister grow up, go to school, and eventually, get married. I wouldn't be there to take care of my parents when they got old and sick. I wouldn't be able to get married one day myself and have children of my own.

I would miss all of that because of someone else.

One day, I was so consumed with the fact that my entire life had been taken away from me, that I just lost control.

Then I escaped.

*   *   *

For an infinite amount of time, it felt like all I could do was run. One foot in front of the other and just keep pushing. I know that eventually my body would give out, but the second I stopped, I know I would be in trouble—not the manageable kind of trouble, but the kind that would get me killed.

If I am going to die, I don't want to give them the satisfaction of doing it. The pain along my leg had gone numb a long time ago, but I am just now starting to feel the blood loss and exhaustion hitting me. I sit down next to a tree to take a break and just think about my life.

I was eight when I was taken. There was an attack in the middle of the night, and nobody saw it coming because we were at peace with all of our allies.

I am a werewolf, and in the werewolf community, it is always important to have allies. A pack can be very large, but they can't defend themselves from everything. Since I was so young, I had never shifted before. This meant I could not defend myself against any of the shifted wolves around me. I was an easy prey.

After I had been taken away from the pack and my family, we traveled for a long time. The first couple of days were very hazy, and I had no idea what was going on. After a couple of years, it was a daily routine for them to keep me to do their chores, make their food, and to take their frustrations out on when life was too hard.

I could barely remember my old life after a year or two.

Almost ten years later, I have managed to escape, and now I have no idea where to go or what to do. They could be right on my trail for all I know, and then the fight and me finally shifting into my wolf would be all for nothing.

Ever since they took me, they tormented me and kept me for years now. I was supposed to cook for them and entertain them whenever they wanted.

But most of them were dead now, all except for their leader.

Realizing I can in no way go any further and that I am not healing quickly enough, I accept my death. It is almost peaceful to think that after my life of torture, I can finally die peacefully. I lie down still in wolf form and curl up into a ball, waiting to die or possibly start to heal and gain some strength back.

About a half an hour later, I hear something walking in the woods. I stand up on all four legs and look around me. Suddenly, a huge brown wolf with a blond-tipped tail is staring back at me, looking fully prepared to kill me.

The wolf starts growling, and out of instinct, I crouch into a defensive position. I put my head down on my front paws and just watch him. He walks back and forth, and after finally deciding I am not going to attack him, he shifts back into his human form and puts some shorts on.

"Shift," the guy says. I put my ears down and whine a little. His strong voice scares me a bit, and I want to shift back, but that is difficult because I don't really know how.

I have been running around the woods for hours in my wolf form because I wasn't sure how to, and I am also faster this way.

When I shifted into a wolf, it was not on purpose, and I don't really know how it happened.

"SHIFT!" he says louder. I whine louder and put my head down. When he sees this, he squints and squats down.

"Have you ever shifted before?" I shake my head, and he sighs.

"Just think about yourself as a human, and you have to want to go back to that form."

I do what he says, picturing my long brown hair down to my waist, my petite 5-foot-tall figure, and my bright green eyes. Seconds later, I feel my bones morphing for the second time that day; it is less painful than the first time, but it still hurts. After I had shifted, I lie on the ground naked and curled up in a ball. Now back in my human form, I can see I have a huge gash on my upper thigh on my left leg all the way down to my ankle.

A few seconds later, I hear the big guy in front of me start to talk.

If you enjoyed this sample, look for
Silent Luna
on Amazon.

ACKNOWLEDGEMENT

I've been incredibly blessed to be able to work with such amazing people to help me live out the dream I've had since I was 10 years old, so before I say my thank yous, I must say thank you to the one who truly made this all possible. Thank you, God, for giving me the opportunity to use the gift You gave me so that I could do something that I love: create stories and inspire others to do the same.

Mom, Dad, thank you for always believing in me and always telling me that there was nothing that I couldn't do. I would like to thank you guys for the never-ending support, love, and the incredible sacrifices you've made not only so that I can have the best that I can, but so I can also push the boundaries and work hard to create my own path. Finally, I would like to thank you guys for always showering me with love and constantly showing me the importance of family.

Paw-paw, I'd like to thank you for always making me feel like I was the smartest person in the world. Your encouraging words drive me to do my best every day, and I can always feel your love showering down on me from above. Your stories constantly inspire me, and I love and miss you very much. Granny, I would like to thank you for always encouraging me when I'm down and never taking no for an answer. I love seeing your face and hearing your laugh. Your bright outlook on life is beautiful, and it matches your beautiful soul.

I'd also like to thank my friends, relatives, and church family who've offered me kind words and supported me through this process. You have made me feel like a superstar rather than a sophomore in high school, so thank all of you.

To Typewriter Publishing, thank you so much for giving me the opportunity to put my story out there and allowing me to live the dream I've had since I was ten years old, and overall thank you for giving me a chance. I'd like to thank my agent AJ for being there with me throughout the entire process to answer my questions and guide me through this exciting unknown territory. My editor, Tinna Conde, for catching all of my mistakes and conversing with me so that this book could be the best it could be and wrapped in a neat bow. Winnie, my launching agent who helped spread this book far and wide, and Malot Aznar for the amazing cover that really pulled everything together. I would also like to thank everyone else from Typewriter Pub whose fingerprints are all over this book. Each and every one of you was instrumental to this book coming together, and for that, I want to thank each and every one of you from the bottom of my heart.

Of course, I can't forget about my OG readers, my beautiful Wattpad family who believed in this story and helped me get to where I am today. You guys helped me fall even more in love with writing with your kind, encouraging words and when I felt low, you guys always knew exactly how to pick me up, so thank you guys for that. I am eternally grateful.

ABOUT THE AUTHOR

Jordan Brown is a student who was born in North Carolina but resides in Missouri. She was inspired to start writing after participating in a creative writing unit in elementary school and instantly fell in love with it which soon led to her putting her works online. Jordan views writing as her therapy and hopes that it not only helps her but others as well. Her dream is to become a well-known author who not only moves people with her words but who also inspires them to work toward their dreams no matter how big or small they may be or how crazy they seem. When she's not writing, Jordan loves to dance, create films, and spend time with friends and family. Her first novel is "The Broken Vow of Silence" and she hopes to publish many more.

Made in the USA
Coppell, TX
28 April 2023

16191364R00229